MORE AND MORE UNTO THE PERFECT DAY

RAY HARVEY

To LINDSAY,
A FELLOW BOOK-LOVER AND
A DYNAMITE CUSTOMER WHOM
I MET AT ACE GILLETT'S.
TATANKAS AND PAPAS.
YOURS TRULY,
Ray

Pearl Button Publishing

Pearl Button Press
A subdivision of the Fort Collins Forum

Harvey, Ray
More and More unto the Perfect Day
p. cm.
ISBN 978-0-9823979-1-6 (paperback)
Copyright © March 2010

Pearl Button Press
305 W. Magnolia Street #162
Fort Collins CO 80521

More and More unto the Perfect Day

That dark morning, when the enigmas began, a foreign sound awakened him. Immediately he was aware of a presence in his mind, a feeling of malfunction coming from deep within. He opened his eyes. He had not meant to close them. He had not meant to fall asleep. He exhaled into the dark and raked his fingers through his hair.

In his room he was alone. He did not know that something had awakened him. All he knew was that he had fallen asleep, and that now he was awake. The foreign sound remained unrealized.

He sat as he had sat before: on the floor of his front room staring through the open window. Insects swarmed the screen. From somewhere far off came the scorching wail of a locomotive. He didn't move. An ovoid moon mounted a star-blown sky. A night raptor swooped in front of the window, and for a moment he imagined that he felt pass by him a gust of wind from the beat of its wings. Already a dull ache had started behind his eyeball. The sound of the train hung for minutes on the still black air and then was absorbed by the gigantic night. He understood now that something was not right, but he did not know what or why.

He thought about it for a long while. Then he rose up from the floor, and after waiting all this time for the job to start, after these endless days and weeks, sitting here like this growing more and more lost in his thoughts, he put on his boots and headed out for work.

That was when he found the puzzle piece on his doorstep. It sat winking in the silver moonlight. It contained the complete image of a red and malignant-looking spider.

1

He was off the interstate before dawn, striking out across the plains and up the Snowy Range to Sugarloaf. In the dark, he could see rags of thermal mist glowing above the roadside grass, but one silvery ghost alone brought a quickening to his pulse. It was large and oddly formed, and for several hundred meters it appeared to keep pace with him, following just beyond his reach, like a phantom ship. Then it was gone.

Thirty miles farther, where they'd instructed him to be, he pulled into a kidney-shaped turnout and waited in his car while the first light started in the east and spread like milk across the April sky. The waxing moon still hung over the western mountains. He sat behind the steering wheel with the engine idling and the heat blowing thickly into his face. He sat with his teeth unconsciously gritted. He glanced into his rearview mirror and saw the sky hulking up behind him, then he turned and stared at the sky over his shoulder, as if something up there watched him in return. A sense of unease crept over him, something he couldn't identify. For several weeks now, since the onset of a mysterious illness the worst of which had passed quickly and yet which, even now, had not fully left him, he'd been falling in and out of this anxious state of mind, a tense, almost paranoid state accompanied by bouts of sleeplessness and a feeling of hypochondria he could not eliminate. It had become his habit to worry about his health.

But there was something more: the entire night before and into this morning, for no particular reason, sad memories of his mother kept worming their way into his brain, coming with a strange insistency. His mother had been a silent soul, elegant and calm. He had imagined himself done with her long ago. Why was he thinking about her again now? What did she matter at this point? At the same time, the nagging notion pressed in around him that there is no God, and these two thoughts seemed connected in his mind; he wasn't sure how. His mother, with her touch of other worldliness, had never been a believer, that was for certain. But he had been once, though gradually as he'd gotten older his religious impulse, of its own accord, had given way to considerations more nearly philosophical. Yet the idea of God as an all-loving, all-knowing presence had always comforted him. And now it seemed gone for good; so that here, at age thirty-three, he was beset by the desire to lie down in his mother's room again, as he had when he was a child, to just lie there on her couch and that was all, not next to her, but with her simply somewhere in the room.

So persistent were these thoughts that fifty miles ago he'd pulled his car over and retrieved from his army bag the one and only letter she had ever written him, a missive slipped inside a book she'd left for him, one of a whole trunkful. Indeed,

1

he'd not looked at this letter in many years, and it was in part this realization—that she should write him in such a clandestine manner—striking him anew, that was troubling him now.

The single page lay folded twice on the passenger seat. He was apprehensive about the prospect of rereading it.

He turned to the window. Cars trickled in around him. He held his wrist draped over the steering wheel, the bone gleaming within. He sat there, watching a kernel of gray light in the northeast swell up and seep out across the sky, negating the morning stars one by one. His eyes were soft, soft as soot, but they contained depths, a metal strength. There was something unbreakable in his features. He had acne scars gouged beneath either cheekbone, but he was good-looking in spite or perhaps because of them. His arms were lean and laced with long azure veins. He had two hundred dollars folded in the back pocket of his jeans. His gaze was pensive and preoccupied. Within the last two hours, without consciously realizing it, he'd become convinced that someone would pursue him eventually. He just didn't know who—or how long it would take before he was found.

Beside him and resting facedown atop his mother's letter was an open copy of *The Complete Novels of Sherlock Holmes,* the same book she'd hid the letter in all those years ago. Glancing at it now, it occurred to him to wonder if there was something significant in this. Had his mother chosen this book for a particular reason, beyond the mere fact that as a boy it had been one of his favorites and she'd read it to him religiously? Had she been trying to tell him something, encoding a secret, perhaps, for him to unravel at a later time? He flipped the book over so that he could read the pages the letter had marked. The left-hand side was blank; the right-hand side was blank but for these words:

The Valley of Fear

He sat scowling. His nerves were jagged and he'd begun to perspire. He could feel his heart hammering below his jaw, in his neck, in his temples.

Was he imagining things? In his foggy state, he couldn't tell. He couldn't process the questions objectively.

He moved his eyeballs back to the letter. Everything suddenly seemed suspicious. He sat staring at the page. Finally, disgusted with himself for his protracted delay, he reached over and snatched the letter up. Its message was brief:

You are my child, bone of my bone, blood of my blood, son of my womb, and you mean more to me than I can say. If anything should ever happen to me and I'm no longer here to remind you of it, remember this always: nothing is greater than life. Remember always: you must live. You must always live. Your life is your own. I love you so much. Your mother...

Her signature looked identical to the rest of her writing: the same fluid unslanted hand he'd always admired. The brittle paper still carried a whisper of her perfume.

He refolded the page and was about to slip it back inside the book and be done with the whole thing, when he noticed something strange: a small drawing on the backside of the paper, block letters printed beneath. It was a child's game, a game of hangman, which he, age six, had played with his mother. He had forgotten all about it; he remembered it now. His mother had chosen a long word for him to figure out and he had lost. The stick figure was hanged.

It struck him particularly that she'd given the figure long wavy hair, indicating, in essence, that the hanged person was female. Another dim memory tried to surface in his mind, failed.

He gazed at the incomplete word:

_ A _ _ I _ E S S

She had written the rejected letters just above the gallows:

Y M U O R T

He felt there must be an important clue in all this, something exceptional, but a clue into what exactly, he had no good idea. He wondered again if it was all in his imagination.

He stared at the game of hangman for several minutes. Then, abruptly, he reached up to his sun visor and extracted a black pen. He filled in the missing letters:

H A P P I N E S S

When he was finished, he noticed, in the gaining light, that more had been written there: a phone number, erased but still faintly readable, which the figure of the hanged girl was partially covering, as if at one time someone had tried concealing the number. He didn't know whose phone number it was. Still, he thought he recognized once again his mother's handwriting, but because of the erasure he couldn't be sure.

He sat there, looking.

The light got darker, then turned violet, and at six o'clock the rain began. Shortly after that, the superintendent drove up in an orange truck and made an announcement. He thanked them all for coming and then said that he was sorry. He said that the job had been canceled because funding had been pulled. He said that a new road was being built outside Gemstone and into South Dakota, and that if anyone wanted to get on with a crew there, they should head out now because, he said, it was a long way off. Then the superintendent climbed back in his truck and drove away.

The rain continued to fall, light and misty. Above Medicine Bow, the clouds were moving rapidly now, disclosing thin slices of baby-blue. Sugarloaf Peak wore a long scarf of mist, a wig of snow. A dark wilderness stood on the mountain below. He got back in his car and sat for many minutes watching the rain burst noiselessly against his windshield.

So it was now that, searching for work, he resolved upon something extraordinary, something he'd first conceived of years ago but never followed through with. He resolved to seek out, once and for all, a piece of evidence that showed with certainty a divine hand at work upon the earth: some incontrovertible fact that mathematically proved the presence of God, whatever

"God" meant. Miracles at Fatima or Medjugorje; faith healings in Oklahoma, India, or at Lourdes; the founding of this nation against the odds; revelations of Joseph Smith, Jesus, Mohammad, even Shakespeare—in his mind, the specific did not matter. What mattered now was that no other proposition apart from God satisfied his requirements for certainty: if any other plausible explanation existed at all, however remote, however near, then for him God could not be deduced.

And that was when it began.

Perhaps even more extraordinary than his resolution was that over the course of the past twenty-four hours, his mind had grown so agitated, and he so consumed with his thoughts, that he himself didn't see anything at all remarkable in his resolution.

He gazed out across the watery lot. His was the only car left. The highway was deserted. He made a hard U-turn and drove out the same way he had come in. The aftermath of the storm straggled off to the north. He accelerated out from under a navy of fat-bellied clouds. The sun cast long bars of light across the earth. Ten miles east of Centennial, he looked to the right and saw, or thought he saw, far down county road 11, a dim sleek-looking shape, approximately the color of quicksilver but tinged with teal. This object, whatever it was, may have been moving or it may have been stationary, he could not tell. It intrigued him very much. There was a liquid-like quality about it which, for all its remove, struck him as indescribably beautiful. It reminded him of a larger version of some vital human organ, perhaps something he'd seen a photograph of when he was young and then at that age suddenly realized: this is inside me too.

He turned onto the dirt road and followed that road all the way into Woods Landing. He never came upon the object. In every direction, inexplicable roads led off to hidden places. It struck him then that he had been in this area once before, long ago, on an extended fishing trip with his mother and father. Or had he? The memory was vague. At the same time, he realized with total clarity now that he could have chosen other roads today, but he had not. He had chosen this one.

He followed a winding highway west, and when he came down off the other side of the mountain, he parked his car and went into a small cafe that doubled as a bus depot; here he drank a cup of coffee. He asked the owner if he knew of an isolated glacial lake anywhere nearby, somewhere above timberline, with water so deep that the whole lake looked turquoise, surrounded with silver rocks. The owner shook his head. He next asked the man about the possibilities of work around this area, tree-cutting, sawmill, anything, but the owner said that as far as he knew there was nothing going on, and disappeared into the kitchen.

Not five minutes later, he stood next to his graphite-gray Mazda gazing for a long time into the pine-scented air. A complicated feeling was mutating in his mind. At his feet sat a cluster of dead white insect eggs, which when he noticed them sent an upsurge of nausea sliding into his throat. He averted his eyes. The sky above looked as though it had been scoured with a stiff broom. To the west and to the south, the land tilted away into a vast parkland, as wide and windy as the sea. Fallow fields still dotted with dirty clumps of snow; tractor roads curving off everywhere into the intricate horizon. Dry wind poured into the cavities of his head. Far away, he could see the curve of the earth pulsing. Pulsing, he thought, like a living organism.

He reentered the cafe and exchanged a ten dollar bill for a role of quarters. The owner, shifty-eyed, silent, watched him warily. Or so it seemed to him.

He went back outside to the payphone.

The payphone stood burning in the knifey sunlight.

He looked around. He couldn't see anybody, and yet he felt as if a pair of hot eyes were following him everywhere. He scanned the trees. They were empty. Wind moved sluggishly through the topmost boughs.

He broke the roll of quarters against the black metal phone box and spilled the quarters onto the shelf below. The sun reflected off each coin, lancing his eyes with thin daggers of light. After a full minute, he lifted the phone from the cradle and began punching quarters into the slot. He dialed the number that he'd seen imprinted on his mother's letter. Then he stood up straight and held the phone to his ear. He closed his eyes and listened to the submarine sound within. After two seconds, before the first ring, another sound began as well, the likes of which he could not recall ever having heard: a droning, not loud but insistent and peculiar, a noise which after a moment seemed to him to be emanating from the very center of the planet. He opened his eyes and listened more closely. He couldn't figure it out. He saw his reflection in the chrome plating of the payphone, his black eyes staring straight back at him, his damp face, almost unrecognizable, looking inordinately warped, acne scars buried like bruises beneath mutant cheekbones.

The phone rang a long time. He kept waiting. All the while, the droning continued without intermission.

He was on the verge of hanging up when someone finally answered—or, rather, someone picked up the phone, though no voice came through.

"Hello?" he said.

There was no response.

"Hello?" he said.

Still nothing. But he could clearly hear breathing on the other end, the droning beneath. He grew anxious. The breathing was rhythmic, muffled, and yet from the clarity of both sounds, he knew that there wasn't anything wrong with his connection.

"Hello?" he said. He spoke louder this time. "Is somebody there? I may have a wrong number, I don't know. I'm not sure who this is that I'm calling. Can you tell me?" He enunciated his words precisely.

Still there was no response; only the steady breath and the continuous drone beneath. He didn't say anything further. He simply stood there, listening to the resounding depths inside. The acute sunlight streaked his long black hair with skeins of blond. After a while, he imagined the droning was a sound not of this world at all: he heard the whoosh of potato-shaped asteroids tumbling headlong through the universe.

"Hello!"

Nothing.

He slammed down the phone and strode back to his Mazda. When he opened his door, he remembered that he had left about five dollars in quarters sitting there. He didn't care. He ducked all the way into the car.

And then the phone rang.

His heart boomed.

He looked over toward the cafe.

The phone was ringing rapidly, stridently.

He got out of the car and walked back across the parking lot. He saw the coins still sizzling on the shelf, the torn and sepia-colored paper of the quarter-roll fluttering in the breeze. He felt that if he didn't answer the phone, it would just go on ringing forever. He absently scooped the quarters into his palm and pocketed them. The phone was still ringing, ringing. He finally picked up.

"Angela Gasteneau is dead," said a cracked voice he did not recognize. "And you're a dead man."

A soft click issued through, and then the only thing he heard was the oppressive drone. He stood holding the phone to his ear. Through the window of the café, he saw the owner inside, glaring at him.

He looped up highway 230, through Saratoga and then onto 71. It was along this isolated stretch of road that he first noticed something sweet-smelling coming through his vents. It was along this isolated stretch of road also that he began questioning if the second phone call had taken place after all. At half past three, he pulled into a parking lot behind a motel in Rawlins and slept in his car for forty-five minutes. He woke alone in the logy air of the afternoon, and into the saddest light he thought he'd ever seen. With a kind of urgency, he began driving northward, straight through until nighttime. He took one wrong turn left which cost him two hours before he regained his way. Late that night, the moon wobbled up in the east and stood in the sky like a giant squeeze of lime, the horizon beneath it a band of xanthic light, furred and radioactive. By midnight, his legs were cramping in fits and starts. He was seeing on the roadside horizontal lines of fuzz that aped the horizon but vanished just before he got to them. He didn't realize it, but he drove the entire night with his teeth clenched and grinding. He had a small scowl stitched into the middle of his forehead, pushing out a fold of flesh above the bridge of his nose. He was troubled now in the extreme, and he sweated, but not from heat.

He slept the remainder of that night outside Gillette in the backseat of his car. He came awake in the full glare of morning beneath the magnifying glass of his rear windshield. His stomach, thirty hours devoid of solid food, felt as if it had a hardboiled egg sitting in it—just sitting there, leaking vapors. He stepped out of the car and into the April breeze. There was no one around. The air, spiced with wild mustard and sage, had the smell of promise in it, faraway grass. Suddenly it came again, the complicated emotion he had felt the day before, but with it now a wingbeat in the back of his mind, a flutter of something frightening, he didn't know what; it slipped away. He stood for an hour in an empty field between the highway and the Union Pacific Railroad tracks, watching the sullen sheep dead on their feet and hearing but not hearing the long iron clang of the morning freight shunting over onto the mainline tracks that went into Nebraska and across the state. The sky hung heavy. Wind poured over and under him. He wore a serious, concentrated expression; staring out across those flat western lands, he did not see them at all—he had forgotten where he was.

The train lurched softly, no outer-space screech as he remembered from his childhood to shatter the vitreous air but rather a smooth clickity-clacking, and then the entire apparatus was gliding away to the south. He watched it move off, down the long diagonal V that had always struck him as so profound. Black smoke from the chimney scrawled itself across the empty sky. He watched the cars diminish. A squadron of purple finches slid by over his head, flying a loose low course above, but although he saw all these things, he registered none of them.

Not that he was an unobservant man by nature. On the contrary, he was uncommonly perceptive, with his 20-10 eyes that didn't miss anything, and in fact his vision had always been a private source of pride with him. Rather it was that now, and for the past two months, he had fallen into this morbid mindset, growing increasingly preoccupied and increasingly trapped in this web of anxiety, until finally it had come to this: he couldn't focus his mind for more than a few moments on any one thing, and yet what exactly was distracting him he could not have said. He didn't know what was happening. He had isolated himself from the rest of the world, so that gradually now, after weeks, only the inward glance existed for him. It was as if all his powers of perception had become pointed within.

Driving across the husk of northeastern Wyoming, a waning Sabbath day. The rain began again. His windshield wipers slapped the water away. He checked his rearview mirror but saw no one. A sourceless anger surged inside him.

He was closing fast on the South Dakota border, rocketing down a humpbacked road south of Devil's Tower, when a loud metal knocking erupted from under his hood and his steering grew stiff. The rain came down. He lifted his foot off the accelerator in an instant, but it was too late. He fishtailed off the road onto a gravel shoulder, sand exploding against his wheel wells and his undercarriage, and as he was plowing in, he saw on the overpass above him a tall thin figure in a black overcoat looking down at him through the rain; it was a young woman. With a concussive jolt, his car smashed into a short but solid berm asphalt, which caused the vehicle to flip. Miraculously, his momentum was fast enough to carry the car all the way back over, 360 degrees, so that as he flipped, he watched the front end of the car turn upside-down and then right-side up, all as if it were happening underwater, a warped, retarded motion.

And came to a stop, twenty feet from the road, upon a slight embankment of sand. The rain for a moment no longer carried any sound. He felt an eerie silence descend about him like a cloak, which his slightest movement would crumble into dust. Then, faintly, "Dark Side of the Moon" began seeping from his car speakers. The patter of the rain resumed. He glanced over at the radio and stared at it for a moment, puzzled. He reached down and clicked it off with his thumb. He felt dizzy but uninjured; his first thought was, I have escaped injury, I have gotten lucky. His mother's letter lay on the floor. He leaned over and picked the letter up. He stuffed it into his breast pocket. He did not see the Sherlock Holmes book anywhere, but looking for it, he found a photograph from an old magazine. It was a black-and-white picture depicting the arklike vessel that had been excavated from King Tut's tomb. No people were in the photo, and the picture was of poor quality. Still, in the very graininess of the image and its primordial feel, there was an enigmatic aura hovering about it that sent an electrical tremor down his spine. He examined the picture for several minutes. He realized then that it too must have been slipped inside the book; for he thought he had a dim memory of it now, from long ago. The doglike figure perched atop the ark chilled him to his bones, and when he flipped the photo over, he saw in handwriting he instantly recognized the following words:

Hound of Heaven

He dropped the photo and left it where it lay. He tried to restart his engine, but the engine would not turn over: his oil was contaminated, and he stood dead in the water.

The rain swayed in diminishing sheets. He sat staring at the overpass, though there was nothing now to see, only gleaming guardrails, a sky beyond of tarnished zinc. By and by, the rain slackened and then stopped, and after a few minutes the sun came out. Blue puddles of mercury or mirage melted across the asphalt: addorsed illusions, like cells, splitting apart before his eyes. He stepped out of the car and felt his legs buckle. To his surprise, he went down on his knees. From this vantage, he glanced once more at the overpass. It was empty. The air smelled heavy and of dirt. He stood and rested his forearms upon the roof of his car. The car was dented and scuffed but not seriously, under the circumstances. He stood squinting into the jellied distance. His anger and his fear had subsided. Far down the road, a dark speck appeared on the horizon. Slowly, it articulated from the rippled heat, hanging for a long moment before it gained solid form and then came blowing past in a cacophony of clanging chains—an eighteen-wheeler thundering by. Wall of wind, the stench of cattle. The grass around him shook. He watched the truck disappear into the simmering wedge beyond. There was something savage in this afternoon light.

Where am I? he wondered. How did I get to this place? At that same moment that he thought this, a peculiar thing happened, something he would think about for a long time afterward but which would never really make any sense to him. As he was staring at his feet, there crawled from the roadside weeds, approximately ten feet from him, an enormous red spider with a green star on its back.

Nikolai's spider, he thought instantly but without knowing why.

The spider came scuttling toward him through the deep sand, moving fast on high hairlike legs, and although still a good distance away from him, the sight of it filled him with a disproportionate sense of alarm, even panic. As the spider got nearer, he felt himself recoil but, as was his way, he gathered himself and moved toward it to crush it into the sand.

But it disappeared.

It disappeared before his eyes, as if the earth had sucked it down. Simultaneously, the twilight swept in around him, and he felt that familiar sense of desolation which so often overcame him at this time of day. What sadness was it, twitching its slow thighs in his mind behind the thin membranes of time? Vestiges of dim memories. He watched them wake.

Off to his left, a herd of anvil-shaped cows stared at him from the open pastureland. He turned back to his brokendown car. Where am I? How did I let this happen?

He moved to retrieve his duffel bag from the backseat, but stopped—he stopped in midstride and stood perfectly still. The shards of a distant recollection had just drifted into his head; he remained motionless for well over a minute trying to bring them together. In the end, however, they would not come, and instead grew more and more remote. But the mere suggestion of the memory was so strong that it had made him catch his breath, and left him also with an empty feeling. He braced himself for another wave of panic, which indeed came pounding over him with the tidal beat of his blood.

He reached into the back of the car and lifted his duffel bag off the seat. He slung the bag over his shoulder, around his head, so that it was strapped across his chest, sash-style, and then he began walking west along the roadside—moving quickly in his feline gait, not hurrying but purposeful, a sure man's walk, but troubled-looking now and sunk in thought. There was something of a military mien about him, in the precision of his posture, the familiarity he obviously had with his physicality, or perhaps he was one of these people self-disciplined enough to have built this sort of bearing on his own. And yet he did not feel right, something had gone wrong. His shadow trailed behind him like a photographer's cloak, and once he even stopped in his tracks and stood for a moment looking at it, watching his shadow suspiciously, as if it contained secrets. It only lay there, a dark puddle quaking upon the high-desert sand. He continued on. His arms, vascular and raw, swung like loose cables at his sides.

Five miles ahead, and well off the main highway, the lights of a filling station appeared, a series of white buildings. He soon came to a nameless motel pitched on the bright edge of nowhere. The first stars of the evening ignited in the east. The sky grew greenish and cool, filled with strange depths. He checked into a room.

And there his sickness returned, more violently.

2

At about that same time, some two hundred miles north, in an oddly similar location but higher up, and in a clearer, more perfect light, a woman with ash-blond hair sat at a small table beside her second-story motel room window. She was reading from a manuscript, not her own, and she appeared deeply engrossed. The honey-colored sunlight as it moved through the room fell across her face, her hair, gilding her whole person with gold. At her right elbow, a cigarette lay burning in a congested ashtray. Every now and then she would reach over and pinch the cigarette up, taking one or two slow drags, all without quite lifting her eyes from the page. She wore a white cotton bathrobe, open at the throat, and her hair was damp and raked straight back off her forehead. Her fingernails were conspicuously long and spear-shaped. Each time she finished taking a pull from her cigarette, and using only her nails, she would tuck her hair behind her left ear, and then she would leave her fingertips resting on her shoulder. Flakes of ash fell on the pages she read from. The smoke from her cigarette swirled into the soft slabs of light. Opposite her, on the other side of the room, a large black trunk sat propped open. This was filled to a surfeit with a number of hardbound books, as well as several notebooks and two or three typewritten manuscripts, all of which looked much the same as the one she now read from.

Presently, the last light of day flickered on the far wall and then expired.

She rose from the table and tamped out the cigarette with rapid stabs. She went into the bathroom and remained there for about ten minutes. When she returned, she wore only panties and a bra. The sun had set. The room was smothered in velvet shadows. The radiator pumped out heat. She did not sit back at the table but stood along the left-hand side of the window, out of view, leaning her shoulder against the wall and staring out at the lowering sky. She searched the clouds, obviously concentrating upon something, for her forehead was furrowed and her expression thoughtful and grave. She was still in this position when, ten minutes later, the phone rang. So engrossed was she in her thoughts that she visibly started from the phone's violent, importunate peal. She turned from the glass and looked to the phone. There it was, crouched blackly on the bedside table. She watched it for several seconds. Then, on its sixth or seventh ring, she strode over and picked up the receiver.

"Hello?"

A woman's voice, even in tone but somehow desperate-sounding, came through the other end. "Hello? Is this Lauren?"

"Yes, it is. Hi, Heather. Thank you for calling me back."

"You're welcome. Is everything okay?"

"Yes, fine. Everything's fine."

"What's going on?"

"Oh, nothing much," said the woman in the motel room. "You know. Thinking and blinking." There was a momentary pause. "The reason I called you earlier," she said.

"As a matter of fact, I'm glad you called."

"Oh? Why so?"

"Well, do you have a few minutes? I mean, can I talk to you for a few minutes?" Heather's voice had become shaky.

"Sure."

"Something happened earlier tonight. Something pretty unpleasant."

The woman in the motel room stood in the narrow space between the two single beds. She was wrapping and unwrapping the telephone cord around her index finger, stretching it so that it cast a large corkscrew shadow upon the wall. She sat down now, unplacidly crossing her legs and leaning forward a bit on the bed. "Continue please," she said.

"Well, it's a little embarrassing," Heather said. "*Now*, I mean. At the time, though, it wasn't embarrassing at all." She cleared her throat. "I became really frightened earlier. I don't know exactly what happened."

"Well, what happened?"

"I don't know exactly."

"Were you raped?"

"Raped? No. God, no. Not at all. I actually haven't been raped in years."

"That's a relief, at least."

"Yes. You see, what happened was…"

"Yes?"

"Well, there's this guy I've been—there's this guy I've had a *thing* for, for quite a while now."

"Uh-huh."

"He's a Christian. That's the first thing I should say."

"I'm sorry, you say his name is Christian?"

"No, his name is Alex. He *is* a Christian. He's a very handsome man … Mexican, or New Mexican, to be precise."

At this point, the woman named Lauren reached over to the nightstand and slid toward her a green package of cigarettes. She shook one out, and with her long fingernails she extracted a folder of matches, which was tucked halfway inside the cellophane. Without lighting the cigarette, she sat on the edge of the bed, still only in her bra and panties, the telephone cradled snugly against her shoulder, the cigarette dangling between her first two fingers. "And how do you know this Alex?" she said.

"Initially?"

"Yes."

"He was a friend of my" (there was a pregnant pause) "of my brother."

"Keith? Is Keith a Christian?"

"No, not Keith. Bill."

"Bill was definitely no Christian," Lauren said. She struck a match and touched the conical flame to the tip of her cigarette. She blew out the flame with a long lilac stream of smoke.

"Well neither was Christ, I could argue. Anyway, you mostly knew Bill in the beginning, when he was young."

"That's true," said Lauren.

"I mean, you would've really been surprised, I think."

"I'm sure." Lauren dragged her cigarette thoughtfully and glanced over at the open trunk full of books and manuscripts, all the notebooks packed with raw poems. "Yes, you're right," she said. "You're absolutely right." She held the dead match pinched between her pinky and her thumbnail and the cigarette in between her middle and index fingers. A plastic cup stood on the edge of the nightstand. It contained about an inch of water. She deposited the match in this, then shaped her ash on the rim of the cup. "So but what exactly happened?"

"Tonight?"

"Yes."

"Well, he took me to a concert earlier."

"Alex?"

"Yes."

"What kind of concert was it?"

"A rock concert, a Christian rock concert."

"I see." Lauren took another drag off her cigarette. "Go on," she said. "I'm very interested." She tipped her ash into the cup and with her free hand tucked a strand of hair behind her ear.

"Well, he'd taken me to a nice dinner before—" Here Heather interrupted herself. "You know what's really odd to me?"

"What?" said Lauren.

"It's odd to me that even though I think Alex is a nice, funny guy, and every time I see him I about die over his good looks, there's always something very *awkward* between us."

"In what way?"

"I don't know for sure. Strained. I mean even at its best, and it does fluctuate. And yet it never completely goes away no matter how long or how often we're around each other. I've puzzled over this a lot, and I can't figure it out."

Lauren said nothing, but manufactured a solitary smoke ring and sent it wobbling into the dark.

"Anyway," Heather said.

"Anyway," Lauren interrupted, "you went to this Christian rock concert with a good-looking guy named Alex."

"Yes. Yes, I did."

"Let me ask you one thing before you go any further: did you know beforehand that you were going to a Christian rock concert?"

"No, I did not. And that was actually the thing that bothered me the most, at first."

"At first?"

"Yes. Because I mean it rapidly got much worse—things rapidly went straight to hell, as a matter of fact. I mean the sad fact of the matter is, he did more or less spring it on me, and that's the truth. Actually, it wasn't until long after I was in my seat that I even realized where we were. Tell me frankly, Lauren. Wouldn't you about come unglued if someone did that to you?"

"Well, I don't know that I'd necessarily come un*glued*," Lauren said. She glanced up and over into a dim corner of the room, where the ceiling merged with the wall. Then her eyes fell back to the floor. She stared vacantly at her peanut-shaped toes, wiggled them once. "Odds are strongly in favor, though, that I wouldn't be overly thrilled about it, I will say that much."

"Right, right. I mean, for a relatively intelligent guy, it was about the most tactless maneuver he could've made. But even then—you know what?—even then, he didn't tell me that it was a Christian function. Because I think at some point he knew that I knew: he just didn't bother to broach the subject. I mean, he was very upbeat and talkative the whole time when we were sitting there waiting (and we sat there waiting for a long while), but he still just kept calling it 'this concert.' I only figured it out, as a matter of fact, because, way down behind the stage, I noticed this white cross on the wall."

"Did you realize beforehand that Alex—"

"I knew he was a Christian, yes, if that's what you're wondering. But I didn't know he was a *radical* Christian. I didn't put that together until I saw the cross. And then, after a little while longer, in this conversational tone, he started telling me how the lead singer in the band we were about to see, how years ago, he said, this man used to be a musician in Jimi Hendrix's band. *Very* big deal. Then he started telling me all this stuff about the guy's former drug and alcohol and sex abuse, but how one day a while back this singer found God, and then shortly after that he became a 'rocker for Christ,' as Alex put it."

Heather stopped speaking, and neither said anything for several seconds.

"I have to tell you, Lauren, talking about this now is making me feel frightened again. It's bringing back the same sense of panic I went through earlier."

"No need to be afraid," Lauren said. "Everything is okay." To the left of her foot, and sitting on the hairlike fibers of carpet, was a small cylinder of ash, resting there perfectly intact. Lauren stared at the ash for a long moment. Then she moved her foot over and, with deliberate taps, pulverized it under her big toe. She glanced at the cigarette between her fingertips. It had burned down nearly to its filter. "Do you want me to tell you what I think?" she said. She sucked a final drag from the cigarette, then dropped the stub into the water; it made a soft sput. "In my candid opinion, I think you've always had this tendency to let things gather in your mind to such an extent that they become so huge that you can't even recognize—"

"You're right," said Heather, "you're absolutely right. I know that I do. I mean, I *do* know this about myself. And I'll tell you the truth, I can't remember a time in my life when I wasn't this way. Still, it doesn't change the fact that I *am* this way. I mean, you know?"

"No, it doesn't, I know. Still—"

"Still, the point is, I was feeling extremely uncomfortable from the get-go. But my discomfort turned into actual anxiety when I realized just what the hell was going on."

"Was it the music that disturbed you so much?"

"No, it wasn't the music. But let me tell you about that music."

"Yes. Please do."

"For starters, it was about as loud as a busted chainsaw, if I may quote your ex-husband."

Lauren smiled broadly. "You may, you may," she said. Unconsciously, she rubbed her big toe back and forth across the carpet.

"To begin with, it had all the earmarks of this heavy-metal-style music, but with *extreme* Christian-oriented lyrics, you know what I mean?"

"I do know what you mean, yes. I know exactly what you mean."

"From a purely artistic standpoint, I hated every second of it."

"Why?"

"*Why?*"

"Why, specifically?"

"Well, for one thing, the words didn't at all match the music. For another, everyone, including Alex, was standing up and dancing. I mean, still remaining in stationary positions, but moving. The main thing is, it was all so weird that I couldn't believe—I truly couldn't believe my eyes. I'm not kidding, either. I also couldn't understand how anyone could seriously buy into it."

"But buying into it they were," Lauren said. She switched the phone to her other ear.

"Yes. At that moment, I came *this* close to walking out, without any word of explanation or anything. Just grabbing my purse and walking out."

"Why didn't you?"

"Honestly?"

"Yes."

"I honestly don't know. I wasn't clear on where we *were*, for one thing. And I didn't know either, at that point, that the worst was still to come. If I had known *that*, I really would've left, I think." Heather stopped speaking: the cataleptic pause. "But, I mean, it's easy to say that now, I know. The thing is, Lauren—and I want to get this across now—a part of me, the main part of me really believes, I mean the main part of me actually understands that all this stuff is basically absurd, despite what I'm about to say, I do understand that. And yet ..." She fell silent again.

"Please continue," Lauren said. "I want to hear the rest—"

"Needless to say, I didn't get up and walk out, and after several songs, there was a long break, during which time the lead singer began exercising his other vocation."

"Preaching?"

"Yes. How did you know?"

"Just took a guess."

"Well, you're right, you're absolutely right. And that, really, was when it started."

"When what started, sweetie?"

"My fear. That is, I went from apprehension *to* fear. Because this man, the lead singer ..." Heather's voice faltered.

"Yes?"

"Well, more or less, he started telling us the story of his life, how he had come back from the edge and so on. I might add at this point that the whole time he was telling us this, he was quoting scripture like crazy."

"Right," Lauren said, "I can picture it."

"And it *was* really just the standard procedure. Next he talked for a long time about how simple it actually is to be saved, how you only have to say in your heart of hearts, 'I accept Christ as my personal savior,' and that's really all there is to it, no matter how many bad things you've done, or will do. On the other hand, as simple as it is, you are *definitely* going to hell if you don't do this—in other words, if you don't become born again. It was then that I took a moment to look around, and I swear, Lauren, everybody, including Alex, was in a trance. I'm not exaggerating. An absolute trance. And suddenly I felt as if I was the only one, out of hundreds of people, not totally brainwashed. Literally the *only* one. It was one of the most horrible experiences I've ever gone through in my life. You know what it was like? It was like a movie or a *Twilight Zone* episode, where everybody except me had been turned into a zombie, or something. I'm being completely serious."

"I can tell that you are," Lauren said. She rose to her feet and began pacing a small circle in the narrow space between the two beds. She stopped once and glanced outside: heat lightening fractured the distant sky. Her shrewd eyes went to the open trunk.

"All I kept thinking," Heather said, "was that there's nothing in the whole universe—nothing—that I could imagine that would be worse than being like these people." She hesitated. "Only here's the thing. When I really started to think about it, I could imagine something worse."

"What's that?" Lauren reached up and pinched the telephone cord, just beneath the transmitter.

"Going to hell." After Heather said it, she fell silent for approximately ten seconds. "You see, Lauren, my entire life, since I was a very little girl, I've had this compulsive fear of going to hell. I know this is an extremely personal thing to reveal about myself. And I know that it's not exactly normal, and I know that it's probably not something at all interesting to a person who has no idea of what it's like to be this way.... I'm sure it even sounds silly to someone not—you know—directly *involved* in it. But it was no joke. I used to have nightmares about hell all the time when I was young, dreams that scared me stupid. For a long time, I was even afraid to go to sleep at night." She hesitated again. "Silly-sounding or not, though," she said, "it was very real."

"I'm sure it was."

"Do you know the thing that used to scare me the most about hell?"

"No," Lauren said.

"It was not the torture or the punishment or any of that. It was the fact that it lasts forever and ever and ever and ever, without end. *Ever*. You know?"

"Yes," Lauren said. "I do."

"*That* is what used to frighten me the most. Infinity in general frightens me, to be totally honest. But infinity in hell is even worse. You know how in dreams, nightmares in particular, things will often seem more real than actual reality?"

"Yes."

"Only, when you've woken up and are into your day, these things usually start to seem half ridiculous?"

"Yes."

"Well, that's how I felt tonight, but without the ridiculous part. That part never came." Heather took a deep breath.

Lauren didn't say anything.

"The best way I can think to describe it," Heather said, "is like this: first there's regular fear, and by that I mean the kind that is not pleasant, certainly, but which you more or less know how to handle from previous experiences. And then there's panic, which ups the ante considerably. And then there's terror. Do you know what I'm talking about? The kind of fear that makes you feel as if you have no choice. As if there's nothing you can do, nowhere to run—although that's about the only thing you can think to do—nowhere to go, nothing to *do*? It's as if your life is finished, and there's no reason to live anymore, and yet you're still alive. And suicide isn't an option, because all the suicides go to hell, and hell is what you're afraid of. That's what I was feeling—"

Lauren cleared her throat. "Listen to me, Heather."

"Just a moment," Heather said. "I want to finish telling you this. I'm afraid if I don't get it all out now, I won't get it out ever."

"All right."

"When I was in the sixth grade, I went through this exact same thing after I saw *The Exorcist*. It scared me so much that for two straight years I carried a crucifix around with me wherever I went. Always. Two straight years. I slept with it, I even showered with it. I know all this is very personal—I know these are very personal things to reveal about myself, and yet I feel I need to *confess* these things now. I feel it's important that I do it now, I don't know why. Can you explain it?"

"Actually, I've heard of such things before."

"You have?"

"Yes. In my experience, though, it's rare."

"I find it comforting to hear that you've heard of it, nevertheless."

"Obsessions and compulsions are frequently religious in nature, Heather. But I'm most interested in your fear. When you were a child, I mean."

"My fear was a complete and pure fear when I was a child, my preoccupation with being possessed by the devil almost total. I do want to be clear on something, though."

"Go ahead."

"No matter how many bad or questionable things I've done in my life—and I've done many—I truly believe that the driving force in my life has always been a desire to be good, to do good. For whatever it's worth. I really do mean that. I've ignored it, or *evaded* it, as they say, and don't get me wrong: I don't pretend that I *am* good. I'm just saying I always go back to this one basic motivation, I really do. I will say this about myself, and I'm certain it's true."

"Yes."

"But as far as my situation with *The Exorcist*."

"Yes?"

"At the time in my life that this was all happening, it never helped me that every person I ever spoke with on the matter, including my mother—including Bill, whom I always went to about such things, he being older, and always so kind to me—it didn't help me that they always said it actually could happen, that demonic possession could take place."

"That's interesting," Lauren said, "because at various points in his life I know Bill himself was obsessed with being possessed."

"Yes, I know."

"Undoubtedly, his alcoholism was a contributing factor on that score. And the drugs, of course."

"Yes," said Heather, "but there was also his Catholicism."

"Yes, perhaps that also, although—"

"Bill wasn't even *raised* Catholic, did you know that? Where did his great devotion come from?"

"It was mostly literary, I think," Lauren said. "At least in the beginning."

"What do you mean literary?"

"You know: Thomas Aquinas, Joan of Arc, Gerard Hopkins, Jacques Maritain, Francis Thompson, and so on. Bill romanticized Catholicism, just as he romanticized about everything else in his life. And in the end, literature was his only mistress, which is why his letters and his conversations are and were so full of obscure literary references. Also, his achieving-the-highest fixation was *the* determining factor for most things he did, as you probably know, and there is certainly something of that mindset in many famous Catholics. I truly think that there are some people, like Bill, with an ultra-driven disposition who turn to religion for the simple reason that religion has always held a kind of monopoly on The Good. Either way, most people do at some point outgrow their fears of demonic possession. I mean, didn't you?"

"I did outgrow it, yes. I mean, that particular thing, I did. But it was this exact same *kind* of fear that I was experiencing again tonight. And that's mainly what I'm getting at."

"What specifically do you mean?"

17

"I mean the fear. To tell you the God's honest truth, I'd almost forgotten all about it—the fear, I'm talking—until tonight. Then it came back."

"*Forgotten* about it?"

"Yes."

"Now *that's* interesting. So what did you do?"

"Tonight?"

"Yes."

"I stood in the auditorium scared to death, is what I did. I was shaking and dizzy, and all while this was going on, I was outwardly having to seem cool, because at the same time, I was afraid, I was also afraid that if I showed my fear, Alex, or someone, anyone, would pounce on me with this stuff about how Christ was just *waiting* for me with open arms and go to him, everything was actually okay, just become born again, like every single one of them."

"Which you would not have done, in any case," said Lauren. "Because" (she reached over and with her agate-like fingernails extricated another cigarette from the pack) "with the exception of hell you can think of nothing worse, correct?"

"Yes."

"And something else," Lauren said, sitting back down on the edge of the bed and lighting her cigarette. "Some part of you worries that these people" (she shook out the match and blew smoke into the darkness) "some part of you worries that these people—and I'm referring to the Born Again Christians—a part of you worries that *they* are the ones who are actually right, yes? That they, the evangelical born-agains, are the ones whom Christ has in mind when he speaks of 'being perfect.' They're his ideal, they're his chosen representatives here on earth, and in reality they're the ones who are going to be saved, while the rest of the world perishes in hell."

"Yes, I *do* worry that. But the thing is, I'm not just thinking of these brainwashed people I saw tonight."

"Oh? Who else, then?"

"It's anyone..." Heather let a moment pass. "I'm sorry, I can't explain it," she said. "I mean, I *do* believe that there's an absolute truth. I believe there's absolute right and wrong. It's not that."

Lauren dragged thoughtfully on her cigarette.

"I need to think for a second," Heather said.

"Take all the time that you need," Lauren said. She squinted her eye against the smoke. "I've never been one who minds a silence over the telephone."

There was a long pause.

"Well, you know how there are about a million different religious groups out there?" Heather said.

Lauren nodded but didn't speak.

"Forget the particular denomination—some may be better than others, I don't know, I'm not talking about that—but in any given one of them, there are always these types who are so completely convinced that their way is the only accurate way, and their miracles are the only real miracles and so on...so convinced, I mean, that their specific customs and stories and *ways* are the only correct ways that for them there is absolutely no question anymore? Do you know what I'm talking about?"

"Fundamentalism."

"I don't know. I don't know what you call it. That's part of my point. My point is, these people are actually beyond convinced."

"Beyond convinced that what?" Lauren said.

"Beyond convinced that their religious group is the right one and all the thousands and thousands of others are essentially wrong. Beyond convinced that all their specific ways and peculiarities are the *actual* way—the actual way that God wants us to behave. I honestly think that if Christ himself were to tell these people 'you are wrong,' they still wouldn't believe it, because their particular religious affiliation, or their religious style, or whatever you want to call it, has become the most important thing."

"I think I see," Lauren said.

"I'm not explaining it well, I know."

"No, you're doing exceptional."

"I'm just saying."

"I know."

"I'm just saying I can't pinpoint exactly what it is about certain religious people that bothers me, but not others. I've been sitting here all night trying to figure out what it is, *exactly*, but I can't. Part of the problem, I think, is that it isn't all religious people."

"There is a clue there, I think." Lauren took a fast drag. "But here," she said, inhaling with a hiss, "is the main problem as I see it, if you're interested in my opinion."

"I am."

"The problem as I see it is, you've gotten befuddled by a middle-class morality. It's really very common." Lauren didn't say anything further but sat there pluming purple in the dark.

"But I am who I am," Heather said, after a moment. "I can't just switch off my personality like that." Gently, she snapped her fingers up near the receiver so that Lauren could hear it, but only just. "I mean, I would that I could," Heather said.

"Yet the fruit of the spirit is first and foremost calm. It's independent, it's relaxed."

Heather didn't say anything.

"Finish telling me your story," Lauren said.

"Well, the real climax came after the concert was over."

"When what happened?"

"When we were all invited up onto the stage to be formally saved—or resaved, as the case may be. At that point, I could feel Alex next to me willing me up there. I could actually *feel* it. Excruciating. It was so uncomfortable that I really wanted to die. I think he was thinking that if anybody could cause an epiphany in me—if anyone could *save* me—it was this singer, whom he thought of as so charismatic and smart."

"I have to ask," Lauren said, "what was the motive of Mr. Alex? I mean, in his mind was he thinking that first you get saved, then you convert, then you marry him, and *then* you two could have sex? I mean, or what?"

"Oh, I don't know about *that*. Regardless, though, what he didn't know, what Alex didn't know, was that I would rather have died than go up on that stage. Nothing could have made me go up there. Nothing in the world. But at the same time, I had lost my entire perspective on right and wrong. I had lost my capacity to judge. I really had. As a matter of fact, I could no longer think at *all*. I've never experienced anything like it in my life. It was almost as if the context I'd spent my entire life developing had been obliterated in the course of two hours."

"Really?"

"Yes."

"Jesus, that's strange."

"It was unbelievable. My brain got so muddled and confused. But I know that if Alex had suspected any of this, he would have said to me that it was satan who was keeping me from going up there, that it was satan putting all this fear and confusion into me, that I need simply resign myself to Christ and not let satan win, and then my confusion would disappear. And ..."

"And you're worried he's right?"

"Yes." Heather stopped speaking for several seconds. Then she blurted out: "Lauren. I lie a lot."

Lauren, in the process of bringing the cigarette up to her lips, stopped in midair. "Beg pardon?"

"I said I lie a lot. I'm sorry. I want to tell you everything."

"There's really no nee—"

"Wait, listen to me. I want to tell you. Do you remember a letter you got once from a guy named Patrick, who was very in love with you? The letter was in your car, you and I were getting ready to go somewhere, and you had just read it, and then you couldn't find it. You kept saying, 'I just read the damn thing, where is it, I just *read* it.' Do you remember?"

"I remember," Lauren said. She looked thoughtful. Silently, she exhaled dual pipes of smoke through her nostrils, then dropped her cigarette into the cup. "I didn't want Bill to see it," she said, "because in actuality Patrick meant nothing to me." She was still squinting at the cup, staring meditatively at the small cylinders of ash, which were floating atop the water like so many logs.

"Yes," Heather said. "Well, I took it."

"Pardon?"

"I took the letter. Moments before you started looking for it, I took it, I don't know why. I didn't mean—I mean, it wasn't my intention to do anything harmful or devious. I really just wanted to read it. And then after I took it, I saw that you were looking for it, and I couldn't bring myself to admit to you that I had it. And that brings up something else, something I've always realized about myself but have never seen as clearly as I do tonight: I'm a slave to other people's opinions of me. And I'm worried that that's the real reason I couldn't just get up and walk out of that concert earlier; because, despite how troubled I was by those people, I didn't want—"

"Listen, Heather."

"No, wait. I want to tell you all this now. Because if I don't do it now ..."

"Okay, Heather."

"Another thing is"—Heather was crying a little—"I've always been jealous of you. Not in a vindictive way, necessarily, but jealous. I would have killed to have gotten that letter from Patrick, for instance. And it wasn't so much that I liked him, although I did like Patrick, I did, it's just more the effect you always have on people, and don't even know it. Or care about it. I've even hated you, many times, for this, despite myself; because at the same time—and I want you to know this as well—I've always loved you. I have and I do. Deeply. Also, I've always realized that this fault is in me, that the jealousy is my problem, not yours." She took an audible breath. "Do you believe me?"

"I want to believe you," Lauren said.

"I want to be sincere now, but I'm not sure that I can even tell anymore. So much of my life has been motivated by my desire to *appear* sincere that I don't even know. There are so many things that I've done in my life, little things, but bad. I've taken money out of your purse—"

"Listen," Lauren said, "it's all right. You really don't need to confess any of this to me, because I don't care. I truly don't. You don't *need* to tell every single thing to every single person you've ever wronged, forget what you've heard from whatever recovery program. This is not a necessary thing for your spiritual health. Only, recognize it within yourself, and then cease to do it. But the first thing you need to do, in my opinion, is take it easy. Go make yourself a nightcap or something. Let me tell you: if you really want your motives to become sincere, it will happen gradually and through a conscious effort on your part, by being aware day by day of how you live. Strive for total honesty with yourself. Just recognizing these things inside you will take you a long way. But you can't change all of a *sudden*—not in the manner you're speaking of, anyway."

"There's something else I must tell you," Heather said.

"All right."

"It's very big." Heather hesitated again, as if to gather herself. "First of all, I don't know if you know it, but your ex-husband Bill was not actually my real brother."

"Yes, I know. Bill was your half brother."

"He wasn't even that. It turns out he had a different mother as well, a woman none of us ever knew. *Our* mother—Terri—didn't tell us this for a long time."

"What?"

"Yes."

"Are you sure? I mean, did *Bill* know?"

"Yes. He knew all along. His father had never hid it from him."

"Really?"

"Yes."

"He never once mentioned any of this to me," Lauren said.

"No, it was not something he liked to talk about. At all. I don't think he told another person. He had a weird obsession with this woman. He was obsessed with finding her, talking to her. He was also obsessed with searching for her, I think."

"And did he?"

"Did he what?"

"Find her," Lauren said.

"Not to my knowledge, no."

"God, I can't believe this."

"This is just the preliminary. My real reason for bringing it up—" Again, Heather's voice broke. "My real reason," she said, crying, "is once I learned this about him, I developed inappropriate feelings for Bill. I fell slightly in love with him, to be honest. And part of that time," she said, "was while the two of you were still together."

"Oh, Heather. That's nothing."

"But I want you to know something more," Heather said. "These feelings were always repressed. I mean, I never acted on them, nor would I have. Still, guilt ate away at me…."

There was a long silence.

"Anyway," Heather said, sniffing, "the books he left you, the ones you just got?"

"Yes?"

"Among them are a few of his manuscripts."

"I know." Lauren glanced over to the table, where the one manuscript still lay, facedown, sprinkled with ash. "That's the reason I called you earlier."

"It is?"

"Yes. You see, there's a rather extraordinary—"

"I know, I know."

Lauren started to say something, but Heather interrupted her:

"Listen, Lauren, I'll be honest with you: I can't bring myself to read through those manuscripts, but—"

"Can't bring yourself? Why?"

"Because," Heather said, "I'm too afraid."

"Afraid of what?"

"Of what I might read."

"But why?"

"Because when I *did* glance at that one …"

"Yes?" Lauren said.

"This is what I'm saying, Lauren: I really don't think that happened. Not like that."

"Don't think what happened?"

"Well, what you read…about Bill and me." They were both silent. "Have you finished reading it?" Heather said.

"No," Lauren said. "I haven't read anything about Bill and you. I think you're talking about a different manuscript. I'm reading about a woman with a spot of blood on her hand."

"Oh, God. Well, I don't think he did *that*."

"Did what?"

"But he might have," Heather said. "I honestly don't know. I can't remember. I sort of half remember something, but it's all very dim."

"What do you mean?"

But Lauren was beginning to comprehend.

"I mean that I'm not sure exactly what happened. It all occurred when I was so young, and Bill was drinking so much."

"But you're saying that you may have fabricated all this?"

"Yes. It's distinctly possible. As I say, it's a vague memory at best, nothing too specific. Actually, you know what it feels like? It feels like it happened to someone else and had nothing whatsoever to do with Bill *or* me—that I'm just remembering how it made me feel when I heard about the person to whom it actually happened. It really does feel like that." For a moment, it sounded as if Heather would say something else, but in the end she held off.

"All this however," Lauren said, "was precipitated by what you had recently read in Bill's manuscript?"

"Yes. And along with the vague memory, I must also tell you that there's this peculiar sensation in the pit of my stomach—peculiar but very real. And *that* scares me."

"Yet the notion had not entered your brain before you reading part of his manuscript?"

"No, it hadn't, I'm certain of that. But, listen," Heather said, frustrated, "none of this is actually why I brought the subject up either. My main point here …" Once more, she broke off and was silent for several beats.

"Go on," Lauren said, "please."

"Lauren, I saw him tonight."

"Saw who?"

"Bill."

"No, Heather."

"Yes, I saw him. He was on the stage, getting saved."

"No. You're mistaken."

"Lauren. I *saw* him. He was by himself. It was him, I know it was."

"Listen, Heather." Lauren rose to her feet. "This is very important: your anxiety has caused a hallucination within you. Your obsessive worrying, along with your guilt, has built a false memory inside your brain. This sort of thing happens. Believe me when I say that I know what I'm talking about here. People see things that aren't actually there but which seem as if they are. Now listen carefully to me, it is so important that you do: you are exonerated of your guilt—your sins are forgiven. I mean that. It's critical that you understand this because you've started to believe in something that *didn't actually happen.* And—pardon? What's the reason? The reason is obvious: you're so afraid, you're so deathly afraid of the What If. But Bill is gone, Heather. Bill is long, long gone."

3

Self-mortification was his secret weapon against despair, a chronic asceticism.

Joseph Gasteneau—Joel, as he was known—a cluster of acne scars brushed like rouge beneath either cheekbone, slatey eyes sharp and tinged with sadness, this was just another nobody kid from nowhere. Only his strength of will was extraordinary. He was fiercely driven.

He was the only child of middle-aged parents, a truck-driver-turned-miner named Neil and Neil's wife Angela, a half Cherokee lady of rare beauty whom Joel loved with all his heart; one younger sister born dead four years after him. Joel grew up silent, a silent child, pale and skinny but healthy. He brought coal from the shed to the stoker. He took out clinkers. He had certain gifts. He was quick with numbers and he could draw. His father had taught him to read when he was only four, and from approximately first grade onward, he developed the habit of counting almost everything he did. Later he began calculating things, it didn't matter what, license plate numbers, prices in store windows, numerals on clocks, and then adding and subtracting and multiplying these numbers, dividing and subtracting, re-adding and so on, endlessly, all in his head, all day long; it brought him comfort. The three of them lived together, on the outskirts of a mining town, in a large house-shaped trailer, fifty meters beyond the backyard of which an undulation of aspen trees fell away across the slopes. He seemed wise beyond his years, and he bore his father's barehanded beatings with a stoicism unimaginable in one so young. Like his father, he possessed an uncanny sense of direction, and also time, but more than anything else, his mind was of a naturally speculative cast.

His father Neil was a hawk-nosed and darkly complexioned man, lean and somewhat haggard-looking but handsome, tall, with a mass of moon-colored hair and high eyebrows that turned thickish as they angled into the bridge of his nose. He was green-eyed, and he wore his mustache long and well-groomed, the tapered tips plunging toward his chin like tiny daggers, which in collaboration with his large cowboy hats and black button-down shirts gave him a dangerous air. He ate very little; he did one-armed pushups first thing every morning and then roman chair sit-ups with a metal weight held behind his head. He had pecs like a prisoner. He was an extremely interesting and complicated man, who had dropped out of school when he was twelve and proceeded from then on to teach himself everything he knew. His conscience was clear. Something of the absolute, the incontestable, moved inside him. For decades, he was the superintendent of a gold mine called the Equity. He possessed all the autodidact's unsystematic and sprawling ways, yet the breadth and depth of his learning were staggering. A light, yes, it shone within him but only, it seemed, in juxtaposition to the darkness of his dark shadows: like fulgurations of insight blazing out at you from inside the blackness of his brain, illuminating that chaos within. He was a sober man who loved astronomy, and the study of great civilizations. Often he made you feel that you would never have thought of the things he thought of, not in a million light years. Inadvertently, he'd instilled within his only son his own conviction that life is a grave thing, neither inherently angst-filled nor silly, and that the accidental is not of primary consequence. Man's fate, he said, is in his own hands, choice everything. He loathed Existentialists, God.

The month that Joel turned seven (September of 1964), it rained for three weeks straight. It rained and rained, morning, noon, and night, and finally it rained so much that after a while Joel thought it would never cease. He stood in his bedroom, in front of the window, watching for hours the low sky flash and weep. The woods beyond lay dripping and lugubrious. It was during this period that he came home from school one afternoon and found his aunt and uncle waiting for him near his bus stop, at the end of a leafy lane. They stood next to their mud-encrusted pickup, under a blue awning, waiting outside despite the cold weather, and despite the rain sizzling in the streets around them. They watched him come up. His aunt Nikki was his mother's younger sister, and she and her husband Peter lived in a town ninety miles north and rarely visited. So when Joel saw them both standing there waiting for him that day, he knew something was wrong.

There came a short break every afternoon when the spongy sky would momentarily dry—an hour or so at three o'clock, the clouds lackadaisically spitting—and then the rain would begin all over again, gathering easily at first, with a sound like the whisper of wind in the grass, and then increasing until soon everything was cats and dogs. It was this that he came home through. He wore his red fireman boots and his golden raincoat. He walked with his head down. His uncle, a kind, phlegmatic man with the hangdog mien of a mortician, stood by the truck, his meaty forearms crossed over his chest, his Army Surplus boots planted widely apart and a butcher's apron still on under his jacket. The apron was stained with brownish blood. His aunt had her head turned, and she appeared convulsive, as if shivering. Her dress clung to her body in the rain. Joel could see beyond them the windows of the house-shaped trailer ablaze with lights, creamy in the burgeoning dusk, and he could see also an orange-and-white ambulance parked out front. The air was purple, the color of thunderstorms. Small bubbles were popping in the puddles he walked through, and box elder leaves lay enameled across the asphalt, tiny frameworks of leaves pitched like ribcages in the grass. An odor of iron hung in the air, mixed with the mealy odor of leaves. Feathers of mist blew off the cliffs above, and these details he would remember all his life.

His uncle did not say a word to him as he proceeded up, only adjusted his orbital eyeglasses and gripped Joel by the shoulder, as if trying to bust a chip off. Joel turned to his aunt, who looked back at him with tear-shattered eyes. She blinked slowly, to gather herself, then told him that he would be spending the night with them, that they would all have dinner together and later a movie, if he wanted, and after that he would sleep at their house, in the guest room, and would not have to go to school the next day. She smiled thinly.

And so later that evening, in a diner eighty-five miles north, while his aunt held onto his dead fingers and his uncle smoked Marlboros without surcease, Joel sat in a crimson leather booth staring out at the watery lot beyond. The table beneath his arms reeked of bleach. Rain had completely stippled the glass, flatworms of water now sliding across the windowpane. A pink replica of the drugstore sign across the street lay slurred over the pavement. The gutters below were sluicing with liquid gold. Joel ate a piping-hot grilled cheese sandwich and potato chips; he drank milk. He watched his uncle crush with the back of his fork a lunar volcano of mashed potatoes and then flood the potatoes with molten gravy. After dinner, they all went to a movie Joel would not remember, throughout the entirety of which his aunt sat weeping in her chair. Thunder trundled down the sky above like rubber wheels across an attic floor.

Next morning outdoors, his uncle told Joel that his mother Angela had died in the night, a series of strokes, he said, these are what had killed her. Joel did not know what a stroke was, but what he pictured were large clots of blood chugging down her windpipe, and glottal sounds, her air totally cut off. He thought: my pretty mother is dead.

He was driven back home that same day and spent the rest of the afternoon alone in his bedroom, staring out the window. The rain was still coming down. His window screen was an incomplete crossword puzzle. He stared vacantly into the gusting sheets, yellow hummingbirds rocketing through. Shortly before dark, the rain slackened and finally the sky began to clear. The clouds whirled away like cannon smoke. The temperature dropped. Joel walked out into the cold. He walked past the caves wherein he often played. Soon, he began to run. And Joel was running, running. He ran north along the river road, toward a sky collapsed over distant lands, where gas burn-offs from an oil refinery cast cherry and apricot tints upon the low-hanging cloud base. Around him, the world went icy and green. The gutters were still sloshing with liquefied ore. Bottlenecked geese splattered up from a nearby river and then ascended high over his head, thin skeins he watched flap madly against the wind, shifting and fading with muted honks. Like that my life has changed, he thought, she is no longer. My mother *is* no longer. He could not wrap his mind around it.

Later that same night, when he folded back his bedcovers, he found something under his pillow, something which astonished him. He found a painting of great delicacy, done in dark watercolors, on a small square of white cardboard. The painting depicted an architecturally remarkable structure, sleek and modern-looking beside a high mountain lake, in an alien land. The lakewater shone of the deepest jade. Over the ragged horizon to the west, a brass-and-bloody sunset leaked out across the sky. In the right foreground, a man with long hair, perhaps a woman, stood looking up at the mysterious structure, and in the window of its topmost room, a silver glow pulsated out. Around the other side of the building, a woman, unseen, stood gazing off at nothing. Her face was detailed, difficult to read. She held in her palm what appeared to be a small pair of scales and also a key, along the side of which, in tiny but very meticulous lettering, were the following words:

In quo sunt omnes thesauri sapientiae et scientiae absconditi

Joel didn't understand the picture, and yet he never asked anyone about it. Nor did he ever show it to anyone. And though this picture was unsigned, Joel knew that only his father, and not his mother, was capable of painting so precisely.

Six years later, two weeks before Christmas, when he was thirteen-years-old, his father beat him so badly that he'd almost not recovered, had almost not been able to make it through. But he made himself recover. He would not give this man the satisfaction of knowing he had won. Repeated blows to his lower back had him urinating blood for over a week, and there were broken bones and something wrong with his guts which for months made him unable to void correctly. The better part of a year is what it had finally taken him to heal, during which time he decided sincerely to murder his father. He had it all planned out, in fact, down to the last detail, and in the end, the only thing that prevented him from doing so was how much he loved the man, who had taught him so many things, who loved him so savagely in return.

Instead he ran away.

He went west, as far west as he could go, riding busses or walking, his hands balled up like two kidneys in the thin pockets of his jacket. He was fourteen-years-old. He sat next to the dirty bus window and stared out at the gigantic shadow of the rig fluctuating across the fields; and always the endless tractor roads curving off into the lonesome horizon, the quicksilver moon watching him from above. He had little money, but some, some which—along with an exceptionally rare stone—he'd stolen from his father, and one week after he left, he stood by the ocean for the first time in his life. He stood watching the slate-blue swells suck and heave. The salty air, rank with fish odors, stung his nostrils. Water lay everywhere—he'd never seen so much of it. He got a job right away washing pots and pans in a bakery. He slept in stairwells, or wherever he could, then he moved into a flat no larger than a closet directly above his workplace, below which large crowds of nutant flowers stood nodding in the open courtyard. The owner of the bakery, a Mormon lady long widowed, was good to him. She liked the way he worked. She taught him her trade. He continued on with her for the next four years of his life. He got back into school.

He was an excellent student who hated every moment of it. But he loved to run. And he loved the ocean, the tireless tide. At night he would stay out for hours, trotting rapidly along the sand, a lone figure moving across the cyanic sky, sea oats trembling.

In school, he learned to speak German, passable Spanish. Most of all, he excelled in sports. He had doglike endurance, and he was quick, a quick study, and already a taste for pushing himself to blinding levels of exhaustion. So that by the time he was finished, he was recruited by colleges all across the country, both for athletics as well as academics.

He did not go.

He took one year off which turned into two, then three. Here followed a period of great profligacy and debauchery, consorting with criminals and degenerates, prostitutes and the like, perhaps the only time in his life that he quit caring. It would not leave him unscathed.

Three and a half years after he'd graduated from high school, he went into the military. He went because it was the last thing in the world his father would have wanted him to do, and because he didn't care, because he was still trying to outrun this man. The year was 1978. He applied for and got into jump school. From there the Army Rangers recruited him, next the Green Berets. In the end, he made it, but not only that: he thrived, one of the best recruits of all time. He was canny. The strength of his eyesight was whispered about among his peers. He made a scientific study of his weaknesses, familiarizing himself in every way with his flaws and predilections, and then he sought to overcome them. Thoughts of being owned by anything began to terrify him, and now the horror of vice, the panic spasms and the coldness of it all, fixed itself like fishhooks into his brain. He became obsessed with certain things, thoughts and acts of self-torture, burning his body slowly, starving himself continually, as he developed a mad desire to strengthen his will. Staring for twenty-four hours straight at a sheer white wall and then trudging the next day through one hundred miles of smothering heat with a 70-pound pack on his back, he himself no more than 140; night jumps into snake-infested swamps, where he was to live for a week, armed with only a knife; hacking through thirty miles of Alaskan wilderness in the Arctic cold, his only equipment a compass, a machete, and two matches; grueling runs up vertical dunes, deadly exhaustions; constant sleep deprivation, yanked regularly from his bed in the middle of the night and strapped and interrogated under the lurid lights of a canvas tent—this and more he endured.

He was twenty-two-years-old.

The military forced him to access a part of himself he might otherwise not have. In the end it gave him a structure that he both needed and secretly craved. He learned greater discipline. He learned languages, maps, weapons, surveillance, hand-to-hand combat. Just another no-name kid from nowhere. But he'd made it. He'd made it entirely on his own.

When, six years later, he was discharged with honors, he swore he would never relinquish his freedom like that again.

Next came days of restlessness, wandering. He drifted for months which turned into years. He worked odd jobs, whatever he could find—loading freight onto barges, laying pipe, carrying hod. He played chess. Or he read all day long. Or drew pictures in pencil. He captured likenesses in lead that astounded the people he drew—astounded them with their perfection, the amount of detail, the longing. He became preoccupied again with the old philosophical questions, questions of freedom, not political freedom but freedom within the soul, questions he'd agonized over in his youth and then put away, questions which came back upon him now with a kind of vengeance. He resolved to follow each of these through to their end. So it was now that he began taking ideas seriously, really for the first time in his life, and on a level he never before had. Thus his reading exploded out in all directions at once. He'd read one thing that he only partially understood, and this in turn would lead him to another, which in turn would lead him to another, and so on, until after two years he developed a turbulent storehouse of knowledge. There was no method to the manner in which he studied, and yet what remained in his mind was methodical.

But more than anything else what he liked was to be alone. He liked walking by himself through the long and level landscapes, not hitchhiking but drifting, at sunset like some solitary figure carved from the coming darkness. He never settled long in any one place. He walked across the entire country and back again. He ran; he smoked cigarettes. He was twenty-nine-years-old.

In Key West, he met a black woman named Lora Hanes with eyes like sloeberries. She was older than him by nine years. She was silent and willowy. She came to his apartment. He watched her pad barefoot around his dusty rooms. She let him draw her portrait as often as he liked, which was often, and for as long. She saw her face duplicated eerily on the pure white pages, saw it come alive with a yearning so great that she felt he knew the very secrets of her soul.

"You make me more beautiful than I am," she said. She reached over and touched his face, his acne-scarred cheek. He turned away.

"You are beautiful," he said to the wall.

"No," she said, "you are. I've never met anyone like you. You're the strangest person I've ever known."

He didn't say anything. She watched him. "Are you haunted, Joel?"

"No."

"What are you doing here?" she said.

"Working."

She stood up and unbuttoned her pants. "You don't have to say anything more. That's what I like most about you: your silence."

He rose up too and gripped her by her forearms, pressing her so tightly against the wall that it made her catch her breath. "You," he said. "You're the one. You're so beautiful I can't stand it." He pressed into her harder, until she couldn't move. She did not resist much. He began kissing her on the mouth. She opened her lips to receive him.

"Do whatever you want to me," she said. "I want you to."

He did.

She came and went sporadically from his apartment. There were no patterns to her visits, no explanations. They spoke very little, or sometimes not at all. Often, she disappeared for weeks on end. Often, she stayed for days and days.

They drank red wine together and stared out across the wide-open waters. Lachrymose music seeped in from the outside, Finnish tangos that mingled with the shriek of seagulls and their pulled-nail cries. The ceiling fan paddled the marine air. Day after day, for hours, she watched him while he drew her face, her anatomy, every conceivable profile and aspect: her interest matched his energy, and matched also his love for the body human. Sometimes while he drew, she talked of this or that particular thing, what she was reading, for instance, or her own work (she grew dark plants in a dark greenhouse), or she spoke of movies or math, the questions of infinity that plagued her. Sometimes they would listen to music deep into the night, and once she said to him:

"Did you know that scientists like music?"

"Where did you hear that?"

"Something I read."

"No," he said, "I didn't."

"I think it's significant. I think it matters."

"Why?" He sounded interested.

"Because it says something. Something about the human brain."

"Yes," he said.

Then one day in the winter of 1987, he left without warning and moved west again. He felt deeply frustrated. He stopped doing all the things he had formerly been doing—reading, drawing, drinking, even, to a large extent, eating. He began running again in earnest; he resumed his religious regimen of pull-ups and pushups, a handful of other exercises, which equaled and then eclipsed anything of this sort that he had done in the military. He thought now incessantly. He would run out into the desert and stay gone for days, taking nothing with him at all, running miles and miles, not eating anything and staying up late under sagging skies, stars everywhere, stars and stars, stars falling all around him, and more stars. During these times, he thought so much that after a while he started to believe that thinking would ultimately destroy him. But by then it was too late: too many questions had been raised that needed answers. He cultivated deliberately his growing compulsion to trace every idea to its ultimate conclusion.

He drifted northward now: from El Paso to Socorro, from Socorro to Grants, Grants to Gallup, always northward, and always working menial jobs. In Lumberton, he worked in a sawmill; in Trinidad, he worked as a baker again; for two months straight, he worked in a slaughterhouse on the outskirts of Greeley. He had this notion that the farther north he got, the better off he would be. He wanted to feel the cold. He wanted to feel the isolation of low populations.

Thus, between the spring and summer of 1990, he walked out of Sterling, Colorado, with sixteen hundred dollars in his pocket and no plan. He bought a car for a thousand dollars cash in Cheyenne, a graphite-gray Mazda with a banged-up body and a rebuilt engine. Shortly after that, he found himself living in a rented trailer just south of Casper, the huge heat of the prairie bearing down on him. Three weeks later, he rolled his car near the South

Dakota border and was subsequently struck down by a brain fever that very nearly killed him.

But it did not kill him. He had lived to pick up the pieces.

Such was the life of Joel Gasteneau.

4

The brain fever had started out as practically nothing: faintheadedness in the early twilight, feelings of hypoglycemic malaise which he was no stranger to from all the years of chronic fasting. Then his nose started bleeding, a watery discharge that took him some little time to stanch, the floor around the trashcan strewn with wads of blood-sopped tissue paper. After that he felt almost entirely better. It was true he had not had a nosebleed in years, he couldn't even remember the last time, but in the end he thought little of it. He continued to sit at the wobbly table, drinking coffee. The air around him turned lavender. A current of wind the size of a child's wrist slid over him, the eastern breeze running through the room and back out across the prairie. He raked his fingers through his hair. He stared out upon the darkening plain. In the east, the sky looked like a draining reef, pale as a green apple. After a while, he rose and went to the doorway. He stood there looking off toward the city of Gillette, which already lay dissolved in the oncoming night, a pall of tangerine light upcast on the clouds like a bomb blast. He went back to the table.

A paperback novel—*The Possessed*—lay spreadeagle before him, a Styrofoam cup of cold coffee and an open notebook beside this. On top of the notebook were several loose sheets of paper, which were all filled with his own handwriting. At this time, he had forgotten about his nosebleed. He did not sit back down at the table but slid the notebook forward and pressed his palms flat upon the page, his arms extended straight. There was a darkling mirror on the wall in front of him; the reflected veins along his inner forearms looked engorged, one glutted vein throbbing on the side of his neck.

He stood rereading what he had last written. There were cataclysmic crossouts and corrections all over the page. He read it through several times. Then, at last, he ripped the page from the notebook and onto a clean sheet of paper copied out the following:

Alone in the dusk of a motel room,
Where angular shadows geometrically
Slice the walls, and a pair of neon signs
Buzz softly outside, glowing rose on pines
Of blackish hue, a traveler looms
Near his window, two stories high. He sees directly

West an oceanic sky spread out cold and vast.
Far off, a tiny wash of white and blue
Fades away in the floods of rising night.
At length, he shifts his sight

Back to the room. The room smells gassed.
He stretches long, cat-like, removes his shoes.

Above him, in the gauzy light, a soft-blue
Seascape hangs. He lies atop an iron bed.
It's springs screech out like guitars. A shipwreck
Gleams as headlights sweep. A gush, in his neck,
Of pain. The moon glides by like a sky canoe.
Silence booms. He lifts his head.

Here he stopped writing and stood for twenty minutes or more, still leaning over the table. His pencil was poised above the page. For a long moment, it looked as if he would continue writing, but in the end he held off. After a while, he straightened up and dropped the pencil onto the table.

He sat down and gazed about him. He was surprised to find the room gone so dark. He stayed in this position for nearly an hour. Then he reached over and snapped on the table lamp. He picked up the paperback and began to read.

One hour later, when he was finished with the chapter, he turned back to the beginning and read it all again, a long, philosophical section he'd been through many times before. After he was finished this time, he stood up and flung the book across the room. The crash shattered the stillness with a violence that spooked him. The seeds of an awful idea were now hatching open in his head, a suspicion he'd stumbled upon concerning his mother and his father which when he stumbled upon it struck him with such force that he couldn't believe he'd not thought of it before. At this time also, things in the room had taken on a curious aspect, patterns of leopardine light shimmering across the carpet, but only on the margins of his vision so that when he turned to look at them straight-on, they disappeared before his eyes.

At length, he gathered the loose sheets of paper into a sloppy stack and stuffed the stack back into his notebook. Then he tossed the notebook onto the bed. He strode across the room and melted into the cretonne-covered armchair. The neural itches of viral delirium were creeping into his brain, but he did not recognize them as such. All he knew for certain now was that the whole left side of his skull was a dragstrip of pain, unusual for him, since he almost never got headaches. With sick surmise, he sat in the leprous chair until dawn.

Dawn found him horribly depressed and unable to sleep still but with a new thought gleaming in his eyes. He sat there. Another hour passed. A rill of sweat slid off his forehead between his eyes. Abruptly, he reached over and snatched the notebook off the bed. Onto a fresh sheet of paper, he wrote the following:

Alone in the dusk of a motel room
Where wedge-shaped shadows geometrically

Tilt the walls, and a pair of neon signs
Sizzle softly outside, glowing rose on pines
Of spinach hue, a sick traveler looms
Near his window, stories high. Directly

West, a darkling sky spreads out cold and vast.
He stands in thought. His eyes are dark. Night accrues
From the khaki light. Gimlet stars ignite,
A gold moon shard. At length, he shifts his sight
Back to the room, where complex odors blast
His face, stretches long, catlike, removes his shoes.

Before him, in Rembrandt dark, a soft-blue
Seascape hangs. He lies atop an iron bed.
Its springs scream out like guitars. A shipwreck
Gleams as headlights sweep. In his neck
A sluice of pain. The moon glides by like a sky canoe.
Deep silence booms. He lifts his head.

Soft are the creatures of night. A clock seeps
Digitals into the room. Through hidden vents
He hears the watery purr of doves outside.
They're balled like roses and throbbing. Now a landslide
Of ice in a pail that's sobbing sweat. He weeps,
Sick and silent. The nighttime grows immense.

He finished writing and slapped the notebook shut. He did not reread anything. Instead, he strapped on his old tennis shoes and headed out for a long run.

But this run was even longer than usual—in fact he didn't come back until he had logged almost thirty miles, by which time the state of his delirium was complete. Now, only now, did he realize how sick he'd become. He staggered back into the room, bouncing off the walls and doorjambs, his jaw spastic with shivering. He felt chills sifting continuously into his bowels, his guts heaving borborygmically, and the tongue inside his mouth swelling to the size of a small fish. He'd tried to shower, and did, eventually, though not before first blacking out and gashing open the whole left side of his cheekbone, which was the least of his problems, however, since from here on in he descended deeper and deeper into fever.

Then, seconds before falling into bed, he saw her again: the young woman in the overcoat whom he'd glimpsed upon the overpass before his car wreck. She was gazing at him now from the empty field beyond the motel's rear window. He froze and stared back at her. Beads of sweat oozed out along his hairline and stood there like blisters. He watched her for a long moment. Her hair, long and flaxen, was pulled back in such a way that it exposed her bruised and bony temples, a large head swaying on a reedy neck. Chthonic woman with a dim intent, her skin so fishbelly-white. She did not turn away or move at all. With a crash, he dropped the aluminum blinds and fell headlong into bed.

And hissed away—in reality only a matter of days, yet what seemed an eternity to his sick mind. By turns sweating and shivering, but at extremes greater by far than any he had ever experienced before, there were dreams, of course, mind-spinning nightmares and hallucinations which conspired, all, to horrify him absolutely senseless. He lay for hours, trapped in a Boschian nightmare, not knowing if he slept or woke. He dreamed repeatedly of health, of a defervescence that did not come. His body began to wither away beneath him. First he grew macerated by his lack of food, then, he came to believe, by a secret longing at the core of his being which he could neither banish nor fully identify.

On the morning of the third day, he opened his eyes for the first time since he'd fallen asleep and found himself haunted by the memory of an ancient odor he'd not thought of or smelled in twenty-five years or more: the inside of his mother's jewelry box, musty and unbearably sad. Moments later, the motel clerk rapped on his door. It took him a full minute to process the sound. It was all he could do to haul himself up and pass her a wad of bills through the chain-locked door. She glanced at the money in her hand, then back up at him with something like concern—his sunken face, his long tangled hair. She said nothing. He bombed back into bed.

He lay naked in his sickness.

Each evening, the ruins of the western sky flickered in the far distance, expiring slowly into a rubbish-heap of purple clinkers piled high in the southwest. He thought he smelled lilies, late at night.

Sometimes, for no reason, his eyes would flip open, and he'd find himself lying there, staring up at the large whorls scalloped in stucco across the low ceiling, and he would think: I may die, I could very well die here, like this. But he was too exhausted to feel any emotion in particular over this pronouncement, save for a distant sadness deep inside his brain which thinking about retrospectively, weeks later, made him want to cry.

At one point well into his sickness, he staggered to the bathroom and threw the switch. He went for water—only to find himself back on his burning bed watching an ominously familiar image spring up inside the meat of his brain. The image had started out small, a sort of malformed, club-shaped kernel, milky and somewhat phlegmy, but then rapidly it began expanding, swelling and swelling, changing forms, mutating, and would not stop growing, until by the end of it, it took up the entire space inside the panorama of his mind: an egg-shaped monolith looming tilted in a bleak and scorched-out wasteland. He did not know for certain what the vessel was, or what it represented, although he was sure now that he remembered it from his childhood, something he had conjured up during a bad illness then; and suddenly, in his motel room, he grew terrified that it was going to break open, spilling all the secrets of his soul, which at some point in his fever dreams he'd convinced himself that it contained.

Deep down but consciously, he knew that the reason he was so terrified of this happening was that he cared very much about the type of person he became.

For he loved himself, he loved his body and all that he had done. He loved his strengths and capabilities, and lying there sick, he felt it all rotting away beneath him, purple and ruby-black scabs, like a venereal leprosy, spreading out across his flesh and eating him alive. Yet at the same time, diverse lusts consumed him, unbelievable hungerings after the female flesh, with attendant images: massive twats, pink and pulsating, with ropes of pubic hair dripping like stalactites onto his face; black orifices and muddy pissflaps, opaque juices splashing across the bone concavity of his skull; humongous assholes, ribbed and infundibular, engulfing him whole but arousing him to orgasms that lasted minutes.

He awoke from dark to dark, pumping out the seed. He fell back in a sexual rage, wild with lusts that simultaneously sickened him.

He cooled his temples against the wall.

Finally, one rainy evening six days after it had all begun, his fever broke open inside him, and he found himself, hungry as hell, staring up at aqueous lights shimmering across the ceiling. His brain felt scorched, and yet it seemed to him that he was seeing things with an abnormal clarity. Almost immediately, he thought of his father.

He arose from his sodden bed and bathed. Standing naked over the sink, he drank glassful after glassful of water, leaking the water out of his skin as quickly as he could take it in. His cheekbone was scabbed-over from the fall he'd taken in the shower.

He dressed carefully in the dark room and then walked out into a fine rain, lurching down to a diner one block away. Traffic was desultory. A car here and there slished by. It was now, walking, that he noticed himself preoccupied again with the same dim memory that had started to surface on the day of his car accident. When it came up this time, it brought with it a much sharper sense of pain, even embarrassment, though he still wasn't quite able to capture it. The worst of the physical suffering was over, he knew, yet within him now he felt a mounting sense of apprehension, as if some terrible event was about to take place.

He ordered a bowl of oatmeal, white toast. Eating slowly. As suddenly as a bone-snap, then, the memory rose up in full before him, and he remembered everything.

The spoon slipped from his hand and plopped soundlessly into the bowl of oatmeal.

5

The river coursed down from the clay hills below the monastery and into a canyon of yellow rock. Along the floor of the canyon, the ground was sandy and the water was torpid and thick, and as the canyon walls rose upward, the cliffs angled closer and closer together so that the sun shone down on the water for only a few hours each day. On the opposite side of the valley, a larger, cleaner river wound down from hidden snowfields and met with this other at a juncture just before the cliffs opened into the woodlands. Very near here there lay a village, a cluster of small homes and other buildings scattered like gingerbread throughout the muscular fir trees. Together, these two rivers slopped out along the westernmost edge of the village, containing a yellow or greenish water, depending on the season, ferruginous and never potable except in a pinch, the entire area a hotbed of geothermal activity; in winter, thus, steam phantoms swarmed up everywhere over the village streets and sidewalks with people passing through the mist, as if in Yellowstone, or New York City.

By midsummer, all the land about the village grew pale in the sharp western sun, when the squash and the melons bloated in the fields and the grasses stood weather-beaten and singed. And then a rumor stained the air; it crept like an illusion over the land: the first nick of autumn blowing down from somewhere far away in the north. The cornstalks stood bronzed and bare, rattling dryly in the wind. The sky spread a flawless blue canopy, which the granite jags tried to puncture and across which jumbo jets smeared their long lines of chalk—diagonals and parabolas only partially erased or pulled to vapors indistinguishable from clouds. The summer raged away. By the end of August, the heat in the sky melted like lead, and everything became rippled and glassy.

Wind from the open pastures to the north poured into the narrow throat that opened into the valley, often carrying with it a dry peculiar scent: the scent of protein. The village was situated at the highest end of the valley, along a deadly but dormant faultline, eight thousand feet above sea level and walled in by a kind of granite-and-basalt cirque. It was an astonishingly silent town, an old mining settlement whose mines were long defunct; so that now it seemed to subsist on its beauty alone. The very air exuded sparseness. In cooler months, sheets of mist that smelled and tasted metallic hung low over the surrounding hills and then blew gently away. Wooden ladders and scaffoldings from the old mining days still stood leaning against sectors of the high cliffs above, duplicating themselves in geometric shadows across the adamantine walls, the hills roundabout thoroughly tunneled and scarred, with tailing drifting down the slopes like snow. As it moved farther along to the south, the valley narrowed and then ascended into the mountains beyond. It was at the foot of these peaks, two thousand feet higher up, that the abandoned monastery stood, its buildings like ships beneath the huge high sky. An insular region, sectioned off from the world on the west and on the south by the great iron-spined mountains, and on the east by the uncultivated fields, it was a landscape of Euclidian perfection, full of vanishing points and far slopes, immense, yet traversed by a single road: an isolate highway humming day or night with Mack Truck tires.

The sky was seamless at dusk, an unbroken bell adumbrating rain. It was the day after his sixty-fifth birthday, and Elias Moorecroft disentombed a large volume from his bookshelf. He paused for a long moment before setting the book on the desk in front of him. He stood gazing out his study-room window. His view ran across a series of variegated fields and then vanished into the great wedge where the landmass merged with the sky. The horizon was wooly. His home was located eight miles north of town, well off the main highway, inside the heart of the pastureland. A lone hawk, blown down from the cliffs, was hovering low over his backyard, and with gritty eyes Elias watched the bird.

Sleep abandoned Elias more and more frequently these days, not occasionally as had once been the case, but nightly now, four or even five times a week. He combated it first by smoking less and cutting back on coffee. When this didn't help, he started exercising more: dips deep into the night, pull-ups on his warm basement pipes, long runs into the iron dawn.

Or he read his way toward exhaustion. He liked long novels with complicated plots. He liked German literature, Shakespeare, formal poems with subtle rhymes and subtle meters, and no doggerel. But more than anything else, Elias loved biology books, and he made it a habit now of delving every night into the intricacies of evolution and the human genome.

He stood holding the dusty volume by its spine. He stared out the window. Beyond him, under a sky swollen with undischarged rain, the tall and tattered rye fell away to the south. These were the wilds of loneliness, he thought, vast, vacant. To his left, the mountains rose up sheer and spectacular into the dusk. After five minutes, with a thud, he dropped the book onto the desk in front of him and blew dust from its cover. Motes exploded into a diagonal block of pewter light. The book was *The Riverside Milton*.

Elias was a tall swarthy man, vigorous and upright in his movements, with austere features, a sharp nose and pleated forehead—one of these men whose age it is impossible to gauge: gray on the head but still fast on his feet, with stone-blue eyes that contained lightning bolts. Indeed, his forehead and his hair both looked as if they had been struck by lightning and still bore the scars. He wore his longish mane high and swept back in a sort of pompadour, his pumpkin-colored scalp visible beneath. He was dressed in baggy brown corduroys and black boots, his standard garb. Moments before coming into the study, he'd crushed out a cigarette, and his fingertips stunk of nicotine and were stained a coppery-yellow.

He stood in the darkling room for a long while but did not bother to turn on the lamp. A pair of half-moon eyeglasses, filled with the muted daylight, sat on a corner of his desk. He looked down at the binding beneath his hand: good solid workmanship, and something he admired, for he was a bookbinder himself. In a moment, he heard a car thump softly over the wooden bridge that crossed the irrigation canal beside his house; then he heard the car stop. Elias walked up to the window. The canal wound by, ten feet below him, silent jade waters with slats of smoky light hanging above the drift. There was a silver glint in the air, an enchanted quality. Near him on his left stood a large rock building, vaguely chapel-like and composed of black stones quarried only fifty feet away. Blue and violet morning glories had overrun the garden. A pale woman in a gray overcoat emerged from the car and stood for a moment staring across the hood toward the flowing water. She wore a mint-green scarf and a mushroom-shaped cap, which she patted now, her long neck swaying like a slender stalk.

Presently she plunged both hands into her slash pockets and proceeded up the yard.

Elias followed her with his farsighted eyes, curious who this woman could be. He went to the door to meet her.

He saw immediately that she was not as young as he had at first supposed. She was of middling age, perhaps not quite. She had an odd face, he thought at once, not unattractive but with something of the science-fictional about it—in the long sleek planes, the shadows her cheekbones cast. Her mouth was calm but conspicuous and consisted of little more than a bee-stung upper lip and a lower one that simply receded away. Yet, for all its simplicity, from the very beginning, he found this mouth almost endlessly complicated, so that by the time their brief visit was concluded he would see many smears of sadness pass across it, mixed with radiance and brightness, and philosophical things, even great gladness. She had a long nose, a trifle too long, perhaps, and rather blasé eyes that were knowing and approximately the color they call hazel.

"Elias Moorecroft," she said swiftly, "how do you do." (Surprising him with her contralto voice.) "To meet you at last, a privilege and a pleasure." She plucked off her mushroom cap and stuffed it into her coat pocket. She rubbed her head. "I apologize for dropping in on you unannounced like this."

"It's okay," he said. "It's quite all right."

"Although I *did* try calling first," she said. "Did you know that your phone..." But she let the last words of this sentence trail off as if they were not worth the trouble of articulating and proffered her pearly white hand instead. "My name is Lauren," she said. "Lake." Her spear-shaped fingernails, unpainted but clear-lacquered and glinting, felt cool as liquid against his skin. Her hair was pleasantly mussed and hung jawbone length, ash-blond.

"You aren't from here," he said.

"No." She paused, frowned; she craned her neck around, gazing back toward her sleek green Audi. "In fact, it's my first time here." She was still looking behind her as she said these last words, and the skin of her neck shone whitely in the muted light.

"Welcome, in that case," he said.

40

"Yes, thank you. But —my God—you must have virtually perfect eyesight to be able read my license plate all the way from here in this light, because I can't make it out at all." Then she turned back to him and smiled. "Or perhaps it's that you don't recognize me, and that's how you know I'm not from here."

"Both, really," he said.

He decidedly liked the lilt in her voice, her languorous confidence.

"Actually," she continued, "the entire past year I've been traveling—that is, I've been *exclusively* traveling. Meaning I've had no real fixed address. The Illinois plates are arbitrary, for the most part."

"I see."

"I like this feeling, you know?"

"Which feeling is that?"

"Being mobile," she said. "I like being mobile. In fact, I crave it. I'll tell you the truth: I like to get in my car and just start driving. Just driving and driving until I'm too exhausted to drive any more, and then I like to pull over and check into a motel room somewhere and sleep until morning, and then get up and do it all over again. I've been all across the country in this way. All across the country and *back*, I should say, south, north, Alaska, Texas, it really makes no difference where. It's the driving, you see." She paused. "The *driving*," she repeated, and again fell briefly silent. "But I am originally from Chicago, and that's why—"

"Oh?" He slit his eyes. "I know the city of Chicago very well, city of the big shoulders, hog butcher for—"

"How so?"

"Well, it's where I matriculated, for one thing … many, many years ago."

"Really? And where did you"—she just perceptibly hesitated— "matriculate?"

"Loyola University."

"I didn't know that," she said.

"No. I don't suppose you would." He frowned. "I mean, would you? But tell me: how can I help you, Miss Lake?"

"Yes. Why is it that I'm here."

"Why, indeed. Although I'm thrilled. I mean, I love it when people just drop by."

"You do? That's good information to have." She smiled again, exposing all her straight white teeth. "I'm here because of my former husband."

"Husband?"

"Yes. Bill Morgan. Do you remember Bill?"

"I do, as a matter of fact, yes." Elias's face visibly brightened—at which point, he seemed to just realize that they were still standing on his front porch. "But, God!" he said. "Won't you please come inside?"

"I thought you'd never ask," she said. And winked at him, but so rapidly that thinking about it later that night, unable to sleep, he wasn't sure if he'd really seen anything after all.

Elias led her first into the darkened foyer and then down an L-shaped corridor that opened up into his living room. In the other direction, a steep staircase ascended into an eerie blackness.

The living room was spacious but cluttered, filled with half-packed boxes and pages of newspaper, nests of excelsior piled against the walls. There was a clean smell in the air.

Lauren stood for a moment upon the threshold, scanning the room slowly. She slithered out of her jacket and stood holding it over her forearm. She had on a white button-down shirt, open to the cleavage, and an ecru summer skirt that came down to her kneecaps. Her shoes were lead-gray and had thin flat soles, no laces. Vaguely, and with a half-cupped palm, Elias directed her to a nearby chair and asked her to please sit. He snapped on a light switch beside her head and adjusted its rheostat. Lauren draped her jacket over the back of the chair and then seated herself, crossing her legs smoothly, left over right. Elias seated himself opposite her.

"Forgive the mess," he said, indicating the boxes with his chin. "I'm moving very soon."

"That explains why your phone is disconnected."

"Yes, that's right." He raised his eyebrows. "Very perceptive." He glanced briefly about him, then back at her. He touched his fingertips to his forehead. "Moving," he repeated with a slight wince. "Sheer hell."

"On that," she said, smiling and readjusting her skirt, "we definitely agree."

Here he flashed her an unexpected smile—an attractive smile, she thought, disclosing his mouthful of nicotine-stained teeth, which contrasted sharply against his claret-colored lips. And now he offered her a drink, which she declined; they sat across from each other, a glass coffee table between them.

"Is your move permanent, then?" she asked.

"Unfortunately, yes. I love it here, but the altitude is too high for really first-rate growing."

"What do you mean by that?"

"Just that. And really, this has only been my summer home for the last ten years or so. My other house, the one I'm moving to, is located in a larger town west of here called Pitkin. That's where my greenhouse is, you see, and my business."

"Business?" she said. "Greenhouse?"

"Yes." For a split second he seemed perplexed. "I'm sorry. I'm a horticulturist and a book publisher by trade. For some reason, I just *assumed* you knew this, but why would you? Yes. I publish horticulture books, and other science books as well. It's a small press, but successful. Why do you scowl at me so forbiddingly, Miss Lake? Did I say something controversial?"

"Forgive me," she said, "but I thought you were a priest."

A look of surprise flitted across his face, and then he understood. He smiled without parting his lips. "No. I *was* a priest. But that was a long time ago."

"You're retired then?"

"No. I quit the priesthood."

She stared at him for a long thoughtful moment. Her greenish eyes gradually widened.

Outside, the light was fading, and the windowpanes were growing increasingly relucent, so that from where they were sitting, their reflected figures appeared to be hovering just above the slope of the lawn. An owl cooed once from the cottonwoods that flanked the canal into its bight. A purple planet swam above the treetops, and the trees stood darkly against the sky.

"May I ask why?" she said. "I'm only curious. If I'm prying, please say."

"No," he said, "not at all. I quit believing in God, is the short answer to your question." He paused for perhaps five seconds. "Insofar, that is, as I ever really believed in Him in the first place—I see that now."

"How interesting."

"Not really," he said. "I'm afraid it's actually very *bor*ing, if you want to know the truth."

But she paid no attention to this. "What specifically made you—I mean what pushed you all the way over, may I ask? If I'm being too—"

"No, no," he said, holding up his hand, "please. If you were, I'd tell you. Science, ultimately. Science demolished my faith."

"Just like that?" And softly, softly she snapped her fingers up next to her ear.

"No. It was cumulative." He paused for several beats. "But you seem so—"

"No," she said, "I'm not."

"What, then?"

"Just intrigued."

"Why so?"

"Because it's almost too good."

"What do you mean by that?"

"I mean too perfect," she said.

He fell silent again, studying her. Her eyes, so unrevealing at first, all at once appeared to him exceptionally bright, but bright with a furtive knowledge. A small green vein throbbed near her left eyelid, curving around the outer edge of the eye-socket where it surfaced for only a moment, like a baby sea-snake baring its back.

She lifted her gaze a little, above him, up to the somewhat glary reproduction of Dali's *Final Judgment*, which hung just over his head. In the subfusc light, the animals in the picture appeared to be stomping through the hoary grass of Elias's hair, Christ with globelike shoulders expounding into his ear, a silver-blue moon resounding in the daytime sky.

A gentle breeze blew into the room, ballooning the curtains and bringing with it the dank smell from the canal, the distant report of a barking dog. The current of air made her turn her head, as if she sensed something there. He took that opportunity to regard her more closely, wondering that her physical beauty should only at this moment dawn on him so forcefully—although her beauty *wasn't* at all obvious, he saw that now as well: there was something too faraway in it, too remote and cold, like a star. Her profile, or three-quarters of it, turned to him now, showed features rather bare, even harsh, a body all points and angles, all disproportion. She was long-legged and thin, easily as tall as he was, but at the same time she was wide-hipped, with a rear-end leaning toward large. In the creamy light of the room, her hair glinted platinum. She still wore the mint-green scarf tied in a loose knot around her neck. She sat leaning forward in the chair, her back ramrod-straight, her legs crossed at the ankles, which were slim and sockless, her shins glinting like two metal rods.

"Miss Lake," he began.

"Regarding my visit," she cut in, "yes. First, did you know that Bill Morgan is dead?"

"No," he said, "I didn't. Oh, I'm very sorry to hear that."

"Yes. I understand that at one time you knew him well." This was a trifle more statement than question.

"No, not really. Why would you say?"

"Well, he always spoke very highly of you, for one thing. You once had something of an influence on him."

Elias seemed genuinely surprised by this, although he didn't actually say anything—or not right off, at any rate. Rather, he tugged at his left earlobe and at the same time downcurled both corners of his mouth, which had the effect of sending his eyebrows halfway up on his forehead. He muttered something incoherent.

"Do you find it so hard to believe?" she said.

"Frankly, yes."

"Why?"

"Well, to be candid with you, Lauren Lake, I only met with Bill on a few different occasions … five or perhaps six times … six at most. He came to me, you see." Elias fell silent a moment, thinking back. "As I recall, he was only thirteen or fourteen at the time. But really, I suppose the main thing is, it's just a little surprising to hear something such as this after so much time has passed."

"Yes, I imagine it would be very odd."

"One never thinks one is doing any good anyway. But you must understand, this was all such a *long* time ago, when I had just come here from San Luis."

"You corresponded after that, though, didn't you?"

"A little, not much. Even that was a fairly lopsided exchange."

"Oh? In what way?"

"Well, I'm a very, very, *very* poor correspondent, for one thing," he said. He hesitated again, scowling at the floor. "But in fact I think it was more than this."

"What was it?"

"I suspected that Bill's motives had become, let us say, not as sincere as they had once been. A not uncommon thing at all," Elias added, "especially in young people."

44

She nodded contemplatively. "May I ask you a personal question?" she said.

"Sure."

"Was your relationship with Bill ever in any way sexual? Explicitly or tacitly?"

"What? No, not at all, not at all," he said. "Our relationship was …"

"Yes?"

"Philosophical. Bill, as I'm sure you know, was an inordinately intense person, and as such he had questions—many, many questions about God, faith, religion, et cetera—as many philosophically minded young people do. It was all quite natural."

"Yes," she said, "that sounds about right."

They were both silent.

"How did Bill die, if I may ask?" Elias said. "And when?"

"Some time ago, actually. A year or more. Alcoholism. Drugs. Fornication. Venereal disease. Confusion. His unquenchable thirst. Whathaveyou. Difficult to pinpoint *exactly* what killed him."

"Are you being serious?"

"Yes and no."

"You are actually a widow, then, not an ex?"

"No. Bill and I were long divorced. We married young," she explained. "I was even younger than him, believe it or not."

"I believe it," he said.

She stood up suddenly now and walked over to the window, her back facing him. She touched her fingertips to the cold glass. In the west, the sky was all dark now, save for a tiny wash of white. Elias could clearly see her head hanging disembodied upon the windowpane. Outside, a butterscotch tomcat was stalking toward her through the grass, moving gracefully in the gloaming, whiskers flashing silver. She raised her eyebrows, held them up. "In any case," she said to Elias's foreshortened image on the window, "the main reason I'm here …" She glanced back at him over her shoulder.

"Yes?" he said.

"Is because Bill left you certain things."

"Beg pardon?"

"Bill left you things," she said.

She turned back to the windowpane. The breeze was pushing back lightly against a hatch of the tomcat's fur, so that from where she now stood, she could see the cat's bone-white undercoat glowing in the darkness. Then the cat moved off into the shadows, his ringed tail up in the air, straight as a rod. "You see," she said, "it's taken a long time for his family to sort out all his so-called affairs—his money, I mean, none of which was really very considerable, despite the fact that his real father *did* leave him certain things of value—"

Again she broke off and squinted outside. The tomcat was suddenly gone, swallowed up completely by this scaled veldt. Then, in the blackness beyond, for a split second, she thought she saw a figure in white; yet when she blinked and looked a second time, there was nothing there at all. She frowned. "To keep it short," she said, "a long, long time ago Bill once told me—he gave me very specific instructions, in fact—that all his books were to go to you."

"Me?"

"Si." She turned to him again.

"What books?" he said.

"His books, as I say. All of them. Bill was the country's Last Great Bibliophile, didn't you know? He had many old books, valuable books, books containing knowledge, and—well, you see, he wanted you to have them. Bill began collecting books when he was just a child. He said that of all the people he knew in the whole world, he thought you'd appreciate them most." She let Elias take this in. Once more she turned her back to him. "He wanted you to *have* them," she said, facing the window.

"Oh, I don't know, Miss Lake. Are you certain?"

"Absolutely certain. Why would I not be? He was very specif—tell me," she said, "who is that man standing over there?"

"Which man?"

"Your neighbor. The one with the ridiculous face."

"Ridiculous face?"

"Yes. I saw him as I was walking up. And then I didn't see him. Now I see him again. He was talking to a group of people."

"Oh, is he back?"

(She thought she may have caught something in his voice.)

"Evidently," she said.

"He's not my neighbor," Elias said, "and he doesn't live here." (She was sure of it now.) "He 'comes around.' He works for me sometimes, but only in an unofficial capacity."

"What sort of work does he do?"

"Well, he likes cars, fixing things. He also likes gardening."

"A factotum?"

"Actually, a stonemason by trade, but really a philosopher of sorts. He's also an amateur arachnologist. He's a very captivating person, but unfortunately he's also quite out of his mind. Tell me, though, is his face really so ridiculous?" Elias sounded concerned.

"Yes, it is."

"Why do you say so?" Elias said.

"Because I can't take my eyes off it, for one thing."

She was still turned away from him, and he narrowed his eyes on her back, more curious about her now than ever before.

"What's an arachnologist?" she said.

"Someone who studies spiders."

"Was he formally trained?"

"No," Elias said. "He's self-taught. And what about you, Miss Lake? What do you do, if you don't mind my asking?"

"Me? I write as well, as coincidence would have it."

"As well?"

"Yes. Just as you do."

He nodded.

She turned from the window and came striding back to her chair. She sat down and drummed her fingernails once on the antimacassars, as if depressing imaginary trumpet valves.

"And what do you write?" he said.

"Articles, mostly. And poems. I'm also a copyeditor."

"Articles for whom?"

"Oh, various magazines about certain subjects on particular themes."

"I see," he said.

"It's all strictly freelance." She blinked her eyes slowly. Her upper lip shone wet and plump. "But I'll be candid with you, Moorecroft. I come from a very, quote, wealthy family, and therefore I really don't need to work. But work? I love to work. Work is healthy, jobs are good for the soul. Work provides an outlet not only for aggression but also expression. That is what I believe. Consequently, I've worked all my life, by choice. I've worked as a lifeguard, a clerk, a bookkeeper, night auditor, waitress—several times doing that last one, in fact. I believe—I mean, I truly believe—that one can tell virtually everything one needs to know about a person simply by how he works. I'm really quite opinionated on the subject—"

"I can see that you are," he said. "But listen, Miss Lake—"

Now she interrupted him: "Don't worry, Moorecroft. Bill wanted you to have them. He honestly did. He told me so. And once, because I loved him very much, I promised him that I would deliver. Really, it's not a big deal. The truth is, you'll probably be disappointed when you see how *little* he actually left you. Though, I admit, several of the books are quite nice—if you're into that sort of thing, I mean."

"What sort of thing?"

"Knowledge and learning, not ignorance. Truth, beauty, brains, that sort of thing."

"But I hardly knew Bill, I must impress that upon you."

"There's really no need. It doesn't matter to me at all."

"And when I did know him," he said as if he hadn't heard her, "I was still a priest. This strikes me as significant."

"Does it? It doesn't me."

"And furthermore I can't help believing that if Bill had known I'd left the church—and that I'd quit believing in God to boot—he would not have wanted me to have his things. You see, when I knew Bill, the priesthood and God, it was all very important to him. It meant a great deal to him. He respected it so much."

She didn't say anything.

"You've come all the way here just for this?" he said.

"No, actually. He left me something here as well—or near here: a small house in the canyons to the north. His father once lived there, did you know?"

"I did, as a matter of fact. I even met the man three or four times. Always somewhat sad, I thought."

"Yes, he was," she said. "That he was. And perhaps for good reason." She scratched the side of her nose with her thumbnail. A small scar lay like a zig-zag along the outer edge of her nostril. Automatically, Elias connected the scar with her spear-shaped nails, as if one of those nails had inflicted the wound. "I will say," she said, "I wasn't quite prepared for how spectacularly beautiful it is here. I mean, I will say that. The rarefied air and so on, all these mountains and so forth."

"It really is. And you never completely get used to it. I know the house you're speaking of, incidentally. It's an excellent location. Are you going to live there?"

"I seriously doubt it."

"Why?"

"It's not really my style, for one thing. Also, there are people who want to buy it, I think. If they really want it, they can have it."

"In the meantime—"

"I'm living there."

"For how long?"

"Not long." She stood up. "Come with me, Moorecroft. I have your books, some of them, with me in the trunk of my car. Trunks in my trunk. Trunks and trunks … which I already have too much junk in my trunk as it is, as I'm sure you've noticed."

Elias, out of eyeshot, smiled but said nothing. She slipped on her jacket and strode ahead of him to the door.

He followed.

Outside, the cool air smelled of water. A pale-haired man, the one she'd seen from the window, sat propped on his elbows at the edge of a steep lawn. He was all alone. He was drenched in a pool of sodium light, his legs outstretched before him. He appeared not to have any bones in his body. He was thin but strong-looking, and yet for all his repose, an excess of energy burned about him, a healthiness that set him apart.

"Thomas," Elias said to him.

"Hello, hello!"

"Could you give us a hand? I have a lady here who claims she has too much junk in her trunk, although personally I don't see it."

"Okay," the man said. "Now you're talking my language."

6

Toward the close of a soft afternoon in southwestern Colorado, during the first week of August, 1990, approximately one hour before sunset, a solitary man with sunburned arms emerged from a passenger train and stood for a long time upon the open platform. The station lay fetched on the western slope of a wide clearing, some twelve miles away from where he had grown up, a childhood home he had not seen in over two decades. No real township existed here, simply an aimless congeries of decrepit buildings, one restaurant, several shotgun shacks each hung with peeling tarpaper and scabrous paint. This was the final stopping place before the tracks again looped away to the east, bisecting the distant fields, away through the canyons, east and south into the dead volcanic country of northern New Mexico and then across the state.

The man stood along the right-hand side of the wooden platform, exposed to the windowpanes of a nearby gas station. The train crackled and zapped behind him. The wind blew about his hair, flapped his shirt. His arms were sunburned, but his face looked unnaturally pale, his eye-sockets bony and encircled with liver-colored rings. A gleam shone in his eyes, a fever gleam, but an odd clarity burned there as well.

Looking west, he could see the old silver mine still flashing on the hill: mounds of white tailing, arsenic burns on the surrounding rock. There was no one about. The dirt streets lay deserted and cauterized. Standing out in the high flat sunlight, he looked as if he might be the sole survivor of some worldwide calamity. The light fell around him like pollen. The day was desolate.

At the end of the street the mountains began, black granite slashed gigantically across the sky. After a while, the train lurched once and then began crawling away, around the great bend, until at last it was gone. Lukewarm wind whispered through the grass. He stood for a long time without apparently thinking, neither did he move; only once his eyeballs flipped over to the right, as if he was searching after something, something.

He stood with an army-issue duffel bag in his hand. His hair was long. His last four months had been spent haunting the hallways of vast libraries, poring over all claims miraculous and supernatural.

At length, as if rousing himself, he jumped down off the platform and turned south, walking away from the depot along the fringes of the settlement. He moved down a dirt road whose tire ruts were deep and baked iron-hard in the sun. The cottonwoods soared above him on either side. He moved swiftly in his worn-out tennis shoes. He had a graceful, coordinated way about him. After half a mile, he came to a larger gravel road that veered at a sharp angle off this one and then swung back toward the southwest. He turned onto it and walked into the narrow valley.

The valley consisted of streams and small meadows, long pastures fenced off with sagging barbed wire. Skunk weed grew along the fence posts, and wild sunflowers blew amid rank shoots of grass. The river flowed, thirty meters to his right, running parallel the road: calm black water, level as a lake. He could hear the faint slap of its shore waves. It was the time of day when the land, still warm, takes on the serenity of early evening. Cattails among the yellow reeds stood clustered along the riverbanks. A deep stillness hung in the air. The sun sat spinning like a little gear far off in the west, yet the eastern sky was already streaked with long lines of red. Bull bats had swarmed down from the caves and were swooping above the river's drift.

He seemed not to notice.

He seemed invested with a specific purpose.

At the end of two miles, the river dropped off into a shallow gorge, and he entered the throat of the canyon. The walls above him turned sheer and sienna. Outcroppings of scrub oak and juniper grew out of the rock, and the smell of juniper spiked the air. One mile farther, he came to a third gravel road, which was a driveway. Here he stopped walking and stood for five minutes gazing up the road. It ascended steeply in front of him, six hundred meters long, and then hooked off to the left, terminating at a flat house he could only just glimpse from where he now stood.

The wind switched on.

He moved his bag to his other shoulder and made his way toward the top of the hill.

Road construction was going on halfway up: halted for the day, a silent backhoe stood reared against the sky like a petrified dinosaur. There were orange pylons and white barrels with flashing lights on top marking off a clean-sliced pit. On either side of him, the entire way, ponderosa pine trees rubbed elbows with pinions and more junipers. Darkness descended gradually. Around the edges of the eastern sky, the light had dimmed to a soft cabbage-green. He walked the steep incline. At last, the driveway funneled into a thin path which led, after all that uphill, into a descending set of stairs. The stairs then opened onto a redwood deck that skirted the north and east sides of the house.

He found the front door slightly ajar and saw a silvery light burning somewhere within. While casting his eyes about, he suddenly got the sensation that he was being observed. He looked around. He could see no one. In the center of the door, an iron knocker hung from the jaws of some ambiguous beast. He used the knocker to knock. He knocked and knocked. Nobody answered. He knocked again. Still there was no answer. He felt sure that if he kept knocking—

Just then, a contralto voice spoke to him from behind.

"May I help you?" the voice said.

He turned.

A tall woman, obscured by shadow, stood at the opposite end of the deck, some fifteen feet away from him. Because of the gauzy twilight and an apricot klieg that burned over her head, he could not clearly make out her features. Yet he saw a pair of smiling eyes beaming at him. Her neck gave the illusion of underwater sway. Neither advanced toward the other.

"Hello," he said. It wasn't until he had spoken that he realized how long it had been since his last utterance, for the word came off his tongue thickly.

"How may I help you?" she said.

He unshouldered his duffel bag and let it lump up beside his right leg. He seemed tired and resigned. "I don't know. I'm looking for someone."

"Whom are you looking for, sir?"

He didn't respond at first. "A woman," he said, but felt right after he said it that the term was somehow not right. "Named Latham," he added. The words, at least, were coming a little easier.

"Latham?"

"Yes. Terri Latham. Do you know her?"

The woman did not immediately answer but for several seconds cast him a long steady stare. "I *did* know her," she said at last. "Terri Latham is dead."

He looked away. Slightly to the left and below him, below the tree crowns sussurating in the breeze, the river opened up into a wide pool, and here the huge evening stood perfectly mirrored, a replica of the red sky, gently quaking. German Brown were rising to the surface of the water, coming faster and faster as the light faded, so that as he looked on, the river became to him a vat of blood beginning to boil.

"Were you a friend of hers?" she said.

He was still looking away, watching the river; watching the small moonlike globes of cotton orbit the riverine cottonwoods and then fall softly into the molecular water. "I was an acquaintance," he said. "I once lived in a roominghouse she rented." He turned back to the woman. "But that was some time ago ... fifteen years or more."

"It was not while she was living here, then?" She raised her eyebrows as she said this, and pointed her daggerlike index nail down, indicating the deck, this very house, from which the silvery light emanated. Then she stepped toward him one pace, perhaps to escape the glare of the overhead light. Her hand was still resting upon the redwood rail.

"No," he said. "I *did* know her here, when I was very young, but I knew her best in Eureka." He closed his eyes and opened them slowly. "California," he added. "Then I'd heard that she moved back here."

The woman's face was sliced with shadows, but because she had moved nearer him, he could more precisely discern the outline of her shape: long legs and wide hips, wide shoulders, like a swimmer. Her nose was long and straight; the milky skin of her face made the redness of her lips more emphatic. Unexpectedly, he felt a sexual surge shoot through him, a hot-flash that made him lightheaded. He looked down at his feet, back up at her.

"Since you're here," she said, "you may as well come inside." She gestured with an open palm toward the front door. "I've just made coffee. A delicious blend of—"

"No," he said. "Thank you, but I must go."

She gazed about, staring out into the falling night. "Go? Where are you going to go *now*?"

But he ignored the question. He reached down and hefted up his duffel bag. She watched him, his ropey arms. He slung the bag over his shoulder, and as he did, she saw his last name stamped in faded block letters across the bottom part of the canvas. She squinted at the letters in the darkness, reading them, as it were, vertically. He followed the line of her sight until he as well was looking down at his own name.

"Is your last name Gasteneau?" she said.

His eyes flew back to hers. "Yes, it is. Why do you ask?"

"Are you related to Angela Gasteneau?"

He was struck by another disorienting hot-flash, this one much more intense than the one previous, and then he felt the blood drain all at once from his head. "Why?" he muttered, with his eyes squished shut. "Why do you ask me that?"

7

He slept that night on the edge of a raggedy field, between towns. In the morning, his stomach felt barren and cold. He lay for a long time mummied up in his mummy bag, watching the mentholated stars burn above him with a pure and gleaming light. The moon was down. He thought of running. He thought of his mother and he thought of running, and after a while he got up and dressed in the open air. He repacked his sleeping bag to the size of a small log, then he stuffed that into his duffel. It was still very dark. On the eastern border of the field, a small stream hissed through the reeds. He walked over to it. He stood for ten minutes along the sandy banks, staring across the narrow water. There were aspen trees on the other side of the stream, and they looked to him like skeletons glowing in the darkness. He turned and walked three miles into the village, following a white gravel road. Diaphanous vapors swirled above the ground. At length, he came to the first building, a brick filling station just now opening, a building still advertised with an old Pegasus beneath which pumpkins-for-sale were piled up like basketballs. He bought a styrofoam cup of coffee and drank it quickly.

He went around to the back of the building and used the restroom.

He dropped his army bag in the corner behind the door. He washed his hands in blood-warm water, then he washed his face. His fingers were stiff; the water felt good. He carefully shaved. He stood alone in the acoustical room with water splattering onto the checked tiles. The bathroom was chilled and smelled of urine and spearmint. He finished shaving and next he brushed his teeth for minutes, flossed, laved more water over his face and head. He clawed his hair straight back and changed into a clean T-shirt and a pair of gray-camouflage pants. By the time he was finished, the narrow window above the sink had begun to lighten.

Outside, the wind had picked up. He walked swiftly through the empty streets of his old hometown. It had not changed much, but what he had forgotten was the stillness, the immediacy of the mountains, the melancholy light. His pants hung highwater, and you could see the flash of his white ankle socks. Unbeloved hounds yapped at him from the alleyways. Passing the butcher shop, he saw skinned game hanging from the ceiling. At last he came to the final houses. He crossed the highway and climbed up a rocky escarpment that led into the cedar trees. One mile farther, he topped out, and then he was high above everything. He could see the entire valley below opening into the canyons, and the canyons beyond opening into the pastures, and after that the thin blue pencil-line of the horizon. The land was filling with light. Still the coldness of the night clung to his bones.

He kept walking and soon he began to sweat. He followed game trails that petered out over large patches of bare rock and picked up again on the other side. In the delicate morning light, the mountains hulked hugely into the tinted air, so close to him now that they subsumed the whole horizon. The sky above grew rose-of-blue, packed deeply with blue, beyond which lay more blue and more, until finally, beyond that, there was only the blackness of space.

After an hour, he came out on a high bluff. He stopped walking and gazed down. A teaky river flashed in the distance. The village, for a time, teetered on the edge of day. The houses stood far below him now, small buildings scattered like tinker-toys throughout the fir trees. Cars were starting to crawl along the highway. He watched for several minutes. Then he unshouldered his duffel bag and stashed it in the brush. He walked off the rock bluff and began to run.

Joel was always the fastest runner. All his life, he was small for his age, but he was always the fastest.

He was ten-years-old when his father first took him to the fair. It was a misty afternoon in early autumn. The ground lay muddy and trampled. Colored balloons floated in the gray air. There were barkers and a Ferris wheel and vats of candy floss, and in the early evening a running race, a three miler. Joel watched the first runners gather around the starting area. He had never seen an actual race before, and after a while he asked his father if he could participate. His father said yes.

Joel stripped himself to the waist. He wore corduroy pants and high-top sneakers, nothing else. With curiosity, his father watched as Joel trotted down among the adult runners: pale and skinny Joel, always so silent and determined, the youngest of the entire group by far and the smallest, perhaps one hundred competitors in all. His father watched as Joel darted off the starting line and immediately into the lead, disappearing around the first bend, going out too fast, far too fast, only a quarter-mile into the race and Joel was already seventy meters ahead of the next runner. To his astonishment, then, he watched as, fifteen minutes later, Joel came pounding in from the other direction, still leading, the gap between him and the second place runner even wider now, up over the brow of a grassy slope, under a half-mile to go, around a smoking pond, Joel in his corduroys and no shirt, his chest beet-red and heaving. Joel moaning from exhaustion. His father exploded off the bleachers and bound down to the finish line. ("Come on," he yelled, "you cute little son-of-a-bitch!") Joel broke the tape in 16:30. The next runner was a full minute behind him.

Seven years later, in high school, all alone at a dog-eat-dog track meet in Salt Lake City, Joel won the metric mile in 4:09.53, four thousand feet above sea level. Three hours later, he won the two mile in 8:55.10, the fastest in the country.

His father nudged him awake in darkness. Neither spoke. Joel rose from his bed and dressed in the icy room. He had just turned twelve. The night before, for a birthday present, his father had bought him a new hunting rifle, a gleaming 30.06 with a Leopold scope.

They left the house before first light. They walked up a steep path that began behind the shed, above the caves, and then zig-zagged into the hills. They moved steadily, his father limping the old limp, but tireless and strong. It was black out and excessively cold. When the first light of day broke over the eastern mountains, they received it upon their backs.

At the end of three hours, they passed the remnants of an old mine, with cables and cogwheels jumbled about the site, huge rusted axles, a dilapidated wooden shack all sun-bleached and gray. The grass blades lay welded to the stones in claws of frost. His father knelt here for a long while and studied the ground. He did not say anything. He once picked up a rock and touched his tongue to it. He stared carefully about him. Joel tried to see what his father saw, but he was not able to. They walked on.

Soon they came to the edge of a dark forest. Here they waited out the rest of the morning, and after that they waited the rest of the afternoon. They waited and waited. The air remained cold all day long. The sky grew blank and gray. They did not eat, they did not talk. They stood. A wild and ancient basin, home of grizzly bear, bobcat. They saw no game. The sun flew by—an irritated eye-rim bagged in layers of smoke—flew past its apogee and then slid down into the smoldering west. Clumps of littered snow stood in the tree bowls. The air reeked of pine needles.

"Keep waiting," his father said to him once.

Toward dusk, Joel caught sight of a pair of golden eagles wheeling away, far off. He watched them for close to an hour. The eagles grew more and more remote, describing slow parabolas across a voided sky. Joel watched them until they were tiny black specks, like flies, one male, one female, shrieking faintly and chasing after the life-giving, meat-eating, thunderously silent sun, which he and his father could no longer see. Then the birds were gone. For a long time, with his sharp eyes, Joel tried to pick them out, but he could not. The sky cleared. It grew even colder. Joel was shivering now. He had given up on the hunt. Just then, a ripple of motion broke across the edge of his vision, and he turned.

A café-au-lai elk emerged alone from the forest and stood in a narrow clearing, two hundred meters to his left. It was a massive bull. It was eating wild apples off a tree, head tipped back, its antlers nearly touching its rear-end. Joel didn't hesitate. He raised his rifle to his eye without any sound, but still the animal turned. Only now did his father realize what was going on. The elk loomed up gigantic in Joel's scope and gazed at Joel without malice and without fear.

Stay calm, thought Joel, hit him between the eyes, or in the neck. The animal stared at him for one second—one second too long.

Just as Joel's father started to hiss something in his ear, Joel squeezed the trigger: a stiff recoil that he didn't feel and an explosion resounding outrageously in the dead silence, the subsequent landscape filled with a diminishing report.

There was a cottony puff of gunsmoke and the bull crumpled. No falter, no misstep, just one moment standing and the next heaped up onto the rocks. Joel took a deep breath and leaned his rifle against a tree. He closed his eyes. "Yes," he whispered to himself.

"By God, you got him," his father said, "like Grant got Richmond."

But Joel didn't hear him, because he was already running up toward the fallen elk. Which was still alive and agonizing on the ground. There was not much blood. Joel had hit him right above the bridge of the nose, a small hole drilled there, as if bored in with an auger, a thin rivulet of purple leaking out of the hole and already drying in the cold air. One of the antlers had been chipped from the fall.

Joel thought: I must cut its throat.

He unsheathed his hunting knife to do so, but as he reached in to pull back the antlers to expose the neck, the elk began twisting its head, swinging the tangled rack back and forth, bawling. In that instant, Joel felt something he wasn't prepared for: he felt revulsion, even fear. For in that moment, he realized how wild this animal was, how living, how vital. The thick fur shirred up at its throat looked impenetrable to him, a brow like brickwork. He could smell the gamy breath, the chemical reek of its urine. The mouth hung open, huge and hinged, with apples mashed between the big cubic teeth, half-masticated chunks of apple and an admixture of pink froth slobbered down into the billy goat's beard. Bloody bubbles popped all around the outer nostrils, and the nostrils were like leather; the eyes crazed and dying: this animal was dying, thought Joel, with beautiful crazy eyes.

Silently his father strode up behind him and took the knife out of his hand. With a strange celerity and sense of timing, he dipped in until he was right up against the animal. In the same motion, he elbowed back the dripping muzzle and sunk the knifepoint deep into the thick hide. The animal screeched. There was a dull ripping sound like torn cloth, and then enormous gobs of blood came spilling out, thick clots dropping forth from the gash with each beat of the heart. The heartbeat slowed. Joel watched the blood come, shining slabs that lay quivering by his knee. Gallons and gallons of blood, he couldn't believe anything could contain so much. His father was pressed right up against the elk, almost tenderly now, almost hugging it, this living vessel no more. The old man finished the job of jugulating and then looked up at Joel. He grinned. He had blood on his hands and blood smeared across his forehead and blood splattered in his hair. His hair was the color of ashes, one thick forelock dangling over his left eye.

Joel's fingers were getting very cold now and starting to ache. Still, he felt elated and would not let this moment—goddamn it!—would not let this moment be spoiled.

"Now," said his father, and showed him how to dress it.

They dragged the animal over to a wide patch of grass—no small job— exposing the midsection as best they could. Without any squeamishness whatsoever, his father grabbed hold of the furry cock and cut out the genitals. Then he made a long slit up to the sternum. The knife slid easily through the glowing skin. Next he pinched up the anus with his first two fingers and carved a ragged circle around the entire asshole, rapidly eviscerating the animal and leaving armloads of blue rubbery entrails steaming beside him in the dirt. He placed the teardrop-shaped heart and then the liver trembling next to him in a patch of old snow, turning the snow instantly to purple slush. It was getting dark now. The moon had risen and it stood on the horizon like a blind eye gazing down. Joel's hands were freezing. His father worked fast, surely. Joel watched him. His excitement had not died—why then this sudden feeling of emptiness?

"Now reach into his chest," his father said, "and pull out his windpipe."

Joel knelt down and went shoulder-deep into the moist cave. His cheek touched the animal's fur. The smell of blood was clangorous. Numb-fingered, he groped around: ridges and more blood, but he was not sure what the windpipe felt like.

"Do you have it yet?" said his father.

"I don't know," said Joel.

"What do you mean you don't know?"

"I mean I feel something, but I don't know if it's the windpipe."

"Well, what is it?"

"The esophagus, I think."

"Goddamn it, Joel, the esophagus *is* the goddamn windpipe."

With that, he backhanded Joel out of the way and reached up into the chest cavity himself, clenching his teeth as he did so, giving him that fierce and dangerous-looking underbite which Joel had so much come to antipathize. In a heartbeat, then, the man yanked out the entire bronchial apparatus, bringing forth the two huge lobes of lung, vascular and raw and complicated, like an alien organism. More blood had gotten smeared across the old man's face. He threw the lungs into the rocks; they wobbled when they struck. Joel's hands were totally numb now, and shooting with pain.

His father quickly finished the rest of the job, and together they strung the animal up over a tree limb. His father, no longer young, displayed his inhuman strength. The remaining animal blood dripped down into the exposed grass. They made a hasty camp and sat down to finally warm themselves beside the fire. The old man, across from Joel, looked at Joel through the tongue-like flames. He smiled. "You did well," he said. His teeth shone phosphorescent in the dark.

Joel did not say anything. He gazed into the pulsating heat. He held his palms out to the fire, as if to halt the flames. His fingers were in such a state of pain that, despite himself, it was all he could think about. Above them, the stars burned blue and bright, and the ovoid moon hung profoundly in the sky. Big sparks popped from the gray wood and went fishtailing into the night. After a time, when his fingers started to normalize, Joel raised his eyes a little, furtively, and stared across at his father whose sleeves were folded off his wrists, disclosing the caked and drying blood all along his forearms. Joel watched him. The mountainous man sat with his legs crossed Indian style; he looked lost in contemplation. Joel could also see now that blood was flecked everywhere in tiny polka dots all across his father's face—a whole constellation of blood—and as his father stared hypnotized into the fire, Joel suddenly thought that the man looked like an abortionist, or a butcher.

Joel slackened his pace now and came trotting into a red forest grove. Incarnadine woods, trees shot with murky light. He passed through. The woods thinned gradually, and the grass gave way to stony ground. Joel came out into the open. He stopped running and gazed about him. A final shadow, the last vestige of the morning, advanced like a wave. He waited for it to slop over him and it did. Rims of rosy-pink stood out upon the western hills, the hills just tipped with sunlight. Then the final shadows of night receded and were swept away, and all the land pressed in around him as, little by little, the whole valley gave way to light.

Below him, a broken heap of rocks lay along the dry floor of an old quarry. He paused for a long moment looking down, catching his breath. His sweat dripped lavender into the dust. An old landfill stood adjacent, two hundred meters to the right: a rusty washing machine foundering in a sea of honeysuckle; a rimless Mercury Cougar that looked as if it had been brought down with a Gatling gun; bottles and aluminum cans scattered all throughout the grass; bald tires; bluish glass like sea pebbles winking everywhere among the rocks.

Joel descended a natural limestone staircase and walked across the floor of the quarry.

On the other side, around a high outcropping, he came to a quadrate pool, deep and emerald, with chalky cliffs inverted on the still waters. He did not stop walking but turned his head to view the pond as he passed. The stones all around were purplish and covered in a thin layer of silica dust. There were dusty smells in the air, a mineral tang. The sweat on his skin began to cool. Mats of algae wheeled imperceptibly across the surface of the water, discharging a lemon light more brilliant than the water itself. A thick cable, powdered with rust, hung from high up on the rock walls and came slanting down into the pool, impaling it. Wind sifted through the grass. The wooden door of a decrepit quarry shack blew open and slapped shut. Joel looked around. Was there someone watching? All of a sudden, he felt sure that there was. Apprehension crept over him with the breeze, an ominous tremor in the gelid light. His sweat dried rapidly. He felt his skin prick.

Quickly, he continued through the quarry and came out onto a derelict logging road. The road led back into the trees. He walked past an abandoned mineshaft that consisted of a ramshackle tin building with a corrugated roof and, at the back of the building, a hole blasted into the side of a black mountain. Small cones of tailings stood around the site like lunar volcanos, and a deep floodwater shimmered just inside the cave. Joel could hear within a steady echo drip, and he saw a railbed vanish into the floodwater, only one-and-a-half of its ties visible. Gray tanagers peeked out at him from the trees but made no sound. He approached the cave.

A dead bat slept at the mouth. It was folded up like an umbrella. The small eyes were closed; pointy ears, a pug nose, the sour face almost human-looking to him, or hobbit. The tiny paws clutched at the magnificent cape. In the trees beyond the shack stood a rank sump the color of blood. The surface of the water was rippled, and a silver-gray tree on the other side lay sand-impacted and bent in the water like a drinking straw. Red leaves fell upon the red water. The wind, the water, and the blood. A vampiric palpation. He passed through. Silence filled the forest.

Thirty minutes later, he stood before an old brick schoolhouse. A rusted chain and padlock hung on the door of the main entrance. The door itself was half ajar on its hinges; all the front windows were starred through with stones. He saw his miniaturized image reflected in the jagged shards: Indian-black hair, acne-scarred face speared horizontally with long daggers of glass. The school grounds had been overrun with weeds and brown jasmine, virid moss and lichen, the front steps cluttered with glass and nails, busted cement, the sidewalks greatly upheaved. He stood for five minutes looking at the facade of the building. Then he mounted the steps and went inside.

Something eerie was seeping out of the walls. The building itself felt cold and empty. Yet, for a split second, he again grew certain that a pair of eyes burned down on him from above. He looked up but saw nothing. As it was, he was not feeling well—dizzy and a little shaky, and he was even beginning to suspect now that his old sickness was there, tugging at him tirelessly, like an undertow, threatening at any moment to recrudesce. Perhaps it is only my imagination, he thought. He went deeper into the building.

He walked through old classrooms completely gutted and smelling of chalk. Each of his steps left full footprints in the dust. The floorboards screeched beneath him, piercing cries that went volleying throughout the long corridors. One-armed desks, a few, stood scattered about the hallways. Black music stands and metal chairs. More dust came snowing down through the cracks beneath him. Insects clambered up and down the mounds of rubble on the floor. There were mice chamferings along the wainscoting, and several sections of the floor had huge warps in it, like wooden swells in a wooden sea. Drifts of dry leaves had collected in the windless spaces.

Presently he came to the library. He stood just inside the doorway, gazing about. Across, on the other side of the room, a slate chalkboard stood propped against the wall. He walked into the room and scanned everything. There were still many books on the sagging shelves, all covered with chalky dust. He sat down in a swivel chair with only three wheels and began sorting through stacks—searching for precisely what, he did not know. At the end of ten minutes, he came upon a large pile of high school annuals, dating from as far back as 1910. He went through each of these in turn, checking them methodically, studying every page. The pages were brittle and discolored, the photos all black-and-white.

And then he found something.

He found pictures of his mother when she was a senior in high school. He did not recognize her at first, not until he saw her name—Kristiansen—and then it became obvious to him. In the photos (and he realized this with a shock) she looked virtually identical to the way she had looked when he had known her, twenty-five years after this photo had been taken. Her beauty, he thought, was ageless: the long sable hair, the Cherokee cheekbones, the lambent black eyes. She was not smiling in any one of the shots, but invariably a trace of amusement played across her lips—something arcane (he thought) and as if directed specifically at him. The year was 1935. Valedictorian. Voted prettiest girl in school. He examined each page carefully.

He came next across a picture of a man holding her hand.

He sat looking at this photo for fifteen minutes.

The man's name was Shelby Morgan. Joel knew it well. Shelby Morgan was a tall and slender man, a handsome man, with a slab of hair hanging thickly across his cheekbone. He was kissing Joel's mother on the forehead. The caption read: couple most likely to get married. As Shelby Morgan kissed her, she stared straight into the camera, the same strange expression stamped upon her face. It was a knowing expression, somehow timeless.

When Joel was finished, he searched the shelves for more yearbooks that might contain her pictures, but he could not find any.

He was in the room a long time before he realized that he was not alone.

He glanced up from what he was doing and saw someone standing in the doorway. For a moment, this person was in plain view. It was a young girl. His heart went into his throat. The girl was dressed all in black, cloaked to the throat in black, a long black dress, little arms poking from the sleeves like the limbs of an etiolated tree. Her hands hung down at her sides, fingers partially bent. Large flaxen braids pinioned like horns her narrow skull. Her face looked blue. She wore a blank expression but stared directly at him. At first she did not move.

Not until he stood up and approached her. Then she turned and went unhurriedly into the other room.

He made to follow her, but when he came out from behind the desk and into the doorway, she was no longer anywhere to be seen. He thought he heard the soft clop of her shoes. He walked out into the hallway and entered the opposite room. He looked about; he saw nothing. Overhead lights lay smashed across the floor. Bird droppings stood piled like young stalagmites beneath the broken windows. Those were perhaps faint footprints tracked across the dust. He followed the tracks to the other side of the room, up a narrow stairway, then down another acoustical hallway. But when the wood gave way to tile, the tracks disappeared, and he could find no trace of them again anywhere. A door of solid maple had slid off its hinges and stood leaning against one of the hallway walls. The door was split its entire length with a fibrous gash. He walked in turn through each upstairs classroom. He could not find her. Finally, at the last room—first grade—he went in and stood before the western window and stared out over the abandoned grounds below. The glass of this window was still intact, though deeply flawed, and like a landscape viewed through heat, everything outside looked rippled.

The land was quiet and empty. Missile-shaped clouds had amassed in the south. A ramulous red apple tree stood up in arms against the sky. Scuffed-up fruit lay scattered all about the cakey dirt. Far off, a pasture of legless cows were grazing in a field of alfalfa.

Joel walked out of the building and made his way down a clay road that ran in the opposite direction from the one by which he had come in. Twenty-five meters away, he turned and looked back.

She stood at the window of the room he had last been in.

Through the warped glass, she looked frozen: a lady locked in ice. He raised his hand to her, but she did nothing in return. She did not move.

Suddenly, then, for a moment's fraction, Joel glimpsed the exact nature of what was happening—and as he glimpsed it, he felt himself seized with a sense of despair greater than any he had ever known before. In a span of seconds, thus, it seemed to him that his entire life could only turn into one and just one indistinguishable color: black, black, and blacker.

But shortly after that, the stranger appeared.

8

Midnight, midsummer, the dry fields draped in shawls of thermal mist. A marble moon hung half crumbled over the western mountains, sprinkling dust onto the peaks.

At ten past twelve, Elias Moorecroft finished the last of his packing and walked downstairs. In the kitchen, he sat at a wooden chair beneath an extinguished lightbulb. He sat at a wobbly card table. A partial cup of coffee stood near the center of the table. Beside it was an amber ashtray with white-chipped edges. He didn't turn on the overhead light but sat at the table in the moon-blanched darkness. After five minutes, Elias slid the cup forward and drank off the last of the lukewarm coffee. He had not slept in over forty-eight hours, and his brain felt fogged, his body beat. Over the past three weeks, he'd developed the sagging tear ducts of the chronic insomniac, the leanness of an El Greco. And yet he was not unhappy.

He slipped off his half-moon glasses and wiped them with worn tissue paper, which he extracted from his breast pocket. He folded the glasses and set them next to the empty coffee mug. Then he closed his eyes and pinched the bridge of his nose. In front of him, beyond the window, thermal vapors crept in like those silken Chinese mists inked upon the calendar above his table. The mist came into his backyard and into the garden. Elias wore denim trousers and a navy-blue crewneck. The kitchen was very warm. A current of air slid in through the open window and lifted a stray strand of his hair. All the rooms of his house were barren and swept clean; they lay now in a wash of ghostly moonlight. He was leaving here tomorrow, and the prospect of vacating this place for good filled him with an emptiness that he hadn't expected.

Methodically, he lit a cigarette.

He sat in the kitchen and stared through the open window. The high clouds slid like quicksilver across the face of the moon, as if the moon were being pulled through the clouds. Elias sat smoking and listening to the crickets in the trees. Inside, the house was still. The breeze channeled noiselessly through the open window. He inhaled smoke, felt the nicotine course through his veins. He closed his eyes and blew smoke into the night.

At one o'clock, he rose from the table and went back upstairs. He was gone for five minutes. When he returned, he went back to the kitchen sink and filled his old copper kettle and put the kettle back on the stove. In the distance, he could hear an eighteen-wheeler heartbreaking it up a steep mountain grade. The kitchen was cooler than the rooms upstairs. The stove smelled faintly of gas. The gas flame cast a soft-blue pall in that corner of the room. The sound of the big-rig rolled away. In a moment, the water started to boil, and Elias spooned coffee into a plaid thermos, then poured in the steaming water. He corked the thermos and jostled it back and forth. He went into the other room and snapped on the light.

It was then that he noticed the three black trunks.

He hadn't forgotten them, exactly. In fact, after he had lugged the trunks into this room, a curious anxiousness had come over him; but he had been so preoccupied with the final details of moving that the trunks and the books had been relegated to the back of his mind.

He saw them sitting there now.

They were pushed side-by-side against the wall of his foyer, and at this stage in his packing, they were about the only objects still left in the room. The light fell on them softly. The light was not bright, but it was bright enough to illuminate the bare walls of the three interconnecting rooms, walls still marked with thin nails, naked electrical outlets, the whiter paint where his pictures had hung. The gray carpet, darker in certain spots than in others, disclosed the phantoms of his old furniture. Echoes huddled in all the empty corners. Beneath the high ceiling, a plate-glass window opened onto his side lawn and, beyond that, the crooked canal overhung with ribbons of mist.

Elias went back into the kitchen and got his eyeglasses. He returned to the three trunks and opened each of them in succession.

Books were packed neatly inside, a great many books, perhaps five hundred in all. He saw right away that he dealt here with a rare and valuable collection indeed: old books bound in leather or even parchment; tomes with small gold studs like expensive thumbtacks hammered into the covers; gilded spines and gold-leaf page edgings; codices, folios, incunabula. He felt a tingle spread through the base of his neck. He set his coffee thermos far away. His fingers wiggled instinctively.

Gently, he began sorting through the trunk on the left. The first thing that struck him was the immaculate condition of each volume: all cleaned and dusted and obviously kept free of heat and moisture and even light. This was the collection of a man pathologically obsessed, he grasped this instantaneously, no mere hobbyist—the woman Lauren had been right—a man, he thought, who suffered for his books.

He came across a mint *Quixote* from 1804.

He came across a first edition (number fifty) of *Quatrevingt-treize*, by Victor Hugo, and he leafed through this right away, his fingers barely brushing the thick pages. He gazed in wonder at the intricate illustrations.

He came across Arthur Conan Doyle's first Sherlock Holmes story, "A Study in Scarlet," in *Beeton's Christmas Annual*, London, 1887.

There was a pristine *Dorian Gray*, dated 1891, the year it was first published.

He was at the process for two hours or more.

He moved on to the next trunk.

In the back corner, a suede cloth lay draped over a small section of spines. He removed the cloth. Underneath was a stack of slim volumes the subject of which was demonology and sorcery, the occult, Lucifer and other princes of darkness. There were books here on ancient magical rites, old books with strange covers, printed, some of them, on vellum or cow uterus and bearing cryptic engravings. Several book covers contained hieroglyphics. Beneath these, he found four books of an altogether different sort. Two of these had similar (but not identical) paintings. These paintings were of an arklike object, which sat glowing greenly beside a mountain lake, in a pristine land, a surprisingly modern-looking man standing next to the vessel, his index finger held up to his lips. Despite the slightly different cover art, each book possessed the same title:

The Secret History

And underneath these words, in a smaller but no less discernable font:

In quo sunt omnes thesauri sapientiae et scientiae absconditi

Elias knelt there, thinking back.

It was he who had published and bound these books, many years ago.

Upon closer inspection, he found inserted into one of these volumes, and looking more than a little anachronistic, a stack of loose-sheaf manuscripts, all typed out on yellowish paper. Without thinking about it, Elias reached for these pages and went with them back into the kitchen. He took his coffee thermos as well. For a long time, he sat at the kitchen table, feeling strangely nervous. He watched a small cockroach scuttle in fits and starts across the entire length of the linoleum floor. The linoleum had hairline cracks in it; he seemed to notice this for the first time. He poured a cup of coffee but didn't drink it. He lit a cigarette and smoked it down. Outside, the crickets in the trees were stridulating with such maniacal ferocity that they sounded as if they might saw themselves in half.

Finally he slipped his glasses back on and began to read:

April 23

Nightfall and the usual grapple with fear and death. But "usual" is not the right word: looking back over the past four years of my life, I see clearly tonight how my brain has grown increasingly lost. I see, in short, what I have become. I remember vividly when the nighttime was not always such a monster.

April 25

The mind has mountains, cliffs of fall frightful sheer no man fathomed...

What hours, what black hours we have spent this night, this year of now done darkness when I wretch lay wrestling with my God! my God?

April 30

Evening. A wire-thin wind blows ghostlike beneath my door. There is new snow, a silvery moon. And again, I'm consumed with thoughts of you - you, my Holy Ghost, my dream, my daemon.

I think I conceived this letter to you, which is not really a letter, I know, and which I can never send you, to be nothing more, or less, than an inquiry into my brain, or a codification of my brain's method of dealing with its thoughts. We are always in control of this methodology, are we not? If we will it? But I ask myself, why you, you of all people, who it turns out I never really knew? I think that your megrims must be my megrims, and that my snowballing hypochondria is something I should address to you, you specifically, I mean, because in reading your words and in thinking of you, you've always brought structure into my thoughts, because of your clarity and your brain, I'm not sure what all, and although it's true that I did not know you, there has always been an important feeling that comes to me when I pronounce your serious name - you in whom are hid all the treasures of wisdom and knowledge. And because for your own sake now I cannot write beyond these words, because your name of agony stings and creeps and cakes my mouth with salt.

May 1

May is Mary's month.

Church today. A pink and blue Sabbath evening. It is the first mass of the week and of the month. I'm next to an attractive blond lady who is by herself. As it inevitably happens when I see a solitary woman of this approximate age, I wonder for a split second, is it you? And perhaps after all, that is what this is about: you, an inquiry into you - my phantom, my ghost.

High above us, the stained glass windows exhale long shafts of light. To my right, through a clear pane of glass, I can see the west sky drain down the estuary like the bed of a pink-champagne river. The woman is much older than me, and she smells nice. She's wearing the same perfume a college professor of mine used to wear, a woman I loved, so right away this lady has me at a disadvantage. The opening hymn is announced, but I don't pay attention. Instead, I sit there. I'm smiling a little, despite myself, because I'm in the mood for church (unusual for me). About ten seconds into the hymn, I notice this nice-looking blond woman can't find her page.

She notices me looking at her, she shrugs her shoulders, more or less asking me, what page? In response, I lean toward her a little (another blast of her sweet perfume) and whisper "I wasn't paying attention either."

Moments later, I glance down at her hands. I notice them because they're folded so precisely. On the back of her right wrist I see a small patch of dry blood. For whatever reason, I'm not surprised to see the blood there. It's almost as if I expected it to be there, or as if I think it belongs there. Not only does the spot of blood not bother me, it excites me. I don't know why. So there it is. And there is where you will begin to glimpse how mad I really am. And yet I have resolved to set everything down with total honesty, tonight and in the days and nights that follow.

The small patch of blood makes me smile at first. But then there enters into my head a photograph I once saw, many years ago when I was about ten years old, of a priest called Padre Pio. Padre Pio was afflicted with a stigmatism, the condition of course in which the person who has it bleeds from the exact same spots on his (or her) body that Christ himself did while he was on the cross. "An issue of blood," they sometimes call it. When I was a child, no matter how many times I looked at this black and white photo of Padre Pio - and I still remember it perfectly - and no matter how many times I read the caption, I could not for the life of me get a handle on it. I simply didn't GET it. For one thing, stigmata are actually recognized by the church as a blessing. You're blessed to weep constant blood from your body up until the day you die.

But here's what I think: blood is overrated.

Or is it?

As I'm staring at the blood on the back of this lady's wrist, I think to myself: what if this lady has stigmatism? It's just a passing thought at first, one of those ideas that come crashing into your mind like a car wreck. But as I start to think about it more and more, I notice that I'm beginning to take myself seriously. And really that's the short story of my life: The What If? my brain so incapable of releasing thoughts that it's come to the point that I must challenge myself to stop thinking about things, and invariably fail. My life in many ways has become a state of constant worrying, constant questioning.

I say to myself now, "What if this woman really does have stigmatism?" I consider it. I consider it and decide (I actually decide!) that if she does have it, it would make me feel—jealousy.

I am devout. I really am. I'm filled with horrible thoughts and even deeds, but at the bottom of it all, I'm devout. More than anything else, all I want is to be good. Or, rather, not just good but The Best. In fact, I want it more than anyone I've ever known (with one or two possible exceptions). This is the reason I'm scrupulous about going to church every day, praying and the like. Don't misunderstand me: I do see the absurdity of church rituals. But what are the options, if you want morality? (No doubt, you have a good answer to that question.) In general, I interpret "the concept," if I may use a bullshit term, of God as nothing more or less than this: The Highest. And by that I mean, whether symbolic or real, God to me represents the best that human beings can possibly be. I'm talking about morally, from a morally objective standpoint. And from this standpoint, He is all of human potential fulfilled. It doesn't even matter to me anymore if God actually exists or not - it's the idea. Or the ideal, if you prefer. I go through this because, morally speaking, I want to reach The Highest. I want to be the best. And despite all the bad and embarrassing things I've done and do, I've never relinquished my belief that I can achieve this goal.

Furthermore, I hate jealousy. That's something else I would like for you to know. I loathe it. I loathe jealousy more than any other emotion, and the reason I loathe it so much is that it's insidious in the literal sense of the word. And because I hate it so much, I am not a jealous person. I'm truly not.

As soon as I realize that it would make me jealous if this woman actually had stigmatism (why her?), I gaze up at the big, glassy-looking crucifix and say to myself, "I don't want to feel jealousy, help me not to feel it."

A bundle of crimson-red roses is attached to the plaster loin-cloth of the crucifix. They are very beautiful. I interpret them as representing not only Christ's love but also his blood. How in my interpretation Christ bled for being a just man. The plaster skin is pure-white and looks vascular and bony and bruised, very realistic. Blood is issuing from his hands and feet, you can clearly see that Christ had bones and veins and skin. Artistically, not all crucifixes are good. This one is. It is excellent, in fact. The juxtaposition of red on white is eye-popping, and the bruises are of the softest blue. I close my eyes and glance at my inward state, trying now to see if I'm still feeling jealousy. Immediately I see that if I'm going to be honest with myself, I am still feeling jealousy. Why doesn't it vanish? Why can't you just will it away? So I say to myself, "Beware, my lord, of jealousy. It is the green-eyed monster which doth mock the meat it feeds upon." As soon as I say it, it occurs to me that I don't remember where it comes from. I got it from a movie I watched in which a group of students was discussing, of all things, the "importance" of colors in literature. This one fellow called Nick comes up with this quote, the teacher responds, "Not bad, Nikolai. Not bad. But what does the passage really mean?"

(Nikolai?)

That question struck me as very smart, because even though it's obvious that the writer is saying jealousy is a bad thing, it is far from obvious what the writer means specifically. What does "the meat" refer to?

What does "mocks" mean?

Why mocks?

In the end I realize I'm becoming obsessed with my thoughts again, and also angry with myself, as stupid as it all is, for feeling this way, and for not being able to shut it all off. I'm frustrated suddenly with God, and for some reason with life in general. I look over again at the lady. She is pretty, but she's not gorgeous. She does have a gorgeous nose, though, long, razor-straight, and on the side of it there's a tiny blue birthmark that looks like a crescent moon. Her skin is pure alabaster. It's so white that it almost appears translucent, much like the crucifix above us. Veins are webbed everywhere just beneath the surface of her skin, a complicated network that I find indescribably attractive. Her head is bowed down a little, her eyes are closed. She is not wearing make-up. Her eyebrows are much darker than her hair. Her lashes are long. After a moment, I start doing the most childish thing. I start imagining her as one of the ladies who was so faithful to Christ during and after the Passion. (There the women are, on the station of the cross directly beside us.) I picture her kneeling below Christ after he has died. I picture her weeping. This in turn makes me think of Christ himself and how one thing for sure that nobody, not even his detractors, can deny: he was one cool breeze, cool under fire. He had the courage of his convictions. One can imagine someone like William Shakespeare or Isaac Newton of greater erudition than Christ, but one cannot imagine someone with greater strength, or someone more able to bring the body under subjection. The crucifix above us emphasizes Christ's humanness, the only part of his personality that really matters to me, the fact that he was a man with blood and bones and skin - I mean, they nearly broke his BONES, for God sake, after he was already dead. And yet he was a man with courage, more admirable to me by far than a courageous God, because to be courageous when you're God is nothing compared to being courageous when you're a man. As I'm thinking about all this, I suddenly realize that it makes me want to cry, the whole image at once seeming so sad and important to me. I even get a totally chaste urge to just reach over and put my hand on your shoulder. But at that moment, we all must rise for the reading of the gospel, and I glance over at the woman's other hand, and immediately I see that there is no blood on it after all, none whatsoever. It's only on the right one.

Elias looked up from the manuscript, and for a long time he sat motionless, gazing into the gauzy morning light. At last, he cranked his head, first to the right, then to the left, the vertebrae in his neck popping mutely, like an accordion straw. The last page he'd read had a partial wine ring on the top corner. He stared at it. Another manuscript—titled "Confession"—lay beneath the one he now held. He removed his glasses and rubbed his eyes. It was four o'clock in the morning. The bare bulb still burned over his head, cigarette smoke piled thickly against the ceiling so that the light of the bulb issued through bleakly like a miniature sun. The house was silent. Outside, the crickets in the trees had fallen silent. He stared at the table for a minute or two longer, then glanced over at his cigarette in the ashtray. He had lit it ten minutes ago, and then, becoming engrossed, he'd set it down and forgotten about it. He pinched it up now and took a test drag. It was out. He relit the cigarette, and then continued reading.

At the end of two hours, when he was finished, he gathered up all those pages and tapped them into a stack. He held the manuscripts on his lap. He rubbed the stubble on his neck. The whiskers on his neck looked like thorns. Soon, he rose up and walked over to the kitchen window. In the east, a rosy wash of light filled a small quadrant of the sky. He stared across the farmlands. Hogs were waking, grunting. The fog for the most part had lifted. Off to his left, the fields looked soft and sugar-dusted. He set the manuscript on the table, and from his thermos he poured himself a cup of coffee. He stood at the window, watching the new day dawn.

After a while, he went outside.

Two horses, one strawberry, one pinto, came wading toward him, shoulder-deep through the deep green grass. That pasture was on the other side of the bridge, just beyond his backyard, and Elias went over to greet them. On his way, he pulled carrots from a side garden along the edge of the house. He cracked the carrots into pieces which shone brightly in his hand.

Draping both arms over the fence, he passed the carrots to the horses. They licked them from his palm. Their movements were gentle and precise. Their tongues were gritty and hot. He combed back each of their forelocks in turn, stroked their veiny cheeks. One, the pinto, had startling gray eyes and a white sunburst exploding on his chest. Elias slapped the strong neck. The other's eyes were brown and bottomless—and to Elias the entirely beautiful. The nostrils were pink and rabbit-like, and with his muzzle he nudged at Elias's hand, snuffing for more carrots.

Elias stood rubbing both horses around the jaws, the shoulders. He felt a cold sadness welling up inside him. He closed his eyes.

By and by, a young man with light hair appeared and stood behind Elias.

"Good morning," the young man said.

Elias turned his head. He smiled—a slight smile, but one that showed affection, even love. "Good morning," he said.

"How is everything with you today?" the young man said.

"I'm leaving in a few hours."

"Yes, I know."

They were both silent.

"You look troubled," the young man said.

"Come closer," Elias said. "I have something I'd like to ask you. Maybe you can answer my question."

The young man moved closer. "I'll try."

Elias stopped stroking the horses and turned to face the young man. He embraced him warmly, and then he stepped back a pace. He paused, as if to gather his thoughts. "Long ago, when you were a boy," he said, "there was an incident in your school."

"What incident?"

"In the fifth grade," Elias said, "Bill Morgan beat a female classmate of his, a girl named Anna."

The horses turned and wandered away. Elias watched them go. "He beat her without mercy, as I recall, and without provocation, and then later admitted that he'd done it. I know that you were a few years younger, but I thought that with your memory—"

"I remember," the young man said. "And I also know why you're asking."

"Oh?"

"Yes. It's obvious."

"Do you know, then, what happened that day?"

"Yes, I do."

"And how do you know?"

"I deduced it."

Elias frowned. "I seem to remember," he said, "that Anna had started a large scandal by *defending* Bill."

"That is true," the young man said.

"What did she say?"

"She said that Bill didn't do it. She said that it was someone else and that Bill was absolutely innocent. She said she could prove it. She said that it was Bill's classmate Carl who had beaten her, and that Bill had taken the blame for it, for reasons she could not fathom."

9

Seven o'clock in the evening. A hot and moth-populated mountain night. Gasteneau sat alone in a rundown motel on the outskirts of town, a cheap room that he'd rented for this reason, because it was cheap, and because he could have it by the day or by the week, and because it was spacious and commanded a view of the outlying plains.

Outside, it was not dark yet, but all his shades were pulled. He sat in a corner of the room upon an old sofa. He sat fully dressed and with his hair combed back, as if he was going somewhere, but he did not move and had not moved for some time. On the arm of the sofa lay a black cigarette lighter and a pair of pliers. He appeared lost in his thoughts, his face haggard and ill-at-ease. An iron band of pain tightened around his head. He was sure now that he had not been imagining things after all, his old sickness was indeed lurking there, just beneath the surface, pulling at him persistently, and it was only with a great concentration of will that he could fend it off.

He had been sitting in the room the entire day, growing more and more uneasy. He had trained himself to wait in this way, motionless, hour after hour, like a prisoner. But something else was happening as well: an old injury to the big toe of his left foot had begun reasserting itself, nothing serious at first, a minor ache, but building and building until at this moment his toe was pounding away with each beat of his heart. It was a running injury caused from his toes banging repeatedly against the tops of his tennis shoes—except this time, as had happened once before, when he was in the army, in addition to the bruising, the toe itself had become infected, so that blood could freely flow in but could not escape. Periungal hematoma. The words kept running through the corridors of his brain, volleying, it felt to him, around the acoustical concavities of his skull.

Half an hour passed, one hour. An moth landed on his face, its touch light and dry. He did not brush it away. The room grew dark. The walls were filled with shadows. Finally, he reached up and snapped on the overhead light. He leaned forward and removed his shoes. He sat barefoot. His big toe, feeling to him now rather like an epicenter from which great waves of pain ceaselessly and concentrically pulsed, had become turgid and huge, the nail obsidian-black.

"Jesus," he said aloud. He'd been afraid to look, and now he grew frightened.

At that moment, his gaze, shifting to the right, saw reflected in the dead cyclopean eye of the television screen a white envelope *as it was being slid beneath his door.* He gasped, turned his head.

He stared for thirty seconds, almost afraid to move. Had he not been paying attention, he may very well have missed it; for it had been pushed beneath the door in such a way as to slide under a nearby dresser, where it might have gone unnoticed, perhaps for years.

But he *was* paying attention, he was always paying attention.

He stood up and hobbled over to the door. He opened it a crack and peered out.

It was very dark. Still, he thought he caught the tailend of a long coat flapping once in the breeze; then it disappeared around the corner of the open hallway. Upon second thought, he was not sure. His palm, still clutching the doorknob, felt clammy. In the east, the moon was hovering, pared so thinly now and with the earthshine so bright that the moon itself looked like silver pincers delicately holding up a large gray ball.

Joel's head swam. He did not trust his vision. All day long, in fact, he had been watching multicolored planets orbit in front of his eyes and then explode without a sound. His toe was a live scorpion hanging off the end of his foot. It even occurred to him that maybe the envelope was not there after all.

He bent down to look.

There the envelope lay, peeking out from beneath the dresser. He closed the door, dead-bolted and chain-locked it. He reached down. He placed his fingernail on the corner of the envelope and eased it out. The carpet had cigarette burns here and there across it. His head as he bent over throbbed in unison with his toe. He slit the envelope open with his pinky. A small note on thick paper fell out into his hand. It said:

God is dead.
You are going to die.

His body went cold. His scalp numbed. He felt as if he might lose consciousness at any moment. He looked down again at the note in his hand. He reread it:

I learned a few things that might interest you.
Coffee at The Clear Sky, 11:00 AM?

L.M.L

He squished his eyes shut and rubbed his eyes. After several minutes, he read the note a third time:

God is dead.
You are going to die.

What the hell was going on? He tried to think; he could not think; he could not process anything. Greatly perturbed, he set the envelope and the note on the dresser and went for the pliers. He reached up and removed a framed seascape from the wall and then wiggled out the thin nail that the picture had been hanging upon. He sat back down on the sofa and, holding the end of the nail with the pliers, ran a lighter flame all along the nail-tip. His brows were deeply knitted.

In the army, they had fixed his toe roughly this same way, years ago.

In no time, he had the thin metal pulsing hot-pink. Large beads of sweat stood out along his forehead and along his upper lip, and the flame was reflected individually in each bead. His brow glowed like expensive wood.

He dropped the cigarette lighter onto the floor and leaned forward. Blood poured into his head. Sweat dripped onto the carpet. He looked once more at his toe: from the swelling, the skin was stretched out so taut that the whole top part of the toe glinted dully, the color of lead, a leaden ball. Another peristaltic wave of lightheadedness coursed through him. He closed his eyes, waiting for it to knock him over or to pass. It passed. He opened his eyes slowly. Concentrate, he thought, you've got to stay focused. He squeezed the pliers as tightly as he was able, and then without further reflection he jammed the molten metal through the top of his toenail and down into the flesh, extracted it. It took three seconds. A tiny geyser of infected pus and blood erupted, the engorged tissue squealing thinly, like a hog fetus, and then a blinding flash of white-hot light filled his vision, and after that all he saw was black.

10

He slept the remainder of the night in his clothes upon the couch. With the first light of dawn, he arose and went to the window. He lifted the blinds. He slid the window wide open and stood looking out across the land. The first thing to occur to him was that his toe felt better. He looked down at it. The swelling was gone, the pain was almost gone. Additionally, his head felt calm and limpid. A soft wind poured into the room. It was a beautiful morning, heady with the smell of cedar and grass. In the distance, he could see the old monastery, still afloat among the oceanic fields. Far off, clouds were dropping like parachutes over the wild mountains. He stood for perhaps ten minutes, thinking and staring. Finally he went over to the dresser and reread the note. He nodded, then went to the bathroom and cleaned himself. He shaved and showered and wrapped his healing toe.

Joel sat at a small table, staring into his cup of coffee. Now and then, he touched the backs of his fingers to his forehead, as if checking the progress of his temperature. Above him, a tight corkscrew of flypaper spun slowly back and forth. On the table beside him were salt and pepper shakers in a chrome caddy, a stainless-steel napkin holder, a cylindrical sugar decanter. A thin vase stood near the inside edge of the table, containing dyed pink flowers. He stared into his coffee cup. He took a small sip. The coffee was the color of licorice and went straight to his head. In the kitchen, a youth in a white tank-top labored under the steam of his dishwasher. Joel sat next to the window. The sky outside was hazy, old fir trees hanging motionless and moss-draped in the morning air.

By and by, a woman with chopped hair came up to the table. She wore a long gray coat, its belt hanging loose, which she slithered out of now and stood holding over her forearm.

She was a tall woman, late thirties or early forties. There was something Western in the shape of her jaw, distinctly American. Her pearl earrings looked like small eggs.

Over her left shoulder she carried a sandwich-sized purse which hung by a spaghetti strap. A thick paperback, bluish-purple, was partially visible inside the purse: *The Portable Nietzsche*.

"Is this to be an empathy test?" she said.

"Pardon?"

"Capillary dilation of the so-called blush response. Fluctuation of the pupil. Involuntary dilation of the iris."

"Excuse me?"

"We call it Voigt-Komp, for short," she continued. She was still standing above him—hovering, he felt—and now she smiled but without parting her lips. She let a moment pass. Joel stared at her. She wore a short-sleeve blouse with red rosebuds cartwheeling across it into space; khaki shorts that had sharp pleats; coffee-colored sandals whose straps went writhing a quarter way up her calves. "I'm only quoting," she said, finally. She moved around to the other side of the table, but still she did not sit down. "Hello, Joel." Her smile widened.

He rose to meet her. "Hello, Lauren. What's your middle name?"

"Marie," she said. "It's good to see you again. For meeting with me, *merci*. I hope that my note wasn't too cloak-and-dagger for you. Apparently your motel is *above* telephones, or something. Whoever heard of such a thing?"

"I don't know," he said. "Please have a seat."

He remained standing, waiting for her to lower herself, which, however, she was in no real hurry to do. First she examined her chair, checking it for food or other sticky substances, and then finding none she sat down. Though sufficiently slim, she turned laterally, in somewhat dramatic fashion, to ease herself in. She draped her coat over the back of her chair, hung her purse over this. For thirty seconds, she didn't say anything at all but, sitting there, regarded him openly. His clothes were wrinkled but clean; she noticed this. She noticed also that as they had shaken hands, his skin felt clammy, yet he was sweating, his eyes red-rimmed and peaceless, like an animal tortured by boys. It struck her as well that he must have access to some unique kind of whitener, for his T-shirt was pure-white, as white as the whitest snow. When he moved his hand from the table, the surface shone with the dampness from his palm. He sat across from her.

"So," she said finally, "how are you? I must say, you don't look very well."

"Would you like breakfast?" he said.

"No, thank you."

"I'm buying."

"Actually, I never eat this early in the day. In fact, I don't eat until the nighttime." (He narrowed his eyes.) "During the day," she said, "I drink coffee; I go for long walks and long drives. I read a lot. In general, I find the concept of eating slightly preposterous, if you really want to know. I mean, when you think about it. Our bodies totally dependent on this stuff which just turns to waste anyway—I mean human existence reduced to *that* … well, it lacks class, in my opinion."

He looked at her for several seconds.

"You have a very quizzical expression on your face right now, Joel. No doubt, you're wondering why I asked you here."

The waitress came and Lauren ordered coffee. The waitress wrote it out on a green pad and tore the top ticket off the book and set the ticket facedown on the counter. Somewhere in back, meat was hissing on a skillet. There was the chink of china throughout the restaurant. Overhead, the honey-yellow flypaper looked as if it had gobs of raisins stuck to it. "As I was saying," she said, "you're not looking so well."

A triangle of yesterday's cherry sat bleeding in the pie case.

"Yes," he said, "I haven't been well."

"You look like a roommate I had once," she said, pouring a long cascade of sugar into her coffee, "the half-mad heroin addict Robert Burton, who had the metabolism of a hummingbird and who hocked everything, including his father's hunting rifle, for just *one more fix*." She added a dash of cream from a tiny pewter pitcher, watched the cream blossom like a cauliflower onto the surface of her coffee. She stirred her coffee slowly, miniature tintinnabulations in the restaurant. "Tell me something, Joel."

"Okay."

"I'm extremely curious to know: what is your opinion of your mother's books?"

"Her books?"

"Yes."

"Which books are you referring to?"

"The ones she wrote," Lauren said. She tested her coffee.

"I don't know what you're talking about."

Lauren let several seconds pass. She eyed him. She was holding her coffee cup with both hands, one underneath, the other with her first two fingers through the ring. Her spear-shaped fingernails, red-painted and bright, looked as though they had been dipped in blood. "May I ask you something personal?" she said.

"All right."

"Exactly how well did you know your mother?"

He glanced down at the table. He caught his reflection in his coffee spoon: wan homunculous miniaturized upside-down in the spoon's concavity, gaunt face, puce acne scars, hollow eyes. He could see her hanging there too, in the background distance, bulletheaded and blurry. He looked back up at her. "Not well," he said. "She died when I was young."

"And your father?"

He didn't answer.

"What I mean is, your father didn't tell you—"

"Frankly it—she—was not something we spoke of."

"Ever?"

"No," Joel said. "Not ever."

"How sad," she started to say, but he interjected:

"He did tell me once he buried her high in the mountains that she loved, but that was the end of it."

"Well," Lauren said, "perhaps it's not my place to say, but if you don't know, your mother was a very remarkable person."

"In what way?" Joel said rapidly. He seemed uncomfortable but interested.

"Several. For one, she was an exceptionally erudite person, but she wore her erudition well. For another, she managed to remain elusive, and still remains so to this day, even as she generated such large amounts of enthusiasm among people. Which is the reason, *I* think, so many rumors surround her, still. Some have even suggested that three people were writing her books, not just her. I don't believe this, though. Does the name Jamie Kristiansen mean anything to you?"

"I've heard the name. What makes you ask?"

"Because that was your mother's nom-de-guerre, the only name she ever wrote under."

He didn't answer. Finally he said: "My mother was a mathematics teacher."

"Only for a little while. At least, that's my understanding."

"Specifically, what kinds of things did she write about?"

"Oh," Lauren said, "philosophical things. Pretty much anything philosophical, she wrote about it. In many ways that was the most remarkable thing about her—how *extensive* her philosophy is."

Joel shook his head. "I'm afraid I don't follow exactly what you're saying." He felt himself growing dizzier.

"Well, I think that people can't quite take seriously the fact that, in the late twentieth century, a woman from a no-name town in the middle of the United States developed an entire philosophy, as sophisticated in its arguments as any philosophy in any century. Or at any rate, that's what some people would say."

"And are you one of these people?"

"Yes and no. I've not read it all, not even close, and yet I admit that her words come at me like silver bullets, they're so appallingly direct. I submit the works. They're right there, for anyone to see and read. Lucid, uncannily lucid, and precise, no one can deny that: she wrote with precision, and her ideas are always stated clearly and forcefully. For many, Joel, your mother represents truth, with a capital T. She was like a vessel for truth, really."

"A what?"

"A vessel. Her philosophy, I mean, was that complete, that persuasive. That's why she has the following she does, although I should add that she did not want a following and even explicitly discouraged it. She believed that this kind of relationship breeds sycophancy and dependence. As a matter of fact, your mother was intensely private, and she always hid herself from admirers. She also maintained almost no correspondence whatsoever. In that sense, her following existed without her participation. I seem to remember her actually writing about this subject, in a sort of grain-of-corn metaphor, saying that *because* Jesus Christ had followers, is why he had to die or his followers would never have come into their own."

Lauren waited for a long moment.

"I'm sure all this is hard to believe," she said, "if you didn't know anything about it, especially. Think of it this way: many people don't believe either that Shakespeare was Shakespeare, and for precisely this reason."

Lauren sipped her coffee. August flies came crisscrossing like chopper fleets through the artificial air. Joel regarded her closely. Her nose was very straight and very pretty, and the baby green vein around her eye matched the hazel of her iris.

"What is the essence of her philosophy?" Joel said.

"That reality is real, first of all, and not created by any one viewer; that reality comes first, and that our brain is capable of apprehending reality as reality actually is, and that that act of apprehension is the word made flesh. That's the beginning. The rest, from metaphysics to esthetics to whatever else, is pretty much an elaboration on this one theme. She has a Spinoza influence, of course, but she surpassed him in scope. And according to something I recently read, she had specific plans to unite neurology, math, psychology, and philosophy into one indivisible theory. This was right before she died."

Lauren paused.

"You see," she subjoined, "your mother was nothing if not mathematical. And yet I think epistemology was her greatest strength. She once likened truth to quicksilver, saying it's very simple to capture, but only when you know the proper *methodology*. But whatever. I will say this about your mother: she completely demolishes all attacks against the senses and the human brain, all attacks against the brain's method of dealing with reality: 'the human mind,' to use her words, and the capacity of reason. Her philosophy is for this world, for living on this earth. Her epistemological philosophy, which she herself called 'a philosophy of relations,' is saturated in Thomism, but she significantly elaborates on Thomas Aquinas, and in so doing, she also outstrips him."

"What do you mean by outstrips?"

"She goes him one better. Her philosophy is properly atheist, therefore, and therefore she is the scientist's philosopher."

For a full minute Joel sat staring into his cup. The waitress came and asked him if he wanted her to dump his coffee and pour him a fresh one, but he said: "No, thank you. It's good just like this. Thank you, though." He looked across the table at Lauren and smiled strangely. For a moment, he looked as if he might say something more, but after all he didn't speak.

"And what about you, Joel," she said, "are you a mathematical person? I'm only curious."

He didn't immediately answer. "I used to be," he said.

"What happened?"

"I don't really know. Something recent. I came down with this horrible fever. I think I almost died. After about a week, once the fever had—you know—burned its swath, I discovered that I had lost my ability to calculate numbers. It was very unsettling for me, because numbers, I mean their perfection, their absolutism, they've always …" He broke off impatiently and scowled at the table. He clawed up his cup and took a large and hasty gulp of coffee, finishing the rest of the coffee in one swallow. "But this is nonsense," he said, "boring nonsense."

"Not at all," she said.

"And anyway it isn't why you invited me here," he said, "I'm sure." He looked up at her.

"No, you're right about that. It's not. I invited you here because when we first—and last—spoke, you asked me a number of questions."

"Yes."

"About your mother. And her connection with Shelby Morgan."

"Yes."

"To begin with," Lauren said, "and I'm assuming you don't know, they were lovers, once, a long, long time ago."

"I do know, actually. Now I know, I mean. I just found out."

"Oh?"

"Yes."

"Perhaps you found out the rest that—"

"No, I know nothing else."

She nodded once. "Shelby himself had told me some of these things years ago," she said, "but it turns out there was a lot more to the story than what he actually said."

"Really?"

"Yes. I discovered—" She broke off. "Let me interrupt myself. How well, if at all, did you yourself know Shelby Morgan?"

"Only a little," Joel said. "He and my father were friends." Joel unconsciously squinted, thinking back. "They were coworkers at the Equity Mine, where my father was superintendent." Joel again fell briefly silent. "I remember Shelby at our house once. I was about four-years-old. Shelby was sitting at the kitchen table talking to my mother, not my father. He was in his work clothes and had just come off shift, which I remember because his clothes were completely covered in muck. It was wintertime. I'm not sure what the two of them were talking about, but I assumed then that it was something about the mine, or my father. Thinking back on it now, I have no memory of the actual conversation, but I can picture them both very vividly, and I also vividly remember standing there watching them, and my mother holding my hand. I don't know where my father was at that time, maybe he was still at work. I do remember Shelby and my mother sitting there for several minutes before they started talking, and perhaps they *were* discussing my father, I don't know. I don't think I ever saw Shelby another time after that."

Again Lauren nodded, as if this made sense. "You see, Joel, long before your mother and father had ever met, Shelby wanted to marry your mother, and your mother, so it seems, wanted to marry him, eventually. But she first wanted to educate herself. First she studied, she studied abroad. Then, for reasons not altogether clear, when she returned, she chose this other man at the last moment, a dark-horse from nobody knew where. Nobody really knew *anything* about him, other than that he was uncommonly smart, and that he'd spent a long time in Africa. It turns out that this man was your father, Neil Gasteneau." Lauren waited while Joel took all this in.

"May I ask, where is this information coming from?" he said.

"Did you know Shelby Morgan's son, my former husband Bill?"

"Your husband?"

"Yes. Many years ago, he and I were married. He was older than you by several years, I realize, and he left town before—"

"I knew Bill Morgan," Joel said, "a little by reputation—he was a great athlete—but later I knew him personally, out in California."

This gave her pause.

"We lived in the same boardinghouse together," Joel said, "one owned by his mother."

"Well, not his actual mother."

"What do you mean?"

"I'll tell you, but let me ask first: when was all this?"

"It was just after Bill had dropped out of college, before I went into the Army."

"I see," she said slowly. "It makes sense to me now." She regarded Joel with what seemed renewed interest. "I must be as blind as a beetle."

"Why?"

"Because I didn't put any of this together when you and I met the first time."

"Put what together?"

"That you're the one."

An icicle skewered his heart. "What do you mean, the one?" he whispered.

"Nothing really." But she'd hesitated, he was sure of it. "Only that Bill mentioned you," she said.

"In what context?"

"In the context of a stone." She articulated that last word with very precise enunciation. "Among other things."

"Pardon me?"

"A stone," she said. "But Bill never called you by name—or not that I can remember, anyway, and I remember everything (unless, of course, I'm forgetting something). This was after he and I had divorced, you see, that he spoke of you. Also, you look somehow different in real life, did you know that? The same, yes, but also different."

He shook his head in confusion.

"So you met Bill out in California by sheer coincidence, then?" she said.

"No," he said, "not exactly. I knew Terri Latham from here, and I knew that she had moved out there. One day, when I was drifting up the northern coast of California, I looked in on her."

"I see," she said. "All told, how long did you and Bill know each other?"

"About one year."

"After which?"

"After which I went into the army and lost complete track of him."

"Were the two of you close?"

"In what way do you mean?"

"I mean—"

"In some ways," he interrupted. "We did spend a lot of time talking."

"What sorts of things did you two talk about?"

"Literature, mostly. We talked a lot about books. In many respects, Bill lived for literature, at least at that time in his life."

"Yes. And later. Did you—I'm very interested to know—did you ever talk about The Prince?"

Joel shook his head minutely. "Whom do you mean?"

"From Dostoyevsky. Prince Nikolai Stavrogin."

"You mean Prince Myshkin."

"No, I mean Stavrogin."

Joel frowned.

"In early drafts," she explained, "and sometimes in the finished product, Dostoyevsky also referred to Stavrogin as The Prince."

"Are you sure?" Joel felt himself growing increasingly dizzy.

"Yes," she said. "I'm positive."

He was silent. "How could you know?" he finally said.

"Because Bill Morgan was my husband. And because Stavrogin had a deep influence upon his life."

"Yes," Joel said, "we did. Many, many times we talked about Nikolai Stavrogin."

"What specifically?"

"You strike me as a very curious person, Lauren."

"You have no idea," she said.

"What I mean is, you strike me as a very thoughtful, very inquisitive person."

She waited.

"Bill had just read a book," Joel said, "*not* a book written by Dostoyevsky but something written by a nineteenth century critic about Dostoyevsky."

"What book?"

"I don't know. I don't remember the name of it. I do know that it was about a novel that Dostoyevsky had planned to write but never did."

"It's called *Confessions of a Great Sinner*," she said.

"As I understand it, Dostoyevsky incorporated much of this novel into his next book: *The Possessed*. But that initial book—the one the critic wrote, in which Bill first read journal entries concerning the novel that Dostoyevsky had planned to write—showed Dostoyevsky's notes for the character who would eventually become Nikolai Stavrogin." Joel was sweating now rather obviously.

"What's wrong, Joel?"

"Nothing," he said, "nothing at all." He paused for a long moment. "Only that Stavrogin figures into things in remarkable ways."

"Indeed?"

"Indeed."

"Tell me: did you know that Bill Morgan is dead?"

"No, I didn't."

"Yes. Bill died some time ago."

"Jesus," Joel said. He looked out the window. The glass was streaked with dust.

Lauren sipped her coffee and stared at him over the rim of her cup. After a moment, she set her cup down and tugged absently at the tiny egg-shaped pearl gleaming on her earlobe. "Forgive me, but I forget," she said. "Did you say that you knew Terri Latham only *after* she had left Shelby Morgan? Do I have that right?"

"Yes," Joel said, "but while she was still here. She used to watch me at night, while my father was working. It's my understanding, though, that Shelby and Terri never actually divorced."

"No, never actually. At least, that's my understanding as well."

"Did Shelby and Terri have any other children?"

"They never had *any* children. Her first two kids, Keith Case and Heather Case, came from her first marriage, when she was just a teenager. But I should mention that these kids loved Shelby as if he were their real father, and he likewise loved them in return."

"Yes, but wasn't he the father of her last child?"

"Justine?"

"Yes." (Joel hesitated.) "Justine."

"No, he wasn't."

"Who was?"

"I never learned. But it wasn't Shelby."

"How do you know that?" he said.

"Because Terri had already left Shelby by then. Terri was unusually silent about the subject of her youngest daughter, especially after Justine's suicide, but I know that Shelby wasn't the father."

Joel didn't speak.

"Of course," Lauren said, "Terri did come back to care for Shelby when he fell ill, and maybe that's what you're thinking of. But Justine was already two-years-old by then." Lauren grew thoughtful. She tapped her nails on the table. "The thing is," she said, "Shelby never *did* get well. Really, when you look back on it, his health only deteriorated after your mother married your father. Also, the mines took a great toll on Shelby's health—did you know that Shelby once died due to lack of oxygen when he was underground, and was revivified by your father?"

"My father brought Shelby Morgan back to life?"

"Yes, with mouth-to-mouth he breathed life back into Shelby. And Shelby never forgot it. He felt beholden. He even told your father that he had never asked for his life back."

"Really?"

"Yes."

Joel considered this information. "Did Terri Latham know of Shelby's feelings for my mother?"

"I've wondered that myself, and I think she must have. For one thing, I don't think Shelby would have hid any of this from Terri, even in the beginning. Shelby was an honest man, he was a good man. Basically, he was a good man." She hesitated. "Joel, how long were your mother and father divorced before your mother died?"

"My mother and father were never divorced."

She lifted her eyebrows. "Are you certain?"

"Yes." Then, very obviously, something entered his brain. "Why would you think they were?"

Lauren didn't immediately answer. "Well, once again," she said, "I don't know if it's my proper place—"

"Please," he said. "I want to know. There are no confidences left to betray."

"Here's the thing, Joel, really the number one reason I asked you here today. Your mother Angela became pregnant long before she had ever met your father. She became pregnant with Shelby Morgan's child Bill." Lauren fell silent.

"Bill Morgan is my half brother," Joel said.

"Was. Yes."

Joel didn't respond.

"In addition," Lauren said, "I recently read—"

"Where did you read?"

"That's a fair question, one I was going to answer a moment ago. When Bill died, he left behind several manuscripts wherein he documents much of this. He references also a number of conversations he had with his father on these exact subjects. His father had never kept any of this hidden from Bill, and in fact was always quite open in his dealings with Bill, as far as they concerned Angela especially. As I was about to say, Bill at one point speculates that your mother loved both men, but that she chose your father because he was more her, quote, intellectual equal. Those are Bill's words. According to Bill, according to Shelby, however, for all your father's undeniable brilliance, he had a fatal flaw."

"Yes," Joel said. "He was violent."

"I was going to say jealous, possessed by the green-eyed monster."

"Perhaps. But that was secondary, a by-product."

"What makes you say so?"

"I have my reasons."

"Fair enough," she said. "'And so the violent shall bear it away.'"

"What do you mean by that?"

She shook her head dismissively.

"Did Bill know that he and I were half brothers?"

"Yes," Lauren said. "He did."

"He never said anything to me about it."

"I know. It's ridiculous, isn't it? Bill was breathtakingly secretive about some things, and this was one of them. Listen to me: there are almost no good secret-keepers in the world, Joel, even if everyone thinks he is, but Bill was one of the few. I've thought a great deal about that lately."

"About what?"

"The fact that he never spoke of this—even with me. It's actually frightening how private he was concerning the subject. And yet, I must say, I love him for it."

"Why frightening?"

"Because at the same time, he was so deeply obsessed with it all—with your mother in particular. Seeking knowledge was Bill's main motive in life, and in so doing he got lost inside the caverns of his mind—lost and then addicted—and he never did find his way back out. It can easily happen, Joel. It happens all the time, in fact, and so let that be a warning to us all." She squinted at him. "May I ask you one more question?"

"Sure."

"Is it true that you had a younger sister? A stillborn named Rachel?"

"Yes. How did you know that?"

"There was speculation that this child was Shelby's as well."

Joel closed his eyes.

Lauren crossed her long legs. She leaned back and folded her thin arms over her breast. She squinted at him.

"If my mother wanted to leave my father," Joel said, "it would have been early on, when she first discovered that he was violent." He sounded as if he was speaking as much to himself as to her. "Is that what you were also going to say before? Or something like it?" He glanced down at her crossed legs, the stretchmarks along her outer thigh visible to him: like vellum, he thought, or sandbars.

"Nobody really knows. Does it actually matter, though, Joel?"

"No. It doesn't. So why can't I stop thinking about her?"

"Because," she said, and started to say something else, but he interrupted her:

"I have this idea that she's not actually dead," he said. "I mean, the notion keeps nagging at me. I never saw her dead, you see." He stared vacantly at the table. "*Is* she dead?" he asked.

"I don't have any reason to think otherwise."

They were both silent. Outside, the sun slipped behind a steaming pile of clouds; the restaurant darkened. She drank her coffee and set down her cup with a click. A red-nosed fly by her pinky fingernail was lapping at a small pool of cream. He was staring out the window, at the stony bluffs which ringed the valley. She watched him closely.

A full minute passed.

"If she discovered early on that my father was violent," he said, "why *did* she stay with him for so long?" He was still turned to the window.

"I don't know," she said.

Another silence ensued. Then Lauren did something that caught Joel completely off balance. She rose halfway out of her seat and reached across the table and ran her pointy index fingernail gently down the entire length of a glutted vein along his inner forearm. This vein was long and tubular; it gave softly beneath her hard nail, then it reinflated the moment she came to the end of it. She closed her eyes and as she did so she exhaled sensuously. "I've been waiting to do that ever since I first saw your veins," she said. She opened her eyes. "Your veins are amazing."

Joel's astonishment couldn't have been greater, but outwardly he didn't react at all. He simply sat there. She then pointed the same nail at the same vein. "May I?" she said. "Once more?"

He didn't answer but scowled and drew back, out of her reach, and turned facing the window again. She held her finger outstretched in midair for a moment longer, then she retracted it.

Two minutes passed.

At last, he turned from the glass and looked squarely at her. In complete silence, they stared at each other for several seconds. Then he swung his eyes back to the window. "Nietzsche is flawed," he said, to the glass.

For a moment she looked mystified. Then she glanced down at the book poking out of her purse. She smiled, but only just. "What do you mean?" she said.

"Raskolnikov refutes the Ubermensch," he said.

"Oh? Ever read *The Pale Criminal*?"

"Pale Criminal?" He turned to her. "What is it?"

She narrowed her eyes and stared at him in silence. "Nothing," she said. But the strange smile was there, hovering around her lips. "And you're right: Nietzsche *is* flawed. But at his best, he isn't. Let's say that without him some very important philosophers wouldn't have come to the conclusions they came to, no matter how hysterically they deny it now."

"Is that so?"

"Yes, it is. It's true that Nietzsche was a misogynist. It's true also that he's anti-reason (not consistently) and that a philosopher's stance on reason in large part defines her. But there's no getting around the fact that Nietzsche had an exalted view of man. Actually, that's the main thing about him: his unique vision of man and of man's potential. This vision shaped a lot of people's conception of what humans could be." She paused. "Besides," she said, smiling openly now, disclosing the serrated tops of her straight white teeth, "haven't you heard?"

"What?" he said. "Haven't I heard what?"

"Could it be," she said, pressing her fingers to her chest, arching her eyebrows, "that he has not heard? Could it be that Joel does not know?"

"What?" he said. He sounded concerned.

"About God?" she said. "Have you not heard that God is dead?"

She smiled again.

He looked away.

11

A chocolate-brown spider sat with pie-eyes in the center of her web. The web was slung like a miniature hammock under the eaves of the trailer, the strands of gossamer flickering blue-to-blue in the soft breeze and the sunlight. Above, the sky was overcast but luminous; far away to the north, sultry cloud-monsters were dissolving and reforming, dissolving and reforming, constantly over the horizon.

He stared at the spider for a long time: lady of the loom, motionless, microcephalic, but with a body as big as a child's fist. He felt the old panic stir in his mind, kicking its legs behind the thin membranes of time. He closed his eyes.

The trailer shone brightly in the cloud-filtered light. It was situated on the raggedy purlieus of town, at the border of an endless aspen grove, the property in complete disrepair: a swaybacked shed with two busted windows; white paint peeled in long strips down the sidings; a tilted porch that abutted onto the massive granite boulders which some glacier had spilled. Beyond the trailer, the white quakies glittered.

There was a solitary apple tree on the stubble lawn, its limbs bent low with the lunar globes of fruit. No flowers, but white apple blossoms lay wilted all across the ground. An old-fashioned thermometer hung nailed to the porch, telling the temperature to be ninety. It was the middle of August. The heat felt smothering. One hundred meters away, at the foot of the mountain, thermal winds swirled up scarves of dust.

He entered the house without knocking.

Complex odors—tobacco, the nick of raw meat, and a musty, almost vinous scent—hit him at once like the blast from an open furnace. Upsurge of memories. All the windows were wide open; currents of air gusted into the minimal rooms. There were no pictures on the walls or books on the shelves. In the room beyond and to his right, he could see a bright orange perched sunlike atop a black coffee mug; beside that, an egg titled in a shot glass, and there also the green telephone crouched expectantly, waiting to ring. Through the far window, a lone poplar stood pulsing in the wind. Something foggy was in the air, and damp. The house was tidy, bare. The ghostly curtains rippled and popped.

By and by, he became aware of music coming from the back of the house: a piano leaking through the fog. He moved toward it. The floors gave slightly under his weight. The smell of meat and cigarettes grew heavier, the air thicker. When he came to the final room, he stopped and stood upon the threshold.

Inside the room it was difficult for him to clearly make out anything, the entire space enshrouded in a Lethean fog. In fact, the fog was a combination of bluish cigarette smoke and mist from a large humidifier which was quietly sputtering out jets of steam. Once his eyes acclimated, however, he saw an old man, very tall and slender, lying supine upon an iron bed. The music was beautiful. This room at the back of the trailerhouse was largely sunk from light.

"Hello, father," Joel said.

In the room, there was a bed and a desk and that was all. This man had little, and wanted less. On top of his desk was a small record player. There was also a sheaf of writing paper and a cup of sharp black pencils standing points up. In the right-hand corner sat a small stack of astronomy books. The black record was wheeling slowly, pumping out a dolorous nocturne that seeped into Joel's guts. The shade of the single window was drawn but had a tear left of center, a wedge of pewter light cleaving the vaporous air, dust motes floating inside like silt seen underwater. Thirty-three leaves on a dying aspen outside.

The man looked at Joel from under the eaves of his eyes. He had his pillow doubled-up under his head. He was fully clothed. He studied Joel with his green gaze that was still bright, then he looked away. His nose was long and lumped, etched along the outer edge of the right nostril with two blood-red lines, like rivers on a map. His chin was still strong, and he still had his thin drooping mustache, though it had turned completely gray. He was smoking an unfiltered cigarette. The smell of raw meat filled the room.

"Hello, son," he said. He coughed once, a phlegmy rumble that sent a cascade of ashes tumbling down the front of his flannel shirt. He was sweating on his narrow bed, listening to Chopin in the dark.

He looked much the same, thought Joel: lean and lanky, but now his face was cross-hatched and caved, with bladelike bones threatening at any moment to slice through the papery skin. When his father was eighteen, he had had his left leg shattered, femur to ankle, in a barroom brawl, the left eyeball partially enucleated and subsequently reattached. He was told he would never walk again. But he had walked again, had made himself walk again, though for the rest of his life he carried his leg like an ancient appendage, and during the time of his long convalescence he had sworn off alcohol for good.

Joel thought of this now.

This is how I remember him best, he thought. My lean-hipped father listening to music in his room. The sheer strength of his will. His eyes gleaming like ice-flows. My father listening to music, day after day, alone in his room.

"You heard that I was dying," his father said, "and so you've come back." It was not a question. He looked away.

"No, father." Just perceptibly, Joel hesitated. "I call you father," he said, "but I've long since ceased to regard you as that."

"Oh?" His father swung his green eyes like laser beams back to Joel. "So that's why you've come." Again, it was not a question, and Joel realized without any doubt now that all the years had not diminished his father's powers of perception. "What is it, Joel?" the old man said. "Have you waited all this time to say those words, to phrase it in just that way? And have you waited twenty-five years for just that? Have you harbored it the entire time? Mapped it out, rehearsed it? Well. How does it feel?" He took a hard drag off his cigarette, then crushed it out with determination and simultaneously gave up an enormous cloud of smoke. Beside him on the bed, an ashtray sat overflowing next to a crumpled package of Pall Malls: his only companions. "But what did you come to see?" he continued. "A reed shaken in the wind, a broken down man, repentant? An ancient relic wrapped in rags, sad, forlorn?"

Joel didn't respond.

"I'm afraid I'll be a disappointment to you," his father said. He raised his eyebrows, his forehead went vermicular. He smiled. Mist continued to pour into the room. The fingers of his right hand moved lobster-like upon the bed.

"I have questions," Joel said.

"What questions?"

Joel didn't respond.

"Speak!"

"I wish to know about my mother."

"Your mother."

"Yes, sir."

The old man gave Joel a strange hiss, a serpent's hiss, and that was all he gave him.

"Please," Joel said.

"Let me tell you about your mother. Your mother was a whore who any man could knock up—and did. Your mother is a cipher of history to me. To me, it's as if she never existed."

Despite everything, his vehemence surprised Joel; Joel winced. "Why do you say that?"

His father didn't answer. The smell of meat was monstrous.

"Did she fall out of love with you?" Joel said. "Did she never love you at all?"

There was a long silence.

"Please tell me. I've never asked you for anything; I'm asking for this. Did you stop believing in her?"

"She cheated us, Joel," his father said, after a full minute had passed. "Both of us."

"How do you know that?" Joel said.

There was no response. The old man seemed to be devising wickedness upon his bed and had set himself in an awkward position.

"Did she carry Shelby Morgan's child," Joel said, "my younger sister?"

"*Younger* sister? What are you talking about? Don't you know that Shelby Morgan raped your so-called mother and that was supposedly the end of everything between them?"

"He *raped* her?"

"That's what she said. Do you believe it? Was she raped, Joel, or was she—"

"When?"

"Before you were born. But I believe you know better."

"I thought that Shelby Morgan—"

"What in the fuck do you know about Shelby? Shelby was a weak man. He was a hard worker, everyone knew that, and I will give him that: he was a good goddamned miner, and I could always count on him for that. But Shelby was a weakling, and that was his undoing. I have no use for people like that."

"What about my younger sister?"

There was no answer.

"Tell me," Joel said.

His father gave him another strange hiss, like a pit viper; but still he said nothing.

"It was the priest," the old man whispered, at last.

Joel glowered.

"Yes," his father said. "The priest corrupted her. And she him."

Neither spoke for a long moment. His father was staring straight ahead, gazing at the wall. Joel squinted at him through the mist, as if with his naked eyes he could penetrate the man's complicated head. "Was Terri Latham's youngest child your child?" Joel said.

For a fraction of a second, his father seemed surprised. "How—" But he cut himself off. He tipped his head to one side on the pillow and squinted at Joel. "Why does all this matter so much to you now, Joel? Exactly what sort of crisis are you going through?"

Joel started to speak but was interrupted:

"Can morality exist after you kill God, Joel? Is man defined by his actions or not? If so, to what end?"

Joel dropped his eyes to the floor. He stared at his feet through the creeping vapors. "Happiness," he said.

"I didn't hear you."

"Happiness," Joel said, louder.

"Why that?"

"Because the opposite of happiness is despair. No man can live for long in despair."

"Why?"

"He needs something to have, to look forward to."

"Which presupposes that life is the ends."

"Nothing is greater than life," Joel said.

"Her words," his father said.

Indeed, it occurred to Joel only in that moment that his father was correct: they were her words.

"But for a man," his father said, "life is not primarily physical. What is it, Joel? Do you remember?"

"Psychological," Joel said. "Man spends the majority of his life inside his own head, and in the end one experiences only oneself."

"Which is a paraphrase of Friedrich Wilhelm Nietzsche, though she would never have admitted it." And then: "Joel, it was you; you were the weak one."

"No," said Joel. "I—"

"You of all people, with *my* blood in you. My blood sloshes through your veins like nitroglycerin, and I only wanted to make you strong, Joel, stronger." He gritted his teeth unconsciously, giving him his old and dangerous-looking underbite. "I wanted to make you untouchable, in the true sense of that word, because you of all people were not meant to be mediocre. Anything—goddamnit—anything but that."

"Blood is meaningless," Joel said. "Your blood, the blood of your fathers... even her blood. By my own decisions, I and I alone determine what I am. I am my own man; my blood is my own."

"Are you certain? Because your tone is unpersuasive. So, then: what have you become, Joel? When you piece back together the broken fragments of your life, what picture emerges? What *are* you, Joel?"

Joel didn't say anything.

"Autonomous man?" his father said. "The eudaimonia of the Stagirite's entelechy? Have you read anything at all yet, Joel? Have you got down to the business of real thinking?" He raked back his moon-colored hair with his long fingers. "Well, Joel? *Speak.*"

"Don't you know that I would have done anything for you, father?"

His father scoffed; his lungs rattled.

"You were my idol," Joel said, "the only one I ever had. I was always faithful to you."

The man fumbled for another cigarette. He fished one out, but it was so desiccated that it snapped in his fingers before he could get it lit. There was a long silence.

"Father, I've come here for another reason as well."

His father waited.

"I've come here to tell you that I know it was you," Joel said.

His father looked up at him. He extracted another cigarette but did not immediately light it. He placed it between his dry lips. He was staring at Joel. The piano pumped out chords.

"I know it was you," Joel said, "that killed her."

"Talk sense," his father said.

"Both of them. My mother and my sister. I know you killed both of them, because you were jealous—you *are* a jealous father, and you are irrational. And that's why I reject you. Because of your irrationality."

The man brought forth a mold-colored lighter. His cigarette wagged tremulously along the corner of his mouth. He touched the flame to the end of the cigarette so that for a moment the slow coal of tobacco crackled and his face glowed orangely through the mist, like a jack-o-lantern in the room. Abruptly, then, the record stopped playing. And in that amplified silence which can seem so bottomless after the music ends, his father said to him: "No, Joel. It was you. You killed her."

90

"I?" Joel said, incredulous.

"Yes," his father said. He looked away and exhaled his green soul against the wall.

"What do you mean?"

His father didn't answer.

"Because she would not leave you, because of me?" Joel said. And suddenly it became clear to him. "She loved me," Joel said. "I remember that she did. She was good to me, always. And I think now that she only stayed with you because of me, because she knew all along that you might one day murder her. And you did murder her. And she knew that you had it in you to do so. She saw it all beforehand. She told me."

"Told you? Come, now!"

"Yes. In a secret letter."

(His father scowled.)

"But she knew that you could never murder me," Joel said, "your own flesh-and-blood, she was certain of this—so certain that she bet everything on it. She was certain that you could never kill me, and in the end she was right. Just barely, but she was right. And why? Because you are the father who can hurt or kill anyone or anything that you come in contact with, it has never really mattered to you either way because you're megalomaniacal, and because you always feel justified in acting upon whatever thing you choose, no matter how puzzling or inexplicable to the rest of the world, expecting us all to just go along with you because you are You. But no matter the lip service you've always given to choice and free agency and even love, and no matter what you've always said about 'man's fate being his own'—no matter this, you could never *truly* bring yourself to murder your own son, because you're obsessed with blood. Blood is the main thing about you. It's your legacy, father. Blood is everything to you. If you exist at all, you exist for blood, and if you doubt what I'm saying, take a look back at yourself, your entire history; point your hyper-perception inward, and you'll see. But hear this first: a man's life consists of more than the meat, and when—"

"Death gives life meaning," his father said, "because there can be no life without death, or the threat of death."

"I could easily kill you now," Joel said. "It would be so simple. I could snap your neck like a reed."

"Except for one thing," his father said.

Joel narrowed his eyes.

"You don't have the guts." The old man rolled his head away. "And Joel," he said, looking at the wall, "you won't be free of me until the day you die. And your mother was never the same after you were born. You ruined her, and her womb."

Joel stared at him through the encroaching fog. He sincerely considered killing him, but the instant he considered it, his father was in front of him, the ashtray capsized on the bed, the giant old man slowly squeezing Joel by the windpipe, shutting his air off, his grip like steel. So quickly had his father moved that it was as if he'd not moved at all, as if he'd been there all along, pressed against Joel, almost hugging him. Joel could smell his meaty breath, his father's suspiration hot and living and not entirely unpleasant. Immediately, Joel clutched his father's hand and began prying back the long thumb. At the same time, Joel brought his knee up to catch his father in the groin, but the old man was prepared for that and simply moved aside—and then with his gorilla strength, which Joel could not believe, he moved Joel out the door.

12

Alone, he stood beside the same narrow highway down which, two decades before, he had made his long, final escape from this town.

He was no longer sure how final that escape was.

He stood for minutes, gazing over the sinuous black road. Light from the luminous sky glanced off a row of solar panels high on the hill, igniting the panels like heliographs. He looked away. His eyeballs felt as if they had small barbs stuck in them. Dark images flitted everywhere along the periphery of his vision—images which when he turned to look at them straight on disappeared instantaneously—and his left eyelid kept fluttering. But worst of all he felt certain now that his keen vision was deteriorating; for he wasn't seeing things as clearly as he always had, a blurry shimmer marring the edges of everything. Away to his right, he could hear the slosh of the sea-green river, but he could not see the water for the screen of summer foliage. He felt a great anxiety mounting within him and he thought: something must give.

Sunlight poured molten lead onto the fields. He stared up at the mountains that were angled so dramatically across the sky. He stared at the stark mountains and he stared at the sky: black basalt tunneled through with mysterious mines of gold, the sky above leaking a melancholy force. Everything felt slightly unreal to him. He stared for a very long time. The road was deserted. After a while, he walked back into town.

He walked and walked. He came up steep sidestreets he was surprised to remember so well. He passed through grubby alleyways, this western town like many western towns, with its Masonic lodge and its crooked river, the hard clean sky above and the cauliflower clouds and the rusting railroad tracks running beside the river.

On the southern end of town, a large goldfish pond stood at the tip of a public park. The fishpond had existed for forty years or more. As a child, Joel had come here often and alone. Bleak Sunday afternoons with a paper bag of dry bread that his mother gave him to feed the fish; smoke coming off the water in ephemeral sheets; clumps of sooty snow about the grass; cold wind. These fish still haunted his dreams, he knew that they would forever: swaying ghostly through the dark waters, these dreamland fish live in wild woodland lakes, where they should not be, and in settings unbelievably picturesque. And always he is fishing for them, even though he knows that to eat them is to court death. Yet he finds himself eating them, raw or only half-cooked, he doesn't understand why, for he's sickened by them at the same time. In his dreams, the waters are foul and contaminated; the fish swim alongside poisonous trout and snakes and black carp and sallow-white suckers utterly packed with bones. All the creatures in these dreams are somehow dangerous, but he doesn't know in exactly what way.

Standing beside the pond now, he thinks of this.

The air coming off the water smells rank, of rotting vegetation.

He watches the goldfish glide beneath the water. Some are orange and some are golden, others hot-pink, their fins ribbed and translucent and rippling in the underwater currents. Many of the fish have grape-colored clouds staining their midsections and many have white tumors sprouting out of their eyes or just above their eyes, chunky growths like weird knots of muscle. The wedge-shaped tails swish through the water, winnowing the algae; winnowing the gunpowder sand. The biggest fish are scarred and have scales so large that they look cobbled with coins.

Once when he was five or perhaps six and the fish were in a feeding frenzy over his bread, he reached elbow-deep into this pond, beneath the fish, and sloshed one out onto the cement. It was fifteen inches long, coppery-orange. It bucked and thrashed on the pavement. Its nostrils were like needleholes, its eyes inky, all-pupil. He stared a long time at the cataphracted body bowing itself back and forth, back and forth upon the concrete, bits of dirt and gravel sticking to its scales. This fish was sleek and dying, and it disgusted him. He kicked it, hard, back into the pond, where except for the silent kneading of its gills and the slow flutter of fins it lay unmoving on its side. Later in the day, he saw the same fish floating dead upon the water. That night, he dreamt of the fish. He dreamt he'd put a stiletto knife through the fish's side, skewering the bean-sized liver like a shish-kebab. In his dream, taffy-soft prolapses the color of sterno began oozing out of the belly and spilling fruit like a cornucopia, fruitlike guts. He ate them, he puked.

He thought of this now, almost three decades later.

He stood watching the fish for several minutes.

He continued walking.

He walked for a long time, sunk in thought, and as if delaying what he would do next.

At the end of one hour, he came to the same building he had sought refuge in as a child, Saint Mary of Zion Catholic Church.

He went around the side of the church, up three cement steps to the rectory door. Through the window, he could see the small yellow office and the secretary's desk and, beyond that, buried in subtle shadows, the priest's living quarters. All the lights inside were off. No one appeared to be home. It was just after four o'clock. Joel knocked. He knocked and knocked. The door was made of a thin metal that resounded clangorously under the heel of his fist. He waited. No one answered; no one came. He knocked again, louder this time. Still nothing. He waited. He knocked again and tried the door. It was locked. Beside him, a set of narrow stone steps descended to the church's backyard, and when he was certain that nobody was going to answer, he followed the steps down.

The backyard was an ovoid lawn bordered on the north and northwest by a profusion of eclectic flowers and, opposite this, a dense garden of raspberry and chokecherry shrubs. From the bottom of the stairs, Joel gazed about him. The berry canes were shot through with pewter daylight. Small gray birds peeped at him from within. On the west end of the lawn, a water sprinkler with a green snaky hose sweetly hissed, and all gone to seed, the moonlike dandelions leaned in the breeze, giving up their parts, piecemeal, to the wind. Joel didn't see anyone anywhere; only a parget Mother-of-Christ, weathered gray on a plinth of slate, smiling at him from her hidden enclave under the northern eaves of the church. Thin dark shapes darted around the periphery of his vision. Bright butterflies blinked on and off like neon lights. He closed his eyes. After a while, he walked back up those steps of crude masonry and around the building into the church itself.

Entering shadows cool and blue. A stony taste hung in the air, and the trace of stale punk. Tides of superior silence. Once his eyes adjusted to the darkness, he saw that inside he was completely alone. He walked through the vestibule, past racks containing religious literature, past the wide marble bowls holding their sacred waters. On his right and on his left, along the church walls, large lancet windows depicted the Biblical dramas, massive mosaics pieced together in multicolored glass. The stained light fell softly to the floor, and so his thoughts like ashes softly fell.

He walked down the plush vermillion carpet toward the front of the church. His steps did not make a sound. He came to the foremost pew and eased in. The wood popped beneath him. The church seemed beyond empty; it felt forsaken, desolate. An enormous bible directly in front of the pew lay hefted open on a metal stand. Slowly, he leaned back into the hard wood. It crepitated with an almost human sound. He stared before him. Pallid Christ crucified on a rust-colored cross, hanging above in a field of scientific shadows; Yeshua-ben-Joseph with his human eyes closed, head cocked to the left, bleeding thin rivulets that issued from beneath a brown and thorny crown. The palms looked nailed down with railroad spikes, the flat, stacked feet. INRI on a crooked wood sign. The plaster loincloth hung loosely about the waist, knotted high at the right hip so that the whole right leg was visible, long and muscular. The ribs were stark and sharply defined, deep oblique muscles below the spear-punctured side-wound from which, two thousand years ago, the blood and water had freely gushed. No candles burned in their lampions around the altar, but long shafts of citrine and winy light slanted to the floor from the high window over his head, and small candles in fruit glasses guttered at the feet of the holy mother. Joel could hear the sound of children playing in the distance.

To the right of the tabernacle, God in vapid gray wafers slept in a ciborium made of pure gold. A creamy candle flame burned steadily in a flume of red glass before the ark. A gust of wind outside blew over the church. The ribbed timber beams creaked. The candle flame remained motionless.

Joel lowered the padded knee-rest at his feet, then knelt down.

He looked at the Bible, which stood open to the New Testament. He read the first thing his eyes fell upon:

The light of the body is the eye: if therefore thine eye be single, thy whole body shall be full of light. But if thine eye be evil, the whole body shall be full of darkness. If therefore the light that is in thee be darkness, how great is that darkness.

He raised his head and squinted.

If the light that is in thee be darkness.

He repeated the words silently.
Light be darkness?
He looked back to the Bible, at the opposing page:

First cast out the beam out of thine own eye; and then shalt thou see clearly to cast out the mote out of thy brother's eye…. Ask, and it shall be given you; seek, and ye shall find; knock, and it shall be opened unto you: For every one that asketh receiveth; and he that seeketh findeth; and to him that knocketh it shall be opened. Or what man is there of you, whom if his son ask bread, will he give him a stone? Or if he ask a fish, will he give him a serpent?

For nearly an hour, Joel sat there thinking. He did not read any more. He shut his eyes so that he would not be distracted by the flickering black lights dancing across the edges of his vision, the barbs of pain.

The church remained empty the entire time that he was there. The air grew increasingly cool. He could hear the wind outside, rushing through the conifers in sporadic bursts. With each burst, the ceiling beams moaned and popped. At last he stood up and left the building.

Outside, the silver sun blazed in his face like pistols. He walked once more around the side of the church and knocked on the rectory door. There was still no answer.

Two buildings north of the church stood a barbershop. He went over to it. Of the blue-smocked barber, a youngish man, Joel asked about a former parish priest named Father Moorecroft. The barber, scissors in his right hand, black comb in his left, said that he did not know a Father Moorecroft and deferred instead to the client beneath his tools, whose back was facing Joel.

Which client shrugged, sending a harvest of hair sliding off his slick shoulders onto the checked floor. The barber suggested that Joel try across the street and gestured vaguely, with his scissors, to a grove of spruce trees fronting a small museum. Joel thanked both men and two minutes later stood before the museum door.

He entered.

In a reliquary room to his left, a curator with a bald head and octagonal glasses sat reading from a dusty tome. He glanced up when Joel came into the room, his dark eyebrows rising semicircular over bluish eyes magnified gigantically behind the lenses. It took Joel a moment to realize that the curator bore an uncanny resemblance to Benjamin Franklin. Joel nodded hello. He asked the curator if he knew what had become of the priest, Father Moorecroft. He asked further if the curator knew whether this Father Moorecroft had perhaps been transferred to another parish. The curator said no, Elias Moorecroft still lived here. In fact, though, he added, Mr. Moorecroft was no longer a priest. Joel scowled. Behind his thick lenses, the curator's eyes swam like two exotic fish. He brought out from a drawer at his right knee a thin phonebook and opened it to the name Moorecroft, the only Moorecroft in the book. Joel scribbled down the address and folded it into his breast pocket. He was about to close the phonebook when his eyes passed over the actual telephone number.

It took him a moment to process where he'd seen this number before.

It took him only a moment longer to remember why and when he'd dialed it.

13

The house stood by the water. A gravel road, flanked on either side by a corridor of cottonwoods, served as a driveway, which, one-quarter mile before it branched off another gravel road, was called county road 45. Beyond the dusty trees, the deep green canal wended crookedly through the fields. Looking westward, a forest of snow-fat conifers gave way to cliffs, and above this, some seven miles from the house, the spiky mountains jutted into the sky.

To the east and to the north, the fields fell off toward the horizon.

With some idea of entering obliquely, Joel followed south-to-north the river that fed the canal. It was a modest flow, sourced in the hills above his childhood house, and in the army whenever he thought of home, invariably what he thought of first was this river, with its cold black pools, its tumbled stones, its sandy eddies and narrow tributaries that he'd built so many dams upon, high intricate structures of clay and rock.

It was Monday, third week of August, a clear, canicular afternoon. The night before, it had rained—misty spates on and off the entire evening, leaving the morning sky rinsed and blue. Outside town, among the low hills and fields, everything lay smothered in leathery shadows, but here where he walked the sun beat down with such intensity upon the water that the sandy riverbed looked like hammered gold. Clouds of quick minnows darted in the shallows near the riverbank. Joel watched a solitary garter snake undulate across the river, chin lifted. A fingernail-sized frog was doing the breaststroke in a pool beside him, with akimbo legs. The air smelled of water and willows.

He followed unreliable paths that dead-ended without warning and then sprung up in the same manner.

Water spiders riding the river's face cast jeweled shadows across the golden sand. He watched them closely. He remembered how once, fishing near here, peering into the tinfoil glare of the current and catching, now and then, the blurry wobble of his lure, there'd come a sudden explosion from a puff of silt, and a giant rainbow trout smashed into his hook, hitting it with a strike so savage that all its subsequent thrashing only ensnared the trout deeper. Joel landed the fish upon the river rocks, dashed its brains out, his hands shaking with excitement. The feel of that strike loomed in his dreams forever: the sensation of a hit that hard, the unexpectedness of it on that particular day; for it had been very hot and the fish not biting at all.

That night, Joel had given the fish to his mother—his father was gone, working the swing shift—and his mother had cooked it with cornmeal and coriander. They had eaten it together, the flesh of the fish coral, not white.

A dragonfly with iridescent wings sizzled past him.

A pair of wasps came gliding in over the river, landing gear lowered: strobic flickers through the tree-cast shadows.

How many days he'd wandered this river alone, walking the same speed as the river, observing all the births and deaths and passages of life that occurred here. How remote and pure the river had once seemed to him, how large, with all its swarming spiders and butterflies, its fat bumblebees and birds and philosophical turtles and the gibbering frogs who spent their entire lives within feet of the riverbank; how clean. He could feel the water breathing beside him now.

He came out of the trees and into the pasturelands. A replica of the overhead sky appeared grayly on the surface of the river. The afternoon was warm. A perfumed breeze blew down from the west. The remains of a bicycle—bent, rusty, missing both tires—lay half submerged in the detritus, a green bottle, like a bottle in the smoke, glintless beside it. He felt the first nick of Indian summer in the wind, saw it in the shimmering air, and with it a trace of bittersweet sadness stole over him.

Twenty-five meters up ahead, the river was intersected by a narrow gravel road, a wooden bridge passing low above the river's flow. A faint path led from the riverbank to the road. There was a pensile wasp burrow beneath the bridge, attached to a jutting rod of rebar. He came to the path and followed it up. From here he continued northwest, across the bridge, walking along the edge of the road, which soon sliced off to the right and ascended up a long hill. He followed the hill to its summit. Then he veered onto a trail that petered out upon a grass promontory. From this vantage, he cast his eyes across the variegated fields beneath his feet. He saw range on range of lilac mountains floating in the far distance, towering clouds, miles high, pounding up above the hills. He could not see the river from here, but the wide canal down below looked like a green serpent sliding through the grass. Mats of goldenrod spilled out across the fields, swaying. Away to his left, the road dropped back down to the west and then straightened out for almost a mile.

Halfway down this road stood the house.

He asked himself now:

If the sum total of nature is God, does God then have consciousness?

"No," he answered aloud.

Then nature cannot be God.

14

The house was a large and looming affair, well-kept but somehow rickety-looking. It was made mostly of white stones and whorled wood. It appeared uninhabited, and yet not entirely. Three big cottonwoods, over a century old, grew in the front yard, a series of S-shaped spruce trees interspersed between and a lopsided catalpa tree on the other side, which stood tickling the eaves of the house. There was a pair of pinkish flip-flops in the grass beneath the catalpa. The lawn was spacious and filled with shadows. To Joel, a heavy air hung here, an almost forbidding air—forbidding in its silence, as if this place contained deep mysteries. Passing under the slow-swaying trees, he felt himself unexpectedly horripilate at the rocking-chair moans.

He came up the porch steps and stood at the front door.

On a narrow rail that ran the entire length of the porch sat a pair of cat-eye sunglasses, distinctly feminine. Next to this was a black ashtray with a long cigarette crushed out in the center. The cigarette seemed fresh. It had lipstick on the filter. Joel rang the doorbell. He heard it resound deep within the belly of the house. Nobody answered. He knocked and waited. Still there was nothing. He knocked again and tried the door. The door was locked. All the window blinds were pulled, and he could not see inside. He turned and gazed behind him.

The land about him was pastoral and serene. Sheep were bleating in the distance. The mountains soared up into the cornflower sky, and a chip of the daytime moon stood there like a lost fragment of the clouds notched within the mountain peaks.

For some reason, then, that familiar sensation he'd come to recognize as paranoia settled down onto him, and yet, also for some reason, neither this feeling nor the recognition of it for what it actually was frightened him. Indeed, he smiled a little, almost, indeed, as if to welcome it. His head swam with a slightly dreamy quality. Perhaps, he reflected, another by-product of my sickness.

He stood for five minutes, just staring. He saw nothing unusual. Still, there was the palpable sense that someone was watching him. He felt absolutely sure of it this time.

Looking across the hushed and shadowy yard, he asked himself: Is it me? Or is it this near-perfect day making me feel so peculiar?

At that moment, a feeling of calm came over him—a calm which for several moments recalled to him his former sense of self: his self at its best. And rising as it did to the surface made him realize (only now did he realize) how far removed from it he'd actually gotten.

He walked around the grounds for an hour more, searching for precisely what, he knew not. All he knew now for certain was that he *was* searching. Perhaps if he waited, somebody would return, something would happen.

He watched lemon-colored butterflies flop sloppily over the clover fields.

In the queer half light, he detected a subtle steam creeping in, heightening the heavy hush. He walked the perimeter of the place, past a stagnant goldfish pond surrounded by limbless, headless statuary. He scanned the landscape in every direction. He saw nothing but a pair of horses far off in the next pasture. When he came to the fence line, the horses lifted their heads in unison and looked over at him, across the grass. He kept walking. Presently, he came to a stone building, vaguely chapel-like and without any actual door but a black doorway carved out of the rock.

A breeze came sliding out of the building and went about his body, stirred his hair.

He walked inside.

Inside, it was as cold as a tomb—moist and with the verdant smell of moss. The building was empty and silent. This was a narrow room, dark save for a long barrel of chalk-white daylight which, halfway down the eastern wall, came slamming in through a chink in the rocks. There were no windows. The floor was wood. At first glance, the building appeared to be a sort of shed, yet it was large enough to serve as a small airplane hanger; so that in the end, Joel wondered at the building's function. A similar doorway to the one he'd entered through stood directly across from him, making this room feel more like an anteroom, an entryway into someplace bigger.

He strode across the floor and looked out through the other doorway.

It was a large garden.

On a small concrete table, beneath the willow trees, a thick book he at once recognized sat atop a stack of typed pages, which pages appeared to be some sort of manuscript. A green apple, approximately the size of a cue ball, sat at the bottom of these pages, acting as a paperweight. The apple had two large bites taken out of it. Joel could see no person, but at the back of the garden, where the grass grew tallest, he caught the rearend of a butterscotch tomcat sauntering through its veldt, tail swishing.

The cat disappeared into the shrubs.

The table stood ten meters in front of him, slightly to his right, and, like a secret plot, this whole section of the property was so buried in foliage that from the outside everything within was hidden. In fact, as far as he was able to tell, the tomblike building he'd just come through *was* the only way to access this place, as if, he thought again, the building were an anteroom after all.

Along the right-hand side of the garden, pink-flowering thorn grew rampantly, and wild roses, and people-sized hollyhocks, just beginning to bloom. The air smelled of flowers and willow bark. Farther down the bower, strawberries lay bleeding like tiny hearts upon the ground. Small tubers bloated beside them, and, farther still, where the shadows thickened, there were tattered raspberry canes, all picked clean. Just beyond the stone table, an exiguous cherry tree grew in the center of the garden and three meters from this, an apple tree loaded with apples identical to the bitten one upon the pages. Magpie with long tails flitted lightly from branch to branch; shadows of birds-in-flight flashed across the ground. The setting sun which had emptied the overhead sky of all but the last of its color was still strong enough to cast yellow polka dots here and there along the grass. A Pentecostal breeze channeled through the garden.

For a long time, Joel stood upon the threshold, neither quite in nor quite out. He felt repelled and drawn at the same time. There was something alluring here, and yet eerie. He felt as if someone were hiding in the shrubbery just beyond, peering out at him. And each time his eyes passed over the book, he grew more certain that he knew it, but from where?

He stood for a long time. Nobody appeared. The probing sun finished its sweep of the garden. The birds grew silent. The leaves shimmered, pulsing with held light. After an hour, Joel turned and walked out the same way he had come in.

It was only then, when he was once again on the other side of the stone building, that he saw it: to the right of the rocks, on a rank chain draped across a mossed-over well:

NO TRESPASSING

The sign had fallen into complete desuetude, with bullet holes puncturing the thin metal and paint flaked off in patches around each hole, showing powdery rust underneath; yet for all its dilapidation, the admonishment carried a weird impact into his guts, and a numbing sensation shot from his stomach to the nape of his neck, nausea rising deep within him. He was still staring at the sign when he noticed, on its top left-hand corner, that someone had pasted here a sticker of a large lavender butterfly. Then, as he was looking at it, he saw the butterfly resituate its wings.

He thought: my eyes are playing tricks on me. He was even quite certain now that he had forgotten his own name, and the only thing that remained within him was the awareness that he was himself. Then the butterfly resituated its wings a second time. That magnificent creature, warming itself upon the stored heat of the metal, lay fully outspread and perfectly symmetrical, with a furred body not unlike the body of its former self, the great wings red-flecked and rimmed with kohl and cream and the long antennae knobbed at the tops, like snail antlers.

Joel stared at it for several seconds, then stepped toward it. The butterfly flickered and in an instant the shadows of twilight had totally absorbed it, leaving him forever unsure if he had dreamed it or if it had been real.

15

For three straight days after that he lay on his bed. He just lay there, sweating. His limbs felt curiously large and detached from the rest of his body. He did not eat. His head swam, and time passed in a confused manner. He had difficulty differentiating between his waking states and sleep.

The window beside him stood wide open, and when the wind blew, it blew hot and dry. He could hear it sifting through the far fields. The noisy grasshoppers of late-summer had begun: hot-rods ratcheting by with their helmet-heads, their gleaming fuselages. He lay and listened. Dog days of August, purple thunderheads hanging static curtains of rain; cotton orbs drifting through the arid air. He grew quiescent.

Seventy hours passed.

He found himself back inside the tomblike building, with no real recollection of how he had gotten there. He stood just inside the entryway. Behind him, the sunlight raged away. It was oppressively warm. The heat in the sky melted down like solder, but once he was inside the building, the stones exhaled great waves of cool, the moist, mossy smell soothing and soft.

He waited minutes for his eyes to adjust. He gazed upon the stone walls. They were whelked and pocky, and to his acclimating eyes they looked lilac-colored. Everything was silent; gales of rich silence. Halfway down along the eastern wall, the same rod of chalky sunlight came sliding to the floor, a galaxy of dust swirling within. The blood coursed through his veins. He could hear the muffled sound of his breath in his ears, like seashell oceans booming away, and the thud of his heartbeat, reptile-slow.

He stood.

Around him, the stones continued to exhale fields of cool. His senses felt hyper-attuned, an abnormal acuity of sound, sight, smell. After an extended period of time, which he no longer had a capacity for gauging, he moved across the room to the opposing doorway. Once again, he looked outside.

Sitting at the granite table beneath the willows was a tall woman. Her head was bent over a book—the same book that he had seen here before. Her hair, silky and Indian-black, hung so long that it masked her face and lay slack about the concrete table. Without any noise, he had come into the doorway. Still, she raised her head. She turned to him.

It was his mother.

In the same instant that he registered this, he registered two other things as well: she had not changed at all; and the book, which before had seemed familiar to him, was her book, her favorite book, not one that she herself had written but one she'd always read, an odd, philosophical mystery story, origin obscure, author unknown, called *The Secret History*.

As soon as his mother looked at him, her lips broke into the soft smile he remembered photographically. She scooped her hair straight back off her forehead, disclosing her whole face. She was very beautiful. He knew in that moment that she had been expecting him all along.

The butterscotch tomcat, couchant and invisible in the grass, rose up and stretched his right foreleg and hind left, then bound up onto the table without a sound. His mother did not take her eyes off Joel, even as she reached out to the cat.

"Hello, Joseph," she said. She stroked the cat between the ears.

Without any warning, he began to cry. He felt overwhelmed, first by her matchless beauty and the love she obviously bore him, which shone in her every feature, and then even more by her eyes, which were so dark and knowing and calm. How had she kept herself so youthfully preserved?

Then, for reasons not at first clear to him but which he now just glimpsed, a great tide of fear started welling up inside him. The tomcat slid against her fingers, pressing firmly into her stroke; then it dropped like liquid off the table and set about cleaning itself, the tiny tongue as pink as candy.

"Mother," he said, "they told me you were dead."

Her smile widened, but her lips remained pursed. Slowly, she shook her head, and slowly she blinked, her long eyelashes beating like the wings of some rare bird. "No," she said. "Not dead. Anyone who lives by my words can't die. Death where is thy sting?"

"Why did you leave me?" Joel said.

"Leave you?" She stood up from the table, graceful, lithe. "I didn't leave you. You left me, Joseph."

He frowned. The cat stared at him. "I would never," he started to say and was about to continue when she interrupted him:

"Goodbye," she said. She turned away. (The cat remained, staring.) "Goodbye, Joseph," she said. She glanced back at him over her shoulder. "I love you. I have always loved you."

At which point, he understood fully now the source of his fear: he was dreaming, and his mother was not real. And just as in his dream he grasped this, she dematerialized before his eyes, dissolving as she walked away into the grainy mist of his psyche, and he awoke.

Awoke to a lavender dawn, and a feeling of hollow that went clear down to his core. Morning wind blew in through the open window and passed over his face. He lay there for over an hour, staring up at the stucco ceiling. Then he hefted himself up and dressed.

Outside, the sun had not yet risen. The land was locked in a state of absolute silence. Wind blew softly through the far fields, flattening the mint-colored grass. There were deer grazing on the hillside below which the monastery stood silhouetted in the neutral half-light.

Down the highway, keeping to the sloped shoulder, he was picked up by a white-haired construction worker in a blue Ford. Joel sat in the back of the truck, hunched over onto the balls of his feet, his tennis shoes wedged between corrugations of steel. The wind went wildly about him. He could feel the sensation of the tires rolling beneath his shoe soles. Five miles later, Joel knocked on the back window. The truck pulled over and Joel hopped out. Grackle, twenty meters away, stood huddled under a lightening-scorched fir tree, their feathers glinting like metal. At once when his feet struck the ground, the birds ascended into the sky. Joel watched them disappear. Then he turned and raised his hand to the construction worker who nodded; who accelerated back onto the road. Then he was alone.

Or was he?

Suddenly, he felt that he was not. He swung around and looked behind him. There was no one there. He studied the trees. They were empty.

He turned at length and walked across the highway, making his away once again down county road 45.

The morning haze had all but burned off the pastures. Wraiths of thermal mist hung dissipating above the grass. Aluminum fence posts, bordering the fields, fired in the fresh daylight, and the grass along the roadside swirled like water around his ankles. He walked through, bursting the browning awns.

He came quickly to the gloomy house, and quickly he went around to the back, through the empty stone building, until he was out in the garden. He did not allow himself hesitate.

The first thing he saw was the butterscotch tomcat again sauntering away into the trees. Joel went over to the concrete table. The air was cool and fragrant. The ground felt spongy beneath his feet. Now the table was empty: no book, no pages, no apple, no one about. There was the same stillness in the air, the same enchanted feeling that he had felt before, but a more mysterious presence lurked here as well.

Something, he felt, was waiting.

He looked at the surface of the table. Written on the concrete, in soft-lead pencil, was a series of mathematical equations, intricate formulas he could neither decipher nor dismiss. He stared at them for a long while. The numbers and letters were faded but still readable. They were written very precisely. Two or three times, he even felt himself on the verge of grasping something important about them, but in the end their meaning eluded him.

He continued walking through the bower, moving slowly under the corridor of trees, glancing to the right and to the left, along a path of small slate slips which lay like lily pads in the grass. The path curved to the left, terminating in a sort of cul-de-sac. Here a thin but well-worn trail of dirt, about the width of something a cat might make, led deeper into the trees and then into a screen of brush.

Joel paused. Then he ducked down beneath the branches and followed the path through.

To his surprise, it deposited him less than a quarter-mile from the river. He looked all around him.

He had never seen this place before. Southward, a cluster of reddish rocks ascended into a water-carved cliff, approximately fifty meters high, down which the river poured in a gentle cataract. Opposite, the river evened out, sloshing away across a long private pasture, before finding its final outlet at the bottom of the valley, seven miles farther along.

Joel turned and looked back behind him. He could see neither the house nor the garden from where he was now: only the soft occlusion of the August flora and the thin trail like sprinkled cocoa disappearing into the undergrowth. Ahead, between him and the river, was a grove of spruce trees, the tallest of which towered to heights in excess of one hundred feet. Above their croaks, Joel could faintly hear the hiss of the river. The trail continued into the evergreens, and as he walked, crumbly black soil, carpeted with rusty needles, consumed the trail completely.

On the other side of the forest, Joel received a shock, the first of many to come: a brown blanket spread beneath a blue spruce tree, with, on the top side of the blanket, a book.

It was the same book he had seen in the garden, on the concrete table.

The book lay facedown and was partially overlapping another book, the title of which he could not make out. Joel searched the soaring trees. There was nobody anywhere that he could see. The only sound he heard was the distant noise of the river, the intermittent knock of woodchucks. Moving only his eyeballs, he stood scanning the forest. Finally he walked toward the blanket.

And here he got his second shock: this *was* the book from his dream, the book his mother had loved, **The Secret History**

Underneath that title, in font smaller but no less discernable, were nine words he had forgotten:

In quo sunt omnes thesauri sapientiae et scientiae absconditi

It had been twenty-five years or more since he had last seen the book, and yet he recognized it immediately. He recognized it from its cover design: a small but precise painting of a lean man, his back to the viewer, looming before the sea, his body blacked out against a coral sunset and the green sea surging everywhere in front of him. The book itself was thick but not large, and it was bound in a wavy cloth-weave that didn't look like cloth.

But there was something else about the book that had struck him at once, and yet he was too preoccupied to grasp specifically what it was.

He stood motionless for many minutes, staring at the picture.

Then he reached down and lifted the book from the towel. He was brought up short by the last words on the first page of the other book: "*Tu! hypocrite lecteur!—mon semblable—mon frere!*"

He stared at this page for some time. Then he raised his eyes and was about to turn his attention to the book in his hand, when he beheld the man.

The man stood three hundred meters away, in the groin-high grass of a green meadow, not far beyond the borderline of the forest. He stood gazing off toward the water.

Joel placed the book back onto the towel and crept forward. He knelt hidden in a cave of trees and watched.

The man appeared to have spontaneously generated. Joel stared at him for several minutes. The woodpecker hammered away. The man didn't move; his eyes seemed fixated on some remote point, across the swelling seas of grass and beyond Joel's ken. Watching him, Joel felt himself transported into a new land, a land of sunlit valleys and fire-green fields.

Abruptly, then, the man turned and began walking. A path led from the meadow down to the riverbank. The man held his left hand laid-out flat, and as he walked, he skimmed his palm over the weeds and over the wandlike blades of grass. The path deteriorated into a jumble of round rocks, which stood piled along this side of the river like so many bloated swine. Joel's eyes the whole time followed the man, who had his other hand stuffed into his front pocket. The weeds he brushed with his palm stood on wire-thin stalks, slender stalks with compact heads utterly packed with seeds. The man moved with a graceful gait, strong-looking and lean, thirty or perhaps thirty-five. Neither handsome nor tall, he was nonetheless so relaxed and so healthy-looking that Joel felt himself instantly drawn to the man.

The man wore faded black jeans and a black button down shirt. He had wheat-light hair. There was an unkempt quality about him, clean but mussed, and curiously catlike. Joel rose at length from where he crouched.

The man came to the river rocks and picked his way up and over them, then stood upon the muddy banks, looking across the river.

Joel moved forward; when he came to the bloated river rocks, he began loping over them. The plash of the water drowned out the noise of his steps. He stopped when he got to the bottom of the stones, some ten feet behind the man.

The man knelt down on one knee to drink. A kingfisher sounded a staccato call. After a few seconds, the man stood and dusted off his kneecap. In the shallows downstream, a black trout drifted silently over the sandy riverbed. A monarch butterfly swooped in and then went wheeling away, off into the undergrowth where whirlpools spun into the deeps and where the fish grew to enormous sizes, fat as pythons, with huge burgundy gills. This was the direction the man was looking off in. At this time, Joel saw nothing more.

The man seemed privately absorbed, but just as Joel was about to announce himself, the man spoke:

"Hello," he said.

Which startled Joel considerably. For one thing, the man still had not turned around; nor had he moved at all. He was still gazing downstream, away from Joel.

"Hello," Joel said. "Forgive—" But Joel interrupted himself. "I'm sorry," he re-began, "it wasn't my intention to surprise you."

"Do you know, it's like very little surprises me."

Joel narrowed his eyes. The man had a slow way of talking, an easygoing voice that Joel found strangely alluring. The man still had not turned around. He was probing the pointy tip of his front pocket with his index finger. Then, somehow instantly, he was looking at Joel.

He was one of the bone-faced.

"It's a sign of intelligence," Joel said.

"What is?"

"Not being surprised by anything."

"Who told you that?"

"Somebody," said Joel. "Some writer, I think."

"Some fool, more like it—or at least you'd better hope so."

"Why do you say?"

"Because many surprises await you."

Joel regarded him closer now. A mordant expression marked the man's mouth, but the first thing Joel noticed about him wasn't this. Rather, it was the capacity of awareness burning in his eyes, or behind the eyes, creating the calm and lighting him from within like twin lanterns. Very suddenly, and with a certainty he did not think to question, it made Joel believe that he could know the fullness of this man's life. In the next instant, Joel understood not that this man would be cut down by the world for being so aware of it, but that he was too deeply aware of it to ever be hurt by anything.

Joel was astonished therefore when, succeeding that, it occurred to him that he and the man looked in some way alike.

For a long moment, they stood in silence, ten feet apart, blinking at each other in the sunlight.

"I know that I'm trespassing," Joel began. "I apolo—"

But the man truncated Joel's apology with a brief and backward flick of his hand and a quick shake of his head. It was a somehow sarcastic-looking gesture. They stood in silence for five seconds more. The water rattled past.

"You see, I'm looking for someone," Joel said.

"Good. You've found someone."

"Someone specific," Joel said.

"Whom do you mean?"

"The father," Joel whispered, and he felt as he said it the familiar sensation of needles come raining down on his scalp.

"Or mother?" the man said. His smile widened. "Don't you know, there is only one who is—"

"I mean the priest," Joel said. "Father Moorecroft."

"Priest? No. Father, okay. But he is not here, my brother."

Or is he mad? Joel thought. It was a real question in his mind. The mocking expression, which had at first struck Joel as so conspicuous, now seemed more just a natural part of the man's bony face. It was impossible for Joel to tell for sure. The man, meanwhile, continued to contemplate Joel with his two wet-looking eyes, like blots of melting chocolate. It flashed through Joel's head that this man was perhaps confusing him with someone.

"Where is he?" Joel asked.

"Moorecroft?"

"Yes."

"He's moved."

"When?"

"Just."

Joel was silent.

"You just missed him," the man said. "And so"—he smiled crookedly—"you were looking for a priest but found me. Hilarious."

"Is it? Why do you say?"

"Because I don't believe in God," the man said.

Joel could see now over the man's right shoulder the china sky, or a long diagonal of it, reflected across the river, late-summer cloudlets riding the current in the same spots, same spots, same spots. Joel squinted at them.

"Yes," the man said, following Joel's eyes to the river, "these days in summer are certainly apt to linger."

Now a cloud passed over the sun and the land darkened. Joel saw a diamond-shaped image stamped on his retina. The kingfisher called. The sun reappeared. Reflections lay everywhere. The man reached down with his left hand and picked up a stone from the riverbank. The stone was about the size and shape of a sand dollar. In one fluid motion, he straightened up and threw the stone, sidearm and with great force, far upriver.

Here, where the water opened into a wide black pool, the stone twice skipped whizzing across the river's surface, then clattered against the rocks on the other side. Joel noticed the man had that peculiar-looking coordination which some left-handers have—a left-handed grace which Joel had always secretly envied. Joel glanced downstream. The anchored trout was gone.

"Follow me," the man said. He just noticeably lifted his chin to the north. Then he turned and began walking over the river rocks, moving parallel the evergreen forest that Joel had come through to get here. Four hundred meters upriver, the man veered away from the water and started up the narrow path that wound through the meadows. He did not look back.

Joel stood there and watched him grow remote.

It was still morning at this time.

In the distance, grape-colored clouds lurched across the eastern sky.

After a while, Joel swung his eyes back to the relucent water and stared. He stared until his eyeballs ached.

16

When Joel finally uprooted himself, he discovered that the man was no longer anywhere to be seen.

Joel followed his path into the meadow and then stopped upon a slight eminence of land. He stood gazing down to the evergreens below. A scattering of small aspen trees fluttered just this side of the grass. At first Joel didn't see anything unusual. He tipped his head back and looked up into the dizzying sky. Directly above his head, the white sun resounded in the burnished blue, iridescent clouds scorching around the edges, very high. He looked back to the borderline of the forest. He let his eyes wander around...suddenly he caught a glare of glass, a flash so bright and brief that he reckoned it to have come from a mirror. Then he saw a small house built against the cliffs, in the spot from which the flash had come.

The house was composed of the same stones that the cliffs were composed of and designed in such a way as to seem a natural outcropping of the landscape, like a cottage hidden inside a scrambled picture.

Joel realized that he must have looked past the house several times, both before, when he was in the forest, and also now from where he presently stood; and yet he had not noticed it. He found this particularly unnerving—in part because once he saw it, the house became so obvious to him that he couldn't understand how he'd not seen it before.

He began walking in that direction. As he reentered the evergreens, the sensation of vertigo that he had felt a few moments before, looking into the sky, increased with unbelievable rapidity, so that in a matter of seconds, a feeling of complete dislocation overtook him. The trees closed in behind; he could no longer see the cliffs or the house or the river.

He stopped walking and genuflected upon the soft earth. He put his head down and shut his eyes. His face dripped with perspiration.

A minute later, when he opened his eyes again, he caught another mirror-like flash, but this one was only a few feet in front of him and tiny, like a spark, or a tooth-wink. He reached out his hand; he was halfway surprised to immediately find a solid object pinched between his fingers: a coral-and-white cameo, framed in gold, about the size of a chicken egg. Hot from the sun, it gleamed there as if new. In fact, it looked so pristine to him that for a split second he wondered if *this* had been the original flash he'd seen from the meadow.

Joel held the cameo in his palm and scrutinized it.

On the face of it was an ivory woman depicted neither in profile, nor quite straight on, but with her head cocked ever-so-slightly to the left. She had a delicate nose and a thick curtain of hair that fell past her shoulders. A thin fracture ran the entire length of the face, dividing the visage roughly in half. This division gave the woman two perfectly discrete sides, which disturbed him.

Even more disturbing, however, was the nagging sense that he had seen this cameo before, except without the hairline split. And then he knew.

He stood up fast, too fast. A white light burst like a flashbulb inside his head, something like an actual lightning bolt but faster and silent and which, for a span of about five seconds, made him feel as if the whole world around him had all gone glitchy and gauche. This was followed by a sluice of heat that poured like lava into his brain, emptying out his limbs and turning his digits cold. He closed his eyes again. A sense of normalcy returned by degrees. At the same time, when he opened his eyes, instead of feeling merely disoriented, he found that his sense of direction had completely malfunctioned, as if (he reflected) his internal gyroscope and everything connected to it had gone haywire. No, he thought, it wasn't quite this. It was more as if, for the first time in his life, it had occurred to him to question if he was moving in the direction that he thought he was, and by the very fact of his questioning it, he grew unsure.

He cast his eyes about, searching for a point of reference. He couldn't find any. The woods became even more sinister and foreign-looking. Long shafts of violet light striped the shadowy air. A Pentecostal wind poured through: an odor of decaying leaves in the wind, slight but profound: auguries of autumn. His nerves stood like hackles. He inhaled deeper, to calm himself.

And caught a distinct whiff of cigarette smoke.

He swung around, first to the left, then to the right. In the distance, he indeed saw a figure in white flash through the woods. But then the figure wasn't there. He closed his eyes and opened them. There was no one. Yet the smell of cigarette smoke lingered in his nostrils. An involuntary shudder wormed up through him. He gazed around for some time and finally glimpsed, or thought he glimpsed, through the mossy evergreens, a mauve expanse of rock, which he took to be the cliffs that rose behind the house.

In a moment, he made his way toward them, suppressing the temptation to run headlong in that direction.

He was right: by way of a dirt path, he came to the house. The sight of a man-made object, however queer-looking it was, eased him. At the same time, the house lay under such a shroud of brooding isolation that his sense of dislocation intensified. The path, bordered on each side by medium-sized boulders, appeared incongruously quaint. Nothing around him moved. Joel went cautiously up the path.

This house was a study of horizontal planes. The base all around was built of solid stone. Rectangular sheets of glass made most of its walls, both front and back, so that up close, the outside world was mirrored piecemeal in a kind of phantasmagorical duplication, which shifted with any shift in his perception. His retinas felt again as though they would scorch from the high-altitude glare.

Coming up the pathway toward the house, he felt cowed by all the glass.

The front door was shut tight, but through the windows on either side of the doorway he was able to see inside: it was a long dark room, spacious and uncluttered. Beyond, through the back windows, the sheer cliffs ascended. Joel knocked with the tips of his knuckles. The bark of his rap swept off into silence. Nothing stirred. He knocked again. There was no answer. He walked along the western side of the house and came to a walnut deck with two iron chairs around an iron table.

On this table sat two coffee cups. A black shadow that the cliff cast down sliced the deck diagonally. The table sat inside the shade. A sliding glass door gave onto the deck. Joel distractedly noted the table for two. Then, glancing left through the glass doorway, he noted also with a disproportionate sense of alarm that the door was now open. Simultaneously, his eyes fell upon a stack of pencil portraits lying on the floor.

Joel stepped inside the house. The temperature noticeably dropped. He was certain that he recognized the subject of the top portrait, yet it took him a moment to understand why. And then he saw that it was *him*—it was a pencil portrait of Joel Gasteneau.

Instinctively he stepped back, as if to distance himself from whatever nightmare he had just stumbled into. His head pounded out another blast, not quite as strong as the one before, but still strong enough to momentarily jar him out of this world.

At which time, a figure strode into the room.

It was the man with the mussed hair.

The man smiled but he didn't break his stride or even hesitate; he kept walking. The knee of his jeans was still damp from where he had knelt in the sand beside the river. In one hand, he carried a silver-and-black coffee thermos and in the other, a tray with cream and a small bowl of sugar. By way of a greeting, he nodded and continued nodding, as if to himself, reinforcing Joel's notion that the man might just be a lunatic. The man's forehead was grooved and heightened, almost diabolically, as from much thought. He strode past Joel onto the deck.

Joel followed.

The man set the tray and coffee thermos down on the table.

"I thought you'd decided to stay away after all," the man said.

"I knocked," Joel began.

"And here you are."

Joel tilted his head.

In the interim since they had spoken beside the river, without knowing precisely why or when, Joel had convinced himself that, mad or not, this fellow was for certain mistaking him with someone else. And more: he was mistaking him for someone with whom he was familiar. The person in the portrait? Joel started to ask this very question, but the man obviated it:

"Please, Joel," he said, "have a seat. This is a...what? It is an opportunity for you, the one you've been waiting for. You mustn't miss it because you're so troubled." The man spoke casually and unaffectedly in his slow voice, and at the same time he began pouring coffee into one of the two cups. He was not looking at Joel, even as he spoke.

A pregnant silence hung in the air between them as it slowly settled upon Joel that the man had just used his first name, after which Joel had difficulty modulating his voice.

"I'm sorry," Joel said, "did I introduce myself to you?"

The man didn't answer.

"You see, I'm very distracted right now," Joel said.

The man's smile widened. And yet he was still looking away, pouring the other cup now.

"Forgive me," Joel said at last, "what was it again?" He stepped forward and extended his hand.

"Tom." The man set the thermos on the table. "Or Thomas, if you prefer."

They shook. Tom's fingers were graceful-looking and felt cool and callused. He pulled out a chair for Joel and then went around the table and sat down.

"Do we know each other, have we met before?" Joel said, in one breath. He frowned and shook his head. Then he wiped his brow with his thumb. "I feel dizzy right now. I get the feeling—"

"Please," Tom said, "sit first and be calm." His expression had not changed: he still looked amused. Indeed, it occurred to Joel that it was this, the mocking manner, the ever-present sense of irony, as if things were not as they seemed, that was keeping Joel most off his guard, and was making him unsure how to take the man. "That coffee is for you," Tom said. He gestured with his forehead toward the other cup and then took a sip of his own coffee. There was a relaxed quality in his movements, a sort of unstudied grace, which for all his preoccupation Joel did notice, and noticed, furthermore, with something like admiration. Tom crossed his legs at the ankles, worn sneakers moving metronomically upon the deck. "I understand that you have many things you want to ask—"

"*How* do you understand that?" Joel said. "I don't know what's going on."

"Get comfortable."

"I must ask you first: I came across two of your books earlier."

"Which books?"

"In the woods."

"I don't know about any books in the woods."

Joel didn't pay attention to this. "I know it's none of my business," he said, "but it's urgent to me that I find out where you got the one book?"

"What one book?" A look of perplexity hovered about Tom's features, and yet he was still smiling. With growing alarm, Joel began to suspect that this fellow really *didn't* know what book Joel was referring to.

"May I ask you something else?" Joel said.

"Yes."

"Do you smoke?"

"No, I don't."

"But this is your house?"

"Not strictly speaking, no."

"What do you mean, not strictly speaking?"

"I mean that stone by stone I built it, so in that sense it's 'mine.' But it doesn't belong to me."

"Whom does it belong to? Elias Moorecroft?"

"Yes, in part."

"But he's moved?"

"Yes."

Joel didn't say anything. He seated himself—or, rather, he crumpled into the opposite chair and took a sip of coffee. He didn't ask the thing he most wanted to ask: he was too anxious about what the answer might be. "Thirty minutes ago under the trees," Joel said, "I came across two books, and I'm certain I wasn't imagining them."

"I didn't mean to suggest that," Tom said.

"I know you didn't."

"Which books?" Tom said.

"One, written in French, I didn't recognize. The other—"

"*Tu parles français?*"

"*Mon français est un peu hesitant,*" Joel said. "*J'avais l'habitude de parler français. Et toi?*"

"*Je pratique un peu.* And the other?"

"The other I've seen only once before, although I didn't realize that until today," Joel said.

"And where did you see it once before?"

"In my home, when I was growing up. It was my mother's."

"What is it?"

"It's called *The Secret History.*"

"Ah!"

"You know it, then?"

"Yes. I know *The Secret History.*"

The blood drained out of Joel's face. He sat there, pale and damp. Neither spoke. Joel stared at the man's fingers upon the table. All at once, these fingers looked hauntingly dismembered and appeared to creep forward and then retreat: they were strong, compelling, beautiful fingers. Joel couldn't take his eyes off them.

"Who are you, exactly?" Joel said. "I don't mean to be rude, but are you the man—"

"No," Tom said.

"Who are you?"

"I'm the man who walks behind the man and whispers in his ear."

"What does that mean?" Joel said.

"Quoting, only quoting, Joel." Tom was momentarily silent. "Joel, have you yourself ever read *The Secret History of the Arche*, as it's also sometimes called?"

"The arch?"

"Yes."

Joel shook his head minutely.

"Some of the earliest printings," Tom explained, "were entitled *The Secret History of the Arche*. Have you read it?"

"No, I haven't," Joel said.

"Do you know what the word *arche* means here?"

"No."

"Do you know anything of that book's history?"

"No."

"What, if anything at all, do you know about it?"

"Really nothing at all. I know that my mother liked it. Why are you smiling?"

"Joel," Tom said, "if you'll bear with me a moment, I'd like to tell you the story—" But Tom interrupted himself. "Joel," he said, "I'd like to tell you the story *behind* the Secret Story, if I may call it that."

Joel did not respond.

"The word *arche* comes from the Latin word *arca*," Tom said. "At one time, arc with a 'c' and ark with a 'k' were virtually interchangeable. The word ark is a variant of the present day word we know as a 'chest' or 'vessel.' There's also a mathematical connotation, and an astronomical one. Do you begin to see?"

"No," Joel said.

"To us," Tom said, "arc with a 'c' means curve, and ark with a 'k' means ship, or perhaps container. But the original meanings were not these, exactly. The original meanings were broader. To put the point explicitly, all these words, and several others beside, once referred to a receptacle or some kind of vessel that might contain anything: good food, for instance, stone, stone tablets, even blood, or a child in the womb."

"*What?*" Joel said.

"Yes, that's right. It was in this sense that Mary the mother of Christ was herself often thought of as *the* Arche."

"I've never heard that."

"Well, it's not well-known. Just the same—"

"No, I don't doubt you."

"I mean, just the same as the Ark of the Testimony was also a vessel thought to literally contain God, so also Mary was a vessel thought to have literally contained God. The metaphor, on occasion, has been extended to symbolize women in general. But why are you wrinkling your forehead at me, my brother? Is something the matter?"

"Yes."

"What are you thinking of?"

"That I don't have any idea what you're saying, or what the hell is going on."

"I'm talking about the book," Tom said, "the one you just asked me about, the one your mother loved." Tom paused in a way that suggested he had more to say, but in the end he was silent.

"Finish," Joel said.

"You'll indulge me?"

"Of course."

"I mean, I know I have a history of boring people to death—"

"I should add," Joel interrupted, "that I don't have any interest whatsoever in any of the Knights-Templar-Illuminati conspiracy talk. To me, that subject is mind-numbing."

Tom sucked his lips, first the top one, then the bottom one, as if to conceal another blossoming smile. "That's good," he said, "that's real good, because none of this deals with that. This is about something much different, Joel, something much different and much more ..." Tom paused for a long time.

"More what?" Joel said.

"Relevant," Tom said, at last. "Let me just put it that way. So please listen closely. I was nine-years-old when I first read *The Secret History*. I understood about a quarter of what I read. It's very philosophical and very complicated, and even scientific. You'd be amazed, I think."

"Where did you initially hear of it?" Joel said.

"My father. He at one time owned several copies, but they all disappeared. It's a rare book, did you know that?"

"No, I didn't," Joel said. "But it makes sense."

"Why do you say that?"

"Because it *looks* so rare."

Tom nodded.

"What is the book about?" Joel said.

"I'd like to tell you."

"Do."

"To begin with, it's as much a character study as it is anything else, and it starts with a fellow named Raddick. This happened some time ago."

"Raddock?"

"Yes. R-A-D-D-I-C-K. Markeus James Raddick. He was a man your father was once—shall I say—closely associated with."

"My *father*? Was he—"

"Please," Tom said, "just listen. Raddick was a tall man, mid-to-late thirties, slim but extraordinarily tough, and surely one of the most melancholy people you'll ever come across." Tom paused in thought. He swept his forelock back with his graceful fingers. "In fact, when Raddick was a teenager, he walked across the entire Mojave Desert by himself, just to see if he could do it."

"Really?" Joel said.

"Yes."

"I'm sorry. Was he ... was this Raddick real or—"

"Listen, please. I promise everything will become clear to you in the end."

116

Joel leaned back into the cold metal of the chair; the metal was twisted like black licorice. Joel took a drink of his coffee, then rested the cup on his thigh. A peacock-colored horsefly buzzed around his head.

"Raddick," Tom said, "was well-educated and well-traveled. From his European father, he'd inherited many millions. But Raddick was no parvenu, not by a damn sight. He was industrious. He was also clever and cerebral. But not too cerebral."

"What do you mean by that?"

"That he was essentially a physical person. Raddick was a man of action and deed. Through a series of ventures—lumber, steel, textiles, and so forth—he succeeded in amassing an even larger fortune than his father." Tom fell silent once again.

"And yet?" Joel said.

"And yet? Yes. And yet. And yet, all this seems to have had little effect on him. He remained almost pathologically morose and taciturn. He did have a wife once, a great beauty of Irish and Gypsy stock named Lillyblade. She was black-haired and younger than him by at least a decade, and he loved her very much." Tom broke off again, as if he had just remembered something. "As a matter of fact, Raddick once wrote a poem about her," he said, "which has only a little to do with what I'm about to tell you, but it does explain something about Raddick. It's short and if you'll permit me, I'd like to recite it to you from my memory, as best I can."

"All right," Joel said.

"It's a formal poem," Tom said, "in the sense that each line rhymes, although the lines are ragged on the page, and so I hope all that comes through." Tom, smiling mysteriously, waited a moment longer and then he began:

He trudged into the desert, taking almost
nothing with him but water and a ghostly old photo
of a lady beside the ocean.
That first night,
he lay above a dry creek bed. Below,
he heard vipers all night moving through the sand
with a side-winding motion,
and
he did not sleep.
He'd grown obsessed with the notion
of walking deep
and deeper into the wilderness. By
the third day, his lips were swollen and dry.
Now he was completely isolated,
surrounded by a desert that dominated
with its glittering sand
and

not high above, a sky so huge and blue
that it scared him to look too long upon.
There was nothing new
now under his sun. By now, his water was gone.
Day five, he quit moving altogether
and sat instead for hours, with his photo and leather
flask, sat coughing in the cool valley of a dune,
watching the daytime moon,
gibbous and gorged, roll by like an eroded stone.
The sky was biblical. The sun was white as bone.
Finally, on the evening of his sixth day,
when his strength had all but slipped away,
a willowy woman in a white dress appeared.
She had long black hair, which stirred in the xeric
air, and though his eyes were watery and bleared,
he knew for certain who it was. And so
it was that she beckoned him. He rose, sure but slow,
up from the ferric
and rust-colored sand,
as if this is what he'd been waiting for all
along. And,
leaving his shoes and other belongings
behind, he followed her into
the drifted dunes, beneath a sky of melting blue.
And that was it. Days later when they found his things,
they saw the photo half-buried in the sand.
It was a black-and-white of a black-
haired woman, very elegant, tall,
whose short life,
two years back,
had been eaten away in a strange
Patagonian land, below a mountain range.
That woman was his wife."

17

Tom remained silent for some time. His compelling fingers lay motionless on the table. "Well, what did you think," he said at last, "taking into account my imperfect memory? Did you like it?"

"Yes," Joel said, "I did. Very much."

"Good. I wanted you to. It's poignant, don't you agree? A little over-derivative, as far as the subject matter goes, but the style is all his. Anyway, Raddick wasn't really a poet, and this was never meant to be published, although it was published. Mainly, it was something he wrote after his wife got sick in the southern Andes, and died."

Tom waited for Joel to say something, but Joel was silent.

"As I was saying a moment ago," Tom continued, "Raddick's melancholia was completely real."

"As opposed to what?" Joel said.

"Put-on or pretended. Raddick once referred to his depressive disposition as his 'taint of blood.'"

"Blood," Joel muttered.

"It's a phrase I suspect he borrowed from the same person he borrowed his poem idea from."

"Who?"

"Alfred Tennyson."

"That's interesting," Joel said. Indeed, he seemed at this point uncommonly engaged, the old scowl now stitched deeply into his forehead, pushing out a fold of flesh above the bridge of his nose; so that Tom felt the momentary impulse to reach over and press it out with his thumb.

"Go on," Joel said.

"His sad temperament didn't preclude a passionate disposition, however, as depressive temperaments rarely do," Tom said. "In fact, in many ways, Raddick *was* intensely passionate. But he was also intensely repressed. So that after his wife died, which happened when he was still relatively young, Raddick proceeded to bury himself in his two main interests."

"What were those?"

"History—Egyptian and Middle Eastern history, in particular—and astronomy. With his state-of-the-art telescopes, Raddick searched the sky for comets." Tom paused. "There was also music," he said, "though I hesitate to mention that because Raddick didn't play an instrument. He didn't play music. But music meant a great deal to him, and I think in order to get an idea of his character, one must know that. I think Raddick's love of music is very important to understanding him."

"What sort of music did he like?"

"Liszt, Louis Armstrong, Duke Ellington, Dvokrak. But what does it really matter? Maybe I'm making all that up. Raddick liked complicated music, let us put it that way. Mostly, it had to have melody. For Raddick, music was melody."

Joel appeared confused, yet he nodded. He was staring down at the deck now, as if engaged in a kind of self-study. Halfheartedly he made a visor of his hand and shielded his eyes, his elbow resting on the table. At the same time, he rubbed his temples and then straightened himself up and drained the remaining coffee in his mug. Without asking, Tom leaned over and refilled Joel's cup.

"Thank you," Joel said.

"You're welcome. We have a lot to get through, so keep drinking." Tom flashed Joel a wide smile which exposed all his teeth; they were slightly snaggled, with one tea-colored front tooth jutting forward like a busted slat. "Joel," Tom said seriously, glowering all at once, "have you ever heard of a Scottish nobleman named James Bruce?" He was topping off his own cup as he said these last words.

"No. I've heard of Robert Bruce."

"Yes. It's not the same man, but they're of the same lineage—or so James Bruce liked to claim."

"What about him?"

"James Bruce?"

"Yes."

"Well, he was a lot like Raddick, in many ways. For one thing, James Bruce was a very wealthy man. For another, he was also a man of action. And he was a complex personality. He was born in 1730, in the lowlands of Scotland. Polymath, polyglot, polyphiloprogenitive, overseas traveler, James Bruce was imposing in pretty much every sense of the word. Physically, he was gigantic. Psychologically, a sport. He had a booming voice and a commanding disposition. He was a Renaissance man, in the old meaning of that term. He was also, I should add, a devout Christian."

Tom waited. Joel was silent.

"Evidently," Tom said, "he learned languages with an amazing facility, teaching himself, among others, the language of *Ge'ez*, which is the classical language of Ethiopia. In fact, James Bruce wrote a famous history of his journey to Ethiopia. That book is called *Travels to Discover the Source of the Nile in the Years 1768-1773*, and his journey, Joel, is indirectly related to the book you asked me about."

At this point, Joel cleared his throat as if to speak, but something brought him up short: another distant but distinct odor of cigarette smoke impinging upon his olfactory. He looked over at Tom, whose face, however, revealed nothing. Joel was on the brink of asking Tom if he too smelled smoke, but for reasons he was not entirely sure of himself, he didn't say anything. He glanced around: he saw nothing—nothing but wind in the treetops, cucumiform clouds scudding in over the mountains like blimps.

"Is everything okay?" Tom said.

Joel didn't immediately answer. "Yes," he said.

"The title of James Bruce's book, as I was saying, pretty much tells us the exact purpose of his journey, doesn't it?"

"I'm getting confused," Joel said.

"About what?"

"Was Raddick real? And James Bruce?" Joel shut his eyes and shook his head.

Tom smiled. "Well, you see, Joel, to complicate the matter further, there's something else I haven't told you yet: the source of the Blue Nile had already been mapped, by two Portuguese priests. And James Bruce, with his great erudition and his methodical ways, certainly knew—"

But now it was Tom who suddenly broke off. He shifted his gaze up and over Joel's head; his eyes widened. "Ah, my little weirdie has finally arrived," he said.

For a breathless moment, Joel just sat there. Then he swung around in his chair, to see what or whom Tom was referring to.

It was a formidable-looking squirrel, perched upon the muscular arm of ponderosa pine, gripping the white stick of an old lollypop, which still had a little candy on it, holding the sucker-stick in both paws, as if he would strangle the thing.

Joel went slack with a kind of relief.

"That guy thinks he owns this place," Tom said. "Curious creatures, squirrels," he went on, philosophically. "In many ways, I hate them. Yet they fascinate me to no end—with their lean faces and tensile-tough tendons, their dangerous claws and bodybuilder deltoids. The cat in me kills them. Do you know what I'm saying?"

Joel didn't answer. He had begun to sweat again. "Not really," he finally said.

"Where was I?"

"You were talking about a man named James Bruce," Joel said. He cleared his throat again. "Specifically, you were saying something about his motives in traveling to Ethiopia." An odd feeling of euphoria, perhaps coffee induced, perhaps something else, was beginning now to course through him.

"Indeed, I was," Tom said, "indeed I was. Thank you for that perfect recapitulation. The squirrel," he murmured, "threw me off." Which squirrel, as he said the word, loped away, plumed tail undulating behind like a fox tail, and so Tom's voice trailed away. He was silent for ten seconds more. "May I ask you your opinion, Joel?"

"Yes."

"Why do you think a man would go through the trouble of learning the classic language of Ethiopia, a dead language to begin with, if—"

"I really don't have any idea," Joel said. A note of irritation he hadn't intended had crept into his voice. "I mean," he continued, softer, "I don't know anything about the man."

Another silence ensued.

"The reason I bring this subject up," Tom said.

"Please tell me why."

"I bring it up because after Raddick's wife died—and I mean *right* after—Raddick then went to Chartres to visit that famous cathedral. Apparently, his wife had been interested in something within. While Raddick was there, he himself became captivated by a small sculpture, which is located on the wall of the south porch, and which depicts the Ark of the Testimony on an oxcart being taken to an unidentified place. Sheba is also in the sculpture, with her little African maid. Raddick studied these sculptures for many hours, many days."

"But why?" Joel said.

Tom, however, didn't answer the question.

"One week after Raddick left Chartres," Tom said, "a mysterious man approached him, on a misty autumn evening. Raddick was in London at this time, and on that particular evening, he was in a coffeehouse. The stranger brought up the subject of James Bruce, with whom Raddick was totally unfamiliar. The stranger wore a slouch hat that partially concealed his face, and Raddick was never able to see him in full. And though the stranger was polite and eloquent, he was not in any way personable. He spoke with a slight accent that Raddick couldn't identify. He was also, according to Raddick, very abstracted."

"What do you mean?"

"Dreamy and detached. After an hour of talking to Raddick in the coffeehouse, he asked Raddick to please come with him. Raddick agreed, and that moment, which changed the course of Raddick's life, is described in great detail: the autumn rain, the silver moon, the bluish mist, Raddick's feeling of loss and desolation at that time."

Tom fell silent again.

"I'm listening," Joel said.

"In the end," Tom said, "the stranger led Raddick deep into the countryside, to a house among the trees. Here he took Raddick down a long set of steps that led to a massive vault behind a titanium door that was thick enough to withstand a blast of dynamite. In this vault were a number of curious-looking artworks, the likes of which Raddick had never seen before. He didn't even recognize their style, or the era. Yet the stranger was not interested in any of these. He led Raddick to the back of the vault where there were a number of deep black corridors. Raddick was getting very confused. The stranger lit several oil lamps and then showed Raddick a huge painting. It was a hyper-real oil that took up the entire twenty-foot wall upon which it hung. It depicted an ancient vessel. The painted vessel sat in a painted room that was *not* ancient, however, but completely modern. The man then turned to Raddick and explained to him that this painting was a painting of the Ark of the Testimony. Raddick asked the man if it was supposed to represent the real Ark. The man didn't answer. Instead, he took Raddick down another corridor and into a chilled white room sectioned off by four glass walls. There, resting on the floor on two long poles, sat a large and dusty wooden container with a doglike figure perched on top. The body of this dog was covered in an old and bloody-looking blanket, and the stranger turned and said to Raddick: 'No, this is.'"

18

Tom stopped speaking and for a long time stared with strange eyes at Joel. Joel grew increasingly uncomfortable.

"What is it?" Joel said. His throat felt painfully dry.

But Tom didn't immediately answer. Instead, he tapped his ten fingers once on the table. The mocking smile worked somewhere along his face.

"The stranger then told Raddick a remarkable story," Tom said, "the details of which I won't go into now. I'll tell you only that his entire story revolved around the Ark, and I mean the real Ark, which some Jewish traditions call the seat of all knowledge."

"I honestly don't have any idea what you're talking about," Joel said.

"But you will."

For another long moment, they were silent. Both of Tom's hands now were wrapped around his coffee cup, the cup overhung with diaphanous ribbons of mist.

"The stranger proceeded to tell Raddick the long and curious history of the Ark," Tom said. "He said that thousands of years ago, the Ark had been smuggled out of Solomon's Temple, during the bloody reign of King Manassah. He told Raddick that the Ark had migrated down from Jerusalem and into Africa over a course of three centuries or more. He told Raddick that the Ark had been housed for over one hundred years on an island in the middle of the Nile, in upper Egypt, near the town of Aswan. The man then said that after leaving this island, the Ark went to Sudan and then down to a large tributary of the Nile called the Takazze river. From here it eventually came to an Ethiopian village called Quara. And near Quara," Tom said, "there's a large mountain lake."

"Lake Tana," Joel said.

"Yes. How did you know?"

"My father," Joel said.

Tom cast him a baleful glance, then took a large gulp of his coffee; when he swallowed, his muscular throat twisted slightly.

"To Raddick," Tom said, "the most interesting thing of all was when the stranger told him that the Ark did *not* contain stone or stone tablets, which the stranger said were merely symbolic, but—"

Abruptly, though, Tom broke off, and Joel held his breath without realizing it.

"But rather a spirit," Tom continued.

"What spirit?" Joel whispered, releasing his breath.

"The spirit of truth," Tom said.

Joel was silent.

"The spirit of truth," Tom repeated. He stared steadfastly at Joel. "The stranger then told Raddick that people gravely error when they interpret symbols as facts. He said that symbols are not lies, but if they're treated as facts, they become lies."

"Lies?" Joel shook his head.

"Don't you understand?"

"No," Joel said.

"Well, what if none of what I'm telling you now is true? What if I'm making all this up as I go along?" Tom said.

"Are you?"

"Would that make it any less true? And if I am lying to you now, then what? Don't you know that amoralism rejects the very concept of morality—lying is neither good nor bad; it simply is. And since I reject God, it's impossible for me to establish any basis for morality, yes? Without God 'all things become lawful.' Therefore I'm amoral. Anyway, what does truth have to do with morality? But perhaps I don't reject God after all, or the truth. Perhaps *that* is the lie I'm telling you. Or perhaps I'm lying to you right now, this instant, to illustrate how it is that morality operates by means of truth, as a necessity of the human brain, with or without God. Or perhaps I'm not lying at all, and none of this has anything whatsoever do with morality, or truth. Perhaps that's the real truth."

"I'm sorry," Joel said. "You're not making sense, and I think you're trying to purposely confuse me."

"Because I tell you the truth, I'm the person to whom you feel you must apologize?"

"No," Joel said. "Why do you keep using that word?"

"Which word?"

"True. Truth."

"Because any meaningful search for God *is* a search for truth."

"But who said anything about searching for God?"

"You did."

Joel shook his head furiously. His temples throbbed with renewed vigor. He was leaning forward now, sitting on the edge of his seat. An unshakable sense of unreality gripped him—unreality about all that he had been hearing and seeing thus far, so that for a moment he didn't believe that this was really happening. Yet at the same time, he felt sure it *was* happening.

"Joel," Tom said, breaking in on Joel's thoughts, "why are you so conflicted? I'll explain everything to you, I promise. God is the light, the way, the truth, no? This, in answer to your query, is the way in which the search for truth is the search for God. And the Ark of Jehovah, as its very name implies, is God. And the Spirit of Truth is the Holy Spirit. And spirit is life—it is mind. Which things are allegories, but the truth is not an allegory. That's why truth is of all three things the most important thing—if, that is, life is the goal, which it is. Truth is the principal thing, Joel. It's the principal thing because truth transcends any one religion or culture. One orange combined with two other oranges always makes a total of three oranges. Truth is universal in the literal sense: it is the universal language. Truth is the one thing that cannot with impunity be blasphemed. As a matter of fact, did you know that biblically speaking the Holy Ghost is almost as often referred to as the Spirit of Truth?"

Joel didn't answer. He sat sweating.

"Do you know what it *means*?" Tom said.

"Truth?"

"Yes."

Joel didn't respond.

"To say of what is that it is, and of what is not that it is not, is true," Tom said.

Joel squished his eyes shut.

"*Veritas est adaequatio rei et intellectus,*" Tom said. "Truth is the equation of thing and intellect. As a man named Thomas Aquinas put it: a judgment is said to be true when it corresponds to external reality."

"True when it corresponds," Joel said.

"Yes. It's called a correspondence theory, but, to be truthful, it's more of a fact, in my opinion. And by that I mean, it's a true theory and therefore no theory at all. That fact—the fact that it's a fact and not a theory—becomes more obvious the more you think about it. Truth and what truth is is actually no real mystery. What is truth? Truth is knowledge, which humans live by means of. And wisdom is knowledge applied. That is ultimately why truth is important. That's why this conversation right now is important. The mark of truth is that it represent reality correctly. It represents what is and it represents what works. Do you understand?"

"Truth is knowledge."

"Yes," Tom said. "Reality is that which is. Consciousness is that which is aware of that which is. Grasping that which is is the discovery of truth. (I use 'fact' and 'reality' interchangeably in this context.) It is the inability or unwillingness of philosophers, religionists, and scientists alike to distinguish between these two—reality and consciousness—that's fertilized the field for all manner of skepticism, relativism, and dogmatism which we see everywhere. Skepticism and its little partners have undercut us all."

"What about the science that tells us that there are no absolutes, no settled facts, and no such thing as true theories, including what you're saying right now?"

"No truth, only uncertainty."

"Yes."

"That's what I'm saying."

"Theories," Joel continued, "may at one time have more explanatory power than theories before, but in the end, all theories ..." his voice trailed off.

"Are built upon pillars of smoke and are always replaced by more inclusive theories."

"Yes."

"'Joel, 'explanatory power,' as you say, implies truth, inasmuch as it implies that explanations are possible. It also implies hard knowledge, which is to say, it implies truth—meaning: if we couldn't hold *any* knowledge as true, there'd be nothing to explain and no way to explain it, and so there would be no such thing as 'explanatory,' let alone 'power.' If something is true, it will always be true, it doesn't matter how many new scientific discoveries come along in the future. The argument you've just sketched illustrates one of the many pitfalls of physicists and other scientists playing philosopher. Philosophy, first of all, comes before science, and the philosophy of science is a species of philosophy proper. What I'd like you to know is that freshly found truths can only expand upon already known truths; they cannot negate it. The method of science assumes this principle by its very definition (though it is seldom recognized explicitly), and in this way, the method of science is self-correcting."

"What principle precisely are you referring to?"

"The principle that newfound truth cannot controvert already known truth."

"Why?"

"Because truth is 'reality accurately identified.' That's what truth *is*. Newly discovered truth cannot controvert the old, because in both cases what has been identified is accurate. The very word 'accurate' *means* true. Do you see?"

"I don't know."

"If it's not accurate, it's not true. And never was. It's false and always was. False is the opposite of true. Anyway, you can't hold a theory without, at the same time, assuming a whole multitude of previous truths that prop that theory up. To start with, for example, that humans have the mental equipment capable of apprehending reality in the first place, in order *to* theorize upon it. You must assume that's true."

"But what if you only assume that it's maybe true?" Joel said.

"Maybe logic, yes. Quantum physics biggest contribution to philosophy yet, maybe. Upon second thought, it may not be. There may actually be no way of knowing (I'd have to calculate the probabilities). Joel, your maybe logic is (or, rather, may be) a bitched up version of skepticism. Like skepticism, it affronts us with its banality. Maybe logic is embarrassing. It's an assault upon the obvious. It asks us to deny the self-evident in the face of all sensory evidence, and it asks this moreover on the basis of no evidence at all. As with all forms of skepticism—and I'm speaking here about skepticism in the philosophical sense of the word, which denies the possibility of real knowledge—your maybe logic immanently contradicts itself."

"Oh? Are you ready to prove that?"

"I'm ready to prove anything. Plenty of people, for example, have noted the following: in claiming that everything is uncertain, you're still claiming certainty: specifically, you're certain that everything is uncertain. And that's actually true—true but boring. What's not so often noted, however, is how many certainties this position actually adds up to. Unavoidably."

"What do you mean?"

"The claim to universal 'maybe' applies to every *specific* counterclaim to certainty. So that when I say to you 'I'm certain there are such things as humans,' you as a maybe logician must say 'I am not certain there are humans; there are only maybe humans.' Yet that is a claim to certainty: you are certain there are perhaps humans. And if that's not enough, you're also certain that I am perhaps wrong. And that you are perhaps wrong. And that I am perhaps right."

Joel was silent.

"And so what more is there to say?" Tom said. "It's an awful lot of certainties for one simple statement, which you aren't even certain of in the first place. The same thing is true of any specific claim to certainty. For example, if in the capacity of doctor I say there is a condition in which bones become brittle, you as a maybe logician must say 'there is only maybe a condition in which bones become brittle.' But this proposition contradicts itself inherently: since you don't believe in certainty, you cannot even believe that there is maybe a condition of brittle bones—you can't believe anything at all because any specific claim to maybe *is* a claim to certainty. Yet by the very structure of your argument, you *must* be certain of this. And so on. I am certain I am alive. I am certain that in order to stay alive, I must maintain my life. I am certain that this same truth is true of all life. I am certain there is physical death—to all these things, and a quadrillion others beside, you, by the very structure of your argument, must claim that I am maybe wrong in saying these things are certain. You must also say that all these things are maybe only maybe. But all those maybes are themselves utterances of certainties."

"A quadrillion certainties."

"And then some," Tom said. "Maybe. Perhaps. If. It adds up. But I actually don't know that for certain. Please remember, though, this is coming from a people who don't believe we can be certain. This insurmountable flaw is, as I say, inherent to the argument, and that's why the argument refutes itself effortlessly, clownishly. That's also why the argument not only can but *must* be rejected, at the very outset, or you're condemned to an epistemological hell."

Joel did not say anything.

"One plus two maybe equals three, but maybe not?" said Tom. "Please. Let us not simply observe how many oranges we get when we combine two oranges with one more: it's still only maybe three. That's absurd. Only in predicting the future, Joel, can we say that certainty is not appropriate. But that isn't news: everyone's always known that predictions are iffy, and one must never confuse the what-is with the what-will-be. That's important. Also, one cannot quantify probabilities without having some absolute from which to start quantifying in the first place, or these probabilities wouldn't be probabilities but random figures without any referent. Your argument is not new."

"It's not my argument," Joel said.

"In the following example," Tom said, "the process of truth-gathering can, I hope, be observed more clearly. Say that a young person is seeking to discover what the act of sex is. As long as his or her observations correspond to reality, the definitions that he or she forms will not be negated by any new truths later discovered. On the contrary, in fact, they'll only be expanded. So let us suppose that our youngster observes that sex is something that takes place in the animal kingdom—for, let us say, purposes of procreation. For this youngster, then, that becomes his or her working definition of sex: something animals do to procreate. Well, that's true, isn't it? Sex *is* this. It may also be other things, but it's this as well. Therefore, this observation won't be negated by any future discoveries, because it is indeed a fact that sex is something that takes place in the animal kingdom for purposes of procreation. It's a true statement. Do you see what I mean so far?"

Joel nodded.

"Next let us say our youngster learns that humans are animals. Well, that's true too. It can be elaborated, of course, but it's true. Say next that our youngster learns that sex has something to do with ... whatever ... genital stimulation. That's also true, isn't it? It corresponds to external reality. Humans are animals, sex does have to do with genital stimulation, and future knowledge can't contradict that. Future knowledge can't just make all the genital stimulation in the world go away. Let us say next that our youngster learns that sex has something to do with a specific kind of genital interaction between partners. Say that he or she then learns that this interaction is often penile and vaginal intercourse. Notice that all these statement so far are true."

"In the sense that they correspond."

"Good."

"Only—"

"Please," Tom said, holding up his hand, "a moment. I feel I'm about to hit my stride. Sex does take place in the animal kingdom. Sex does have something to do with stimulation of the sex parts. Sex often involves penile and vaginal intercourse. All these things are true. And their verity derives not from arbitrary constructs, nor from the nature of the human brain alone, but from reality."

"As observed by the senses."

"Yes—as observed by the senses and as *processed* by the human brain, which is conceptual. All knowledge must start and end with observation: the observation of what *is*. That is knowledge. The facts of reality are what tell us finally whether things are true or not. And the fact that we have brains and the sensory perception to feed those brains doesn't mean knowledge is therefore *in*valid."

"That's what modern physics and philosophy and even religion tell us."

"Yes, I know. I've heard it many times. Too many. The argument is this: we can't know reality not because we don't have the equipment. Rather, we can't know reality because we do have the equipment. What, then, I wonder, would constitute a legitimate form of knowledge?"

"God's knowledge."

"Hardly. God must also be conscious by *some* means, otherwise He's not conscious at all, and a God who's unconscious is no kind of God. And so since God must be aware by some means too, His knowledge is automatically invalidated as well, just by virtue of the fact that He's conscious. Consciousness, which on the one hand makes knowledge possible, also, on the other hand, negates it. So they say. So say the quantum scientists and all the other philosophical fools and agnostics. But wait a moment: all this knowledge of the invalidity of knowledge must itself be invalid, and for the very same reasons."

"That's true," Joel said.

"And are not our eyes, ears, and brains, are not these also part of 'ultimate reality'?" Tom said. "And in learning about sound or sight or sonar, and how these things tint nature in their own certain way, are we not also then learning about ultimate reality in *relation* to these things, all of which are also part of ultimate reality? So there you have it. Say next that our youngster learns that aphids do not engage in partnered sex. Say he or she learns further that there is such a thing as sex with yourself, gay sex, oral sex, anal sex, and so on. Are you with me?"

"Yes," Joel said.

"Why do you look so concerned?"

"It's your choice of subjects I find peculiar."

"The subject is not the subject here. Chiefly, I wish for you to notice how none of the new things that he or she learns controvert anything he or she has already learned. Those previous things remain true, regardless of any new discoveries. Do you see?"

Joel nodded.

"As long as the discoveries are true in the first place, as long as they accurately correspond—"

"There can be no future conflict."

"Yes. You do see, then. Good. That is a crux. To say that later truth always or even sometimes controverts earlier truth is to say that reality controverts itself. Which it does not and cannot. If our hypothetical youngster had, for whatever reason, defined sex as the act of drinking water, well that *is* an inaccurate observation and therefore later truth will contradict it. Reality, to put it another way, will expose it."

"As false."

Tom nodded. "Probably at the exact moment the youngster asks someone to have sex—and hands the person a cup of water. Knowledge *if it's true* is only expanded by future discoveries, not crossed-out and begun anew. Never that. Knowledge is truth. You must not ever forget that. It's the basis of everything—everything you're about to learn, Joel."

"What?"

"If it's not true, it's not truly knowledge. Only in this way can knowledge happen. Because only in this way is future knowledge made possible."

"Only in what way?"

"What I just said. The pursuit of more knowledge assumes, and so builds upon, all previously gathered knowledge and so on, backwards. The knowledge-gathering process doesn't begin at the beginning every time. A great number of truths are assumed, even (and especially) by scientists and philosophers who deny truth. I repeat: if it's true, it will always be true. The contexts may and often do change, but the old and known contexts remain true, and they are therefore the building blocks of expanding contexts—which is to say, further knowledge. Science doesn't fully understand this yet, however, and until it does it should stay completely out of philosophical and political discussion`. But let us return to these recondite subjects later on, if at all."

19

"Would you like more coffee?" Tom said.

Joel glanced into his cup. The leaden sky was reflected on the surface of the liquid. Joel nodded. Tom reached over and poured. The coffee struck, and the reflected sky wobbled away and then wobbled back. Joel raised the cup to his lips and drank. "Thank you," he said, swallowing.

For some time, they were both silent, but the woods about them were alive with insects now, and insect noises, spindly-legged jays screeching like monkeys from the topmost tree boughs. Tom refilled his own cup. As he poured, Joel could see the muscle striations along the top of Tom's thin forearm flex and squirm, and the veins running just beneath the surface of his skin, like little underground streams, shallowly buried. A distant passage started to surface in Joel's mind, but for a long moment it eluded him. He was just on the point of dismissing it when it came:

This living hand, now warm and capable
of earnest grasping, would, if it were cold
and in the icy silence of the tomb,
so haunt thy days and chill thy dreaming nights
That thou wouldst wish thine own heart dry of blood
so in my veins red life might stream again,
And thou be conscience-calm'd —

"In many ways," Tom said, once again breaking in on the drift of Joel's thoughts, "the issue of the Ark *is* an issue of blood."

"Pardon?" Joel said.

"I said the issue of the Ark is in many ways an issue of blood."

Joel's heart paused, then released a big beat.

"And the issue of blood," Tom said, "refers to more than one thing: death, for instance, and life, of course, violence, war, regeneration, the female cycle, fertility—"

"What does any of that matter?" Joel hissed. "What in the hell does it have to do with me?"

"Can I ask you to please refrain from questioning me further for now?" Tom said. "I don't mean to be rude, but you're slowing everything down, and even more than that your tone is beginning to accumulate a slightly distracting interrogative force." Tom stared straight into Joel's eyes as he spoke. Joel stared back. They watched each other silently for some time, and soon Tom's liquid eyes lay upon Joel with such unwavering fixity that Joel began to feel these were not human eyes but the eyes of a stuffed elk. At last, Tom broke the silence:

"The stranger explained to Raddick at length that the ancient ark with the doglike figure perched on top was not, in the end, the real Ark, although, he said, he had at one time thought it was. He said he had spent a good deal of time procuring it. He told Raddick that, after everything, he had stolen this object precisely because he believed it was the real Ark. He said that he and a few other women and men had sought to liberate the Ark, because (he said) the Ark had been shut up and hidden for several centuries, and the damage this had caused was inestimable. The man said that liberating the Ark meant liberating knowledge and abolishing faith. Their whole goal, the stranger said, was to liberate truth, and in so doing to cultivate civilization and learning, which according to the stranger is what the real Ark contains. He said he knew for a fact that the Ark contains this, but he did not explain how he knew. The stranger furthermore explained to Raddick that prior to the discovery of these things, the human race was crude, barbarous, cannibalistic, uncultivated. But with the discovery of knowledge came understanding—understanding of agriculture, understanding of how to domesticate, how to plant and grow and cultivate, how to build. Knowledge brought manners and civility to humanity. It brought trade and free exchange. It brought the division-of-labor and the transmission of knowledge. Most important of all, it brought humankind a system of objective laws which were built upon one unshakable foundation. Do you know what foundation I'm referring to, Joel?"

Joel's body went icy. He did not say anything.

"I'm referring to justice, of course," Tom said. "The foundation of justice. Please let me explain something important to you: justice is a political idea and also an ethical idea, and the thing in nature that gives rise to justice is the fact that each and every person is his or her own person. No one has *rightful* jurisdiction over the person or property of another—property being an extension of person. Do you know what I'm talking about?"

Joel still didn't say anything.

"The stranger's story," Tom said, "is also an allegory. It's an allegory for the person who brought civilization to the world and who civilized humankind. But, like truth, justice is not an allegory: it is a specific and very literal thing."

Tom fell suddenly silent, and his eyeballs jerked over to the left. His hands upon the table lay motionless. A small breeze came out of the woods and passed over them both, stroking Joel's hair as with gentle fingers. Joel turned his head and followed Tom's gaze but saw nothing.

"At the end of their extraordinary meeting," Tom said, "the stranger told Raddick that it was up to Raddick now to liberate the truth. When, with quiet astonishment, Raddick asked why him, the man responded with, and I quote: 'Because you possess the means, sir, but more than that you possess the drive.' The stranger said no other word after that, and these two never met again. But before Raddick left that night, the stranger went over to the vessel in the chilled white room—the vessel with the jackal perched on top—and he opened it up. From within, he removed a large book, which was one book among many books. Then, without any explanation, he gave this large book to Raddick. It was James Bruce's *Travels to Discover the Source*—"

But here Tom interrupted himself yet again, and yet again his eyes jerked over to the left. His ironic smile intensified, though his mouth remained closed.

"What is it?" Joel said.

Tom didn't answer, at first. He was still looking away when he finally did: "Joel," he said, "everyone has a history. This happens to be yours."

"I don't know what you mean."

But Tom's only response now was to smile a little wider—not altogether pleasantly, Joel thought—and at the same time, he leaned forward, only a fraction, but enough so that Joel suddenly saw the pine trees behind invert upon the convexity of Tom's silky eyes, spearing the eyes like arrows sunk to the quivers. Once again, he stared straight into Joel's face and did not blink or speak. He stared for what seemed minutes. Finally his lips broke open:

"I think it's time now for you to go," he said.

20

Two days later, while Joel was sitting in his motel room, a book arrived. It was James Bruce's *Travels to Discover the Source of the Nile in the Years 1768-1773*. Inside the book was an old journal, the *Journal Asiatique*, and inside the journal, a folded note had been inserted. Joel opened it up.

It was an invitation from Tom asking Joel to return the following day.

The page that the note marked contained an article titled *Etudes sur l'histoire d'Ethiopia*.

But Joel didn't return the next day, nor did he return the day after that. Or the day after. He waited. He waited because he wanted to prove that he didn't care about any of this. He wanted to prove it to himself. He wanted to show himself that the conversation had not mattered, that it was not in any way personally relevant.

Yet over and over, his thoughts returned to the strange meeting, in the strange house, with the strange man, and over and over he longed to go back to it.

In addition to that, however, something else was happening: a part of him was convinced now that someone else was indeed living or lurking around the property, although he was far from sure who or what this person might be—sex slave, insane cousin, someone or something even more terrible.

But even more unsettling than this was that he had also grown increasingly afraid that when he returned, there would be no house after all, no man, no anything.

So he waited.

The following day, he did spend hours investigating the historical sources concerning Ethiopia's history and Ethiopia's extraordinary claims. He read long passages from James Bruce's *Travels*, a number of which described the comets and eclipses and other interstellar activities observed over the decades and over the centuries from the continent of Africa. To Joel's extraordinary relief, he found that what he read in these books corresponded more or less exactly to what the man Tom had said. In fact, in a book called *Ancient Cities and Temples of Ethiopia*, Joel read an account of a man named Iyasu, who was both King and priest, and who, because of this, was granted permission to open the lid of the Ark and gaze inside.

Curiously, though, Joel could discover no person named Raddick.

And that worried him.

One week later, on a Sunday afternoon, Joel returned.

He made it a point to first walk above the highway, above county road 45, and out onto a high escarpment in the hills, so that he might gaze down across the property from a higher perspective, the perspective of distance. He saw it down below, one mile away: the gloomy house clustered among the trees like a knot of secrets. He saw also the angular rooftop of the empty stone building, and the conifer forest skirting the western side of the hidden garden, and then the river beyond like a river of liquid lead. Deep in the north sky, blue banked clouds appeared to be undergoing a complicated metallurgic transformation. Distant rumors of thunder issued from there, as if Weylan the Smithy stood just beyond the mountain peaks, pounding away in a random grim forge, upon a random grim anvil. Joel came down off the ridge.

From the highway, he looked once more across the farmlands. He could no longer see the house or even the housetop. He frowned. Under the pewter sky, the August grass was blowing. Dry cottonwoods moved sluggishly in the wind, tossing their heads like horses. Far off, he saw workers in the fields alongside fat Herefords, all marbled rust-and-white. A deep silence hung about the land. He looked twice over his shoulder, but there was no one there. He felt now it was only a matter of time—and thinking this he realized that he himself didn't fully know what that meant.

He turned and walked down the gravel road.

The instant he stepped onto the property, he was struck by the same feeling as before: a feeling of anticipation mixed with dread. Radiating from the catalpa tree was a forcefield of strangeness. The big leaves burned with a greenness of such intensity that they looked artificial to him. They were etched in hard lines against the sky, legumes hanging down everywhere like lean emerald snakes.

He walked around the south side of the house. All the shutters were drawn. Joel again looked over both shoulders. The house loomed gothic against the sky. It wasn't until he passed by the stagnant goldfish pond, with its jade-colored algae and headless statuary all tattooed with red lichen, and came through the empty stone building that the first living thing appeared: the tomcat loping across the path in front of him and disappearing into the undergrowth. After that, everything stood motionless. The wind died; the willows went slack. Shadows lay like liquid on the garden grass. Joel walked over to the cement table and placed the palm of his hand flat upon the surface. The concrete was cold and webbed with spidery cracks. He stared down at the gray cement. The mathematical equations were still there, indited in soft-lead pencil and nearly expunged by weather, but he was able to read them. He still couldn't understand them, however: they were too complex. Yet seeing them again now made him feel vindicated. And then he noticed a new formula at the bottom of the equations, written in the same designer print as the others:
GOD = BREADTH, DEPTH, HEIGHT, WIDTH
Why was this so familiar?
And what did it mean?

While he was staring at the words, he became aware of a sound like breathing coming out of the building behind him. He swiveled around and gazed into the big empty room. Blackness was all he saw. The sinking sun was buried in mercury clouds, and no daylight entered in through the chink in the stones. Joel approached the doorway. A steady current of air poured out over him. He waited for his eyes to adjust to the darkness; they never did. Perhaps there was no sound after all. Then two white objects appeared like eyeballs within the liquidy black; yet when he closed his eyes and opened them again, he didn't see anything.

He stood peering into the darkness of the building. He was no longer sure what he was seeing and what he was hearing and what he was imagining. For a time, he thought he could discern a pallid willowy shape watching him from the far end of the room. But the shape just hung there and didn't move.

He turned from the building and walked swiftly through the garden and then came out on the other side of the shrubs.

The last of the daylight lay dappled like egg whites upon the forest floor. The trees towered high above on either side. Everything here was silent and shadowy. There was a heavy stillness in the woods. Then an enormous gray heron swooped in front of him and went cruising low above the ground, legs dangling behind like sticks. The bird was bony and big, like a lank white hound dog soaring breakneck through the trees. Joel watched it light into the misty river foliage, three hundred meters away. He gazed around. An amber-brown butterfly came flopping in and out of the shadows, and there, off to his right, the steel-and-glass house shimmered into view.

He advanced toward it.

One hundred meters away, through its prominent front windows, he saw someone sitting on the floor of the front room. This person was facing the opposite direction from which Joel was coming, so that Joel couldn't tell if the person was a man or a woman. Whoever it was did not move at all but simply sat there, staring, apparently, at the floor. Joel approached. The light was poor, but Joel soon enough realized who the person was: it was Tom. And even as Tom sat there, motionless and blurry in Joel's deteriorated vision, the quietude that was his quiddity emanated from him like radioactivity.

Joel advanced; still, Tom did not move. The window next to Tom stood wide open, and Tom's left arm was hanging outside, holding, in those graceful fingers, what appeared to be a small Libra on a chain. Joel went around to meet him.

He was still twenty feet away when Tom spoke:

"Hello, Joel."

Joel didn't respond.

"I'd given up on you," Tom said.

"That was your first mistake."

"Ha-ha!"

But the queer thing was, Tom still hadn't moved at all. He was still looking in the opposite direction, still sitting on the floor. Once more, Joel wondered if this fellow was not right in the head. Presently Tom slipped outside through the open window and dropped fluidly to the ground like a cat. Immediately, he bent down to tie his sneaker. When he was finished, he stood in one motion, without any hitch or hesitation at all, just one moment kneeling and the next upright; so that watching him Joel felt that his eyes had missed something, an intermediate movement in between. The Libra was gone. Joel blinked. Tom proffered his cool callused hand. The two men shook. Tom's uneven half-smile dilated a little. He wore what looked to be the same faded black jeans as before. His shirt, untucked, was a rhino-gray crewneck with long sleeves pushed back off the wrists, revealing the bottom third of his veiny forearms.

They stood for a moment, regarding each other in the silent sun.

"Shall we walk?" Tom said.

"Yes."

Tom turned and began moving along the faint path which circumscribed the house. Joel walked beside him. After a moment, the path split off into another; this path wandered west, away from the house, and then it began climbing a gentle slope that rose around the edge of the cliffs. Neither man spoke. When they came to the hillcrest, they moved away from the cliff's edge, along another well-worn path, which ran on for another fifty meters and then terminated into a bosky glade. The fir trees gave way to medium-sized aspens. Long blades of grass grew along either side of the path, forming a miniature archway that swished against their pant legs.

Joel stopped walking a moment and gazed over his head. The sun had set, and the sky was growing cool. A skein of geese flew blackly by. Tom led them deeper and deeper into the aspen trees, a sweet-smelling glade filled with the grainy light of dying day. There were large white boulders among the grass. Near the far end of the glade was an extinguished firepit. The dirt around the firepit was chocolate, cakey, and three large tree stumps stood nearby. Tom lowered himself onto one of these stumps, and Joel seated himself across from him. Swallows wheeled low above. Still, neither spoke and soon there descended upon the glade an oppressive silence, which seemed to Joel like a foreshadowing—a foreshadowing of death. Joel's skin began to crawl.

"Joel," Tom said at last, "if you don't mind, I want to ask you once more why it is that you've come back here?"

Joel pointed toward the ground. "Here?" he said.

Tom shook his head and whirled his index finger lackadaisically round and round. "No," Tom said. "Here. To your old hometown."

Joel looked about him, as if he'd just realized where he was. The aspen leaves were blowing gently, showing silver undersides and shifting all at once in unison, like schools of silvery fish. "It's difficult to say," he said. He was staring at the blowing leaves as he spoke, and he continued to stare at them.

"You mean, because you don't know?" Tom said.

"No."

Tom waited.

"I don't mean to sound evasive," Joel said. He turned back to Tom. "Or less than forthright. As I mentioned before, I've been looking for someone."

"Yes," Tom said, "so you did. Elias Moorecroft."

Joel didn't respond. He was lightheaded.

"No?" Tom said.

"It's true I was led to believe that Moorecroft had information concerning my mother," Joel said. "But—"

"Then it's as I supposed."

"What?"

"Your mother," Tom said.

"Where?" Joel said. At which point, another sunburst exploded inside Joel's head, bringing with it this time a razorous pain that came in a series of quick slices. "I mean, what about her?" Joel managed to say. He shut his eyes and ground the heels of his palms into his eye sockets. "Do you know her?" The pain gradually subsided and was replaced by a deep chill. Joel opened his eyes and peered up at Tom, who sat thinly before him.

"I *did* know her," Tom said.

Joel shut his eyes again.

When he opened them, he saw that he was staring straight at the ground, the hyper-acuity of hearing and vision upon him at once, accompanied this time with a sense of torpor that made even lifting his index finger feel like an effort. In that moment, it seemed to Joel that he could count each individual particle of dirt below, so clearly did he see them all. And indeed he did begin to count them, and he continued to do so until Tom interrupted:

"Joel," he said, "do you believe the dead persist?" He was watching Joel count. But as soon the question was asked, Joel stopped counting and looked up at Tom.

"Persist? In what way?"

"In any way," Tom said.

"I...no." Joel spoke slowly, softly.

"I hear hesitation," Tom said.

"No. I just don't understand your question. I don't understand where it's coming from." Joel shook his head and swayed dangerously from dizziness. "Look, my man," he said as loudly as he was able, "what exactly are you getting at here? Goddamn it! What the hell is going on?"

"Nothing, Joel. Nothing. Are you all right?"

"No. Something has gone wrong. It seems like everyone is dead or dying, for one thing, that's what it seems like." The image of his father came unbidden into his brain.

"I think that's true," Tom said. "Everyone is either dead or dying."

"And I don't understand you," Joel said. "Or your questions. At all. Who the hell are you?"

But Tom was silent. He watched Joel closely. Joel held his gaze for thirty seconds, then looked away, up at the blowing trees. It was getting very dark, but the big white boulders held onto the light. Joel again started to question the reality of all this.

"Joel," Tom said, "I can tell you this much: you'll never find what you're looking for, unless you actually know what that something is."

"I *do* know what it is."

"What is it?"

"It's...it's all very personal."

"Please share it with me."

"I made a resolution once—"

"When?"

"Several months ago."

"What resolution?"

"I resolved to search out a piece of evidence that indisputably showed God's hand at work upon the earth."

Tom waited. "Is that it?" he said.

Joel didn't answer.

"I might have saved you the trouble," Tom said.

"What do you mean?"

"There is no evidence for God. There cannot be, by definition. You can convince yourself that God exists, but that's much different from proving it."

"Why?"

"Because proof requires evidence—in fact, proof *is* evidence. But evidence belongs to the natural world, not the supernatural."

Joel didn't say anything.

"And so if there's evidence," Tom said, "it must be natural. And yet if it's natural, it obviously can't be supernatural. So it can't be God, because God is supernatural."

"But there are so many things that have never been explained," Joel said, "like the origins of life."

"That doesn't mean there's not a natural explanation. It only means the explanation hasn't been discovered yet. In the absence of omniscience, you don't suddenly conclude God. That's a fallacy. If omniscience is what you require, Joel, I can tell you right now, absolutely, that you require an impossibility: at any stage of learning, no matter how erudite you become, there will always be more to learn and more explanations to uncover. Omniscience is not possible. Knowledge progresses incrementally. No one can know every single thing there is to know, and using the natural limits of knowledge to try to prove God is a very serious error."

Both men were silent. A blue spider leg of lightning twitched over the stone hills.

"Lightning," Tom said, "was once thought incontrovertible evidence of God. Now no one in her right mind believes lightning anything other than a natural phenomena."

Still Joel didn't speak.

"If there's evidence," Tom said, "it can't be God. Fideism is your best bet, really, although that too is fraught with difficulties."

"But if God is responsible for human existence," Joel said, "or even connected to it in some way, He must somehow be able to touch this world."

"Touch this world. Yes, I like that. You mean the natural world?"

"Yes."

"So God must be natural?"

"Yes."

"That's exactly why God is *im*possible."

Joel shook his head minutely.

"You assume that God *is* responsible, Joel. But true knowledge isn't gotten through such problematic assumptions: we grasp through the data that our senses receive. Ultimately, we apprehend reality through that sensory data. That's how knowledge happens. It happens when new sensory evidence swims into our ken, and we incorporate it. But the sensory evidence always comes first. Please remember that. And yet you are correct: if God created us, He must in some way be able to, as you say, touch this world. He must somehow be connected to or with the natural world, or He wouldn't have been able to create us from nature, and our chemicals would not be a part of nature, because He could not touch them."

"What does 'natural' mean?" Joel said.

"It means of nature," Tom said.

"And what is nature?"

"Nature is that which exists. If it's not natural, therefore, it doesn't exist. It can't. Nature is everything. There is no such thing as a super-nature."

"God," Joel began, but fell silent.

"God what?" Tom said. "Is in the details?"

"No, that's not what I was going to say."

"What were you going to say?"

"What about morality?" Joel said.

"God is in morality?"

"Yes," Joel said. "Or if God does exist, perhaps that's where He's to be found."

"That, then, means your whole resolution is a resolution about morality."

"Yes," Joel whispered.

"That puts a whole new slant on things."

"Why?"

"Because morality requires a step more than the mere grasping of facts. It requires that as well—it requires that first—but it also requires something more. And that step is a step which psychology and even philosophy have long been afraid to take. And so they've recklessly left it up to religion."

"What step?" Joel said.

"Estimates," Tom said.

"What do you mean?"

141

"I mean judgments. I mean evaluations. I mean how can bad and good be determined by what *is*? How can the grasping of facts tell us how to behave and how to act rightly, or if there even is such a thing?"

"Perhaps it can't."

"Perhaps not. Then again, perhaps it can."

Joel swayed on his stump. "What's your point, then?" he said.

"My point is that if God *is* morality, then you may very well find what you're looking for." Tom squinted at him through the creeping darkness. "Or you might not."

Joel started to say something, but another wave of nausea rocked him through and through and made him almost tip over again. He held onto the stump with both hands and sat gazing into the cold ashes of the firepit. Tom watched. A charred beer can sat inside the ash. Next to it was a green bottle, like a bottle in the smoke. Overhead, thicker clouds rolled in. A cold raindrop smacked Joel on the back of his hand. Joel looked down at his hand for a long moment, quizzically.

"But maybe you've come back here for another reason as well," Tom said. His brown eyes beamed. "Maybe," Tom said, "you've come to see me because you've guessed that the Ark is here."

Joel raised his eyes from the ashes.

"I mean the real Ark," Tom said, "which some Jewish traditions call the root of all knowledge."

"What are you telling me?" Joel said.

"Why do you speak so softly to me?"

"I find that description—"

"Which description?"

"The root of all knowledge."

"You find it what?"

"Odd," Joel said.

"Why?"

"I don't know."

"Would you like me tell you?" Tom said.

"Yes."

"You find it strange because an object of faith can't actually be described as 'the root of knowledge,' since knowledge and faith are incompatible."

"Are they?" Joel said.

"Yes."

"Yet there's faith in the sense of confidence," Joel said, "as in, to have faith in one's abilities."

"That's not what we're talking about," Tom said.

"What are we talking about?"

"We're talking about faith in the religious sense, the philosophical sense, the sense in which it is used most weightily. And in that sense, knowledge is evidential, whereas faith is belief even in the absence of evidence. That's what faith *is*."

Joel was silent.

"Faith is the substance of things hoped for," Tom said, "the evidence of things not seen. Faith by its very definition is blind belief—there's no other way around that. We could volley semantics forever on the subject, and many people do just that, but in the end faith *is* blind belief. As such, faith is not concerned with things that can be observed, tasted, touched, felt, heard. Those things belong to the tangible world, the world of knowledge, which in turn belong to the world of evidence, which is the only world by definition. The Ark, then, Joel, is the root of this? But how can it be?"

Joel stared vacantly into the darkening air. "I don't know," he said.

"But maybe you've been thinking that Raddick somehow succeeded in wresting the Ark away from Africa after all, and that he placed it here, in a remote corner of the Rocky Mountains, and that within the Ark he found strange awesome secrets. Now: what do you imagine those secrets were, Joel?"

"I don't care!"

"No? But what if those secrets proved beyond all doubt that knowledge *does* lead to morality? Would you then be vindicated in your search?"

"No," Joel said. "Because then people like you would be legislating morality, like Inquisitors."

"Legislating morality? Who besides you brought in politics? Church and state should properly be separate, if that's what you're saying, and morality is properly a personal issue. In fact, victimless crimes are unjust for this very reason: because there is no victim. Which is why any attempt to 'legislate morality,' as you say, *is* for good reason unconstitutional. Rape, cold-blooded murder, expropriation, progressive taxation and other forms of theft—these things are illegal not because they're immoral but because they're unjust: specifically, because they infringe upon another's right to life and property. An absolute ethic, derived from the facts of nature and not 'God,' wouldn't change the principles of political freedom, as you imply, but just the opposite: your freedom, government's freedom, anyone's freedom stops where another's begins."

Joel didn't speak.

"I say what about it?" Tom repeated.

"What about what?"

"What I asked. What if those hidden secrets showed that alongside knowledge—because of knowledge—morality as well grew on Eden's gnarly tree, only deeper down? What if these secrets were able to demonstrate *how* morality functions, the precise way in which? How morality is not some whimsical invention created for 'the disenfranchisement of the strong by the weak,' nor some arbitrary thing whose purpose is mind-control, but instead is a discovery that shows not only the way humans may live, but the way humans may live most abundantly?"

"You must prove it."

The rain picked up.

"Yes," Tom said, "but if proven, where would it leave you in your search? If your search for God yielded only nature? If you found that absolute morality, far from merely ramifying into some nebulous afterlife, is a necessity for the here and now, a thing whose main function is to abolish confusion within the human brain, to abolish rage and discontentment while alive on this earth, and, most of all, to abolish man's dependence upon other things?"

"What other things?"

"Any other things," Tom said. "Anything that puts one's happiness in other hands."

"That means that happiness is the goal."

"Didn't you know?"

"I thought I did. Now I don't."

"It's a kind of happiness, actually."

"What kind?"

"The kind that is kind," Tom said.

"What do you mean, what does that mean?"

"To be kind?"

"Yes."

"Very often, to be kind simply means to not be unkind. The kind of happiness I'm speaking of is a far profounder thing than run-of-the-mill happiness. To be specific, I'm speaking of a happiness that is serious, yet relaxed, that is not self-righteous or intolerant, that is calm, that is cool—the same way you might feel when you're most happy with yourself. I speak of a happiness that's not vulnerable, that's not easily made anxious or angry, that's laid-back and yet mature, self-developed. This is the natural state of the person who possesses the kind of happiness I mean. Still, these things are side-effects, not causes."

"What are the causes?"

"What we've been talking about," Tom said.

"Morality."

"Yes."

They stared at each other steadily.

"So what of it, Joel?" Tom said. "I know I keep asking but—"

"What of what?" Joel said.

"What if in your search for God, you discovered that the only purpose of the very God you've been searching for is nothing more, or less, than the divesting of your mind from anything that lays claim to it? Like drugs, whores, killing, stealing, lying, raging, pornography, cheating, genocide? What if in your search for God, you discovered that the absence of morality does not free men from arbitrary constraints, as you've been told, but on the contrary enslaves man, unwittingly, by stripping him of the real rules he must live by in order to live freely? Not politically free, mind you, but psychologically free. So that if you're dependent upon lying, killing, stealing, raping, masturbating, starving, drinking, cheating, whathaveyou—if you're dependent upon these things for your happiness, for your life's worth, for your income, for your gratification, then your happiness and gratification are not possible without those other things, and so you *belong* to these other people and things. You are unfree, in other words, and your life is not your own."

"What if, you ask?" Joel said.

"Yes."

Joel didn't answer.

"What if you live in sin," Tom said, "are you then a slave to sin? Or let me put it another way: if morality is a necessity for long-term happiness—which is to say, if the psychology of the human brain needs this sort of happiness to maintain its desire to live—is morality then a psychological law since the brain is a reasoning thing, long-range in humans *because* it reasons?"

"You could not demonstrate that. Not by an ultimate test."

"No?" Tom said. "Try this: suppose that I'm lying to you right now, and that I have been from the beginning (which I have). Well, what is a lie? I'll tell you: a lie is a willful and deliberate departure from fact. Now suppose I've been lying to gain your approval, or to impress you. Where does that put me?"

Joel shook his head vaguely and as if with great pain. Tom waited, but Joel did not answer.

"Assuming I've succeeded with my lies," Tom said, "and you *are* impressed by my stories (and how could you not be), in order, then, to maintain my status in your eyes, I must always lie now about these things—and about anything that might expose me as a liar. As a matter of course, a way of life, I must continue to depart from the facts, so that in this particular arena, and any connected to it, I'm at odds now with what's real, what's *true*. Truth has become a threat to me; the Actual is a threat; reality is a threat. But more than that: what does it say that I'm lying to you in the first place in order to impress you?"

"It says that you get more satisfaction from another person's opinion than you get from things as they are."

"Precisely. That was very good, Joel. Very well put. And isn't that a moral question as well, whose ramifications are easily demonstrable? Your approbation gives me more satisfaction than reality, and therefore I'm willing to alter facts to gain your approbation. But perhaps that's not my motive here. Perhaps I'm lying to dupe you out of something. Motive hardly matters, because the principle remains the same: anything or anyone that can expose me is a threat; reality is a threat. I must therefore take pains to maintain my lies, or risk being discovered. The more lies I heap on, the more lies I *must* heap on. So that if happiness and fulfillment are what I'm after here on this earth, how could I possibly reach these things if I'm at odds with the world as it really is? My brain will soon become too preoccupied with the business of deception to have time for unsullied enjoyment."

"Unsullied?" Joel said.

"Yes, unsullied. And, to address your previous comment, it's in this way that an incorrect morality *is* demonstrable through an ultimate test. In fact, it's in this way that an improper ethic *does* lead to hell. But that hell is on earth. It is a grave error to mistake symbols for facts."

"But there have been so many people," Joel said, "who've committed crimes far worse than your lies, and have even prospered in doing so, and yet they've never been caught or even suspected and have gone on to live happy lives."

"I think that's beside the point, isn't it?"

"What? How could it be?"

"Because it's the principle that matters. And yet to the extent that, proportionally speaking, any person does not live in accordance with reality, that person will be at war with what's real, whether he knows it or not, whether he admits it or not. It's graded, yes, morality is a spectrum—there are degrees of goodness and badness—but in the end it doesn't really matter how successful a person becomes at the business of deception: the number of things threatening exposure always increases his need to cover up deceptions. Successful or not, facts for the immoral person become by definition the enemy, and these facts must then be avoided at all costs. Now tell me: how happy will this person be? How happy can he be? His disposition will be marked by things like paranoia, or depression, or anger, or logorrhea—"

"What is that?"

"Too much talky-talky. Like me. Even in the best of circumstances, the immoral person is not really his own person but a slave to others, and to his own vices as well. These things sully his happiness—necessarily—because they rule him; because without them he is, to the extent he relies on them, unfulfilled. From a psychological standpoint, self-sufficiency, which in this context is a virtue—"

"Why is self-sufficiency a virtue?" said Joel.

"Because if the goal of life is to live, each person must individually live it. This means each person must initiate the process and sustain it. No one else can perform that fundamental act of will for another."

"But the initial choice *to* live comes first? Before morality?"

"Yes."

"Then morality depends on a choice that's built upon something arbitrary," Joel said, "which makes morality whimsical."

"Whimsical? Not unless you consider non-existence equal to existence, life equal to death, being to non-being, which it's not. Or maybe you're just playing the devil's advocate. Okay. Consciously or unconsciously, that initial choice to live is made in order to *live*. And isn't the desire to fulfill the potential within, to cultivate the life you have, a non-whimsical reason? To have life, to generate it, to enjoy it? Joel, the choice to live or die is not, ideally, made upon a whimsy but just the opposite: if you want to live, you must choose to live, and morality is a guide and standard for life, because human life is predominantly psychological."

"I believe the choice of suicide is as legitimate as the choice to live," Joel said. "Under some circumstances."

"Under some circumstances, but certainly not ordinary ones. Life and death aren't equal, if that's what you're asking. Death gives life meaning in the sense that death is what life strives against, but it's not the other way around."

"What do you mean?"

"From the perspective of the dead, life doesn't carry any particular relevance."

"But that's not what I'm asking."

"Choosing death over life *is* immoral if it's, as you say, 'whimsical'—or, in other words, if it's without a reason. It helps to have one."

Tom paused for Joel to speak, but Joel did not.

"Self-sufficiency is a virtue because nobody can perform the long-term act of living for another," Tom said. "If one wants to live, one must ultimately maintain one's life—psychologically and physically—over the course of a lifetime. That's what morality is for. Don't regard things as good or bad because God says so. Regard things, rather, as good or bad if they will benefit your life over the long term, or if they will harm it. If life is the goal, self-sufficiency is therefore the means. Everyone must to some degree be self-sufficient. Which of course doesn't mean one is a slave to food because one must eat to stay alive. Neither does it mean that one is a slave to work because one must work in order to live."

"Why doesn't it?"

"Because those things are outside the realm of choice, and morality only applies to what's chosen. Within the realm of choice, the self-sufficiency of the chronic liar is hard hit: to the extent that he's lied, he's tied to those lies, until he quits caring if he's exposed. As a matter of fact, the same is true of any other vice (or sin, if you prefer). It's in this way, to finally finish addressing your concerns, that each individual is the real measure of morality, and not 'society as a whole,' and not the so-called community. The reason for this is that the individual is the chief beneficiary of morality, not others. Morality has become synonymous with helping others and so on, I know, but that doesn't mean that that's the correct definition. In fact, it isn't. In fact, the idea that morality is exactly equivalent to helping others is a very destructive idea. Morality is *first* the need of each individual person. The need, I repeat. The function of morality is to show humans how best to behave *not* because humans will be punished or rewarded after this life, but rather so that humans can have life now, in this world, and have it most abundantly. This is what morality is about. Morality brings order into the human brain. It brings consistency with reality, and order and consistency are the things from which all other good things flow, from which *life* flows. We are each individuated, Joel. We must not let our lives be ruled by drugs, or money, or masturbation, or rage, or lies, or other people. Your life is yours to shape, but *you* must shape it. Your life is putty in your hands—or the hands of other things. Morality determines which. Do you see?"

Joel did not respond. A very long silence ensued. Rapidly the rain increased.

21

The rain increased, and the woods about them were suffused with purple night. Joel squinted continuously as from a deep head pain. The raindrops felt inordinately cold. Suddenly, Joel reached out his hand, as if to touch Tom; as if to check whether Tom's presence were real. But Tom, across from him, was too far to reach, so that Joel's hand flailed once, then dropped against his own leg.

The whole time, Tom regarded him impassively. They both sat blinking in the rain.

"If it means anything to you," Tom said at last, "Raddick didn't believe in an objectively verifiable morality either, a fact that figures prominently into his story and yours. You see, Raddick had a passion for facts, for that which he could see and feel, for details and logic. That's what he cared most about, and I believe it's that which drove him to Africa in the first place: his passion for facts, the facts of history. In that sense, Raddick's search was a literal search for truth—historical truth, at the very least. And so with his iron will he resolved to follow the Ark's trail wherever it led, and that's precisely what he did. And do you know what, Joel?"

Joel shook his head.

"Raddick found it," Tom said.

"He found what?"

"Your guess was correct. He found the Ark, but not only that."

"Shouldn't we head back?" Joel said.

"Head back? Why?"

"It's starting to rain pretty hard."

"Let it come down," Tom said. He stared at Joel for some time. "There's no going back now," he added.

Joel nodded, as if he saw some sense in this, or as if he would now believe anything. He tipped his head and gazed up into the enigmatic sky. He did not see God. He saw camera-flashes of lightning igniting everywhere around the mountaintops and silver raindrops sailing down from high out of the troposphere and smacking him squarely on the face. Far away, a wispy protuberance had dropped from the clouds and was angling toward the ground like a mammoth's snout. Joel straightened his gaze. An outcropping of rocks, which he could only just make out from where he now sat, stood in the grass like fins: the fins of prehistoric fish, circling slowly beneath the waves of grass. He turned back to Tom.

"Do you remember me telling you," Tom said, "that just before he met the strange man in London, Raddick had spent a good deal of time hanging around the north porch of Chartres Cathedral, studying a mysterious sculpture there, a sculpture that depicts the Ark on an oxcart?"

"Yes," Joel said.

"Well, you might also be interested to know that Raddick first heard about that sculpture not from his wife but after his wife died, through a telephone call."

That brought Joel up straight. "A telephone call? What telephone call?"

"An odd one. Raddick was in Paris at the time. His wife had died only days before. He was in the process of liquidating a large share of land he owned on the southern outskirts of the city when, one frozen night in the middle of that brutal winter, he found an anonymous phone number written on a slip of paper. The handwriting might have been his wife's, or it might not have been, he wasn't sure. The slip of paper was tucked inside a journal he'd found in his wife's studyroom. It was an oriental journal published in France called the *Journal Asiatique*."

"I want to know about the phone call," Joel said.

"It was a phone call. Why are you so hung up on it?"

"Whom did he talk to?"

"I don't know. He never said, exactly. He dialed the number out of curiosity, because of the handwriting, and said later only that he heard an 'unearthly sound' on the other end of the phone."

"What was that sound?" Joel said, breathless.

"I'm sorry, I don't know."

Joel shut his eyes. The rain tapped upon the leaves and filled the glade with a gentle drone. Joel was suddenly struck by the unbearable beauty of life, and the unbearable sadness.

"After Chartres and after his encounter with the stranger in London," Tom said, "Raddick became rather monomaniacal. The story of the Ark fascinated him endlessly. But I want to reiterate something at the outset here: it was *not* the religious aspect that captivated Raddick. Raddick's interests were archeological, historical, and especially astronomical."

Joel shook his head. The rain fell from his hair. "Why that?"

"Because there's discussion in James Bruce's book of all the comets and eclipses and other interstellar goings-on that have been observed throughout history from the continent of Africa, and from this discussion, Raddick got an idea."

Joel looked up at the sky. Away to the northwest, a jumbo jet plowed soundlessly through. Was this really happening?

"Raddick began poring over all the literature he could find on the subject," Tom said. "He studied the Old Testament, and he read the *Kebra Negast* in its original language, *Ge'ez*. He read James Bruce's hefty *Travels*—two times consecutively, as a matter of fact. The more he read, the more obsessed he grew. The mystery of the Ark consumed Raddick, and so did his search."

Tom fell silent. He wiped his wet face with his shoulder. His graceful hands were splayed on his thighs, and they shone whitely. His fingers looked disembodied. Joel stared at them glassy-eyed. Tom squinted at Joel.

"As I mentioned before," Tom said, "Raddick above anything was a man of action. He was a physical man. If he decided something, he did it. Often he had long spells of lassitude and depression, but always in the end he came out, and he moved forward."

Joel pushed his wet hair out of his eyes.

"And so," Tom said, "Raddick resolved very early on that no matter how long it took or how much money he had to spend, he *would* see what the Ethiopians claim is the Ark of the Covenant—either that or he would die trying."

Tom stopped speaking. The rain began to slacken. Everywhere, the blades of grass were degged with silvery raindrops like jewels.

"And what happened to him?" Joel said. "Did he die?"

"No," Tom said. "But others did."

Joel was shivering.

"Raddick hadn't intended to spend five years in Africa," Tom said. "And yet that's what he did. He visited many different places. He spoke with countless natives. He was three times in the city of Axum, and each time he was there it was during the middle of January."

"For *Timkat*," Joel said.

"Yes, that's right. How did you know?"

Joel didn't answer.

"Oh, I see," Tom said, "I see. And so it was after his third visit there that Raddick discovered for certain that the Ark brought out for the *Timkat* celebration is only a replica."

"How did he discover it?"

"A few months before, in September, he'd met what they call the Guardian of the Ark. This man stood on the other side of the gate outside the sanctuary chapel, and he answered all Raddick's questions. According to Raddick, this man was very gentle and very polite, still in full possession of his faculties, although he was well over one-hundred-years-old. He answered Raddick's questions with complete clarity. By this time, Raddick had become fluent enough in the Ethiopian language to be able to converse with the natives directly, and that was a huge advantage. They trusted Raddick more because of it. The Guardian told Raddick that under no circumstances would Raddick ever be allowed to see the Ark of the Testimony, not even from a distance. In answer to Raddick's direct question, the Guardian said that indeed the very Ark of the Testimony, built in the time of Moses at the foot of Mount Sinai, was housed only fifty meters away, that it was there right now, but that only the Guardian was ever allowed to see it. Not even the other priests, he said, could lay eyes upon the Ark. The knowledge that the Ark was so close to him and yet so completely out-of-reach almost drove Raddick mad. Did I say almost? It *did* drive him mad, as you will see. The Guardian explained that as Guardian he could never once leave the Ark's general presence. And it was this that finally tipped Raddick off, a few months later, at *Timkat*."

"Because the Guardian wasn't with the Ark when it was brought through the streets," Joel said suddenly.

"That's right," Tom said.

"That was shrewd," Joel said, "on Raddick's part."

"Shrewd on *your* part, Joel, to figure it out. But Raddick was shrewd. He was nothing if not shrewd. Specifically, though, it was after the celebration, while Raddick was still in Axum, that he put all this together. You see, he didn't glimpse the Guardian outside the sanctuary gates any more, not even from a distance, as he had in the past. That was when Raddick began to suspect. He even went out of his way to find the Guardian. He asked the other priests if the Guardian had died; they said no. Then something occurred to Raddick."

Tom paused for several seconds. Joel waited anxiously.

"The persistent rumors of war," Tom said, "had become more than mere rumors now. The Italian army invaded Ethiopia, and it was ultimately this that led Raddick to the truth."

Joel felt his pulse quickening.

"Raddick returned to Lake Tana," Tom said, "where he'd already been, on a number of different occassions, to interview the Falasha priests who inhabit this lake's many island monasteries."

"Falashas?" Joel said. "I'm sorry, I don't know that word."

"It means an exile, or a stranger, and it refers specifically to Ethiopian Jews. Before this, the Falashas had treated Raddick with utmost respect and courtesy, answering all his questions. But when he returned now, they did not seem to him so kind or so friendly. They eyed him suspiciously. Or so he thought. Actually, he couldn't decide. By now, you see, his obsession had begun to overtake him, and he was paranoid—in the true sense: seeing things, real or imaginary, he wasn't sure. A kind of chronic fear had settled in upon him, and he wasn't able to evaluate things properly. For some time now, Raddick, understand, had felt himself pursued."

"By whom?" Joel said.

"He didn't know. But he felt certain of it."

"What made him so?"

"Odd glimpses that came at unexpected times. Unknown people staring at him. Raddick had already resolved upon something terrible, and perhaps that exacerbated it. At Lake Tana, he stayed for twenty-four hours on the island of Tana Kirkos."

"What was he doing?"

"He was there asking the priests a different set of questions now. He asked about places in history that the Ark had been moved during wartime. The answers were all vague. Raddick grew more and more wary. In a papyrus canoe, he paddled to other islands. He was beginning to think that the Ark had been taken to someplace else entirely, perhaps beyond the Rift Valley, thousands of miles away, where he would never be able to trace it. He grew afraid that the Ark had been removed to a place so secret that only two or three priests would know its whereabouts. And now he felt himself sinking into his blackest depression of all. But you know what? He fought it. Raddick didn't yield to it. He kept moving, searching. That's what you do, Joel: you keep going, you continue on, you keep trying, and you never say die."

Joel was very silent.

"At the same time, Raddick was seeing more and more shadows behind him, wherever he looked. He stopped sleeping. He felt he was in a land of overwhelming beauty, but also overwhelming deception—a land of reflection: the water reflecting the sky, the African moon reflecting the African sun, the sky reflecting oceans of light, optically devastating. He started hearing things, as well."

"Seeing things, hearing things? *What things?*"

"Things, you know. Natives moving in the shadows. Voices that came to him without a source. In a way, Joel, Raddick was beyond everything now except the Ark. His desire for it had eaten him alive."

Tom stopped speaking and clawed back his wet hair. Both men were very damp. But only Joel was shivering; and try as he might, he couldn't decide if two people talking like this, in the middle of a dark wood, was in any way out of the ordinary. Tom certainly did not appear to think so, which meant nothing to Joel, however, because he was convinced now that this man was out of his mind.

Then Joel heard something, distant but distinct: it was the dying strains of music, a dying flute. The sound came and went, and came again. It was so faint that he wasn't sure he heard it after all. He looked at Tom. "Did you hear that?" he said.

"What?"

"A flute. For a moment, I thought I heard flute music."

Tom cocked his head to listen. "I get nothing," he said.

Joel sat motionless. The only sound he heard now was the steady drip of rain. "Continue."

"In the end, Raddick visited many of the island monasteries, but in the end he found nothing significant. He didn't know what he would do next. Then he caught his big break: along the hidden shores of Lake Tana, there's a tiny settlement set back on dry land among the trees. This place provided him with temporary respite. He'd never seen or heard of this place before, primarily because there's no monastery there. To his surprise, though, he did find something of interest."

"What did he find?"

"He found a chapel that was actually more like a half-finished structure carved into the rock-wall behind it. The front part of the structure was not totally enclosed, and inside, there were a number of passageways that went back into the mountain. The stones that made up the front part of the structure were covered in lush undergrowth, so that the whole thing was well camouflaged. For a long time Raddick didn't even notice it. There were only a handful of people who lived there, all men: a silent and primitive people, devoutly Christian, but existing in such savage isolation that they looked upon any visitor with mistrust.

They did, however, feed Raddick and allow him time to rest. Which was the biggest mistake of their lives: after looking upon the chapel the entire time without actually seeing it, Raddick as he was about to leave noticed that this grouping of stones formed a room. He stared into the room with a mounting sense that something important was about—what's wrong, Joel?"

"Nothing," Joel said. "Please go on."

"What Raddick at first saw was just a lot of clustered religious iconography. But as he sat staring, a pair of white eyeballs suddenly emerged within the room. Then a tall figure came into the opening. Do you know who that figure was?"

"The Guardian," Joel whispered.

"That's right. That's exactly right. He stood half-hidden in the shadows, and at first he did not see Raddick. By the time he did, it was too late. Raddick didn't hesitate. He murdered the man. He murdered the Guardian, and then he murdered the others as well. Specifically, he scrambled the man's brains with a stiletto knife, inserting the knife into the nape of the neck and wiggling it around, and he killed the others about as easily. Raddick had been a soldier, you see, and as I mentioned, these were a primitive people, a peaceful people, and there were not very many of them. So now Raddick had plenty of innocent blood on his hands. But what did he care? And yet even after he'd killed them all, he was *still* seeing people swarming everywhere in the shadows. He was not at all calm, yet he knew that the Ark was now within his grasp. The tunnel was pitch-black, profound—"

"Did he *find* it?" Joel said.

"Yes. I've already told you that. He found it down an offshoot corridor: the Ark of Jehovah sitting in a small stone room, sectioned off by rock walls. It was wrapped in many layers of cloth, and it sat upon two long wooden poles that were skewered through four rings which were attached to each corner of the Ark. The poles had small pegs underneath, and these pegs fit snugly into four corresponding divots in the stone floor. The room was lit by a tallow candle as big as a beer keg, and everything smelled of incense. Raddick went directly over to the Ark, and, using the same knife that he'd used to murder the Guardian and the others, he slit the ancient veils that wrapped the ancient vessel."

Tom stopped speaking for several minutes. The rain had ceased, but the woods still dripped and dripped. To the east, the clouds pulled apart, and the first stars of evening shone through, Venus rising. Something complicated hung between them.

"Goddamnit," Joel finally said, "what did he *find*?"

"Joel," Tom said, "Raddick found something that exceeded his most extravagant speculations, something that changed his life forever. He found first, beneath the golden mercy seat, a totally unexpected thing: He found cats."

22

Someone coughed. Joel opened his eyes. He was in a foreign room with gray walls. Several minutes passed before he'd fully reoriented.

It was late morning. He lay upon a single bed beneath a high window. The blinds were drawn, the room submerged in sea-colored light. The bed was the only furniture. There was a tiny bathroom across the way.

In one motion, he folded the covers back into a large dogear and swung his legs out of bed. He sat on the edge of the bed for another five minutes, thinking. His vision was clear but for the innumerable bugs hopping along the outermost periphery of both eyes.

At length, he stood up and went into the bathroom. The carpet felt firm and cool beneath his bare feet. Ten minutes later, when he reemerged, he had cleaned himself, and he quickly dressed.

He was in the basement of the steel-and-glass house. The bedroom door opened directly to the outside world, into a narrow concrete ramp that rose steeply up to ground level. Joel mounted the ramp and then walked around the house. He came to the walnut deck. There was no one anywhere that he could see. A coffee thermos stood steaming in the center of the table, next to ripe bananas in a clear glass bowl, oranges, figs, and hothouse grapes. Under a plexiglass bell, there sat a plate of fresh rolls. Joel poured himself a scalding cup of coffee; he did not eat. He did not sit down. He stood drinking his coffee and looking about. The grounds were silent and very still. Shallow puddles of rainwater stood like pots of quicksilver in the depressions of the walkway, giving back a pale-blue image of the cobalt sky above. Similarly, the glass windows of the house reflected the sky and all its egg-shaped clouds, so that it occurred to Joel that he was in a land of reflections, but reflections, he thought, that mirrored nature actually, through the reflector's lens—tinting and shading nature, perhaps, but not distorting it beyond knowing. He inhaled deeply.

The air smelled rinsed and cool. The summer was dying. The conifers stood shagged and gnarly. The half moon hung bone-white over the western mountains, and it too was reflecting the sun and the daytime heavens.

Joel stood staring for a long time, and then he walked back into the house.

There was nobody home, and Joel could see outside through the windows much more clearly than he could see inside from without.

A clammy draft channeled soundlessly through the room. Joel went over to the pencil drawings still stacked upon the carpet. He approached the pictures cautiously and picked up the first one.

His suspicions were confirmed.

These portraits were indeed portraits of him, uncanny reproductions of his face and body—moles, pores, muscle striations, acne scars, individual strands of hair, no detail too small—drawn from many different aspects, and with an almost miraculous touch, but the artist was Joel himself. He sorted through each picture, all but one of which was of him; that one depicted the haggard face of a handsome man, with the exophthalmic eyes of a prophet or a killer. The man had ash-colored hair and a thin drooping mustache. It was his father.

Joel stood looking at it for some time. The veins in the whites of the old man's eyeballs looked like miniature explosions of blood. Joel cast his thoughts back, remembering when he had drawn it, well over ten years ago, in California. He turned now to the sunlight. An illuminating ray came gliding through the reflective glass and revealed handwriting on the back of his father's portrait. Joel turned the portrait over. A short passage had been scrawled there, in black ballpoint, which said:

> We bless with brief thanksgiving
> Whatever gods may be
> That no life lives forever;
> That dead men rise up never;
> That even the weariest river
> Winds somewhere safe to sea.

Beneath that, in soft-lead pencil and handwriting totally different, were these words:

> For a little while we live, and life hath mutable wings.
> A little while and we die; shall life not thrive as it may?
> For no man under the sky lives twice, outliving his day.

Joel recognized the handwriting of the first passage—that spidery, angular script was unmistakable: it was Bill Morgan's.

The second passage, however, was not in the hand of anyone he personally knew, but the designer print was particularly fresh in his memory. It was the exact same writing he'd seen on the cement table. But the biggest surprise of all was still to come:

In a corner of the living room, on a cherrywood table under a gooseneck lamp, there was a sprawling jigsaw puzzle. The puzzle was all completed but for a single missing piece. Joel stared down at it; seeing up close what it depicted, he felt his mind reel, his skin crawl: it was a gallery of spiders, a taxonomic puzzle for school children, and Joel knew instantly and without any doubt what the missing piece was.

He reached into his front pocket and brought forth the puzzle piece he'd found on his doorstep that dark morning many months ago.

He placed the piece into the puzzle.

It fit perfectly.

23

Thirty minutes later, as he was walking out, he met Tom halfway down the gravel road. Tom was dressed in worn jeans and a black T-shirt. He was smiling, coming toward Joel, his hand extended even from twenty-five meters away.

"How did you sleep?" Tom said.

"Like the dead," Joel said.

They shook hands.

"But dead men rise up never," Tom said.

"It was you who wrote that second quotation, then?"

"What second quotation?"

"On the back of my father's portrait."

"No, it wasn't."

"How is it that you of all people ended up with those pictures?" Joel said.

"You have an artistic gift," Tom said.

"Thank you."

Joel stood waiting.

"Those pictures were given to me," Tom said, "because I asked for them."

"Given to you by whom?"

"Elias Moorecroft."

"Who gave them to him?"

"Lauren Lake."

Joel was silent.

"Do you find that surprising?" Tom said.

"Yes. How—" But Joel cut himself off.

Tom was smiling crookedly.

"I'm sorry," Joel said. "There are still many things I must ask you. It's very important to me. I feel as if I'm the victim of a joke."

"Let us walk."

Joel nodded. Side-by-side, they strolled back down the gravel road. Presently they came to a wide path that ran parallel the deep green canal. They walked at a leisurely pace.

"Did you know Bill Morgan?" Joel said.

"Yes," Tom said, "of course."

"How did you know my mother?"

"By her fruits."

"Please," Joel said impatiently.

"Please what, Joel? I'm completely serious. How does anybody know anyone if not by her fruits?"

Joel didn't answer. He had stopped walking. Five feet to his left and below him, below the mossy banks, the green canal rocked gently by. In a moment, Tom also stopped walking; he turned back to Joel. "People are defined by their actions, Joel, yes?"

Joel narrowed his eyes. He was staring at the flowing water. He didn't answer.

"And actions are defined by thoughts," Tom said. "But what defines those thoughts?"

Joel still didn't respond. He began walking again.

"May I quote you something?" Tom said. "It's from a book called *Love and Will*, by a man named Rollo May. I've committed this to memory because I think it's so very important."

Joel nodded.

"When we analyze will with all the tools that modern psychology brings us, we shall find ourselves pushed back to the level of attention or inattention as the seat of will. Close quote. Do you hear what he's saying there? He's saying the seat of free will is contained in this tiny question: should I pay attention or not? That's the only choice we have, and all the rest come from it. The work of willing, I call it. The work," Tom repeated, and then fell silent. "The effort, Rollo May says, which goes into the exercise of will is really effort of attention; the strain in willing is the effort to keep the consciousness clear, i.e. the strain of keeping attention focused." Tom again fell silent. Then, after ten seconds, he added: "So. Life is work, life is effort."

Joel said nothing. Tom watched him.

"Tell me, Joel," Tom said, "are you in shape?"

"What kind of shape?"

"Running shape."

"How would you know if I'm a runner?"

"Because if you don't run, you can't win," Tom said. "Run therefore every race set before you." Tom paused. "In answer to your question, Joel, we all know. How could we not? You were our hero, and we followed your running career very closely. We thought you were going to be a superstar, a gold medalist."

"We?"

"Yes. All of us."

Joel stopped walking, and so did Tom. They stared at each other seriously and in silence for several seconds, until Joel averted his eyes. Joel gazed off toward the south. Small clouds were coming up like smoke signals over the sawtooth mountains. His black hair stirred in the breeze. He turned back to Tom.

"My feelings about running are very complicated," Joel said. "I tell you that candidly." He hesitated. "Maybe I could have been an Olympian, if I'd wanted, if I'd tried. The truth is, you've got to want something like that with your entire being, because there are so many other people, with at least as much talent as you, who want it so much. On that level, the winner is always determined by who wants it the most. I didn't love running enough, is the short answer. But that's not quite accurate. I hated running too much. Or not running, exactly, but racing."

"Why racing?"

"Because losing, or even the thought of it, terrified me. The psychological toll, the obsessive worrying day and night, the thought that *I might lose...*" Joel broke off.

"Please finish," Tom said.

"Well, people who aren't this way can't really understand it—not really, I mean. But I can tell you this much: some people are driven to always be first. It's not necessarily a good thing, and I'm not self-aggrandizing. It does have its good side, but I think now that it's more of a curse. I think it's pathological, an actual compulsion, like food purging. Here's what it was like for me: it was as if not being first in a race was a reflection of my self-worth as a human being, and that *is* why I always wanted it the most. That's how I felt. This wasn't a societal or religious imposition but something I had set up in my own mind—although that makes it sound deliberate. It wasn't. It's just always been a part of me. I felt I had to win every time, no matter the suffering I endured, or I was an inferior person. No athlete—I don't know if you know this or not—wrestlers, boxers, football players, no athlete suffers like the runner. So each week of racing was psychological warfare conducted at a gigantic cost to me, and I grew to loathe it. That compulsion," he added, "still resides within me, but dormant."

"Oh?" Tom said. "Well, nevertheless."

"Nevertheless what?"

"Nevertheless, if you resist to blood the desire to stop, afterward the enduring will yield up something greater than if you had not exercised thereby."

"I don't understand what you mean."

"How can you obtain the prize," Tom said, "if you don't run? How can you bring your body into subjection?"

Again, Joel shook his head. "Look," he said, finally, "are you out of your mind? Or is it me? I feel as if I'm dreaming every time I talk to you."

"Thank you," Tom said. "I take that as a compliment." He reached down and unsheathed a long brown stalk from a circular cluster, a series of which grew along the banks of the canal. They resumed their walk. With his muscular fingers, he began to shape a little noose out of the stem. "Neither of us is out of his mind," Tom said. "I'm simply answering your initial question, Joel, the one you asked me several days ago. This is about *The Secret History*. It's about your father. It's about you."

"My *father*? What does he have to do with it?"

"A lot."

"Do you know him?"

"Yes. Very well."

"How? How do you know him?"

"I visit him, for one thing."

"*What?*"

"I said I visit him. He's an extraordinary man, as I'm sure you know. But are you really so shocked?"

"Yes." Joel paused. "It beats everything I've ever heard, and I think I should warn you: my father can be very persuasive, but don't allow yourself to be fooled."

"Fooled in what way?"

"In any way. Nothing is ever what it seems with that man. He's a fascinating person, and articulate, and more than anyone I've ever known, he can bring complicated ideas down to the level of complete comprehensibility—when he wants. Yet he rarely wants, and that's the thing: he purposely obscures. He obscures far more than he clarifies. Why? I don't know. I've never understood. I've thought about this so much that I think I've thought it into the ground. Why can't he just talk straight? Why does everything always have to be such a puzzle with him? But even more than that, my father has no human conscience. He's the type who would profess infinite love for you on one day, and then damn you to eternal hell the moment you cross him."

"But would he *really*?" Tom said.

"Yes, he would."

"That leads me back to what I was saying last night."

"What's that?"

"You remember that Moses was as much Egyptian as Jew?"

Joel didn't answer, but he couldn't hide his look of confusion.

"From here on in," Tom continued, "it's important for you to remember that, because so much that Raddick found inside the Ark was Egyptian."

"I don't understand what this has to do with my father."

"You will."

Joel stared steadily at Tom for several seconds.

"The Egyptians regarded cats as the guardians of all that is just and good," Tom said. "Which is why two intricate stone cats stood perched on top of everything inside the Ark. Those cats were symbolic."

Their walk led them now to a stone bench beside the water. The pastures lay spread out before them. Tom seated himself and tossed the tiny grass noose into the water. Joel remained standing for a moment longer. He watched the looped stem whirl away into the deeps. Then he too sat down.

"As I mentioned before," Tom said, "Raddick was well acquainted with ancient Egyptian civilization. History, as I said, was his passion." Tom scratched his cheekbone with his thumbnail. "And so he understood. Or at least he thought he did: anyway, as soon as he saw those two Egyptian sculptures, it all dawned upon him."

"What did?"

"That Moses' entire upbringing was Egyptian. His formative years were spent among Egyptian royalty. This, of course, had an inestimable influence on him."

Joel turned his head and looked across the water. He watched the husk of a dragonfly glide airily over the current. The clouds reflected on the surface of the canal looked like miniature moons. A soft breeze blew down from behind and wrinkled the water.

"But this is not about Egyptology," Tom said, "any more than it's about Knights Templar or Illuminati. This is about something more universal. Raddick carefully began unpacking the Ark. And what he found there, to his surprise, were books. Books and books, and more books."

"What sort of books?"

"All sorts: books containing knowledge, old books, valuable books, books written on parchment and leather; books written on cow uterus. But his greatest surprise of all was that there were even a few books written on paper."

"Are you speaking seriously?"

"Very seriously. And yet this was paper of a kind he'd never seen before. There were, by the way, no stone tablets anywhere inside the Ark—did I tell you?"

"Yes."

"Nothing to even suggest them. That stone is purely symbolic as well."

"What does it symbolize?"

"It symbolizes the unsearchable riches." Tom himself, staring down at the water, seemed for a long moment to consider his own words. "On second thought," he said, "that's not incidental. In fact, it's most singular to this story."

"Which fact are you referring to?"

"The fact that the stone symbolizes the unsearchable riches, and that instead of stone tablets, there were books on paper."

"Why singular?"

"Because what Raddick discovered first and foremost about the Ark is that it had once been a living growing thing—a little but living library. The Ark at one time, and for a long time, had been added to constantly. New discoveries and new knowledge from around the known world were continually contributed. The Ark was a live body of knowledge, and, like knowledge itself, it was continually expanding, continually evolving. And then—" Tom broke off and was silent for a long moment. A gray serpent came rapidly downstream, sidewinding with the current. They watched it pass.

"And then at some unknown point," Tom said, "the Ark was shut up and hidden away from the entire world, including from those who held it. No one at all was permitted access to the Ark. That, of course, is when everything went straight to hell."

"What do you mean?"

"I mean knowledge stagnated, and faith took over, which ushered in the Dark Ages. Knowledge is not faith, Joel, contrary to what you may have heard, and omniscience, as I also mentioned, is not the goal, nor ever was: at any level of learning, no matter how erudite a person becomes, there's always more to learn. Do you see the significance of that?"

"I don't think I do."

"The significance is in the fact that the focus shifts from all-knowing to always learning. The things we do not yet have answers for don't suddenly presuppose that answers are not possible or forthcoming eventually. It just means we don't have enough knowledge yet. That was the first of four critical things Raddick discovered inside the Ark. The next was that many of the documents, which were written in an outlandish tongue Raddick had never seen before, described something much like what we today call natural selection, but more than that—"

"How could he have known it described that if he couldn't read the writing?"

"Very good, Joel. The answer to that question is that there were many pictures and diagrams, all done with extraordinary care. These pictures showed over and over again a gradual process of living species evolving."

"But these diagrams were old?"

"Very. They were Egyptian-like but not Egyptian. They were done on a tough fabric that rolled up and didn't easily tear. Raddick didn't recognize the fabric. The drawings were so thorough that by the end, Raddick was not left in any doubt: these pictures showed animals of almost every kind—fish, fowl, insects, reptiles, even dinosaur—*progressing* toward other species. This ancient understanding of natural selection came about exactly as our current understanding of it came about."

"How?"

"Through observation. Which is how all learning advances. But the most remarkable thing that Raddick saw in these diagrams were the pictures that focused exclusively upon the human larynx. Some of these drawings even showed dissected throats. Raddick deduced from these pictures that someone had discovered that it's the tilt of the human larynx, occurring through an evolutionary process, that's given us our voice box. And more: it's our voice box that's given us our freedom of will."

Joel shook his head impatiently.

"The evolution of speech," Tom said, "is what's given rise to rationality, because it's given us the power to store knowledge by means of words which has in turn freed us to seek out more knowledge. Our rationality is what's given us the power of choice, because speech has brought us to this point: the point that we must will ourselves to pay attention or not. The spoken or written symbolization of words (also known as language) gives us the power to subsume any number of things under a single word. Written language came afterward, but in this context written language serves the same function as spoken language. We learn what 'rock' denotes, and thereafter we hear or see the word 'rock' and immediately *know* what's being referred to. This power of recognition through words, stored by means of words, frees the brain to pursue more and ever more data, which is knowledge, which is truth. The voice box, in collaboration with the primate brain, is what makes all this possible. But it's not an automatic process. The process must be willed by each individual person, and it is the strain of attention, of keeping the attention focused, that is the seat of this fundamental act of will. Humans have free will as a result of which humans must concentrate to stay alive."

"He found *that* inside the Ark of Jehovah?"

"Yes. The Ark, which is the seat of all knowledge, according to some traditions."

"What else did he find?"

"Something written on leathern scrolls, in a language he *could* read."

"What language was it?"

"Greek. He found a detailed explanation of what this particular group of Greeks considered the foundational principle of human cognition."

"What?"

"He later began referring to it as 'the law of evidence.' Others have since termed it 'evidentialism.' It's a formal declaration of the obvious, really: every theory, proposition, claim, hypothesis, or whatever must proceed first from data and not the other way around, never ever that. *The evidence must always come first.*"

Tom was silent for several seconds; he waited for Joel to interject, but Joel never did.

"That's what the law of evidence is," Tom said at last. "It's very simple, in a way, and yet in a way it's not: that simplicity is deceptive. And the implications run deep. The law of evidence in essence restates a well-known phrase: 'there's no reason to think otherwise.' It is the first epistemological rule you must *always* abide by. It's the first and also the final argument against God because it is irrefutable. The law of evidence forbids faith in any long-term form, including so-called 'revelation,' because it's the exact opposite of faith. Do you understand, Joel?"

Joel didn't respond.

"It means that if there is no data, any assertion that's made about anything not only can but *must* be dismissed. You can't even entertain these claims as possible, forget probable or certain. If I say that there are submicroscopic men inside our brains who pull levers that control consciousness, you in the absence of evidence must dismiss it. The reason for this is that knowledge *is* data. To entertain claims for which there is no evidence is even worse than a contradiction in terms. It is to invite chaos into your brain."

"How so?"

"In such cases, everything becomes equally valid, since you've done away with the evidential. Any claim becomes legitimate. Nothing is more credible than anything else, nor can ever be established as such. Black hell teeming with demons beneath earth's crust is as cogent as plate tectonics. Photosynthesis is no more valid than Jack-and-the-beanstalk. Flat earth is as plausible as gravity. Raddick right away came to grasp the gigantic significance of this, the supreme importance of the rule of evidence. The rule of evidence, Joel, applied consistently, upends the rules of knowledge you've all along been taught. Obviously, it has incredible implications concerning God, as well."

"God is a non-evidential claim," Joel said.

"Yes. The burden of proof applies as much to God as to anything in a court of law—or, for that matter, in a scientific laboratory. It doesn't make the slightest difference that billions *believe* in God. The rules of cognition do not change: evidence must come first."

Joel didn't speak.

"Never forget that," Tom said. "Observation is a precondition of knowledge, and all knowledge must stand the test of evidence. Among other things, that means the data must precede the theories, and the theories must never precede the data. Hypothesis and propositions—including the proposition of God—must conform to facts. Facts are gathered through observation. The fact that God has become sacrosanct changes absolutely nothing in reality. I know legions of doctors, lawyers, pastors, priests, scientists, and so on who indeed accept the validity of reason and proof and the law of evidence—up to a point: until it comes to religious or spiritual matters. And then reason is shelved. Yet this is precisely when it is most needed, because these are the ideas that form our epistemological groundwork, the ones upon which the rest of knowledge are built. Let he who would reject reason and sensory perception try driving or walking down the street for thirty seconds without using reason or his senses. The truth is that there's no good reason at all why proof and evidence should not be applied as rigorously to things spiritual and noetic, and I say that to you in all sincerity. As a matter of fact, the greatest enemy of human cognition is blind belief."

"If God did not exist," Joel said, "man would have invented him."

Tom didn't answer. The wind came steadily off the water. They were both silent for a long while.

"Joel, cognition operates in a specific way, and that way requires an effort: the work of willing, which is the work of keeping the attention focused. It is so much easier to simply believe than it is to apply the rigorous rules of evidence to everything we think."

"That's true," Joel said.

"If you're ever in doubt about something," Tom said, "refer back to reality, back to the concretes, where knowledge begins. You do not conclude God on the basis of insufficient knowledge. In actuality, the law of evidence is what's truly sacrosanct, Joel, much more so than God. Why? Because the law of evidence is the guardian of truth. Everything epistemologic depends upon the law of evidence. Even God Himself could not be beyond the laws of reason and logic or He couldn't have created a species who must conform to those laws. That, incidentally, is one proof of God's non-existence."

"What is?"

"If God is truth, and if truth is the accurate identification of reality—which it is—then God would not require faith. And yet God does require faith. God, therefore, cannot be truth since learning truth requires the opposite of faith: it requires reason. Not only does truth *not* require faith: it cannot exist until faith is abolished. Why so? Because truth is the observable, the actual. It is the antonym of faith. Try adding numbers by faith. Try doing long division by faith. In fact, God is no more exempt from the rules of logic than ghosts, green men, Grendel, the Great Spirit, or ESP. And for the same reasons. If you claim God, if you claim green men, *you*, not me, must provide the evidence for it. If there's no evidence, you must dismiss the claim. If you don't dismiss it, you court the anti-mind, the anti-life. The law of evidence is the third thing Raddick found inside the Ark."

"There is no evidence for God, you say," said Joel. "Evidence, you say, is natural, and God is supernatural."

"Yes."

"So God is impossible."

"That is what I've said, yes."

"But surely you don't mean to suggest that inside the Ark of Jehovah, Raddick found that Jehovah is impossible?" Joel said.

"That's exactly what I mean to suggest—and more: the final thing Raddick found, which is very closely related to the other three, is really the principal thing." But here Tom broke off and was silent.

"Go on," Joel said.

"The principle thing," Tom said, "is that for the sake of which everything else is done. *That*, sir, is the principle thing, and it is the thing that finally destroyed Raddick, just as it destroyed your father, and for the same reason."

"What in the hell are you talking about?"

"That's right," Tom said. "Wisdom, which requires incorporating your knowledge into actual practice, means among other things that you must bring your body and your brain under subjection, or you'll never find those unsearchable riches. If you don't know what you must do, Joel, or if you don't see it clearly, you'll never attain it, but then, on the other hand, it won't matter because you won't really know it—or, if you do know it, you won't care enough. If, though, you *do* know what you must do and if you *do* see it clearly, failing to act in that way will lead to self-destruction—or sociopathology."

24

Overhead, the blue sky had grown bluer still, so that tipping his head back and gazing upward, Joel felt as if the heavens were rushing down at him, ready to smother him to death. He continued looking up. Tom sat watching him. The breeze lifted and fell. After a while, Joel's head began to spin. He lowered his gaze.

Tom stood up and gestured with his chin to the summit of the nearest peak, which was poking at the rubbery sky. "From here," Tom said, "the summit of that mountain is about seven miles away. The first mile, leading to the trailhead, is flat. But once you hit the trail, the way grows steep." He turned to Joel. "So," he said, "what do you think?" His tea-colored front tooth jutted and flashed.

"About what?" Joel said.

"Shall we?"

"Shall we what?"

"Race."

Joel seemed astonished at the suggestion. And yet he stood up as well. "Are you kidding?"

"No."

Joel glanced down at his worn-out tennis shoes, his gray-camouflage pants. He then looked back to Tom, who was dressed in jeans and a pair of sneakers even more raggedy than Joel's own. Tom shook his head, proleptically. "Don't worry about any of that," he said.

Joel looked perplexed.

"If you don't run," Tom explained, "you can't win. Run therefore every race set before you."

Joel started to speak, but before he could say anything at all, Tom had darted off and was at a dead run.

It took Joel a quarter-mile to catch him. Even then, he lagged about ten feet behind. Tom ran with a liquid-like motion. The warm breeze blew. At the trailhead, Tom, increasing his speed as he hit the first big hill, stripped off his T-shirt with one hand, and in so doing didn't miss a stride. He ran from then on with his shirt balled in his fist. Watching him from behind, Joel saw with shock that Tom's entire back was covered with long thick scars. He saw also the pale and lean upper body, so that in his faded denim, Tom looked bluish and silvery. Just then, the first wave of exhaustion swept over Joel, and he wondered how he had gotten into this.

Coming into the first switchback, the way grew excessively steep. Each switchback was short and sharp. Joel closed the gap to five feet. Singlefile, they churned up the inclines. Their breath came hard. Both began to sweat.

Joel estimated the grade at fifteen percent. They ran among dwarf oak and ilex. Then these trees disappeared, and there were only rock walls and dirt. The sun bounced heavily off the rock. From below, the two men looked liked insects scaling the verticalities. To the south, the valley was ringed with stone bluffs. Low yellow hills lay across the northeastern horizon. The gingerbread village could not be seen.

The switchbacks kept coming. Joel fixed his eyes on the small of Tom's scarred back. There was no fat there whatsoever, and Joel could see each striation of each individual muscle squirming just beneath the skin. The blue sky brooded above. Just over two miles up, the switchbacks ended, and the way grew steeper. The trail went relatively straight from here to the top of the mountain. Joel realized then that he was right up on Tom's heels. He surged and went around Tom on the right, giving himself as wide a berth as possible, as if to avoid contact with Tom.

He paid for his surge: exhaustion swamped him so severely that he feared he would now not make it to the top.

The summit loomed miles away still, and yet the thought of enduring even another half-mile felt inconceivable. At that moment, everything about running that Joel hated and had forgotten about came back to him. In his mind, the miles ahead seemed insurmountable, his situation as grave as life or death.

He could hear Tom breathing right behind him, the crush of his footsteps.

He ran on.

He did so by fixing his eyes on a point fifty meters ahead and then telling himself:

Make it to just that point, fifty meters, and then perhaps you can stop running.

Then, when he came to that point, he repeated this same process.

In this way, he passed the next mile.

Joel thought: you must simply make it through the next moment before you decide anything. Make it through the moment.

Tom, meanwhile, did not fall off the pace at all, so that when, at last, they came to the top of a very long and very steep grade, peaking out at just over 11,500 feet, and the trail widened slightly, Joel saw Tom coming up on his periphery. Then the trail widened more, opening into a meadow of yellow grass and columbines. There were aspen trees on the other end. For five hundred meters, the gradient went from fourteen percent to four percent, and Joel recovered his breath somewhat.

"You're wearing me out," Tom said.

He caught up to Joel and ran shoulder-to-shoulder with him. He, like Joel, was sucking deeply at the thin air, but the mocking manner was still present.

Tom was gleaming with sweat. Still, there was an effortlessness about him that sent another wave of fear through Joel: fear that he would be beaten by this man. He lifted his eyes to the summit; it loomed high above, incredibly remote. The sky hung oppressive, and he didn't see how he could possibly hang on.

"Well, are you going to make it?" Tom said, displaying once again his uncanny purchase on the drift of Joel's thoughts.

Joel didn't answer.

Together, they pounded up through the aspen trees, and then they came into a higher meadow, a mountain glade alive with insects and yellow butterflies. The air around them was rippled with heat. A light breeze poured out of the black conifers above. The sun in the sky stood like iron. The higher they climbed, the thinner the air, the hotter the sun.

A quarter-mile later, they entered the dark evergreen forest. The air smelled thickly of pine pitch. The trail narrowed gradually and grew increasingly steep. Tom fell in directly behind Joel. Overhead, a pair of crows deployed downwind. The steepness of the hill took a stupendous toll on Joel's body, so that any sense of recovery he had felt going across the meadow now vanished. Joel was growing sick, his head as heavy as a cannonball. He imagined himself slogging through quicksand. Purple flowers lay on the ground at his feet; he wondered if he were really seeing them. Then they were gone.

The next mile was the most excruciating yet. His breath came harder and harder. He went fifty meters at a time again. At the end of each fifty meter block, he believed his body would shut down, and he would be forced to stop. But somehow, through sheer strength of will, he managed to put one foot in front of the other, continuously.

Two thousand meters before the summit, he thought that he must quit running or die. He felt that these were his only two options now. His breathing had become so labored that his lungs felt as if they'd been scorched out with bleach. And still, the thud of Tom's footfalls banged loudly behind him, striking Joel's ears with inordinate clarity. Soon Joel came to regard that relentless sound as malevolent, intentional. He glanced over his shoulder. Tom was right there and he was staring straight at Joel, staring in an oddly serious way that made Joel feel alarmed.

Tom was panting madly, he was sweating, and yet his body looked so muscular and lean, so capable, that to Joel Tom at once took on the aspect of an alien organism without any skin or tissue at all, something bred down to pure bone and blood and sinew—not a robot of titanium and tungsten but an organic thing that would rip apart solid steel. And somewhere along the line, Joel in his half-delirious state grasped that what was happening here was much more than a running race and that the man he was running against was deadly serious.

Joel looked up. The bald summit hung there, less than a mile away now, but with the steepest section still to come: the final ascent. The vertical rock had no ending. Each breath for Joel was laced with broken glass. His lungs felt bloody. Against the hyaline heavens, the steel-colored sun resounded in the bottomless blue. As they ascended, the summit seemed simultaneously to recede. Before him now, the last trees reared up like raggedymen against the sky. And then Joel noticed something remarkable: the steps behind him were not quite so audible.

He listened closer. Indeed the pound was not as pronounced.

He glanced over both shoulders. He could not see Tom on either side. Thus, in spite of his overwhelming fatigue, the knowledge that he'd hung on longer than his opponent, and that he was pulling away and winning now, this knowledge gave him a shot of adrenaline—enough, perhaps, for him to make it all the way to the top.

Joel kept listening. The sound of Tom's footsteps continued to recede, until after two hundred meters, Joel could not hear them at all. Tom's voice then came to him loud and clear:

"Don't worry," Tom said, "I'll catch you later. You can run, but you can't hide."

Upon hearing which, Joel's guts liquefied. Yet he pushed on. The way grew steeper. Joel climbed higher into the mountains. At thirteen thousand feet, his exhaustion wiped out his sonic sense entirely so that he no longer heard any sound whatsoever, including his own footfalls, his own breath. He was reeling with vertigo. His nose bled steadily, although he didn't know that, and his vision had gone dangerously tunnel. Wherever he looked, he saw a greenish fuzz like a bloom of mold all around the edges of his sight.

In this condition, and still running, but only just, he came stumbling into the final ascent. The trail leading up to the mountaintop flattened for approximately seventy meters, during which time Joel managed to breathe a little easier. It helped, but it was too short-lived: the headwall rose up in front of him like the hull of a huge ship; he mounted it. The trail went away, the final six hundred meters a field of slick talus, the land barren and black.

No trees grew this high up, and there was no vegetation of any kind. The lupine sky hung immediately before him now, close enough (he felt) to reach out and touch. And Joel was running, running, though barely so, one oozy foot in front of the other. Tiny ptarmigan with feathered feet veered through the rarified air, watching after him, he thought, piloting him. Ten feet now took on astronomical proportions. Blood ran from his nose. His hair hung lathered and ropey, and clung thinly to his skull.

Halfway up the headwall, he stumbled. But the hill was so steep that he fell only a short distance, down onto one knee; and for that brief moment, out of his mind with exhaustion, he thought he would just stay there.

That's when he heard the footsteps coming up behind him again.

He went completely numb. He didn't dare look back. He rose to his feet instantly and staggered on.

"I told you I'd catch you later," the voice said behind him.

The footsteps grew louder.

Joel stared at the black ground passing beneath him. He felt himself stumble once again, but he didn't fall. He lifted his eyes. Fields of scree bordered the sky. And there stood the isolated stone summit, releasing heat into the air. Joel was hee-hawing for breath. Still the footsteps grew louder. Still the sun burned down. He could feel Tom gaining by the second, ready to overtake him at any time.

"Do you understand yet, Joel?" Tom's voice sounded like a whisper in his ear.

Joel jerked his head to the right, but he didn't see anyone.

"Do you know what it means to bring your body under subjection?"

Joel shook his head to shut him out. Joel was forty meters from the top. He surged with the last of what he had, which wasn't much. His thighs were fire and ice. To his despair, the footsteps behind him matched his surge. Thirty meters to go, now twenty, now ten. And still the footsteps held fast. With five meters left, Joel lunged—and made it to the summit first.

He immediately swung around.

All he saw was open space; wind thrashing in the trees far below.

Tom was nowhere.

Joel couldn't believe his eyes, he *didn't* believe them. He stood gazing about frantically. He was bleeding; he was starved for air. The sky hung right before him, throbbing. Sweat leaked out of his every pore and dripped onto the stony ground. Joel scanned the landscape below. No one was coming up the hill. He turned a slow 360. In every direction, there was nothing but mountains, vast ranges of lilac peaks stretching away into the rim of the wooly world. In one valley far below, a kidney-shaped lake, white with sunlight, lay glowing as if the light were sourced within the water.

"Thomas!" Joel shouted. "Tom!"

His voice was swept instantly away by the wind.

Joel swayed from dizziness. His nose still bled, and he noticed this only now. He took off his sweat-soaked T-shirt and pressed it against his face. He started to tilt his head back, but vertigo walloped him like a club blow. He understood at this time that he was not in his right mind, but he didn't understand the extent to which. In a sudorific daze, he sat on the rocks. The air was absolutely pure. After a moment, he lay down on his back. The sunlight crashed silently around him, shattering the vitreous air. His nose stopped bleeding, yet his fatigue was so great that each time he blinked, he felt it more and more difficult to open his eyes.

Sprawled on his back under that murderous sun, the sky pressing like a pillow against his face, Joel began to shiver uncontrollably.

"Tom!" he yelled, from his back.

But the only response was the whistle of the wind.

That was when Joel knew he was in deep trouble.

25

He rose unsteadily from the rocks. The ground beneath him was made mostly of black basalt whose surface bore the scars of ancient lightning bolts, great gouges that scored the stones like hatchet marks. The wind blew dry. There were no clouds; around the sun, the sky shone like brass.

His shirt in his hand was drenched and clammy and smeared with his blood. He tugged it on. On legs of rubber, he wobbled off the shadowless summit. He slid on his rear down the steep scree slope. Then he entered the relative cool of the evergreens. His breathing had calmed, but his lungs felt hot and raw. He was mad with thirst and feverish and unsure of his way.

In the middle of the evergreen forest, he found the path he had run up—or so he thought. He began trotting again, down the path, the quicker to make it to the bottom. The sunlight thundered above him through the screening trees, long shafts of sunlight crisscrossing everywhere through the shadowy air.

One mile later, the trail forked. It was a fork he did not remember from the ascent. Both paths down were steep. He stopped and gazed about him, searching for a point of reference. He could not find one. He looked behind. To the north, high above, he saw rising through the trees the windy cliffs of nowhere, where eagles made their nests, and below, dark spruce interspersed with the apple-green quakies, and a slow-churning river that went meandering away at the foot of the cliffs. Joel chose the path on his left.

At once the way grew very rough. Within fifteen minutes, he found himself slogging through a damp marshland, which smelled of mulch and mushrooms. Silver deadwood lay strewn about him, one massive pine tree, dead from top to bottom, capsized on the ground and yet perfectly intact as if crystallized. The daylight had not diminished. The sky remained empty.

The path twisted down through slips of slate and buck brush, scrub oak and gorse, and he remembered none of this at all. Then the path faded away entirely. Joel did not know where he was. The vegetation grew so inimical that he was forced to stop moving completely. He stood there. He looked behind him once again. Retracing his steps was out of the question, so steep was this mountain, so fogged his brain, so weary his legs and his body. From the lay of the land, he thought he knew more or less where his hometown was located, and yet he wasn't sure. He'd never been here before. The undergrowth grew almost impenetrably thick, but he clawed his way through.

A half-hour later, he came into a desolate wood. It seemed unlikely to him that anyone had ever gone here before, so forsaken was it, so dark. He stepped into a stagnant stream. It lay dying in its messy bed, the small hard river stones fossilized like eggs. The smell of dust was strong. He felt it coating the insides of his nostrils. He was so parched that he momentarily considered drinking from the scummy water, knowing it would make him sick but knowing also that it would take a day or more to manifest. He did not do it. There were crunchy leaves among the river stones that crackled beneath his feet. Joel walked beyond into yet another stand of evergreens, and here he came upon a rotting mule deer corpse that sat stinking in the dirt. A huge hole had been blasted through the left side of the deer, as if the animal had been brought down with a cannonball. Dry blood lay thickly beneath the carcass, old blood, brown blood, blood webbed with hairline fissures. The deer was a small spike with velvet antlers just beginning their inward curve. The loose square teeth leered at him in a ludic grin, wooden ribs poking from the carcass like a shipwreck. The deer hide had grown whangy in the vigorous sun, and all along the face, the skin was peeled back like rotten fruit, disclosing mossy patches of skull. A steady plume of beetles scuttled from one side of the nose and emerged from the opposote nostril. Joel nearly retched from the reek. This was followed by more chills.

Hours later, in the auburn dusk, he stumbled out onto a chalky road. He was cold to his bones yet perspiring. The road ran vaporous in the twilight. Mist swirled around his ankles. His face looked pummeled, his lips crazed with cracks. He bled from cuts all over his hands and arms and neck, and the spit in his mouth was a small chewy bolus. For the last two hours, his legs had been cramping so severely from dehydration that each time he reached to his hamstrings, he felt knots the size of ping-pong balls embedded in the muscle. He rubbed them now and stood tottering in the cool tinted air.

The last of the light faded away. Tiny insects snapped on the ground by his feet. Above the black mountains to the west, the sky was awash in bloody light. Distant dogs bayed. Joel continued down the spectral road.

He came at length to a small creek he knew. The water ran swiftly. He walked along the grassy banks. The blades were flecked with foam, and the fog looked creamy in the darkness. He knelt before the water and dunked his head under. It took his breath away. He emerged dripping. The water was icy and black. He then drank breathlessly for a long time. When he raised his head again, the water ran in rivulets down his chin and from the ends of his hair. He scrubbed his face; he drank more water. Then he stripped off his shirt and submerged it. The air around him smelled willowy and cool. Among the mossy banks, river doves unseen cooed with watery voices. Joel stood. He wrung his shirt and wiped his face with it and then pulled the shirt back on.

While he was standing there, he saw in the braided current downstream the surface of the water suddenly turn pale. He stared wonderstruck at the whitening water. Then, slowly, he lifted his eyes. He stood motionless, watching. There, over the eastern mountains, a gibbous moon climbed into the night, suffusing a small quadrant of the sky with its soft unearthly light.

26

It was in a state of unmitigated delirium that he stumbled back onto the yard. He collapsed on the grass beneath the giant trees. Chills consumed him. The big bleak house cast shadows across the lawn. After a while, Joel rolled under a row of low shrubs, which partially concealed him. The night was warm, yet he was freezing. A perfumed odor laced the air. Over his head, the cottonwoods moaned. Thermal mist glowed in the moonlight. He shut his eyes.

When he opened them again, he didn't know how much time had elapsed. He heard now gentle strains of flute music. His eyes might have been closed for one second or one hour or even one day. Then he noticed that his shirt was wet, and that he was still shivering, and that his hair was soaked with his own sweat. He lay there on his back, listening. The flute was coming from somewhere nearby, a lonely piper in the summer night, but he could not pinpoint precisely where the music was coming from. He strained his ears. The music was soft but distinct. Hidden crickets also strummed their chords. Joel remembered clearly when he'd heard this flute music before, and Tom's words came back to him now:

Do the dead persist?

In the next instant, Joel thought of the poem Tom had recited to him, the poem in which a grief-stricken man, dying in the desert, was in the end visited by his phantom wife. It came to Joel again—this time more strongly—that everything he was experiencing now was a demented trick some madman was playing upon him, a sick sophisticated masque orchestrated to punish Joel for all the bad things he had done. Perhaps, Joel thought, this madman, whoever it was, had also, like Raddick, lost a dearly beloved, and that loss had unhinged him. Or perhaps his loved one had not died at all but was instead the victim of some catastrophic incident, like a brutal rape or a severely disfiguring accident.

Joel strove to abolish these thoughts, but he could not do it. The possibilities loomed up before him—possibilities that now seemed endless.

The dolorous flute piped on.

He considered that he might still be sleeping. His head was far from clear. And yet the longer he heard the strange sound of the flute, the more certain he grew that he was awake.

He lay there in delirious conjecture, shivering on the grass.

He breathed very shallowly, to coddle his shredded lungs.

At length, he eased himself out from under the shrubbery. The granite statuary watched him with blind stony eyes. He followed the sound of the flute. He walked around the north side of the house and soon came to a cement stairwell. It was a stairwell he'd not ever seen before, at the bottom of which stood a heavy metal door the color of stone. This door stood slightly ajar. Silvery light sprayed out through the partial opening, a pall of glowing mist hanging motionless along the floor of the stairwell. The flute was coming from behind that door. The music sounded so slow, yet so sophisticated. It was pitch-perfect. He started to think it was perhaps coming from a stereo.

In a state of dislocation, he stood for many minutes at the top of the stairwell. Then the flute player made a mistake and went back to replay the same notes. His heart leapt, the mistake confirming what he already implicitly knew: this was living music.

He stood for what seemed hours. Every second that passed increased his dread. The flute played on. The crickets panted. It was a gentle night. At last Joel crept down the cement steps.

All about him, the concrete exhaled its waves of cold. The walls seemed alive. Spiderwebs lay like little trampolines in the corners of the stairwell, and they glinted in the pewter light. At the bottom of the steps, Joel paused for an even longer time. He listened to the lulling sounds. Eventually he stepped over to the right so that he might catch a glimpse of who or what was playing, but when he set his foot down, a dead leaf exploded beneath his sneaker.

The music immediately stopped, and Joel stopped breathing. His heart pounded fiercely behind his sternum wall. At length, a rustling sounded from behind the door, as of pages being rearranged. Still, Joel didn't move. He kept his eyes riveted upon the door. Nothing happened. After thirty seconds, the flute resumed.

Joel did not move for a full fifteen minutes. Then, cautiously, he crept toward the open door until at last he was right upon it: he felt he must at any cost see who was inside. A current of air poured steadily out of the room and passed over him—through him, he felt. Very slowly and very carefully he leaned forward and looked in.

His eyes went huge: A slender woman stood playing her flute in the middle of the room.

This woman looked almost identical to his mother, and yet somehow she looked different. She was younger. Her long eyes were downcast. She was focused upon sheet music on a metal stand. She wore a white flowing dress with short sleeves, her arms bare and suntanned. Her straight hair hung silky and black, like the hair of a Japanese woman, down past the middle of her back. There were no rings upon her fingers, no bracelets upon her arms, no earrings in her earlobes. She was taller than Joel. She had a dark bony face, and she possessed a melancholy beauty.

There was something famished-looking in her cheeks, as if a great illness had once beset her and left a lasting mark there.

Joel felt his knees buckle.

He could imagine nothing in the world that would account for this slender swaying figure, and he sought frantically now to grasp what was happening, but his mind refused to focus.

Still playing, the young woman lifted her eyeballs from the music.

She saw Joel watching her.

She stopped playing at once, her eyes widening. Joel stood immobilized on the concrete floor. The steady stream of air passed over him. The woman seemed as astonished as Joel. And yet the first thing she did was glance to her left, at something outside the scope of Joel's vision. Then she looked back at Joel and raised her index finger to her lips, as if beseeching his secrecy.

Joel just then heard something else come from within the room, something like a growl or the low growly voice of a man, but he couldn't tell for sure what it was.

Instantly, Joel jerked back and pancaked himself against the cold hard wall of the stairwell.

His head spun.

His brain searched for explanations, and his pulse raced. The poem Tom recited flashed once again into his mind—the black-haired wife, her dress, her death by disease, so that for a moment's instant, because of the resemblance, Joel believed that indeed this was a sick man's game somehow being played out upon him. He understood furthermore that if this *was* a game, the woman inside the room must also be aware that it was a game—her finger raised to her lips suggested as much—and she was probably playing her flute now not out of pleasure but to indulge the game's orchestrator, under coercion or not Joel didn't know.

None of which, however, explained her astounding resemblance to his mother.

Then the horrifying implications flashed into his mind of the flute player *not* knowing this was a game, and he found that thought most chilling of all.

These things went through his head in a matter of moments.

Before he could consider what he would do next, the stone-colored door swung all the way open, spilling more silvery light out into the stairwell and over Joel, who was pinned against the wall; and then of all people Tom appeared in the doorway. Joel saw behind him the woman still standing in the same spot. She held her flute down at her side. In her other hand, a fresh cigarette was burning furiously between her fingers. She was watching Joel with black beautiful eyes. By now, Joel had grown so disoriented that he felt he was on the verge of collapse.

Tom smiled at him and spoke:

"You did run well," he said. "You beat me fair and square." Then his tone changed. "Joel, I'd like for you to meet someone. This is my sister Lia. Lia, this is Joel."

The woman did not speak but inclined her head. She seemed uncommonly interested, and she eyed Joel from head to toe and did not once avert her gaze. Then she took a slow drag from her cigarette and exhaled her silver soul upon the ceiling. She continued to stare. Joel swayed from dizziness. His face registered nothing but shock, which Tom noticed.

"What is it, Joel?" Tom said. "Oh, I see. We're twins," he explained, "but we're not monozygotic, of course."

That was the last thing Joel remembered of that strange summer night.

27

He opened his eyes to pitch black. His body was slick with sweat. His windpipe felt split down the center. He groped blindly for a light switch, but he felt nothing at all: no nightstand, no table, not even a wall. He swatted the empty air.

"Hello!" he said. "Hello! Is anyone there?"

His voice sounded hollow in the darkness. No answer came.

"Hello," he said. "Hello!"

There was nothing.

He waited a long time for his vision to acclimate to the darkness. It never did. At length, Joel closed his gritty eyes and sunk back into stormy sleep that lasted for days.

He was not, however, that whole time completely unconscious. It even seemed to him that at a number of different points someone was in the room with him, a presence he could not identify. This presence felt as if it was hovering right beside or above him, perhaps more than one person. Yet each time he tried to open his eyes, he was unable to: he felt totally paralyzed, from head to toe, and no matter how much he strained, he could not move a single muscle. In his confusion, he began to wonder if he'd been drugged. First he heard tiny voices, then angry voices, voices perhaps shouting at him, voices that grew in a wild crescendo of violence. Still, he was powerless to move or speak.

Then everything went quiet. He could move again. He partially woke from a vivid vision fraught with venomous fish and snakes and spiders; he woke partially to a human weight tilting the mattress he lay upon, someone sitting beside him. But when he opened his eyes, it was so dark that he could not see anything. After a while, he was not sure if he dreamed or woke.

Two or three times, a cool hand cupped his forehead. Joel simply lay there. He was soaked. A voice came to him out of the blackness. It was the voice of one he recognized, a voice that spoke calmly and at length about many things.

"What did you discover, Joseph?" the voice said. "What did you find in your quest for God? Did you find the evidence you were looking for? If so, where did you find it? Near-death experiences, astral dreams, transcendental Buddhist and Hindu claims of reincarnation? Old Hag, Ouija boards, 11:11, UFO sightings, ESP? And is that all? Do the claims add up, then? Do they constitute proof? Do they meet your criteria for certainty? Does the Old Hag live in the light of reason? And do the claims need no faith? Is the phenomena apprehended by observation? Tell me what's more convincing, Joseph: Mohammed moving a mountain, Christ resurrected, or mankind as an experiment in an alien's laboratory? Answer: it's a trick question. They're all equally unbelievable. No evidence exists for any of them. They all require an act of faith. You must reject them for that reason, and so must I. How otherwise would we know which to choose? And why? Why this over that?"

The voice went away. Joel listened. He heard no more. Then he fell asleep.

When the voice returned, the room was still pitch black, and he at first thought it was the voice of his mother. The voice said:

"Morality is inescapable for humans, even the amoral human, because convictions and thoughts and judgments are inescapable to a thinking brain. In this sense, the amoral life lived whimsically or violently or passively is still a life lived according to a certain moral code, be that code a code of violence or whimsy or passivity. Only an adversary ethic would tell you that others are the final standard of good and bad behavior: otherism means death to each individual person. There is something that comes before others, Joseph. Do you know what that something is?"

"Yes," Joel muttered.

"What is it?"

"It is the word made flesh."

"Yes," said the voice that was no longer female. "It is the word made flesh. It is the spirit made physical. Only the individual can perform that fundamental act of willing—of willing the word into flesh—of translating the mental into the physical, of defining oneself through one's thoughts that determine deeds. Morality—true morality—is the standard that guides human choices and decisions. It doesn't matter if you live alone upon an island, or if you live among millions of others. Morality in any case is necessary to human life. Life requires thought. Thought requires effort. Life therefore is effort. Life is work."

The voice fell silent. Joel could hear soft breathing in the dark. The presence beside him was motionless. At length, the voice resumed:

"I ask you: what within the human clay gives rise to good behavior and bad behavior? And why do we act at all? Is there some one phenomena we can pinpoint that unites these things? The answer is yes, there is something we can pinpoint, and that something is called *life*. Life is the thing that unites existence and consciousness and human action."

The voice stopped and was silent for so long that Joel thought it had finished. Then it spoke again:

"To live, we must all act. And more: we must act in a certain way."

"In which way?" Joel said. He felt himself barely able to speak.

"In a way that fosters life. *The things that nourish and give warmth and enhance life are deemed good, and those that frustrate and threaten are deemed bad.* The moral is the thing that promotes one's welfare; the immoral is the self-destructive. Don't think in terms of is this act moral or immoral, but ask instead: will this action harm me over time? Will it enhance my mind and my life? Or will it not? That is true morality. Prudential ethics reject the deadly assumption that morality is rooted first in others. It rejects the assumption that morality involves living for others, which is an assumption that puts the happiness and well-being of each human out of reach and opens the doors wide for every manner of faith and faith-based ethics and arbitrary decree and more, each one ultimately and equally unverifiable. There is a great enemy upon the earth, Joseph, and that enemy is blind belief."

"What of those who *want* to believe?" Joel said or thought he said.

"Anyone can believe whatever he wants about anything. That doesn't make it true. Santa Claus, or the Tooth Fairy? I do not demur. But remember this: ignorance is not bliss, and force is the ultimate refuge of blind belief. You cannot claim allegiance to rationality and blind belief at the same time. A house divided against itself can't stand."

The voice ceased, and Joel slept. He was awakened by a cool cloth upon his forehead. He opened his eyes but saw nothing except black. The voice spoke:

"Religion has tricked the world into believing that morality cannot exist if God doesn't exist. What a sorry joke for us to discover after all that morality not only can exist if you kill God, but that morality can *only* exist if you kill God."

Moral law (the voice quoted) *is as real as human nature, within which it has its existence. Strange, indeed, if man alone of all living beings could realize his highest welfare in disregard of the principles of his own nature. And this nature, we must remember, is what it is—is always concrete and definite. Indeed the sceptic nowhere else assumes the absence of principles through obedience to which the highest form of life can be attained. He does not assume that a lily, which requires abundant moisture and rich soil, could grow on and arid rock, nor that a polar bear could flourish in a tropical jungle. No less certain than would be the failure of such attempts, must be the failure of man to realize, in disregard of the laws of his being, the values of which he is capable. The structure of man's nature, as conscious and spiritual, grounds laws just as real as those of his physical life, and just as truly objective.*

28

The quality of the darkness changed. A warm breeze passed over him. Joel's eyes flipped open. He found himself staring wide-eyed at a mysterious green moon. He was fully clothed except for his socks and shoes, and he lay on a small iron bed. The covers were soaked. He scanned the room. It was a place he'd never seen before. Across from him, through the open window, the moon shone so brightly that it hurt his eyes to look upon. Each time he blinked, pins of pain radiated outwardly behind both his eyeballs. He hung his leg out of the bed: the bones inside him felt dislocated, the meat tightly packed inside. At length, Joel rose from the bed and went across the room. He stood in front of the open window.

He was two stories high. He did not recognize the township below him. There were no streetlamps outside, and yet the moon illuminated everything in a strange greenish glow. Instruments of labor lay strewn across the ground: wheelbarrows and lumber, pallets of brick, barrels of mortar, cement, masonry, sod. There was nobody around. The town appeared deserted, dusted in a thick coating of lime.

Wind blew through the empty streets and came up the building and over him through the open window.

Beyond the town, the mountains stood darkly against the sky. Bats were swarming across the face of moon. Joel pulled on his socks and shoes and climbed out through the fire escape. From the light of the moon, the metal staircase lay duplicated in isometric shadows across the brick building. Everything was silent.

Down on the street, the air smelled even more strongly of dust and lime. Above the crooked silhouettes of the buildings, the green moon hung engorged. Joel had the unshakable sense now, just as he had on the day of his car accident, that there was something urgent he must attend to. Yet no matter how hard he tried, he could not recollect what it was. That was when he saw the man watching him at the end of the street. This man was sunk in shadows. Joel could tell from his size alone that it was a masculine figure. The figure stared at Joel steadfastly, and he was slender and exceptionally tall. He was dressed in a long black cloak. His bright eyes beamed. Then suddenly those eyes jerked past Joel, above Joel's shoulder, and Joel turned to follow his gaze.

On the opposite street corner, a smaller figure stood like an old crone. This figure was also cloaked in black, a wide cowl draped over its head. While Joel was staring, the crone-like shape extended a bony arm, sliding the arm out from somewhere within the dark folds of the sleeve, exposing a skeletal wrist. The figure beckoned him. Joel approached. Every step increased his fear. The warm air blew against his face. There was dust upon everything, and everything appeared radioactive in the unearthly light.

Halfway there, a rasp sounded from the other corner. Joel looked back. The tall figure had scraped a matchstick on the brick building beside him. He brought the match up to his face and lit the cigarette hanging from his mouth, and in the glow of the flame, Joel saw him in full. It was his father.

"Come here," the crone hissed. Just swung back around. That voice came at him like a voice from his buried past.

Joel continued walking toward the cowled figure. The closer he got, the more shadowy the figure grew. The figure even tucked its head deeper into its chest, as if to avert its face. Joel's anxiety intensified, until he stood in front of it at last.

The figure lifted its head.

Inside the cowl, Joel saw only blackness. Abruptly, then, the figure opened the cloak. What Joel saw was an emaciated female form all smeared with blood. Gobs of blood were caked and hanging in the matted pubic hairs and in the gashlike cleft. There was fresh blood upon the breasts, and upon the pale thighs, and upon the bony shins. This blood was sourced in a massive wound that ran the entire circumference of the neck. Even now as he watched, that wound pumped out jets of blood which were vomiting down the front of her body. The figure hissed at him again:

"Murder," it said. And it pointed not at Joel but at his father.

Yet Joel could not avert his eyes from the bloody body, because he also knew who this woman was: it was the girl Justine.

When he finally looked back to his father, his father was no longer there. He turned again to Justine, but it wasn't Justine anymore. It was his mother, who stood naked and smiling at him with blood smeared all over her body, her gashed-open neck disgorging shiny slabs of blood.

29

He came up gasping. He lay on his back, drenched with his sweat. His breathing gradually normalized, and his eyes gradually acclimated. He watched the room compose itself out of the ashen light. He did not know where he was, nor how long he had been unconscious. He did not know if it was morning or evening. Yet he remembered everything else: he remembered running to the rarified summit, the aftermath, the flute player who Tom said was his twin sister. He touched the back of his hand to his forehead. His fever had broken. On the floor beside him, someone had left a large pitcher of iced water.

Joel reach down and lifted the pitcher off the floor. He drank all of it. Then he dropped back onto the pillow and fell asleep.

When he opened his eyes again, he didn't know if it was the same day, or even the same week or month. The window facing him opened to rough-barked trees and a draining sky. There was a bathroom across the way. Joel swung his legs out of bed and stood up. His head whirled. His lower back, his rear end, every muscle in his body felt shattered from the run. He hobbled over to the window and saw immediately where he was. He was in the basement of the big gloomy house that belonged to the expriest.

In the bathroom, there were clean towels and a pair of clean socks and a long-sleeved thermal shirt. Joel showered carefully. After he was finished, he tugged the socks on and then the shirt. He went back into the bedroom and slipped on his pants. He left the room.

Outside, the sun sat throbbing in a wide notch over the western mountains. There was no wind. Shadows lay like water upon the grass. The great trees were laved in light.

Joel walked around the house to the chapel-like building. The more he moved, the more his muscle soreness lifted. At the doorway of the building, cold air came sliding out over him. He walked through the building and into the garden. There was no sign of life. He approached the stone table and once again scrutinized the intricate equations which were written there. These equations fascinated him endlessly. Once more, he felt himself on the verge of apprehending something important about them, but in the end, their meaning remained just beyond his reach.

He looked down at the most recent equation of all:

GOD = BREADTH, DEPTH, HEIGHT, WIDTH

What did that mean?

Why was it so familiar to him?

Before he had time to actually consider the question, he became aware of a sound like breathing once again coming from the dark room behind him. He knew in a heartbeat that it was that same breath he'd heard before, except it was more pronounced now.

Joel hesitated, then turned.

And there she was.

She stood at the far end of the building, in the small cube of light that filled the opposing doorway. She wore the same streaming white dress that she had the night he'd seen her playing the flute. Her sable hair hung loose and flowing. She stood blinking at him in the dying daylight. He could think only of his mother, so much did this young woman resemble her.

After a moment, she entered the building and vanished, absorbed by the blackness within. Yet he could hear the sound of her breath the entire time, and he could see a vague outline of her ghostly shape. Quickly she reappeared—a white figure advancing toward him through the dark—and before he knew it, she was standing in front of him in the garden.

He was very conscious the entire time of her breathing, how audible it was, how strange.

She did not smile at him, and her face was absolutely calm. There was something almost animal about her, animal and shy, like a giraffe. Her eyes were liquid with life. He thought again and again of his mother and his mother's gaze, which he remembered perfectly, and which contained the same calm, the same burning intelligence. The woman wore black canvas shoes. In her left hand, she held a black pencil and in her right a spiral-bound notebook. Almost unnoticeably, she bowed to him. Then she stood there, slender and remote.

"Hello," he said. His voice seemed to him inordinately loud in the stillness of the garden.

She passed him the notebook.

Before anything, he saw that this was the same writing that was on the stone table just behind him—and the same writing on the back of his father's portrait: the dark designer print without flaw. He didn't give himself time to consider the ramifications of this but read the words she had written:

Hello, Joel. I was born without at voicebox. I must communicate with you through the written word. My lack of larynx distorts my respiration, and that is why my breathing is loud.

Yet it wasn't loud, not exactly. It wasn't labored or raspy enough to be loud. It was to him deeply comforting, he wasn't sure why. Just as he remarked this to himself, it dawned upon him, rather like a revelation, why the sound of *her* breath in particular was so familiar to him. Perhaps at that moment she detected something like a catch in his own breath, for she looked at him with a slight narrowing of her eyes and a just-perceptible tilt of her head. He didn't say anything, but he thought of the finger she'd held to her lips, whatever night that was, when he'd seen her playing the flute. That gesture suddenly took on whole new dimensions in his mind.

She wrote:

Are you feeling better?

"Yes," he said. "Thank you for the water."

She nodded.

"How long was I there?" he said. "I have no idea how much time has passed."

She wrote:

You've been very sick.

"Yes," he said.

She watched him.

"Is August over?" he said.

She nodded again. And then with the same peculiar purchase on his thoughts that her brother seemed to have, she wrote:

Hearing you speak now confirms what I knew all along.

"What?" he said.

She wrote:

It was you who called that day in April.

He read those words not with shock but a disconcerting confirmation of the revelation he had just had: because he himself had deduced that very thing.

"Why did you answer the phone," he said, "if you can't speak?"

She wrote:

My father used to call that number to give me instructions. He reported them to me and I listened.

"What instructions?" Joel said.

She wrote:

For his garden and his business.

She handed him the notebook and watched him. Then she reached over and wrote:

I've been curious about you for a long, long time. I've never seen you before.

That sent another tremor down his spine. But a part of him was beginning to understand. They were both silent for several seconds. Her breathing remained rich, resonant.

"Are you a mathematician?" he said.

She wrote:

I'm an arithmomaniac, more accurately. I can't help it. I was born with the gift of math and no voice. Numbers have always comforted me.

He closed his eyes. "Do you do math for a living?" His eyes were still closed.

She wrote:

Yes, I do.

"What do you do?" he said.

She wrote:

I'm a code-breaker.

He scowled. "Do you write music as well? Was that your music I heard the other night?"

She nodded once. Her flute fingers moved unconsciously. He noted the thick writing callous on her index finger. "I've never heard music like that before," he said. "I felt as if I were dreaming."

She wrote:

Perhaps you were.

She smiled.

He frowned and shut his eyes again, half expecting that she would not be there when he opened them. But she was there. She was still standing before him, staring at him with her dark gaze.

She wrote:

Did you know that music is mathematical, Joel?

He shook his head. "I don't know anything about math," he said. "Not anymore."

She narrowed her eyes on him. She wrote:

Anymore?

He didn't say anything.

Then she wrote:

Joel, is math an invention or discovery?

"It is an invention," Joel said.

She wrote:

See, you do know something about math. Now tell me why it's an invention.

"Because numbers don't exist without humans," he said.

She wrote:

Math wouldn't exist, then, if humans didn't exist?

"Yes," he said.

She wrote:

And what is math?

He was silent for several beats. "Math is quantification," he said.

She wrote:

That's correct. Math is the science of quantification, the science of computation and measurement.

He didn't say anything.

She wrote:

Do you know why that's significant?

"No," he said.

She flipped the page over and proceeded to write for a very long time, filling up more than two full sheets. Joel waited. He watched her. He was struck once more by the speed and fluidity with which she wrote, a small scowl of concentration knit into the middle of her forehead.

At last, she handed him the notebook. This is what it said:

Numbers are language, and language is abstraction. But language refers to concrete things. Definitions are ultimately self-evident: when you want to show someone what the word "water" means, you pour water over that person's hand and say: This that you feel on your hand is what I mean by the word water. The "this" is reality; it is the concrete. The word water is the abstraction. Refutations of all other forms of agnosticism and pragmatism are similarly straightforward. The pragmatist's basic error is in not realizing that language refers to actual things in reality. Math is a microcosm of this method. Math in pared-down form exemplifies the human method of cognition. But math is only a model. We live by knowledge, Joel. And epistemology is the science of knowledge. Epistemology starts and ends with three simple words: consciousness is awareness.

Joel looked up at her. She was staring at him intently. He turned back to the notebook:

Consciousness is awareness. That is an epistemological fundamental which can't be refuted or denied, since any theory of knowledge that tries to refute the fact that consciousness is awareness must rely on the awareness of consciousness to refute it.

First comes the external world which each consciousness is born into. That world is also known as reality, or existence. Then comes the awareness of it. These two things are separate, but not equal: by definition, the external must come first, before there can be an awareness of it.

Reality is existence, and existence is everything.

There's existence, and there's essence—or, in the language of Thomas Aquinas, esse, which is identity. To be, in other words, is to be some THING.

Thomas Aquinas taught us that the only alternative to that which exists is that which does not exist. But that which does not exist doesn't exist.

The universe, said Thomas Aquinas, is the sum total of everything. And there is no nothing, said Victor Hugo.

For this reason, there cannot be "the possibility of many universes." Nor is there anything "beyond the universe": if something exists, it is by definition part of the universe. If it does not exist, it does not exist.

Metaphysically, the fact of existence is the peg upon which the entirety of human knowledge hangs, and any attempt to deny existence refutes itself at the outset, because even the barest and most laconic denial of existence implies some kind of existence.

"Nature is what we call everything that can in anyway be captured by the intellect, for a thing is not intelligible except through its definition and essence," said Thomas Aquinas.

Look around.

(Joel looked.)

All the things you see now are existing things. They are all different, but they have one essential thing in common: they all exist.

Metaphysically, the facts are these:

Existence is everything.

There is no nothing.

Existence is reality.

Reality is what's real.

Nature is reality.

The universe is everything.

Nature is the universe.

There is no super-nature.
All else proceeds from that.

Joel stopped reading. He looked up at her. She had not moved at all. She watched him patiently. Her breathing was very pronounced and soothing. He read on:

Consciousness by its very definition is always of or about something apart from itself. Consciousness by definition is relational. "No one perceives that he understands except from this, that he understands something: because he must first know something before he knows that he knows," said Aquinas.

"Consciousness, is irreducible because consciousness can't be reduced to other facts or broken into component parts. Consciousness is an ultimate datum of experience...at the very root of all mental activity."

There exists an external universe, which human consciousness does not in any way create but only apprehends. It measures. And that is what math does.

"Today's scientists have substituted mathematics for experiments, and they wander off through equation after equation, and eventually build a structure which has no relation to reality."

Do you know who said that, Joel?

Joel shook his head but didn't look at her. He continued reading:

You CAN easily live without math, but you cannot live without reality. Math measures reality. But math is just a tool, one of many. Never forget that, Joel.

It took him ten minutes to read it all. The entire time, while he read, they stood in the diminishing daylight. The sound of her breath eased his mind, and her dreamy presence eased him too. The more he heard her breath, the more he wanted to hear it. Thus, without quite meaning to, he muttered aloud but very quietly:

"Your breath."

In response to which, she took the notebook from him and wrote something else, something he would never forget. She wrote:

Spirit is breath, breath is life, and the fruit of the Spirit is in all goodness and truth. These words I write to you are spirit, and they are life.

While he was still reading from the notebook, she reached over and wrote:

It's time now, Joel.

He looked up at her with surprise, but she had already turned away.

"Time for what?" he said.

She turned back to him and reached once more for the notebook and wrote:

Time to murder and create.

30

He followed her back through the empty building.

On the other side, under an indigo sky, the big house sat brooding among the trees, and the sunset was pinking all the front windows. The membranous moon floated up over the eastern horizon.

She walked with purpose. She did not look back to see if he was following. Joel stared at the small sharp stones that snapped beneath her shoes. They went past the stagnant goldfish pond with its headless statuary submerged to the waist in water. She moved with deceptive speed and did not appear to hurry, though her stride was swift. Only after they'd stopped did it occur to Joel that her manner of moving was, in a complicated way, as much like her brother's as it was like his mother's. She glided up the porch steps, and then she turned to him. She stared straight into his eyes.

"What is it?" he said.

She didn't respond.

"What are we doing here?"

Still, she didn't in any way acknowledge that she'd heard him. She only breathed and watched him. He listened and looked back into her eyes, like bottomless wells. She held the notebook at her side. The window behind her was filled with coral light. The silence was finally broken by the croak of a crow. Joel looked up. A huge black bird pounded by, sunlight glinting off its back. When the crow was gone, Joel looked away. He stared at the fat moon on the other side of the sky.

Then Lia opened the front door, and he entered.

She led him down and L-shaped hallway at the end of which was a steep staircase. The steps terminated in utter darkness. She mounted them. The rhythm of her breath increased. At the top of the steps, the darkness about them grew fur. Lia stopped and stood. His eyes refused to adjust to the dark. At last, he discerned a yellowish doorknob, like a miniature moon, hovering at her hip.

"Is this your room?" he said.

In response to which, she pinned him to the wall again with her enigmatic eyes. He could see her eyes faintly gleaming. He listened to her breath and very soon it came to sound to him as if it were sourced within *his* own body. And when he realized this, his pulse raced even more, and his anxiety intensified— at which moment he thought he caught the suggestion of a dim intent upon her face: an intimation that she might suddenly club him, or kiss him. His blood went cold. But she did neither. Instead, she lifted the notebook and scrawled something in large letters and passed the notebook to him. He had to squint to read it. It said:

No, Joel. It's *your* room.

With that, she turned the glowing doorknob and flung open the door. Gales of moonlight came spilling out like nacre tides over his shoes and his pant legs.

The butterscotch tomcat bolted out of the room and disappeared into the darkness.

31

The room was penitential. A single lamp sat extinguished on the window sill. Beneath that were three dark objects that Joel couldn't make out. The window was open. The evening breeze poured into the room, puffing the curtains like sails.

Joel stood on the threshold and turned to her. She gestured with her chin toward the three dark objects. He hesitated and then entered. She followed. A gust of wind came into the room, and the door behind them banged shut. He swiveled around. She was still right there, breathing over his shoulder. He faced forward again and approached the objects.

They were three large trunks. Their lids were down but unlatched. Atop the first trunk sat a stack of four small thick books whose titles he couldn't make out. Suddenly, the lamp ignited beside him, and a flame-like tongue of light flickered against the window. The lamplight sent a bolt of pain through his eyes. He squinted against the glare. Once his eyes adjusted, he saw a bluish-white glow that filled the room and fell out through the open window down onto the grass below. He could clearly see all four books now, and he picked up the one on top:

The Secret History
In quo sunt omnes thesauri sapientiae et scientiae absconditi

He opened to its title page. No authorship was listed, but a publishers name was:

Great Redactor Press

The paper was brownish and very coarse, durable, the kind of paper that lasts forever. Joel flipped back to the front cover. The art was much different from the previous book—the book he'd seen in the woods—but the artist was clearly the same.

On this cover, there was no man and no surging sea but a woman who stood intently reading beside a high window, beyond which, in the night sky, a solitary star pulsed above a slender moon. She was reading from a titleless tome. Her blouse was badly torn, both her breasts completely exposed. At her feet, a sinuous serpent with a triangular head lay half erect. There was a lank and drooling hound hidden behind the door of the room. The woman's forehead was wrinkled in concentration. The quality of the craftsmanship took Joel aback.

He moved to look at the other three book covers and indeed glimpsed the very book he'd come across in the woods. But just as he went to lift it from the trunk, Lia passed her notebook to him. He jerked back in surprise. He'd been so engrossed in the picture that he'd not expected her. He heard her own breath catch as well, and then he saw her grave face flickering in the lamplight. At that moment, she looked to him more like his mother than ever before. He grew nervous. Still, she held the notebook out to him. Her lips were slightly parted. Her teeth shone with a bluish cast. At length, he reached for her notebook, and as he gripped it, his fingers brushed against hers. He felt he had touched a ghost, her skin so icy and so soft.

He looked down at the words she had written:

There were printed one thousand copies of this book. Each one of them had a different cover design, which was hand-painted by the author. Now there are only five copies left. Of those, four are right here in this room.

"What became of the others?" he said.

She wrote:

They were burned.

"Burned by whom?"

He saw a nerve twitch along her cheekbone, or perhaps it was only the play of the licking lamplight. She wrote:

Your father.

"What?"

But she didn't respond.

"How do you know that one other book remains?"

She stared at him for a long time. Then she wrote:

Because you have it, Joel.

"I?"

She nodded minutely. She took the notebook from him and left in its stead something else.

He looked down at what he now held:

It was a typewritten manuscript.

It shone with the same bluish cast as her teeth.

Outside, the dead moon hovered.

He glanced out the window and stared at the moon, then he looked back to her, then down at the manuscript in his hand. For a full thirty seconds, he stared apprehensively at what he held.

When he lifted his eyes to her again, she was not there.

She wasn't anywhere.

32

And yet for several minutes, he thought he could still hear her breath, distant but distinct. Then he didn't hear anything.

"Lia?" he said. His voice reverberated through the empty room.

He waited. She did not reappear. He stood there for some time, staring at the floor and listening. Eventually he moved closer to the window. The bluish lamplight was leaping against the glass. The door to the room stood wide open now, and beyond it lay only darkness. Then, for a split second, he thought he saw her sitting in a room across the way, watching him. Except now she had no mouth, only a smooth lump where the mouth should have been. He caught his breath, and blinked, and she was no longer there. A spasm went through him. For minutes he simply stood.

Finally, with dread, he turned to the pages he held in his hand. This is what he read:

CONFESSION
by William Michael Morgan
(to no one, to everyone)

Small things happen, minor events occur, details emerge...

In the spring and summer of 19--, I was living in northern California, in a boardinghouse owned by my stepmother Terri Latham. All three of Terri's children lived with her, I was number four. Terri's real children are Heather Case, Keith Case, and Justine Latham, who is her youngest, and about whom this letter (which is not really a letter) is so singularly concerned. Of them all, I'm the oldest by far. I should note that Terri is not my blood mother, and yet I love her dearly, and never once did Terri treat me any differently than she treated her real children.

At that time in my life, I was drinking a great deal. In fact, I was drinking more than ever before, and I was also suicidally depressed. My beautiful wife Lauren had left me not too long before, and it was during this time that I felt her absence most profoundly. In addition to this — or perhaps I should say because of it — my lifelong tendency toward hypochondria had escalated out of control. I worried constantly about my physical and psychological health. I worried about everything from hepatitis to head lice to herpes to the hypochondria itself, and many days and nights I spent gnawing my nails in the chemical light, reeking of booze and bleach, in rooms full of broken glass and razor blades. I worried about cancer, I worried about death. Death. Always death. And yet sometimes, suddenly, I would see with total clarity how far gone I was, how obsessive my worries had become. And then the cycle would begin anew but in a different way: my worries would shift to my mental health. I worried very much that I was losing my mind, and I worry that up to this day, this exact moment.

None of what follows would be intelligible without some knowledge of my binge drinking and drug abuse, yet those periods were always intermixed with periods of great lucidity and sobriety. Even more significant, however, is that it would be impossible to comprehend any of this without addressing this central fact: throughout my whole life, starting when I was a young boy, my sexual desires have been at the root of virtually every frustration, vice, and sin whose motions have worked inside my members. Obviously, I refer to lust, but more specifically I refer to lust for the female — the female flesh.

This isn't unique — I don't pretend it is — the omnipresent and overbearing male sex drive. On the contrary, it borders on the banal. Still, it is the predilection that men have for the visual, for visual stimulation, that is the driving force behind pornography, and all other such things. In a very real sense, pornography and the apparent ridiculousness of it is not so ridiculous after all, insofar as it all derives from purely biological forces that stimulate the sex urge in men. And yet even though I do believe it's natural in this sense of the word, as I suppose everything is at root, it does not make pornography any less insidious.

Porn, prostitution, strippers, masturbation, lust in general, it has a hugely destructive potential, as many natural things do, and for one simple reason: it's habit-forming. Like all compulsions, lust can own you in full if you're not fully vigilant. The power of this particular addiction is among the easiest to underestimate, though it must never be underestimated, because sex and lust is such a vital and even healthy part of the human condition. And that's what makes it so easy to underestimate — to rationalize, even as it gains power over you — and in fact, when I was fourteen, I remember very specifically thinking it was okay to indulge myself in pornography and the like because I believed then that it would not be a problem to do away with when I wanted, when I chose. And then, about one year later, I found, to my horror, that I was NOT so easily able to give it up. Since that time, I've been addicted to an almost endless number of different things, and I can say for certain now that lust is for me the profoundest addiction of them all. The so-called physical or chemical components of addictions — nicotine, heroin, alcohol — these are comparatively easy to overcome, primarily because the physical withdrawal goes away in a matter of days. The hard part of addiction is the psychological component, because it lasts years and may never completely go away, lust especially, as it never has with me, though I ceased to indulge in it long ago.

Some people love food, some people love drugs, some people love violence, some people love lust.

And yet if reaching the Highest is the goal — which it is, and I WILL one day reach the highest — everything, including lust, must be exorcised from the human brain and the human body.

I, William Michael Morgan, was never meant to be under the control of lust and pornography and masturbation. That is not what I wanted from my life, which is the one and only life I have. I was meant for more. Yet I've walked around lust-crazed for most of my life.

Reading over what I've written so far, I see that I must clarify something: the lust that burns within me and that is such a huge part of me is not uncontrollable, and I do not think it's inordinate in my case. From the time I turned twenty-two, I've almost always been able to control my lust, inasmuch as I have not indulged it. But even in not indulging it, it haunts me: my preoccupation with and my desire for the female flesh looms at the forefront of my brain, and I sometimes feel I've lusted my heart away.

In June of that same year, J came to town. J is a man about whom I could write volumes but won't.

I loved J very much, and I still do to this day. He doesn't know that he and I are half brothers. I've never told him, because I think it would be an act of great disloyalty to my father and to my mother — and to that monumental act of lust and violence by which I was conceived and which ultimately brought me screaming through the bone-carved gates.

Terri of course remembered J very well, from the days when he was a child and she watched after him. Terri has always had a special place in her heart for J — she told me so herself. Why is this? I think because there is something in J that's infinitely tragic. Terri invited him to stay with us and he accepted. He and I became very close during this time. It was literature that cemented our friendship. J loves literature. He is an extraordinarily complex person, and I do not pretend to understand him. He's strange, remarkable. I don't exaggerate when I say that I've never known anyone else like him. And the more you get to know him, the more you realize it is impossible to ever truly know him. He is in some ways the sanest person I've ever met. But in other ways, he is the oddest. There's a scripture that reads: "If any man offend not in word, the same is a perfect man, and able to bridle his whole body." That is what I think of when I think of J.

He has the ability to multiply five digit numbers in his head. He can draw likenesses more exactly than anyone I've ever seen. His sense of direction is almost freakish. And yet none of these are really what sets J apart. What sets him apart is the sheer strength of his will. Surely this comes from his unbelievable father.

I once read a real-life account of a stonemason in the days of the Spanish Inquisition who was tortured on the rack almost every day for over a year by his Inquisitors. That man never broke. He never renounced his Pagan beliefs, even though he was badly crippled for the rest of his life. In the end, the Inquisitors relented. I thought of J when I read about that, because that's the kind of willpower J possesses. He has something inherently inside him, something closely related to will but not quite will, something beyond will, which in any given endeavor strives after The Highest. Very probably, I think, that is why J turned to religion when he was young, despite the fact that neither of his parents were religious. Yet the sadness J carries within him is sourced so deeply that he and he alone knows how far down it goes — and perhaps he himself does not even know.

J was eighteen years old when he came, one year out of high school. He was restless and dispossessed. He and I drank a great deal together, and we associated during that time with a motley and dissolute crowd. J's smallish stature made him an easy target, and so did his silence, but J is not one to trifle with. He's an elite athlete, wrestler, runner, and more, and many was the time that I saw him beat bloody grown men twice his size. Undoubtedly J has been one of the four most important people in my life, and that's why I dwell at such length upon him here. Still, I believe he figures into this story in some other significant way, though I do not exactly know what way that is.

J and I spent many hours discussing books and poems. I can say now in all sincerity that those conversations are among the most treasured and most influential and most satisfying conversations of my life. Books are as much a passion with J as they are with me, though he does not share my love of book-collecting and bookmaking and so forth. He reads constantly, however, and he remembers everything he reads.

That day J left for good — the last time I ever saw him — he gave me several pencil portraits that he himself had drawn. Most (though not all) of these are self-portraits, and I've always privately regarded his near-obsessive self-portraiture as symbolic: symbolic of him seeking to understand himself, to see himself more clearly, more fully. I loved his artwork. I loved it more than any other artwork I've known, and I once told him so. It embarrassed him. There are many people who can draw realistically, but I've never seen the quality of longing that J injects into his faces. His portraits are much more than mere likenesses. They contain a passion that outstrips portraiture. J gave me these drawings without my asking for them. He gave them to me because he knew how much I loved them. It was a gesture on his part that meant a great deal to me. J is not demonstrative. He gave me something else as well, a thing of truly inestimable worth. He gave me a large and precious stone, ovular and heavy and whelked, with small depressions like the moon. It consisted primarily of incorruptible gold mixed with something I'd never heard of, something J said was extremely rare, a mineral that was blue-colored and silver. J had gotten this stone from his father — he stole it, he said — who had once given it to his new bride. But J told me something else about it, which I found incredible, but my father corroborated the story before he died. J told me that my father had once stolen this same stone from J's father, claiming that he, Shelby Morgan, was the rightful owner, because he'd seen it first, in the mines. But J's father is the one who excavated it, did all the work, because (as Neil claimed) my father didn't understand the value and complexity, the sheer rarity, of what he'd found. Neil was the man who brought that stone out of the earth and into the light of day, that much is true. According to J, his father stole it back from my father.

In the end, none of this matters (probably) because they're almost all dead now. In any case, I believe that this precious stone had become a heavy, heavy burden to J and was no longer beautiful to him at all. I believe it became nothing more than a sad reminder, and not of any worth to him now that she was gone.

So he gave it to me.

I later learned from my father that Neil had discovered this stone in a small mine that he himself had staked and built, with my father's help, a mine hidden in a remote section of the Purple Mountains.

"It's just a rock," are the last words J ever spoke to me, that day he left, in the midst of the worst case of katzenjammers I ever had, a black bitter day the memory of which, even now, these many years later, brings a great sorrow upon my heart. And then a mysterious thing happened: that stone simply disappeared.

It vanished. Where? I do not have any idea. I truly don't. Obviously it was taken, but taken by whom? I kept it under lock and key at all times. No one — and I mean no one — knew where it was. Apart from sweet, sweet Lauren (and T, of course) nobody in the world knew anything about it. I showed it to no one else. Even Lauren only saw it once, the day she last visited me, not long after J had left, which was some time after she and I divorced.

Out of respect for J, I've not ever mentioned him by name to anyone, and I've done so because J is an intensely private person—more so than anyone I've ever known. So that even if Lauren never set eyes upon him, as she never will, I believe that J and the tiny part of his private life I was privy to should remain secret. Yet I did tell Lauren the story of how according to J that stone was found, though I did not use real names. I thought Lauren wouldn't believe it. I underestimated her, as usual. She not only believed it — she was fascinated by it, and fascinated by the stone itself. She even drew a picture of her idea of the hidden mine as she conceived it. I thought that her picture possessed a great power, and many times I've wanted to look at it again, to see it. It haunts me in a way, but Lauren has that picture, and never the two of us shall meet again.

I would note also that Lauren fell in love with the incorruptible stone that J gave to me. She adored it so much that if I still had it, it would be hers in a moment, because no one in the world would treasure it more.

The stone was with me for a total of three months, and then it vanished. I told Lauren once that it had disappeared, and she was shocked, saddened, as puzzled as me.

My lifelong trouble in the flesh has caused me to commit countless crimes of the flesh — for they that are after the flesh do mind the things of the flesh, but they that are after the Spirit the things of the Spirit, and to be carnally minded is death, but to be spiritually minded is life and peace. Live after the flesh, and your spirit will die. But through the Spirit mortify the deeds of the body, and you'll live. Two flesh-crimes in particular condemn me most. First, I am almost certain I inappropriately touched with my hands and mouth my stepsister Heather, on a night I eventually blacked-out drunk. At the time, I believe Heather herself was not fully conscious either. It makes me sick to admit this, and even more sick to admit that I simply can't remember for certain what exactly happened (I could never ask her), and yet I've resolved on total honesty.

As reprehensible as that is, however, it's only a prelude. I've committed and even greater flesh-crime.

Terri Latham's youngest daughter Justine was a shy and quiet girl who was also exceptionally sweet. No one but Terri and the man who impregnated her knew who Justine's actual father was, including, I believe, Justine, and yet I've always had my suspicions.

I note also that Justine was not overly shy with me, in part because she trusted me, foolishly, it turns out, and also because she liked me, and even confided in me on a number of different occasions.

Physically, Justine was very mature for her age, and I confess now that I was aroused by Justine, in spite of myself. She was only fourteen years old then, but she looked much older, not that that matters. She was also exceptionally beautiful.

At this time, a man named Philip Lambert was boarding at Terri's house. Lambert was a man in his late thirties, a dockworker, like J, but unlike J, he was a complete boor. He was also violent, and from the beginning I saw him as a dangerous person. He had eyes for Justine.

One day, he called for her to bring a glass of water to his room. He did this on the pretext that he was sick and could not get out of bed. When she came to his room, he tried to kiss her. She clawed his face, which infuriated him. He beat her across the back with the buckle on his belt and hit her several times before she got free, and still he came after her. He thought that the two of them were alone in the house. He was wrong. There was one other person there, and that other person was J.

J made Lambert seriously pay for what he'd done to Justine. He broke both of Lambert's arms and threw Lambert out of the house, and Lambert never came back.

Justine was upset but, curiously, not overly so, it seemed to me. Not long after that, on an afternoon when I was alone in my room, she came to me. I lived in the basement of that house and had the whole downstairs area to myself. There was a network of pipes and plumbing down there that made a lot of racket, so that from above you could not hear anything happening in my room. Justine knocked on my door. She described to me in detail what had happened with Philip Lambert. She spoke frankly, and even laughed once in sheer disbelief at the whole situation, which she could not believe. Then she asked me if she could have something to drink, as she sometimes did, and I gave her a beer, as I always did whenever she asked. I should also say for the record that I was very drunk myself at the time. Justine was not crying or anything. I however had been crying, for reasons of my own, unrelated to her, and I'd also been drinking for three days straight, but I wasn't anywhere close to incoherent. That fact is important to note: I was in full possession of my faculties. I'd almost drunk myself sober, in fact, which I mention because I want to make it perfectly clear that I was in my right mind. I also remember everything clearly, and at every point I was in control of myself. I even at one point asked myself: can I stop? The answer was yes.

Justine was an affectionate person by nature, with those whom she trusted, and I was one of those people, probably because I'd known her for many years. I'd lived with her, on and off, since she was a baby, and all throughout that time I can honestly say that when she would hug me, or kiss me goodnight, my feelings were always chaste.

But something changed on this particular day, I don't know why, and it happened when she hugged me. I then began to touch her all over body.

That afternoon is when I raped Justine Latham.

It was I who raped Justine. It was not Philip Lambert.

One week later, Justine hung herself, and the only thing she left behind was a note written in her own blood that said:

When that unspeakable episode was over, Justine left my room in shock. She could not even cry or cry out for being too stunned. I lay back on my bed and stared up at my window overhead. It was a narrow window that opened to a large garden. Children were playing outside. The afternoon sun came in through the window, it was very warm. I lay there staring. After a while, a spider came crawling down the window, on the other side of the glass. It was a large, poisonous-looking spider, fire-red, a spider I'd never seen before. Watching it crawl, I felt a sudden sense of panic and a great sickness at —

Here Joel broke off reading and crumpled to the floor. The impression this manuscript made on him was indescribable. He wondered now not *if* someone was playing a perverted joke upon him, but who and how. In this state of mind, he ran again and again over every single possibility he could conceive, but nothing made sense.

He did not understand what was happening.

He sat there on the floor and stared vacantly into the bluish light that ran like water across the bare wooden floor.

He closed his eyes, but he did not sleep. Nor was he quite awake, however. He watched a long parade of images pass on stilts across the dark screen of his mind. Bill's manuscript lay on the floor beside him. Joel sat with his head tipped against the wall. At one point, he thought he heard noises outside: the cry of a raptor, the dull pop of gravel, an automobile, the soft gurgle of the canal flowing inexorably by. At another point, he heard a hiss in his ear like the one from his dream:

Murder!

Half-delirious, sweating, crouched upon the floor, he believed now that the voice was correct.

His eyes flew open. He sat looking into the far corner of the room. An expression of horror crept across his face. It was as if he saw crouched there in the corner of the room a wild-eyed hag who would pounce on him if he moved a muscle.

That's when the butterscotch tomcat trotted into the room.

It came over to Joel and stepped daintily onto his lap, its long whiskers glowing slivery in the metallic lamplight. The cat rubbed against Joel. It pressed its warm body firmly into Joel's arm, his midsection. Joel could feel the small motor within, the humming lifeforce emanating from down deep inside the cat's body, the cells. Joel reached over and stroked the cat from head to tail. The soft warmth soothed him. With languid eyes, the tomcat turned and looked into Joel's own eyes, then yawned, disclosing a mouthful of razorous teeth. Joel petted the cat longer. After a while, the cat hopped from Joel's lap. It cast its jeweled eyes once more upon Joel, and then it left the room.

By and by, Joel rose from the floor, to do the thing he knew he must, at which moment a tall figure darkened the dark doorway.

When the figure saw Joel, it stopped in surprise.

It was a man. He stood just inside the room. His white hair shone in a silver-blue penumbra around his head. He looked strong and imposing. A hand-rolled cigarette fumed between his first two fingers. He dropped the cigarette now. It lay smoking on the wooden floor.

"Who are you?" the man said. "What are you doing here?"

Joel groped to remember. His mind reeled.

It came to him at last.

"Elias Moorecroft," he said, "my name Gasteneau. You would not remember me, but we once knew each other, many years ago."

"Bloody *hell*," Elias said. With the tip of his big boot, he ground the cigarette out and stepped deeper into the strobic room. "Joel?"

33

"I've been looking for you," Joel said.

"How did you *get* here?" Elias said.

Joel didn't immediately answer. Elias waited. He wore baggy trousers and combat boots. His black shirt was collarless and coarse-looking. He was a bulky man, and standing there in the livid light, he cut a commanding figure, his face craggy and handsome. Outside, the stars and the planets swarmed in the sky. The moon rose higher.

"Here?" Joel said at last. "I was brought to this room by a woman named Lia, who cannot speak."

Elias's eyeballs flicked to the left and then to the right, the whites gleaming stone-blue. "Lia?" he said. "Where is she?"

"I don't know," Joel said. "She disappeared. It may be that she was never here to begin with. I'm not sure."

Elias tilted his head, like a dog. He stared at Joel. They stood approximately five feet apart in the bare blue room.

"Did you know my mother?" Joel said.

Elias hesitated, but only for a moment. "I did," he said.

"Did you love her?"

"Yes," Elias said. "I loved her very much."

"Did she love you?"

"Yes."

"Why did she not go away with you, then?"

Elias didn't say anything.

"Or *did* she?" Joel said.

"Pardon?"

"I said, did she go away with you?"

"I heard. But I don't understand what you mean."

"I'm asking you, did my mother leave my father and me and go with you?"

"Joel," Elias said.

"Do you have her with you now?" Joel said. "Hidden away, but *alive*?"

"No, Joel—"

"Do the dead persist, Elias?"

"Persist?" Elias said. "The dead persist in the legacy of the living, and that is all. The dead do not live, if that's what you mean."

"But how does their legacy survive?"

"In the thoughts and words and deeds of the living. But dead is dead."

A long silence fell.

"Was it because of me?" Joel asked.

"Was what because of you?"

"Did she not go with you because of me?"

Elias hesitated again, longer this time. "Yes," he said.

"Then my mother died for me."

"What do you mean by that?"

"Do you not know?"

"No."

"My mother was murdered—"

But here Joel broke off because he was brought up short by a brand new thought. Retrospectively, it was the moment he'd come to regard as the watershed moment in all that was about to happen. It was the point at which a whole new possibility opened up before him—and it came to him now not as a new course but as a much deeper level down the very passageway he'd already been following, an elaboration upon the same thoughts he'd already been thinking, so that it struck him also, in virtually the same moment, that he would never have found this new thing if his previous thinking had not led him this far. The moment, he realized, was cumulative. And despite his deep agitation, the significance of this fact was not lost on him.

And then his father's mining claim flashed into his head; and Shelby Morgan; and the drawing that Lauren had done, which Joel had never seen.

"Murdered?" Elias said. "What are you talking about?"

But Joel didn't answer the question. "Do you know my father, Elias?"

Elias nodded yes.

"I must ask you something very important: did you know about his mine?"

"Mine?"

"Yes."

"No."

Joel was silent.

"I'm afraid I don't know what you're getting at, Joel."

"Equity," Joel said.

Elias shook his head.

"Was my dead sister Rachel your child?" Joel said.

Elias didn't answer. Then he said: "I don't know."

"My father *thought* she was, though, didn't he?"

Elias said nothing.

"And my mother wasn't sure either, correct?"

Elias remained silent.

"The old man told me that my mother was a whore. He said that Shelby Morgan raped her and impregnated her."

"Shelby Morgan?" Elias said. "No. *He* raped her—your father did—and that's why she did not know for sure whose child Rachel was."

This thought had not occurred to Joel. He considered it now. "Did you not know that Bill Morgan was her biological son?" Joel said.

Elias knitted his brows. His eyes moved from Joel to the three trunks and then dropped down to Bill's manuscript on the floor. He didn't speak.

"You didn't know," Joel said. "The old man told me that Bill Morgan was conceived through rape. He told me that that's what my mother had told him. Bill also intimates the same in his manuscript."

"Yes," Elias said, "he does. But I had never heard that, and I don't know the answer to your question. She never mentioned it to me. Your mother was difficult to fully know. She was incredibly private, Joel."

"It is a fact that Bill Morgan was her son," Joel said. "I'm not asking that. I'm asking did you know it?"

"No," Elias said. "I didn't."

"Knowing it now," Joel said, "what do you think?"

"What do you mean, 'what do I think'? I don't think any less of her, if that's what you're wondering. How could I? How could *you*?"

For a long time, Joel didn't respond. "I couldn't," he finally said.

"Every person has a secret side. And your mother was no different. She was rare, she was complex. But she was a human being."

Silence prevailed. The room throbbed with light.

"That's true," Joel said at last. "What you say is true." Then his face clouded over. "Elias, do you believe there's such a thing as sin?"

"Yes," Elias said. "And I believe that it's wages are death."

"What is sin?"

"All unrighteousness is sin," Elias said. "Sin is any willful or deliberate departure from the things that foster human life. Sin is that which frustrates human life."

"Human life," Joel repeated. "Because life for humans is not primarily physical."

"Yes," Elias said. "Why?"

"Because we live inside our minds."

They were both silent.

"Will you hear my confession?" Joel said.

"I'm no longer a priest," Elias said.

"That doesn't matter."

"I no longer believe in God," Elias said. He hesitated. "Are *you* religious, Joel?"

"No," Joel said.

"Then why are you looking for a confessor?"

"Because it's by knowledge that the just shall live—isn't that right?"

Elias narrowed his eyes.

"It's for the truth's sake," Joel said, "the truth which dwells inside and will be with us forever, that I seek a confessor. As nearly as I'm able, Moorecroft, in the spirit of truth, because I don't want to be afraid of the truth any longer."

"Those are hard words to understand. What do you mean?"

"Three bear record," Joel said. "Isn't that correct? The Father, the Word, and the Holy Ghost, and those three are one, yes? Those are the three that bear witness, not by water alone but also blood."

"You're speaking in riddles and half-quotes," Elias said. "And circles." There was impatience in his voice. His white hair glowed in the throbbing lamplight.

"Not at all," Joel said. "I'm speaking in allegories. And yet the truth is not an allegory. It's the opposite of that. That's what the man Tom said. Besides, whether it's metaphysical or metaphorical doesn't change a thing. The spirit bears witness because the spirit is truth, and spirit is mind. I want to tell the truth at last."

"You keep saying 'the truth,' but I don't understand what you mean by that."

"Naming it," Joel said.

"Naming what?"

"The facts as they are, as they happened. I mean putting into words what *is*." Joel paused. "Or what has been," he said.

Elias shook his head, but only a little. His high hair trembled.

"Words complete the process of identification," Joel said. "*That's* what I mean by naming. To know something is to know how to put it into language. I want to be afraid of that no longer. I want to no longer be afraid of the truth, and the spirit of truth."

Elias stared seriously at Joel. Neither spoke for a long time.

Finally, Joel gestured with his chin to the manuscript on the floor. "Have you read what Bill Morgan wrote in those pages?" he said.

"Yes," Elias said. He started to say more, but something very specific made him stop. What that something was, he could not have precisely named. The lamplight licked his face, his black-clad body. For a full two minutes, neither man spoke; they just stood in the center of the bare room, regarding each other in the wild glow of the lamplight. The moon shone brightly through the window. In those two minutes, Elias felt Joel's eyes burning into his brain: a fierce and fevered gaze. Abruptly, then, a sort of transference took place, something twitching behind the thin membranes of time, so that in that moment Elias understood it unequivocally. He caught his breath. "Oh, no," he said.

"Yes," Joel said. "Now do you see? Will you hear me now?"

"As you wish," Elias said.

"It was me," Joel said. "I raped her. I raped Justine and killed her."

Outside, the black water unspooled endlessly by.

Elias waited.

"It was not Bill Morgan," Joel said. "And it was not exactly as Bill described. Justine loved me very much, even though she was just a child. And *that's* what I betrayed. That love is what I took advantage of."

"What did you do?" Elias said.

"That's the question I've asked myself a million times these past four months."

"Only four?"

"Yes. Because the strangest part about this whole horrible thing is that I forgot it."

Elias shook his head in perplexity.

"For over a decade," Joel said, "for fifteen years, I forgot the entire thing. I don't mean that I pushed it out of my head and refused to think about it. I don't mean that at all. Nor do I mean that I repressed the memory. I mean it was gone. I mean I literally forgot it. I had no recollection of it whatsoever. It was as if I'd never done it at all. Have you heard of such a thing happening?"

It took Elias a moment to answer. "In fact, I have. Psychologists call it a psychogenic fugue, I believe. But my understanding is that it's extremely rare."

"But you have heard of it?"

"Yes, I have. How did you eventually remember?"

"I don't know. I got very sick. I even came close to dying, I think. But I didn't die. When I came back, it was there, the memory was there. I remembered everything."

"Tell me precisely what you remembered." There was now suspicion in Elias's voice.

"I remembered every last detail, with pure precision. May I tell you?"

Elias nodded. "I said so, yes."

"Bill's facts are correct regarding Philip Lambert and regarding my stay there. But on the day following the incident with Lambert, Justine came to *my* room. You see, at that time in my life, I was under the influence of a number of harmful things, just as Bill mentions, but none of those things were as harmful as the one—the only one—that's relevant to what happened."

"You mean alcohol?" Elias said.

"No."

"Crystal Methedrine?"

"No. Far, far worse than any of those."

"What?"

"I was under the influence of an incorrect philosophy," Joel said. He was momentarily silent. "It was an amoral, relativistic philosophy that resulted in nihilism, as such philosophies inevitably do. Moorecroft, if there's only one thing I want get across, it's this: philosophy matters. It matters the most. I've lived it, and I know what I'm talking about on this."

"Tell me exactly what you mean."

"I mean that the ideas a person holds determine precisely, mathematically, the actions that that person will take—and how that person will view those actions and feel about them afterward. Convictions determine actions. Philosophy is the source from which every subsequent thing flows. Whether the idea is scientific, political, aesthetic, technological, or anything else, philosophy is the source. Thoughts shape deeds. Those thoughts spring from the ideas one forms about existence and the universe around us. And that is philosophy. Of course, I didn't know any of this then," Joel said, and fell silent.

"Go on," Elias said.

"I'd convinced myself that nothing mattered except fulfilling my desires. I was therefore indulging in many things that brought me no pleasure, things I didn't really care about, but which I thought were as good as life got. Because I was without purpose, and because I didn't really care, I persisted in this lifestyle for almost two years. For two years, that was my philosophy: a rootless anomie. And since I'd convinced myself of its validity—because, in fact, I had come to *believe* in the philosophy—it gave me mental permission to wrong others at any expense: I felt there was an ideological justification in doing so, and conversely I felt there was no ideological justification in refraining from doing so. I didn't believe morality could be demonstrated by any ultimate test. Do you see?"

"Yes," Elias said. "No man chooses evil because it is evil; he only mistakes it for happiness, which is the good he seeks."

"Yes," Joel said. "Is that yours?"

"No."

"It's a correct thought. It's accurate. In fact, I never did *feel* I was doing evil. How could I? I didn't even believe there was such a thing. In any case, I wouldn't have embraced evil solely for its own sake. In the same way that tyrants seize control and don't think there's any injustice involved in their control but are merely elaborating their philosophy, so was I. In essence, I was under the influence of an adversary ethic: the ethic of amoralism. Which led to a pleasureless sort of hedonism."

Joel paused. The blue light pulsed.

"As terrible as it is to say," Joel said, "I think this whole crime happened out of something like boredom."

He waited but Elias didn't speak.

"The most inexcusable part," Joel continued, "is that this so-called philosophy of mine wasn't even particularly important to me: I'd not reasoned it out, I did not hold it dear. It was something I went with because I was contrary and bitter."

"Bitter toward whom?" Elias said.

It took Joel a minute to answer. "My father," he said. Elias waited. "Even though I grew up loving him," Joel said. "Also, strange as it is to say, I grew up religious, in my own way. I mean, I believed."

Elias watched him.

"I don't know for sure why that is," Joel said, "since neither of my parents were believers. It was all uninfluenced by them—meaning, I came to it on my own. *You* know. I remember you used to see me when I was very young, in the back of church, at night. Somehow the idea of God—of an all-loving, omniscient presence—comforted me. The fact that my later philosophy, if you can even call it that, was adopted so nonchalantly on my part is in some respects the greatest crime of all. I've even considered that *that's* why I forgot about the horrible thing I did."

"Because the philosophy wasn't important to you?"

"Yes. Because it was so meaningless, so insignificant." Joel fell briefly silent. "I do not say that to justify myself," he added. "It's just something I thought of."

Elias nodded.

"I'll not torture you with the details of the actual deed," Joel said, "except to note that on many crucial points, Bill is wrong. He is right that Lambert was a boor, as he says, and I did not care for that man at all, and I did gladly throw him out, and I did break his arms. But I was not trying to be a hero, as Bill makes it sound."

"No? I didn't think Bill necessarily made it sound—"

"I just didn't care enough about anything to want to be a hero, that's all I'm saying. But later, when Justine came to *my* room, it was because she was still frightened, and she was grateful to me—though, I say again, she needn't have been, and also Bill was correct when he said that she was curiously calm after the incident with Lambert. The fact that Bill recognized this brief period of time when she was not overly upset is, I think, highly significant."

Joel paused, thinking back.

"Justine wore braces," Joel said, "she had freckles. I specifically noted, even then, when she came to me afterward, that she had taken time to powder over her freckles, as she usually did, because she was shy around me, and she cared what I thought of her appearance. There was even a time when I found that habit endearing. Later on, it came to anger me."

Joel closed his eyes and was silent for a long while. Elias shifted from foot to foot. The floor beneath him creaked. The room was filled with bluish-silver light.

"There's a moment," Joel said, "when every person decides what he's going to do next. That moment of time always exists. It's the moment of final choice before the act. You face an alternative in that moment when you can choose otherwise. In that moment, you make your choice, and you follow through in deed with what you've decided. That night, when she was in my room, is when I chose to force myself upon her."

Joel was silent again.

"Let me be clear, though: I *don't* think that that part—the physical part—is what hurt her most," Joel said.

"What did?"

"My coldness toward her after the fact."

"What do you mean?"

"When it was all over, and her hands were still weakly pushing against me, I got this almost overpowering sensation such as I had not felt before, to *not* be touched by her, to not even be near her. It was pure revulsion. She was crying, and that suddenly enraged me. I didn't ever hit her, but I felt the urge to. And yet the sensation I'm talking about was *not* primarily one of violence but of revulsion. Still, there was an element of violence mixed in with it. It's difficult even for me to describe—and for me to comprehend. I've thought about it a great deal, and I've not been able to ever quite grasp it. I believe, though, that my revulsion and my coldness is what ultimately killed her."

Elias shook his head. "I don't understand."

"There's more to say," Joel said.

"Go on."

"From that day forward, for the next six days, I didn't acknowledge her. I refused to even look at her. That's what finally drove her out of her mind, I believe. And she *did* go out of her mind. Bill doesn't get into that, but it's true."

"Maybe Bill didn't know about it."

"He knew."

"What makes you so sure?"

"Because everyone knew. I mean, everyone in the house. It was obvious."

"How so?"

"For one week, it was Justine—and not Bill—who sat gnawing her fingernails in the chemical light, reeking of bleach and broken glass. She was beside herself. She was beside herself in every way and at all times—wild but silent. The rage shone like blood in her eyes, in her every movement. I remember it now perfectly. From head to toe, her skin, including her pretty face, was scratched bloody. She had cut her whole body to shreds. Once and only once after the incident did she come to my room."

"Why? What did she say?"

"She said nothing. She stood in the doorway bleeding and staring at me until I shut the door. Even then she still stood there for another hour. I could hear her breathing just outside the door. Later that same night, at dinner, she did not eat a single bite but stared at me the entire time. Murder was in her eyes. Not once did she take those eyes from me. I left the table early. As I stood to leave, Justine began screaming. Not actual words, just shrieks. She screamed and screamed, and continued to scream for a long time after I'd left the room."

"What did Terri and the others think of all this?"

"They thought it all had to do with Lambert. They thought that that incident had unhinged her. I know this for a fact because Terri told me. She told me that they didn't know exactly what was in Justine's mind, but that Philip Lambert with his belt buckle had traumatized her."

"No one suspected it was you?"

"Not that I know of. It was never mentioned to me, anyway. Still, I grew very afraid that I was going to be found out. That became a source of great anxiety with me. In fact, at one point, I got so scared that she was going to tell on me that I was unable to sleep for several nights straight. One of those nights, I was seized with a sense of panic so overwhelming that I sincerely thought I was going out of my mind."

"But she never did tell?"

"No, she didn't. She never said anything to anyone. This is perhaps not as remarkable as it might sound. Justine was an uncommon child, and like many such children she possessed a strength of will that's terrifying to observe in someone so young."

Joel looked outside. He could see the lamplight from the room leaping across the grass below. The moon hung among the stars. Finally, he turned back to Elias, who stood with his boots planted widely apart, arms crossed over his chest.

"That went on for six days," Joel said. "For that entire time, Justine was in the state I've just described. Then, on the afternoon of the seventh day, a Sunday, I was lying in my room when I heard the back door of the house open and close. I got up from my bed and went to the window. My room was in the rear of the house, so I could see Justine crossing the backyard. She was empty-handed. She walked to the shed at the far end of the lawn. I watched her enter the shed and shut the door behind her. I stood there at the window. I stood for a very long time, waiting for her to come out. But she never did."

Joel stopped speaking.

"At one point," he resumed, "I thought I'd heard a noise like pounding from within the shed, but that didn't last long. I wasn't sure I'd actually heard it. I stood at the window for hours. The afternoon wore on. There were dead flies on the window sill and dead moths. I remember them vividly now. It was hot. Just before sunset, I left the house and went down to the shed. I was frightened and even shaking. It turned out that she'd barred the shed door. It took some doing, but I managed to force the door open. Inside, the first thing I noticed was an oppressive gloom that frightened me more yet. This wasn't just in my imagination, either. There were beams of sunlight crossing the heavy air, motes of dust in the light. I see all this with photographic precision now, even as we speak. It has somehow come back to me in every detail."

Elias narrowed his eyes again, suspiciously.

"At first," Joel said, "I didn't see Justine anywhere. I even called out her name. There was no answer. I knew she had to be in there, though, because there was only one door to the shed, and I'd stood watching for hours. I went to the back of the shed. And that's where she was: hanging high above from the rafters, from a tangled coil of barbed wire. She was naked. There was blood all down the front of her body. She'd folded her clothes very carefully and placed them on the wooden floor below. That detail struck me profoundly, then and now. You may have heard that Justine died by hanging herself with barbed wire. That's true, but I want to say something about that: I saw it, I was the first one there, and it was not just a single strand of barbed wire. It was far worse, and far more gruesome. This was a whole coil of barbed that she'd gotten from somewhere and had not bothered to unroll all the way. I believe she did this deliberately, as a symbol of some sort, a symbol of the horrific act of violence that had been done to her. She wore the coil of barbed wire like a wreath of thorns around her neck. Just handling it, getting her head through, had gouged fresh wounds everywhere upon her face. Her hands were still bleeding. She'd stood on a high ladder and wound the other end of the wire several times around the ceiling beam, then she hammered a couple of large nails through the wire and into the beam so that the wire was mashed under the nail-heads. She was not faking this: she didn't have any intention of surviving, she did not want to. And she didn't."

Joel paused.

"Is that everything?" Elias said.

"No," Joel said.

"What more?"

Joel didn't answer immediately. "Why did Bill confess to something that he knew he didn't do?" he said.

"He didn't know he didn't do it," Elias said. "Dostoyevsky's book—*The Possessed*—had him beside himself." (Joel's pupils dilated.) "Bill grew convinced and afraid that he *could* do such a thing, and he began obsessing over it endlessly, until he actually believed that he *did* do it. Understand, Joel, Bill's confession was written long after the fact. Years after. As a matter of fact, his 'confession,' as he called it, was written not really that long ago, I've just learned. In any case, he wrote it well after that event took place. The memory of Justine's rape and suicide was history, but it came back to him when he was very sick and vulnerable with his obsessions and his fears."

"How do you know this?"

"I was told."

"By whom? Bill himself?"

"No. By the one and only person Bill was in contact with during that time."

"Lauren Lake?"

"No, not Lauren Lake. It's not important. Listen, Joel, I don't mean to presume, but I must say something about this: the episode you've described has such parallels with *The Possessed* that I can't help wondering if something of the same sort of thing that happened to Bill is now happening to you."

"What do you mean?"

"Have you fabricated that this happened?"

Joel shook his head. "No," he said. "It was I."

"Do you know the book I'm talking about, *The Possessed*?"

"Yes. I know it well."

"And you're sure that what I'm saying is not true? You're sure it wasn't Philip Lambert after all?"

"Yes. This happened. And I did it. Psychologists might say that it was self-fulfilling because I'd read holes through that book, but I consider that complete nonsense." Joel hesitated for a long moment. "Do you want to know something else, Elias? Something very horrible? I believe Justine was actually my sister, the daughter of my father and Terri Latham."

Elias didn't say anything, but his face was grave.

Joel was silent for thirty seconds more. Then he said: "I also don't understand how Bill knew."

"How Bill knew what?" Elias said.

"That Justine was raped. As I said, she would not have told anyone, so I don't understand how Bill could have known. Because more than anything else, Justine was ashamed of *herself* for this. She blamed herself."

"The note," Elias said.

"There was no note. I know Bill said there was, but there wasn't."

Elias scowled. Then he went around Joel and strode over to the farthest of the three trunks. The wood floor quaked beneath his heavy steps. Joel watched him. Elias brought forth a small book which had a sheet of paper inside. He handed this book to Joel. It was the *Biathanatos*, by John Donne.

The loose sheet of paper inside, which Joel opened up to, was written in Justine's actual blood, and it contained a single word:

RAPE

Joel stared at it with goggle eyes. A shard of ice punctured his heart. Justine's blood was ancient and cracked and shone fantastically in the silver-blue light of the room. Joel knew in an instant that it was real. He stared. The planet wobbled beneath his feet. He felt as if he were holding a scroll from the Satanic Sea. "I never knew about this," he said at last. He let the book close upon the note, and he held the book down at his side.

Elias watched him carefully.

"Where did he get that?" Joel asked.

"It was in her bedroom," Elias said. "Bill was the first one to go in and therefore the first to see the note. He kept it. He stewed over it, apparently."

"What do you mean?"

"It is my idea," Elias said, "that finding the note in blood in some way contributed to his later belief that he had done this thing to her."

Joel was again silent for some time. He was thinking of a puzzle piece and growing increasingly troubled.

"There's one other thing," Joel said, "something that no other person could possibly have known—because I've never told anyone, and I'm the only person who *could* have known about it."

Elias inclined his head. Joel held off for several moments more. "The spider," he said finally. "*That* actually happened. The red spider was real. And something else: it was very much the way Bill described it, only the spider was bigger and more frightening and had a green body. Watching it crawl down the glass outside, there came over me such a sense desolation and despair..." But Joel didn't finish. He stared down at the ground, the lamplight swarming between his feet.

Elias uncrossed his arms and placed a hand upon Joel's shoulder. Joel shut his eyes. That human touch, that touch of warmth, eased his chronic anxiety. After a moment, Elias let his hand drop.

"Literature became reality for Bill," Elias said. "And that spider is literary."

Joel looked up at Elias.

"The spider," Elias said, "is from Stavrogin's confession, don't you remember? *If* it actually happened to you—"

"It happened," Joel said. "I promise you that."

"Then it was purely coincidental—and also coincidental that Bill included it; because I know definitely that Bill got it from Stavrogin. I know it for a fact."

"No," Joel said, "I'm not referring to Bill."

"Whom are you referring to, then?"

"Tom," Joel said. "I'm referring to Tom." His voice was very soft.

This was evidently not what Elias had expected to hear. "Tom?"

"Yes," Joel said. "He's known all along. He's known about it even before I remembered it."

"How could he have?"

"I don't know. That's what I'm saying."

"But what makes you think he does?"

"Because he's a fiend, a devil. And because he left a puzzle piece—" Joel broke off and scowled down at the floor. "Nevermind," he said impatiently. "It doesn't matter, none of that matters."

"But I don't understand," Elias said. He raised his eyebrows. His forehead glowed like pewter, and Joel watched the light ooze out over him.

"I suppose he might figure something like that out," Elias said. "I mean, I'm not saying he did, but I can see him piecing it together, from the literature and Bill's manuscripts, and other things." (Elias pointed at the trunks.) "He'd probably think about it for days, and he'd probably not sleep that whole time, and then he'd figure it out. That's how he is. I don't know that it happened this way, but I can envision it."

"But how would he have even *known* to think about it in the first place?" Joel said. No sooner were these words out of his mouth, however, than he understood. His breath caught in his windpipe. His eyes widened. He turned and stared at the manuscript on the floor. The lamplight streamed across the page. He stared at the light without seeing it. "Moorecroft," Joel said, "do the dead persist?"

"You're repeating yourself," Elias said. "Why do you insist?"

"I've been seeing her," Joel said. *"Really* seeing her."

"Your mother?"

"No. Justine. It's not my imagination. I've been *seeing* Justine. Always she's watching me." Joel turned now and looked toward the other side of the room, into the dark corner where the liquidy light did not penetrate. "Look," Joel said. "She's there right now."

Elias followed Joel's eyes across the room. He stared for a long time. "There's nothing there, Joel," he said. "Nothing at all. You're hallucinating her."

"No. I know what hallucinations are. That's not what's happening."

"Yes, it is."

"Can demonic possession take place?" Joel said. "As a priest, did you ever once come across something like that, something you couldn't explain?

"No," Elias said. "And possession cannot happen. It's another superstition. I promise you that. Knowledge alone obliterates superstition. Bad ideas, the 'insidious philosophies' you spoke of earlier, *those* are what possess people; those are what inhabit people. Not demons. Demons don't exist."

Joel was silent. "Only ideas inhabit the human soul," he repeated, "not demons." It wasn't a question, but Elias responded nonetheless:

"Yes," he said. "Wisdom is the principal thing. Wisdom is knowledge made flesh, it is knowledge actualized. I'll tell you again: there is no devil and there is no super-nature. There is no God. There are no ghosts. There's no ESP. There are no haunted houses. There are only haunted people. I have many times seen exactly what you're describing now—the hallucinations you're having. Do you hear? What is happening to you, I've *seen* this many times. I promise you that hallucinations like yours *are* real—to the person hallucinating." Elias paused once more. "The dead," he said, "do not persist." He reached out his hand again and placed it on Joel's shoulder. Joel looked down at his feet. Elias said: "Why have you come back here, Joel?"

"I've come to confess my crime to Terri Latham. Because to confess it is to acknowledge the truth, in full and in spirit. I've come to tell Terri Latham that it was me who raped and murdered Justine so that justice would be served at last for the rape and murder of her daughter."

"Terri Latham is dead."

"I know that now."

"And you're not guilty of murder."

"I am."

"You aren't. You're guilty of something as horrible, perhaps even worse, and no one here can mitigate that. But that thing is not murder."

Joel was silent.

"If your repentance is sincere," Elias said, "if your *desire* is sincere, your sins are forgiven. One needn't be a religious person to understand that, or to accept it."

Joel shook his head angrily. "You've completely misunderstood me, Elias. What is it you think I'm talking about?"

"I think you're talking about forgiveness," Elias said.

"Nein!"

"Exoneration," Elias continued, "and mercy."

"They are all the same thing," Joel said, "and the essence of justice precludes every single one of them. They are *not* what I'm talking about."

"Are you sure?"

"Yes. Why, now, do *you* insist?"

"Because I believe that you are seeking forgiveness, Joel. *Her* forgiveness."

"I would never have Justine forgive me. Ever."

"I'm not speaking of Justine," Elias said.

"Whom are you speaking of?"

"Your mother."

Joel was silent.

"Is that not why you're really here?" Elias said.

"I'm here for the reason I stated: because I want to be totally honest at last."

"But why is this so important to you now?"

"Because I don't want to live in bondage anymore."

"Bondage?"

"Yes."

"To whom?"

"To reality. Justice requires disclosure in full."

"What do you mean by justice? You keep using the word, Joel, but—"

And then Elias understood. Immediately his eyes dropped down to the book that Joel still held at his side.

"An eye for an eye," Joel said.

"But is that really justice?"

"Don't you know?"

Elias didn't answer.

"I'll tell you what Justice is, Moorecroft. Justice is proportionality."

34

At 11:30 PM, Lauren Lake left off writing and stood up from her chair. She was barefooted and wore a loose white T-shirt and Capri pants. She walked into the kitchen and poured herself a glass of red wine. A clock on the stove leaked green digitals into the room. Her arms glowed palely in the kitchen light. She went with her wine back to the living room. The living room was lit by a halogen lamp, which she extinguished now. Her windows were all open to receive the soft September air.

She sat down upon her couch and lit a cigarette. Millers swarmed the screen. She was alone in her house. The breeze blew gently around her head. She stared outside and sat smoking in the dark. The starlight above cast dim shadows into the room. Those shadows fell across her piled books, across her feet, across the creamy skin of her arms, her slender swaying neck. She took a thoughtful drag from her cigarette and then appeared to consider the brightness of the stars among the mountains. The big dipper hung directly before her: cartwheeling across the narrow valley gap. In the dark, she saw distant headlights swinging down off the mountain pass. She sat listening to the soft tick of the moths. Her ash-blond hair hung chopped across her jaw. Outside, far below her, the rippled river flashed so brightly in the moonlight that it looked as if white water serpents were dancing everywhere upon its surface. Lauren blew smoke into the room and clawed her fingernails through her hair. It was late. The night was warm.

By and by, there came a knock upon her front door. Lauren took a slow drag from her cigarette.

"Who is it?" she said, exhaling.

"Joel Gasteneau."

Lauren's lips opened into a smile. She ground out her cigarette and then like a praying mantis unfolding, she got up from the couch and went to the door to let him in.

He stood in the doorway with his haunted eyes. His face was very gaunt.

"I was hoping it was you," she said. "Please come in." She stepped aside so that Joel could enter.

"*Merci*," he said.

"*Avec plaisir. Il n'y a pas de quoi.*"

He nodded. He stood in silence, staring at her. His upper lip was damp.

"Stay with me awhile?" she said.

"No, I don't have time."

"Why? What's so urgent?" she said.

But he didn't answer.

"At least come in for a minute, then," she said.

"Merci," he said.

She led him into the kitchen. It felt very good to him to be indoors— indoors with her—inside her nighttime kitchen among the food and warmth and musty wines. She snapped on the overhead light.

"Sit," she said, "please." Then she got her first clear look at him. "Oh, my," she said.

"What is it?" he said.

"Your face."

He remembered the lashings he'd taken stumbling off the mountain, the spills, the subsequent sickness.

"You're bloody gorgeous," she said.

He scowled deeply. "Please," he said, and was silent. She watched him. "Lauren," he said.

"Yes, Joel?"

But once again he didn't answer. He sat down in one of her kitchen chairs and ran his fingers through his hair. In silence, she prepared him something to eat. She fed him: black bread and brothy beef soup with potatoes, carrots, croutons. He ate it; he ate it all. He realized only then how long it had been since his last meal. Neither spoke. He drank red wine and so did she. She poured him iced water from a glass pitcher. When she opened her refrigerator door, glacial light spilled out into the kitchen, glowing all around her as if this door were the entryway into an alternate universe.

Afterward, when he was finished, she cleared his dishes and then sat down at the table, across from him. Still they were both silent. At her elbow was a shallow ashtray made of clear glass. The ashtray was clean. Beside it, in one of the table grooves, there sat a tiny cylinder of ash, perfectly intact. Lauren noticed it now; with her long lacquered fingernails, she picked it up delicately, as with pincers, and managed not to break or damage the fragile tube. Joel watched her closely. Lauren did not deposit the ash in the ashtray, as he expected she would. Rather, she dropped it into the palm of her other hand, where it burst soundlessly. With her index fingertip, then, she massaged the ash into her palm, out of existence. This entire process took no more than five seconds; she performed it apparently without thinking, so that when she glanced up and saw the interest with which he regarded her, it made her doubletake him. She smiled. "All ashes in the end," she said. Her teeth were very straight and very white.

"I need to ask you something," Joel said.

"Go ahead," she said.

"It's not really my place."

"I'm sure it is." She then stood up and cleared his dishes away. She put them in the sink and rinsed them. After that, she went over to the kitchen cupboard. Among the many glass tumblers, she selected two. Then she exhumed a quadrate bottle of tequila. In each glass, she poured out two fat fingers and gave one to him and one to herself. "Continue with what you were saying," she said. She raised her glass to him. Rather obliviously, Joel drank but without haste. She sipped her own.

"Do you remember years ago," Joel said, "a precious stone that Bill had?"

"Remember it? How could I forget it? I fell in love with that rock."

"Did you steal it? I'm not accusing you, and I'm not asking because I care—"

"I?" she said.

"Yes. Were you the one who took it?"

"I wish I was."

"But you were not?"

"I was not."

"Do you know who was?"

"No."

Joel was silent. "The story behind it," he said.

"I never *knew* the story behind it."

"I thought Bill had told you," he said.

"No. He was horribly vague about it."

"In what way?"

"The usual way: speaking without details, only generalities."

"Bill didn't know the details."

"But you do," she said. It wasn't a question.

"Yes. A lot of them, anyway. Because that object—that stone—was my mother's. And I'm the one who gave it to Bill."

She considered this. "But Bill knew about it first and foremost from his father. There was something like a deathbed confession, as I recall, though nothing quite that dramatic. Bill once intimated to me that he knew exactly where that mine was located—or, as he put it, 'the place in which the treasures are hid.'"

That brought Joel up straight in his chair, despite the tequila now coursing through him like morphine. "Are you sure?" he said.

"I'm sure that he intimated that, yes. I don't know that he actually knew. In fact, I doubt he did. But it's possible that Shelby told him what he knew."

Joel fell silent. Neither spoke for several minutes. Lauren watched him the entire time.

"You drew a picture once," Joel said. "A picture of where you imagined that stone was found."

"Yes. How did you know? Oh," she said, "I see."

"I read about it," he said.

"Yes."

"Do you still have that picture?" he said.

"Yes, I do. Would you like to look at it?"

"Yes. Very much."

She stood up from the table and left the room. She was gone for several minutes. When she returned, she carried under her arm a large sketchbook, which she set down on the table. She opened up the book.

Inside were hundreds of her drawings, some small, some large, some on cocktail napkins, some on pieces of grocery bag, all sheathed in the clear-plastic covering of the sketchbook. She flipped through the book quickly. At one point, Joel glimpsed a picture he definitely recognized, but Lauren was flipping through so rapidly that she didn't herself seem to notice it, and he said nothing.

Finally she came to the picture he'd asked about. She passed him the book. She sat back down at the table.

The drawing was done in dark-gray pencil, with some color, on a small sheet of lined white paper. It had been drawn with a degree of haste, offhandedly. And yet there was care in it. The picture depicted the mouth of a cave at the base of a high black cliff. The maw of the cave was gigantic—large enough for a tall human being to easily stand up straight in, and indeed just such a man was there. The man wore dark clothes and long gloves and high black boots with buckles. He stared not into the cave, nor out at the viewer, but with his head tipped far back, up the verticalities, at something a thousand feet above, perhaps the remote cliff-crest itself, or perhaps the powdery sky, which Lauren had so delicately and so carefully shaded in. The mountain cliffs too contained an element of blue—or rather an ethos of blue, so gentle was her artistic touch. The man staring upward did not seem to know about the woman on the ledge behind him, nor did he seem to know about the other person, in the middle distance, on the left-hand side of the page, a person watching him as well, someone indistinct and half-hidden behind the tall conifers. A bluish light throbbed deep within the belly of the cave, like an immanent force. The evergreen trees all around were gnarled and shagged.

This was a line drawing without shadow and without flaw. It possessed an uncanny power that Joel was drawn to.

He looked from the drawing to Lauren. He didn't speak. They stared at each other. Joel turned from her to the sketchbook. Then he flipped back to the previous drawing, the one she'd passed over, the drawing he'd recognized.

It was a drawing of him: one of his own self-portraits.

And yet it wasn't—he saw that at a second glance. The style was different: it was gentler, less pent-up, but no less precise. She'd made his long hair even longer, adding something indefinable around his mouth and around his eyes, enhancing his acne scars, so that in the final analysis, her rendition of his self-rendition made him look strange even to himself.

He unconsciously placed his fingertips on the plastic covering, blocking off the scarred parts of his own face.

She did not once avert her eyes from him. She stared at his real face, his bony fingers, his veiny hand upon the sketchbook. Around the outside edge of her own eye, a green vein pulsed like a fuse. A delicate film of sweat had formed along her forehead. A rill of sweat slid down the thin blue shadow between her breasts. Lauren now was breathing deeper, her chest rising and falling in a soft pneumatic heave. She waited and watched for his reaction; none came. He stared at the picture and that was all.

"It's from your self-portrait," she said.

"Yes, I know." He looked up at her. "Why did you choose it for a subject?"

"Do you really not know?"

He shook his head slowly.

She rose up from her chair and came around the table. She stood before him. "Do you really not know that I'm crazy about you?" she said. She moved even closer to him, hovering right above him.

He didn't look at her. He was staring at the table. She stepped closer still, so that she was now pressed against him. His eyes were riveted to his own face that she had drawn.

"You're one a million," she said. "I saw it in your face the first time I laid eyes on it."

He raised his eyes to her at last. He saw her ash-blond forelock capsizing like a wave over her cheekbone. She looked like a lioness.

"I'm very sorry," he said. "I'm not what you think."

"Don't worry about that," she said.

"There are things about me—"

"No," she said, "there aren't."

He started to say something else, but she did not let him: she leaned directly over him, so that the last thing he saw was the pendulous swing of her bare breasts inside her shirt, and then she covered his mouth completely with her own as if she would suck the life right out of him.

35

Joel woke with a feeling that he must hurry. He sat up quickly and swung his legs around. He was shirtless but still in his camouflage pants, the front pocket of which he immediately checked. The object was still there: small and egg-shaped.

The taste of tequila lay like a clot of salt inside his throat. Sitting up so quickly had made him aware again of how sore he still was from the run into the mountains. His lips were dry. Hooks of pain tugged at his eyes, behind his eyeballs. The black bugs were still jumping along the margins of his vision, and his ears were ringing mildly.

He stood and went to the window. A bluish light glowed around the edges of the drapes. He opened the drapes and looked outside. To the right and below, the river lay like a slab of pewter in the dawn. It appeared not to move. In the east, a wash of rose seeped across the sky. He stared. And then it came again: the sensation that someone was watching him. For an instant, he even thought he saw a dark figure, minute but unmistakable: a shambling shape moving through the trees. When he blinked, however, he saw nothing. His stomach churned.

Presently Lauren came into the room and walked up beside him. She stared at his bare torso.

"How lean you are," she whispered. She brushed against him.

"Lauren, I have to leave now."

"Why?"

"There's someone I have to see again."

"Who must you see?"

"A woman," he said. "My sister."

"Sister? I didn't know you had a sister."

"I didn't either."

"Christ, your mother must have been one fertile egg—" But before she was quite finished with this last word, a loud knocking at the front door interrupted her.

Joel cast her a baleful glance.

"At this hour?" she said.

She strode into the living room to see who was at her door. Joel put on his shirt and followed her out. When Lauren opened the front door, the sun hung like brass over the eastern mountains, and she saw it burning right above the mussed hair of the man who stood upon her doormat.

"Oh, hello," Lauren said. "Please come in." She turned to Joel. "Joel, I'd like you to meet my good friend Tom. Tom, I'd like you to meet my good friend Joel."

"Hello, Joel," Tom said.
"Hello, Tom," said Joel.

36

"It's good to see you again, Joel," Tom said. "It's been a while." Tom proffered his muscular hand. His wet cow eyes shone like jewels in the dark hallway.

"Again?" Lauren said. "Are you two acquainted?"

Tom turned from Joel back to Lauren. "Yes. Joel and I go *way* back. What's it been, Joel? Three, four weeks now?" He was looking at Lauren the entire time he spoke.

"Something like that," Joel said. His mouth was very dry.

"Joel," Tom said, still staring at Lauren, "did you know that Lauren is one of the greatest exponents of your mother's philosophy that you'll every meet?"

"Pardon?" Joel said.

"Yes," Tom said, "that's right. And the ridiculous thing is, she doesn't even know it, or really care about it." Only now, Tom turned back to Joel. The half-smile hovered around the corners of his mouth.

"Doesn't even know what?" Joel said.

"Your mother's philosophy," Tom said. "She knows it a little, but mostly it all comes to her naturally."

"Actually," Lauren said, "he doesn't know what he's talking about."

"Lauren, my dear, will you excuse Joel and I? I don't mean to be rude, but we have some extraordinary business to attend to." Tom paused. "Unfinished business," he added. "Rather urgent."

Lauren was silent for a long moment. Her shrewd eyes went from Joel to Tom, then back to Joel. Joel's forehead was damp. She smiled at him kindly and said: "Don't worry, Joel. He's a pussycat."

37

The two of them walked side-by-side behind their attenuated shadows. They went down the steep road that led up to Lauren's house. Road construction was complete, the instruments of labor, the tools of industry, all packed up and gone. To the left and to the right of them, the evergreens soared up into the still morning air. The sky was teeming with light. For almost a quarter-mile, they walked in silence. Finally Tom spoke:

"I never finished telling you," he said. "I'd like to."

Joel didn't say anything. He was staring straight ahead. They did not stop walking.

"The issue of the Ark," Tom said, "is really an issue of blood. I repeat that, Joel, because Raddick, as I may have mentioned, had a lot of blood on his hands now. And so in the cave beside Lake Tana, Raddick remained with the Ark for a long time. How long? He didn't know. He lost total track of time. He was absorbed with the task of inventorying everything that the Ark contained."

"What was the final thing?" Joel said.

"The final thing?"

"Yes. You said that the final thing he found destroyed him."

"Oh, that. It was an ancient book that had been compiled by an ingenious redactor, whose name Raddick was not able to discover. The message in that book replaced, in effect, the Ten Commandments."

Joel stopped. He looked steadily at Tom, who continued walking. The morning breeze blew. Joel resumed his pace.

"That book," Tom said, "did not sanction murder, or lying, or theft, or adultery, or any of those things—I don't mean that. I mean, it laid out systematically a complete secular philosophy—a philosophy of ethics—and in so doing, it did away with authoritarian decree, the decree of God, superstition. It laid it to waste. It abolished those ten commands that are given without explanation or reason, and it replaced them with principles and with thorough explanations backing them. In other words, it codified clearly the *reasons* behind ethical principles—why, for instance, cold-blooded murder is morally wrong. It greatly expanded upon the reasons behind immorality—how immorality frustrates human life over the long run—and it showed how reason (by means of which humans live) does not operate by decree. On the contrary, the human brain thinks, reason is also a choice, and not only that: the human brain thinks in principles. This book showed Raddick the *why* of ethics. It showed him that ethics is a science, the science of human action, and it showed him how morality is grounded in natural life, and not supernatural. This book disclosed how *is* implies *ought*. It showed how the capacity of choice gives rise to moral agency, how goodness is chosen, and so is badness. It showed, in short, the reasons behind morality and the virtue of justice. This book patiently laid out the case for the morality of killing—if, for example, your life or the life of a loved one is threatened by a malefactor. It gave principled explications of the insidiousness of jealousy. It showed why self-reliance is good, and why kindness is virtuous. It showed all this and more."

By now, Tom and Joel had walked almost two miles. A small wind arose. Joel was so caught up in Tom's words that he didn't realize where they were. His insides, therefore, liquefied when he looked up and saw, fifty meters away, the house-shaped trailer gleaming in the sharp morning light.

"What are we doing here?" Joel said.

"I've brought you here to show you something," Tom said.

He led Joel over a stony path that went into the aspen trees, behind and away from the trailer house. The leaves of the trees clashed dryly in the wind. It was still very early. Soon they came to an abandoned building. Joel remembered this building from as far back as his early childhood. He was surprised to see that it was still standing; for it had been in such a state of dereliction twenty-five years ago that it seemed to him then on the very brink of collapse.

Tom took Joel into the heart of this haunted house, down a set of soggy wooden steps, which descended to the basement. The floors, above and below, were punctured everywhere with gaping holes through which the early morning sunlight softly fell. They stepped carefully. The basement smelled of mold. It was lit up strangely with the crisscrossing cylinders of light.

At the far end of the room, an intricate spiderweb lay at a steep angle from wall to floor. The web was immense. In the top right-hand corner of it, there was a large and malignant-looking spider perched upon shelved legs. Joel recoiled. He felt an almost overpowering urge to bolt. Instead, he made himself stand there. The spider's eyes looked like gig-lamps. A molted exoskeleton, her twin, sat chitinous and intact right beside her. There was a small twig snagged like a chicken bone within the web. The spider didn't move. She had red legs and a green body, a silken sac slung beneath.

Tom didn't say anything. He gripped Joel by the forearm and led him to within two feet of the web. Joel's heart hammered. Tom turned to him.

"This is my spider," Tom said. "I raised her. She's very rare, and she has a very short lifespan. Wait with me and watch."

Tom didn't explain anything more. They both stood staring at the exotic spider in its web of silk.

They waited for one hour. The sunlight poured molten glass across the rotted floor. The strands of gossamer turned lavender. Two hours passed. The room was quiet. Still they waited. They did not speak. Nor did they move. They stood. The spider stood motionless as well.

After almost three hours, something happened: the spider twitched. And that was all. She fell motionless again. Fifteen minutes later, she twitched once more, and again. All at once, the translucent silk sac beneath her opened like ripping cloth, and all the little eggs hatched. Joel gasped. An army of baby spiders came pouring out, marching across the web, and immediately they ate the mother. It took little time, every second of which, however, Joel's stomach surged. His skin crawled. He made himself watch.

When, at last, the spider feast was finished and the baby spiders had dispersed, Tom turned to Joel.

"*That* is how the dead persist," he said. "The only way."

"By giving up life?" Joel said.

"No. In the legacy of the living."

Joel stared at Tom in amazement.

"Have you heard that the earth is an egg that contains all good things in it?" Tom said.

Joel shook his head.

"Life is an organic process," Tom said. "Life is everything. *There is nothing greater than life*. All entities, sentient or insentient, have an essence, but only living entities pursue values. They do so for one reason: life. Nietzsche said that life is a process of valuing. 'When we speak of values,' he said, 'we do so under the inspiration and from the perspective of life.' Life gives rise to knowledge, which is truth, and knowledge in turn gives rise to more life, and so on, reciprocally. But life comes first. And there is no lie in the truth."

Joel said nothing. Tom watched him in silence for several minutes.

"Choice is the locus of morality, Joel, and morality is the locus of human life. The most fundamental choice there is is the choice to pay attention or not. That choice is the precondition of thought. Aristotle asked: what is the good? He answered: the good is that for the sake of which everything else is done. The good is the end object of an action. The good is the goal, the pursuit of which must be chosen. The source of the good is located in the pursuit of values, which refers to the goal-directed nature of all life, not just human, though here specifically I mean the fact that the *good* also resides in goal-directed human action, which resides in the nature of human survival, which is chiefly psychological."

Still, Joel did not speak.

"If there were no morality," Tom said, "we would have nothing to worry about, no matter what things we did: genocide would be exactly equal to honesty, and fulfillment and happiness would be purely arbitrary. But there *is* morality—acts of cold-blooded murder and acts of kindness are not equal: one is good and the other is bad. Morality is a roadmap for living now, while you're alive. Will this or that act promote your life in the long run? That is the fundamental moral question. Human life, the power of choice, the potential that resides within each of us—these are what give rise to morality. And morality—or ethics, if you prefer—gives rise to goodness; it gives rise to truth and wisdom. The excellency of knowledge is that wisdom gives life to them that have it. But faith is the opposite of truth: Faith is belief in the face of knowledge to the contrary. Faith is the substance of things hoped for, the evidence of things not seen. Consider that no animal in the wilderness could survive long if it tried to live blindly, without raw sensory data and a brain to process that data.

So man for the same reason cannot survive by faith. If you believe in life, you must reject faith, in any form, other than a temporary, transitional state while knowledge accumulates. Do you understand?"

Joel didn't answer.

"If Christ be not raised, then your faith is in vain?" Tom said. "No. Faith is always in vain, and yet the life that is lived most abundantly is the life that is lived through the application of sound morality. That is how humans flourish. Morality requires a process of learning knowledge and then of disciplining yourself to live by the knowledge you've learned. Our lives are predominantly psychological because we live inside our brains."

Joel closed his eyes.

"Life's goal is emotional," Tom said, "but the means are not."

"What is that goal?"

"You know what it is."

"I'd like for you to say it."

"Happiness," Tom said.

Joel stared at him.

"Self-development is the aim of life: fulfilling as much as you can the potential within," Tom said. "*That* is the means by which we reach the goal. The goal is human happiness. It's the work of achieving this—the *work*, I say—that makes morality not merely factual but necessary. Life should not be endured but lived. I've spoken all this to you now so that the potential joy of life might remain in you, and so that your own joy might be full."

Tom fell silent. He stared at Joel for a long while. Then he turned and gazed off toward the south, where a mass of clouds had piled up over the mountains. The clouds were edged in gold and looked like white flames burning against the blue. Tom stared at the clouds. Then he turned back to Joel.

"By now," Tom said, "I'm sure you've figured out what I haven't yet explicitly said."

"What do you mean?"

"I mean Raddick's story. I mean Raddick's story is the story of the book you asked me about in the beginning: *The Secret History*. What I've told you about Raddick and his search for the Ark, his wife, everything, is all from the book your mother loved so much. Or did I tell you that?"

Joel didn't say anything.

"The final thing Raddick found," Tom said, "is what Raddick later began calling the 'autotelic nature of life,' which presupposes death, and which the great redactor of this book systematized into a complete secular morality that *could* be demonstrated by an ultimate test—the test of human life. That is what destroyed Raddick."

"Why?"

"Because morality requires self-control. Self-control is the basis of character. Morality requires work. Every single day, whether we want to or not, we must each go to work."

"Or?"

"Or we don't have life most abundantly, and death—spiritual death or physical—creeps in, slowly but inexorably. Morality means bringing the brain and the body under subjection, because not all pleasures are good; because vices and predilections must be guarded against, or the happiness that can only come through fulfilling the potential within won't ever be fulfilled—if those vices aren't controlled. Morality is a spectrum; there are degrees of fulfillment, and there are degrees of the virtue which lead to fulfillment, and life is a set of scales weighted for or against happiness, and happiness—true happiness—makes up for the multitude of sins."

Tom fell briefly silent.

"In the end," he said, "for all his incredible strength, Raddick could not control his violence, or his rage, or his deep predilection for despair. Raddick was unable to bring himself under subjection, which is what goodness requires."

A long silence ensued.

"And is that how it ends?" Joel said. "Unhappily?"

"Yes," Tom said. "I'm afraid so. The author was an unhappy person, you see. And yet there's a little more to the story that you might find interesting: Raddick's idea that he was being followed *wasn't* purely in his imagination after all. In fact, he was being followed—by the footsteps of the dead, by his past, among other things. Nonetheless, he did succeed in smuggling the Ark out of Africa, just as he swore he would. As unbelievable as it sounds, Raddick singlehandedly brought the great vessel across the ocean and into the United States, where it exists to this day. The search and what it uncovered destroyed him, because it showed him in a way that he could no longer ignore all his sins and the crimes that pursued him relentlessly. And yet at the same time that search yielded up truth, which is no small thing."

Tom stopped speaking and looked off toward the south again. Far away, an eagle pivoted against the flame-like clouds.

"The end?" Joel said. His head had begun to throb.

"The end," Tom said, still looking away. He turned back to Joel and then astonished him by embracing him firmly. "Goodbye," he said. He stepped back a pace and turned to leave.

"Wait a moment," Joel said. "I have to ask you something else."

"Go ahead," Tom said.

But Joel didn't immediately speak. His headache intensified. Tom patiently waited. Above him, the irregular mountains loomed.

"How did you know?" Joel murmured.

"How did I know what?"

"About the spider," Joel said. "*My* spider, the one on the windowpane, the one on the puzzle piece that I know you left on the doorstep—how could you possibly have known?" Joel spoke through cracked lips. His voice was so quiet that his words were barely audible.

But Tom heard him. He was not smiling now. "Isn't it obvious?" Tom said.

Joel shook his head.

The mocking smirk slowly crept back over Tom's face, exposing the tea-colored front tooth. "Your father," he said. "The old man spilled the beans."

Whereupon Joel saw another camera-flash explode noiselessly inside his head. Tom turned away and began walking down the road. By the time Joel recovered, Tom was twenty meters away. Joel called out to him:

"I have something that belongs to Lia," he said. "Will you give it to her for me?"

"Who?" Tom said.

38

But even as he said it, his eyeballs flicked away from Joel, up over Joel's shoulder, at something behind Joel. Joel turned.

She stood one hundred meters away, near the entrance of the black cave beyond the backyard of his childhood home. She lifted her hand to him. The breeze blew through her black hair. She wore a white summer dress that had indigo stripes. Joel's heart began to pound. He stared for a long while. Then he turned back to Tom, but Tom was gone. Joel could see him in the distance, moving over the humpbacked river road, gilded in the armor of light. Joel watched until Tom was a speck on the horizon. Then the horizon snuffed him out. Joel turned back to Lia. She was staring at him. He advanced toward her. Even from fifty meters away, he could hear the steady rhythm of her breath. He could feel her transcendental repose.

She stood just outside the cave entrance. Even in shadow, her black eyes brimmed with light. Joel reached into his front pocket and brought something out. He passed it to her. It was the cameo he had found in the forest, the cameo with the hairline fracture that divided the face into two hemispheres of light and shade.

She extended her pale hand, and Joel took her hand and pressed the cameo firmly into her palm. Her fingers felt cold and yet soft upon his abraded skin.

"I found this," he said.

She looked from her palm back to him. Her breathing was steady and alive. He realized only now how he had come to crave the sound of it. She held her notebook in her left hand, and she wrote something down. She passed it to him:

Where did you find it?

"In the forest," he said, "behind your house."

She wrote:

I thought I'd lost it for good.

He didn't say anything. They stood for a moment in silence.

Then she wrote:

Do you remember this cave?

"Yes," he said.

She wrote:

What do you remember about it?

"I played here all the time when I was a child," he said.

She took the notebook back from him, but she didn't write anything else. She breathed. Joel stared behind her into the darkness.

"It was my secret fort," he said. "My hiding place. My childhood. The tunnels go back very far. No one even really knows how deep they go. They're endless and unexplored. But nobody knew them like I did. They were my caves."

She wrote:

Childhood is a private garden, Joel, sometimes a terrible one. Every person's childhood is unique. The adult carries childhood with him through life, until the day of death.

Joel read and reread these words. He felt overcome with sadness. He looked up from the page.

She took the notebook from him and wrote:

"Experience coming too early constructs, sometimes, in the obscure depths of a child's mind, some dangerous balance—we know not what—in which the poor little soul weighs God."

And then she wrote words that amazed him even more:

He can't just get away with what he did, Joel.

"Who?" Joel said. "Who cannot?"

She wrote:

You know who. And you know what. That man did something monstrous, something unspeakable. He must pay for it. For the sake of justice, he must.

Joel felt himself slipping away. He glanced over at the house-shaped trailer that he'd grown up in. It stood fifty meters beyond, crouched in the massive shadow of the mountain. "I'm very sorry," he said, "but I don't know what you mean."

She wrote:

Yes you do. We've waited a long long time, Joel.

He grew increasingly afraid.

She wrote:

If not you, who?

"What? What do you mean? Why do you say that?"

She wrote:

Because you're the only son, and because your strength and endurance are very great. Time now, Joel, to murder and create.

"Murder?" he said. "What are you talking about?"

But he was beginning to grasp.

She wrote:

Yes. He shut up the truth. He understood it, and yet he killed it on purpose. He repudiated it and replaced it with his thunderous authority.

Could this really be happening? To Joel it suddenly seemed impossible. He closed and opened his eyes slowly. He stared at her in silence. Then he looked away from her and peered into the dark cave that went back into his past, into his childhood, into the hidden places where he used to play.

She wrote:

The flesh is a wind that passeth away and cometh not again.

He shut his eyes, his face charged with suffering. "I don't know what you mean," he said again. His eyes were still closed. "I wouldn't know where to begin."

And yet when he opened his eyes, his gaze immediately and as if of its own accord swung over, so that he was once more staring at the house in which he had grown up. She saw his glance and touched him lightly on the arm. Her fingers were cold and ghostly. He looked at her; she shook her head. With an open palm and a slow sweep of her arm, she gestured back to the cave that gaped open behind her. Suddenly the thought of going back there, into those mazelike corridors of his past, frightened him beyond measure.

Then he felt something slipped into his hand. He looked down.

It was a tightly folded piece of paper, around which she was now closing his fingers, as if she would not have him look at it in her presence. As she closed his fingers around it, her breath quickened, and she stared into his eyes. He was once again struck with the sudden fear that she was going to club him or kiss him.

But her black eyes simply moved away until she was again looking back into the blackness of the cave behind her. He followed the line of her sight. Together, they stared for a long time into the darkness. Joel began to sweat. He unconsciously tucked the folded paper into the front pocket of his pants. He turned to her, as if to receive further instruction, but she shook her head and stepped back. She lifted her hand to him in a sad gesture of farewell.

"You look so much like her," he said, "it's unbelievable."

She responded not at all.

"Goodbye," he said to her.

She bowed.

Joel turned from her and walked alone into the black caverns of his past.

It was at this time approximately 10:30 in the morning.

39

The rock creaked over his head.

An odor of iron hung all about the cave, a taste in his mouth like old coins. At the back of the cave, a narrow corridor plunged southward into the mountain. Joel entered. Immediately the darkness overtook him. He went deeper in.

Twenty years since he'd last been here, yet he remembered it perfectly. He did not look back. He could hear her breath for a long time; it was like a comforter to him. Mustiness seeped from the stone. He made his way carefully down the ungiving corridor. For guidance, he slid his fingertips over the walls on either side of him. The stone was icy cold. There was a purple glow in the distance by which he could faintly see. He did not know where this light was coming from. After a while, the light vanished. Still he could hear her, and he soon began imagining that her breath was emanating from the rock itself, as if, like her, this cave were a living organism, inhaling, exhaling. Then, very abruptly, the sound of her breathing ceased, and he was left there all alone. He continued on.

Several times he stopped and just stood, listening. Each time he stopped, he could hear no other sound, and yet each time he resumed his walk, he was sure he heard a low noise behind or beside him, like a growl.

He went deeper into the mountain.

He never saw the shape that watched him from the dead black corners.

At the end of one hour, a yellowish light appeared in the distance far ahead. The light grew clearer by degrees. As he advanced, the roof of the cave sloped lower and lower. Soon he was on all fours, crawling toward the light. Then he was on his stomach. By the time he finally made it into the opening, his shirt was sloppy with mud.

He stood in a large stone room. A fat rod of sunlight descended from a smokehole in the ceiling of the cave. The mud along the floor was marked here and there with small animal tracks that looked like runic symbols in the earth. Joel approached the column of light and stood inside it. It was very warm. Dust motes swarmed within. He stood motionless, listening. He heard nothing. He could see clearly now the cave walls around him. They were webbed with white fissures of quartz, which crazed the rock like crumpled yarn. At the back of the room, three separate tunnels angled away into the darkness. Joel hesitated for a long while, loathe to leave the light. Then he entered the tunnel on his left.

The rock was high but excessively narrow. For several hundred feet, he had to turn laterally in order to squeeze between the walls. After a while, the passageway widened. The walls still shone palely in referred sunlight from the room he'd just left. Gradually, though, this light diminished, and he was once more swallowed up in total blackness. The ground sloped downward beneath his feet; it was sheer lumpy rock, slick with mud.

He eased his way through. He pressed his hands into the cold walls on either side of him. The darkness was like an immanent force. Once, fleetingly, he thought he tasted something sweet, like protein in the darkness. It was gone as quickly as it had come.

The deeper in he went, the colder he grew, the more cramped the quarters.

The only sound now was the sound of his own breath. It rebated back at him off the ungiving stone. Joel advanced with great caution. He could not see anything. Yet he was not lost. In fact, he knew exactly where he was and remembered it all with photographic exactitude.

After fifty more minutes, he came to a thin cleft in the rock. He reached his hand inside. All he felt was cold empty space. The air was damp. The darkness around him pulsed. Joel waved his hand through the gelid air of the other room, feeling for something solid, though when his fingers brushed over a solid wet object, he jerked his arm back in fright. Then he realized what that object was: a cone of calcite growing down from the ceiling of the cave.

Joel sat down on the stone floor and dangled his legs into the darkness below. He had the sensation that he was sitting upon a precipice. He placed his palms flat on the ground and lowered himself down into black space. He went as far as his arms would allow, both shoulders hunched up to his ears. Still, his feet touched nothing. All he felt was cold air beneath him. Momentarily he panicked—until the toes of his sneakers brushed against solid ground.

He dropped. The short landing sent a shockwave of pain blasting up through his cold feet and into his legs. He waited a moment. In this room, the air smelled even more strongly of minerals. It was freezing cold, and the coldness crept into his bones. He could see nothing, and he moved forward with both arms outstretched and groping blindly, like a madman or a mummy. Eventually he came to yet another rock wall. He shuffled to his right, sidestepping with care, feeling his way with his fingertips. His shoes made a soft scuffing sound. Several times he tripped over the small stalagmites that grew haphazardly from the ground. Then he found what he was looking for: an offshoot corridor that opened out of this room.

He squeezed through that hollowed rock and came at last into the room that used to be his private fort.

Before his eyes passed multicolored wands of light that the retina creates in places of plenary darkness. He was freezing now. A sound of gurgling water, almost unnoticeable, reached his ears. Once more he shuffled forward blindly.

At the end of ten minutes, he located two rock slabs that covered an old hiding hole.

He pushed the two slabs aside and groped around. Small life scurried away beneath his hand. Within that depression, resting upon the ground, was a bulky object encased in a plastic bag. This, in turn, was wrapped in a musty old blanket. The wrapped object was a suitcase that Joel had once lugged all the way back here, by himself.

He extracted the vessel now.

He unwrapped it slowly.

He could not see anything.

The air inside the cave was motionless. The only sound was the sound of gurgling water; it came to him continuously. The damp blanket that wrapped the vessel smelled of mold and had not been touched in decades. Joel balled the blanket up and placed it on the floor behind him. He unlatched the vessel and felt around inside. The first thing he exhumed was a heavy cylindrical stick, which he broke open and tossed on the ground, well away from him. Instantaneously, the room ignited in a hellish glow. The flare hissed loudly, a smell of sulfur filling the room.

Joel looked slowly around.

A pall of blue flare-smoke hung about the cave. Long columns of calcite grew in clusters both above and below him and dripped like teeth. The light of the flare leapt over the moist misshapen pillars of stone, which, in one section of the room, rose up hugely from the floor. Dripping pools in shallow basins lay across from him. The water looked like blood. Joel gazed about as one amazed. Old childhood sorrows swamped him.

Nearby, a ring of stones marked the last firepit he'd ever made in this room. Just beyond that was a pair of toy trucks; they sat atop two mounds of dirt he'd built alongside a polystyrene ship with a plastic sail and tin anchor. The small boat was beached beside the flowing water. There was a long-dead lantern on the ground as well. The hardened mud of the dam he'd made was well-preserved. Joel stared at all these things. On the walls behind him, the shadows slithered and crept. The stone glowed scarlet in the light of the flare. The gurgling spring stood on the other side of the room, welling up endlessly in a calcite basin and emptying into a limestone aqueduct that ran along the back of the room and then into darkness. The bell-shaped ceiling arced low over his head and was clustered with stalactites that gleamed and dripped.

The lurid light of the flare began to fade.

Joel knelt on the ground before the open vessel. He removed a sealed can that contained a number of votive candles, all white and glowing. He lit one candle from the fading flare, and then he lit another from the flame of the first. He placed them both on the open lid of the vessel. The flare diminished and winked out. The stone room grew dark but was lit now with creamy candlelight whose twin flames burned before him like cat eyes. The smell of sulfur still hung thickly in the air.

On the left-hand side of the vessel was a rolled army blanket and, next to this, a leathern flask with a long nylon strap. A large hunting knife, sheathed in black, poked from the center of the blanket-roll, pale-green fishing line wrapped around and around the knife hilt, two small fishhooks hanging visibly from the leather sheath. A metal flashlight was stuffed into the other end of the blanket. The flashlight batteries had been brand new when he bought the flashlight, twenty years ago. He did not think they would still work. He was therefore surprised when he punched the switch and a cone of dim light appeared on the rock in front of him. He extinguished the flashlight and stuffed it into the deep thigh pocket of his pants. A stack of newspaper and a bundle of dry sticks were piled beside the blanket. There were also two other flares. Opposite these was a clear-plastic bag, sealed and folded over several times. It contained 500 wooden matches whose tips Joel had dipped in hot wax long ago. The hardened wax still preserved each match tip.

Facedown on the other side of the vessel was a framed photograph. He lifted it out and held it under the candles.

It was a photo of him, when he was perhaps five-years-old, standing between his mother and his father. All three of them faced the camera. His mother and father both looked very happy and so did he. His mother held onto his left shoulder, his father held onto his right. Both were faintly clutching, as if they would tug at him. His father looked mountainous and magnificent, with his great marmoreal brow and his lean handsome face, his defiant eyes. His mother too had never looked more striking—or more strange. His own young face stared back at him, so foreign and so clear, so unscarred. He did not recognize himself at all, even now as he stared and stared.

At the end of five minutes, he placed this photo back into the vessel and began sorting through the other things, most of which were books.

He found a small *Othello;* a rare edition of *Hamlet;* an ancient-looking copy of *Henry IV*, Part One and Part Two. There was a *Dr Jekyll and Mr Hyde* with a glossy hardcover that glistened in the candlelight; underneath that, a forgotten copy of *The Red Pony* and *Of Mice and Men*. There was also *The Secret Sharer* and *Heart of Darkness* contained in one book. He disentombed *A Dead Man's Memoir; The Time Machine; The Scarlet Letter; Moby Dick*. He found a slim volume of poems by Lewis Carroll, which he had forgotten all about but which he remembered now. A pristine hardback of *Alice's Adventures in Wonderland* was also there together with *Through the Looking-Glass, And What Alice Found There,* both of which his mother had read aloud to him, two times consecutively, because he'd loved them so much.

Then, near the bottom of the vessel, he came upon a rare King James Bible whose pages were edged in gold. This was a book his father had given him.

A thin cord, sewn into the top of the binding, served as a page marker. Joel opened up to the page it marked.

Underlined in dark black pencil was a brief passage that he had to squint to read:

Ye have not yet resisted unto blood, striving against sin.

He himself had not marked this passage, and he didn't have any idea who else would have.

His father?

Joel stared up at the ceiling in thought. After a while, still kneeling in front of the vessel, his knees began to ache. He became aware also of how very cold he was. He moved to sit and stretch his legs out before him, and as he moved, he felt an object in his front pocket. He fished it out. It was the tightly folded piece of paper that Lia had given him.

He unfolded it now. In her perfect printing, these words were written:

The path of the just is as the shining light, which shines more and more unto the perfect day.

He frowned again in thought. Then he began flipping rapidly back through the open bible, tearing pages, he did not care. He flipped and skimmed. The onion pages crackled loudly in the windless silence of the cave. Fifteen minutes later, he found what he was looking for.

In the book of Proverbs, Chapter 4, the following words and the following words alone had been underlined:

Wisdom is the principal thing.

Let her not go: keep her; for she is thy life.

The path of the just is as the shining light, that shineth more and more unto the perfect day.

Upon reading this, Joel stood up quickly and paced an anxious circle around the room. His brows were knitted. At length, he sat back on the ground. The candles had burned down, and wax stood pooled on the inside of the suitcase lid. Joel was freezing, and yet he was sweating.

He sat in thought. The candles burned. After a while, he reached over and pressed his thumb into the pooled wax. It was warm and firm and retained the imprint of his whorled thumb. He then lifted one of the two candles and poured hot wax onto the note Lia had given him. He covered in wax the words she had written, as if to preserve them. He waited for the wax to cool. Then he refolded the note and slipped it back inside his pocket.

He lit two fresh candles and continued sorting through the suitcase.

The last book he came upon lay at the bottom of all the others. It was a lean but heavy volume, bound in a strange cloth-weave that did not look like cloth. It lay glinting in the candlelight. He lifted it out carefully. His fingers trembled. On the cover was this title:

The Secret History of the Arche

Underneath that, in smaller, darker font:

In quo sunt omnes thesauri sapientiae et scientiae absconditi

Upon reading these words, a sudden insight made him catch his breath, and the sound of his own air intake startled him. He swung around. The stone walls swarmed with light and shade, but there was no one there. He peered deeply into the dark corners but saw only the mute columns of limestone. Gradually, he turned back to the course-grained pages in his hand.

What he found inside astounded him.

He found pictures of embryos and insects. He found intricate woodcuts depicting snakes and vivisections, fetuses and flowers. He saw detailed illustrations of skinned humans with split craniums, the sepia-colored locomotor system of the human animal, the vast plexus of human veins and nerves, bloated brains with bulbous tubercules, and more. He saw the inverted tree of the human bronchial apparatus, and penciled below it these words in quotation marks:

"The wind, which is spirit, the breath of God, was breathed into Adam, conferring life; but it is no less the whirlwind out of which God speaks to Job, the sign of His destructive powers."

Joel was buried in this book for so long that he lost all track of time. He kept lighting new candles. He might have been there for days.

Finally, he flipped back to the front cover.

The artwork and the artist were unmistakable. In dark watercolor, painted with the same miraculous precision, was a very thin child sitting alone at a kitchen table. The child's bare feet did not quite touch the floor. A small fire burned in a scullery to his left, the white flame casting a cold glow across the wooden floors, which shone like dark ice. The child sat before a chessboard the pieces of which were in their starting position. The child stared not at the chessboard, however, but through the open window, at the nighttime sky beyond. The sky was vast, oceanic. An ovoid moon, silver-blue, stood in the left foreground. Fish-shaped clouds glowed in the moonlight. The artist had given the moon a partially hidden visage—a feminine face—elegant and soft. In the distance, beyond the moon, buried deep within the stars, a green galaxy burned like a wildflower. Apparently unbeknownst to the child, a black serpent beneath the table lay poised to strike his foot. In the right-hand corner of the painted room was a large wooden chest. On the side of the chest were these tiny words:

GOD = BREADTH, DEPTH, HEIGHT, WIDTH

He studied the picture for many minutes. The strange material that bound the book spread a faint circle of extravasated light onto his lap. He opened the book to the last page. A thin volume fell out. It was *The Hound of Heaven*, by Francis Thompson. Inside this thin volume was yet another insert, a loose-leaf page, folded over once horizontally. He was about to unfold it when an alarming realization struck him: for some time now, he didn't know for sure how long, he'd become half aware of a presence behind him. And the moment he realized it, he heard, or thought he heard, a noise deep within the corridors of the cave. The noise sounded like the baying of a distant dog. Joel did not move, and no other sound followed.

For a full fifteen minutes, Joel heard nothing else but the gurgling water. Perhaps I'm only imagining things, he thought. Or perhaps there are indeed dogs, but those dogs are loping down the hallways of my head.

His eyes went back to the loose-leaf page that was trembling in his hand. He unfolded it.

It was a map.

It was done in black ink on unlined paper, drawn simply but not crudely. On the contrary, in fact, there was a sophisticated, hypnotic quality in the spare dark lines. The map was a topography, but a very odd sort of topography. He saw that it depicted the entire area surrounding him and his childhood home. It covered about a hundred mile radius. Joel had no memory of ever seeing this map before. Still, there was something familiar about it. Then he grasped what that something was: it was done in his mother's hand. She'd drawn the mountains as angular M's. Smaller angles, like capital A's but without horizontal bars, depicted the trees. Tandem lines beneath the mountains were mining tunnels or perhaps caves, like the very one he was now in. The rivers she had drawn as thin snaky lines. There were even a few words written on the map:

Purple Mountains
Equity Peak
Crystal Caves
Monastery

His greatest shock of all came when he saw that deep within her depiction of the Purple Mountains, a certain section was marked with a large black X. Joel grew breathless. The longer he stared at the map, the more uncertain he grew over the precise location of the X; for in many ways, it didn't seem so deep within the mountains after all. It was a disconcerting illusion, almost like a puzzle-picture. Decidedly, the map was having a disorienting effect on him. He felt he could not gain true perspective, could not get the directional bearings that normally came naturally to him. He closed his eyes. At which time, he heard the noise again. His heart skipped, then released a thunderous beat. The noise came a third time. It was still distant, but unmistakable now, so that the following two things hit him simultaneously: that whoever or whatever had been pursuing him this entire time had been with him from the beginning; and that this moment right now, the point at which he'd unfolded the map, is the moment his pursuer had been waiting for all along.

40

Joel stared at the map for a few seconds longer, striving to memorize it. But he was not able to concentrate, so great was his horror. With quailing fingers, he held the map over the candle flames. The brittle page flared once in the darkness of the room, then collapsed in a cluster of ashes and orange worms that squirmed in his hand. Joel snuffed out the candles. Darkness engulfed him. He snapped the suitcase shut and checked to make sure that he had the flashlight in his thigh pocket. He slung the long strap of the suitcase over his shoulder and then went without light across the room, exiting opposite the way he'd come in. He could hear the soft slosh of the underground stream, and that's what he made for.

He followed the flow of the water to an opening at the base of the farthest wall. First he pushed the suitcase through the opening, away from the water. Then he lay down on his stomach in the icy stream and forced himself through the constricted opening. The passageway was relatively high, but it was very narrow. Halfway through, he was seized with claustrophobia, yet he wrenched his way deeper in. He at one point had to turn over on his side, in the freezing water, to force himself though the center of the passageway, and there he banged his elbows bloody, twice whacked his head. Extricating himself at the end, he felt something tear inside his solar plexus, and he reckoned he'd damaged the network of nerves there. At last, he stood up dripping on the other side of the stone passageway. His breath came painful and ragged. He was in another room of absolute blackness. The flowing water beside him poured down a stone throat that went deep into the center of the mountain.

Once more, Joel strapped the suitcase over his shoulder. He turned on the flashlight. He pointed the light at the water, which was so black that it completely absorbed the light and gave back no reflection at all. He passed the beam in a slow arc around the cave.

He was in a small cubic space. It was musty and filled with frangible spires above and below him, watery walls glistening in the mushroom-colored cone of his flashlight: glistening like the innards of some great beast. Across the room, a wide fissure in the rock gave to another room of darkness.

He abolished the light and gathered himself. The pain in the pit of his stomach paralyzed him, and for some time it made each breath exceedingly difficult. He stood for minutes, waiting for the pain to pass, watching the greenish motes of retinal light trace before him through the darkness. He was wet and shivering. The pain subsided slightly. He advanced toward the fissure at the other end of the room and eased himself through.

On the other side, a breeze as light as a bat's breath passed over him. It lifted his hair as with little fingers. Joel walked into this breeze, seeking its source. The floor of the corridor sloped upward. He could see nothing. He was in a section of the caves that he'd never been before. It was foreign territory. His way grew increasingly complex. He could no longer hear the flow of water. The only sound now was the sound of his breath and the scuff of his footsteps. He felt utterly alone. At the same time, he felt an indefinable presence looming in the caves. Several times, he stopped moving and turned on the flashlight, shining it around him. In every direction, he saw nothing but black rock and limestone spire.

He used the flashlight until it was nearly dead.

He grew colder.

The passageway grew more intractable.

After what he thought was one hour, he imagined himself locked in a labyrinth of malevolent devising. The rock growled above him. With each step, the pit of his stomach pulsated. He was dizzy. He came at length to yet another offshoot corridor through which the feeble breeze passed. He continued moving into the breeze, but he'd grown so cold and so lightheaded now that he was no longer sure that any such breeze existed after all. A number of times, he considered turning back—and with a kind of horror realized that even if he wanted to, even if he was prepared to retrace his steps and face whatever was behind him, he would never be able to remember the way by which he'd come to this spot.

He now began to think himself irretrievably lost. He feared that he might wander around in this stone maze until he died.

Then he heard something else.

It was a sound that in the first instant kept his panic at bay, and in the next amplified it. It was a soft hissing which came to him like the murmur of underground voices. He spun around.

In the deep darkness way back, he thought he saw a pinprick of light, although he wasn't sure. His eyes were no longer reliable. The light vanished. He stood there unmoving. Then he began pushing forward again into the feeble breeze, which also went away. The murmuring sound ceased as well. Joel stopped.

Had he been imagining them both? And was he after all imagining something behind him?

Or were there perhaps spirit voices in the earth after all?

Very carefully, he stepped back five paces.

The murmuring returned.

The breeze passed back over him.

He knew then what had happened, and he cursed himself for almost missing it.

He snapped on the feeble flashlight and passed it over the slick rock wall on his right. He was just able to make out another corridor, this one opening directly above his head. As he'd guessed, the breeze was blowing through this tiny passageway, and he'd walked by it in the dark.

He unshouldered the suitcase and started to shove it through the high passageway. The instant he lifted his arms, however, a searing pain tore through his solar plexus. He gasped. He pressed his face against the cold rock. Then he forced himself to shove the suitcase partway through. After that, he hefted himself up, pulling with his arms and scrabbling with his feet, hitting his head on the rock ceiling. His midsection went numb with pain. Inside the passageway, he had to headbutt the suitcase forward since it was too narrow for him to raise his arms above his waist.

Three-quarters of the way through, he got stuck. He couldn't move forward or backward. He tried to keep calm but did not succeed. He thrashed wildly, berserk with claustrophobia, until at last, somehow, he extracted himself from the tunnel and came through the other end. His ribs felt shattered. The pit of his stomach was radiating pain. There was a mound of rubble before him. It had fallen from the rock ceiling above, a mound of many years. Dripping, muddy, wheezing, Joel stood upon it and moaned. In this room, the murmuring sound was much louder, the breeze much stronger. A lemon bar of light stood in the distance. He began moving toward it. The muddy ground grew gradually visible beneath his feet. His sneakers slapped through. He was able now to see how grimy he was, his gray camouflage pants and his dark thermal shirt all smeared with mud.

The lemon light leaned in through an earthen hole, about the size of a charger. Joel poked his head through. He found himself gazing out at a collapsed roof of stone beyond which hung the breathing bell of the sky. On all four sides, walls of granite stood partially crumbled. Above, affixed to a wooden beam along the front end of the fallen roof, a small iron cross like a sword hilt toppled forever backward into the sky.

He knew instantly then where he was.

41

The monastery stood on the edge of a wide clearing, a lonesome field that stretched away from the foot of the spiky mountains. Some nine thousand feet above sea level, these granite structures, with their prow-shaped roofs and orthogonal lines, stood shiplike among the oceans of wind-troubled grass. Around them, gales of sunlight crashed mutely down, and the land was clean and vital.

The buildings had been constructed in the spring and summer of 1854 by a schismatic sect of Jesuits, radical penitents and misogynists, all, who, one by one, began perishing of an unidentified illness, so that by 1877 the entire compound stood desolate. Thus it remained for over one hundred years: eight stone structures adrift upon the high field.

For a brief period of time, trappers had used the rooms as lodgings, had, like the Jesuits, slept on the hard straw beds, but when the fur trades died, everything soon faded from within, and never again would anyone inhabit this monastery. The ghosts of mutilated monks wandered the windy rooms. The grass beyond grew heavy and lush.

Across the open acres, the rocky wind incessantly poured. A pure, invigorating wind, it had the smell of distance in it, and grass. It mussed the feathers upon all the hawk heads. It ruffled the fork tails of the barn swallows perched along the fence lines. It muted the magpie's croak. Blackbirds with red-rimmed wings squinted into it. It originated high above, gathering at the summit of the bald mountain peaks, and then came sliding down in one solid current, down, down through the narrow gaps and canyons, over the ragged tree crowns, and finally out across the long blond grass. The grass was boulder-studded and wind-bent; in collaboration with the light, it flickered with shadows and shapes that made it seem as if schools of fish were always passing through.

High above, the mountain basin loomed wild and remote. The basin was webbed with a multitude of spring-fed tributaries, the water of which flowed icy and green and cut far beneath the mossy banks. Salamanders and frogs populated the hidden coves.

At the western edge of the basin, a much larger river fell off the cliffs and exploded into a great crucible of vapor and bubbles below. From here, the river pounded on. It pounded down through the jumbled mountain timber and then leveled out at last under a shaggy bluff, just behind the monastery.

To the south and to the east, the landscape fell away into an intricate horizon, and in the very far distance, dry purple hills floated above the earth.

There was still plenty of daylight. Joel swiftly made his way to the river whose roar had come to him as a distant murmur in the caves. And now that he was back outside, he noticed a remarkable thing: the strength of his eyesight had apparently returned in full. The gelatinous blur was gone, the hopping insects on the margins of his vision were no longer there. He could see sharply for miles.

He knelt down in the sand upon the riverbank. Just as his knee touched the earth, he saw a reflection in the shallow shore water—an image not of himself but of someone closely resembling him. Yet this person was clothed differently than he was. Instead of his dark thermal shirt and camouflage pants, the figure had on a long crimson cloak of such extraordinary brightness that the red reflected bloodlike upon the water. A gnarled juniper tree grew horizontally from the rocks above, and one of its reflected branches bisected the red doppelganger, skewering it perpendicularly. All this lasted less than a second. Even as Joel saw it, the reflected image turned away on the rock ledge above and disappeared. But in the moment before Joel's real face came swimming before him on the river water, another image flitted by, this one even higher, like a shadow, or a quicksilver shape, wobbly and fluid. Joel's eyes flew upward. Nothing was there at all—nothing but the real sky and the real cliffs and the real and solitary tree.

He unshouldered the suitcase and opened it. He brought out the leathern flask. He unscrewed the cap and submerged it in the river. A chain of silver bubbles rose from the lip of the flask to the surface of the water. When it was full, Joel tightened the cap and slipped it back inside the suitcase, then he latched the suitcase shut. He leaned over the river and drank. The river was ice-cold and bathed his bruised diaphragm.

He stood up with a knee-crack. The water sloshed in his stomach. He was not entirely clearheaded, but he didn't know that yet. He knew, however, what he must do next.

He glanced back once more at the place from which he had just come: the abandoned monastery of crumbled stone. There was no one there. He saw at his feet the china sky reflected diagonally across the river. He slung the suitcase strap over his head and across his chest. He adjusted the strap so that it lay tightly across his injured midsection, immobilizing movement there as best he could. In this manner, he set off up the side of the mountain.

He was in deep woods before he knew it. The light here shone like jade. Game passed silently before him. Game trails crisscrossed everywhere, a maze of paths that disappeared into the lush undergrowth above. Joel walked rapidly. His injured stomach made his breathing shallow. By degrees the sun sagged down into the thick-piled clouds, and the sky went purple and pink. The day was waning, but there was still good light.

One mile above the monastery, he executed a series of complicated loops. Next, he doubled back on his trail, and then he did so again, and then again.

By and by, he came to an ancient fir tree whose plaited roots lay exposed upon the ground. Joel stood beneath the tree and looked up through its long branches at the treetop swaying high above. The trunk was so large that the actual limbs didn't start until several feet over his head. To his right, five meters away, a rock wall ascended parallel the tree.

Joel stood on the highest of the exposed roots and once more readjusted the suitcase strap across his midsection. Nimbly, then, and with as little movement as possible, he leapt from the root and grabbed onto the lowest-hanging branch, which was well over nine feet off the ground. A great pain ripped through his diaphragm. The swinging suitcase came up and hammered him in the face. He didn't let go of the limb, which was almost as big around as his leg. The rough bark abraded his hands. In the next motion, he swung once and pulled himself up, straddling the limb. Then he climbed up to the limb above, then to the next one above that one, and so on. In this way, he went seventy feet into the heights of the tree.

The suitcase was cumbersome and heavy and made for difficult climbing. Ten feet from the treetop, when the tree began to sway, Joel stopped. He strove to quiet his breath but only partly succeeded. His hands were sticky with tree sap, and the smell of pitch stung his nostrils.

Next to him stood a similar tree. Its branches brushed against the branches he was now crouched in. Long pinecones were clustered like bananas in the uppermost boughs. Beyond that tree, the rock wall rose, and Joel saw upon the cliff a number of narrow ledges. He eyed them all closely. Then he cast his gaze down below. He saw no one coming. His vision felt even sharper than before. It felt powerful, bionic. His eyes went back to the tree beside him and then to the cliff just beyond that.

At length, Joel stood carefully on the limb below him, positioning his feet as firmly as he was able. The limb gave slightly under his weight. With his left hand, he held the branch at his forehead. With his right hand, he readjusted the strap across his midsection. He paused, braced himself.

Then he leapt into the adjacent tree.

The first limb he struck felt as if it would impale him. The suitcase swung and hammered him again. Pinecones everywhere fell to the ground with muted clops. He'd led with his uninjured side, but the impact jolted his entire body, so much so that the searing pain went through him again like a lance. Simultaneously, the strap of the suitcase came off his shoulder and hung heavily from his forearm. He hugged the tree and waited for the pain to subside.

Eventually he slid the strap back over his shoulder and then scuttled over to the far side of the tree. From here he was able to reach out with his tennis shoe and touch the cliff.

He unshouldered the suitcase and dropped it down onto the cliff ledge, which was perhaps three feet wide. With his pitchy fingertips, he nudged the vessel as far back as he was able against the wall. He then climbed out of the tree and carefully hopped down onto the ledge. He stood beside the bible-black vessel, gazing down below him.

The land was empty as far as he could see. The sun was sinking. The evening wind blew through the treetops. He didn't linger. He squatted down and opened the vessel. Everything inside had been badly jostled. He removed the knife from the rolled blanket, then unbuttoned the pocket flap on his thigh and shoved in the sheathed knife alongside the flashlight. He lifted the blanket roll and looked up.

The top of the cliff swayed twenty-five feet above him. He inserted his fingers under the twine that bound the blanket and with poor leverage and a narrow purchase, he leaned back and then flung the rolled blanket toward the summit of the cliff.

Blinding pain ripped through his midsection, and the blanket barely cleared the clifftop.

Joel took the bag of matchsticks from the vessel and stuffed those into his front pocket. He strapped the water flask over his shoulder and around his head. For a moment, before shutting the suitcase, he paused over the beautiful watercolor on the cover of the book, and he stared even longer at the photo of his mother and his father and him.

He then latched the suitcase and stood it up on its spine. He pushed it flush against the cliff wall, so that it was not (he hoped) visible from above or below. He cast his eyes once more across the country to the east. When he was satisfied that no one was coming, he began scaling the cliff.

The cracks were narrow and the footholds loose. He was very frightened. He climbed slowly, methodically, the water flask sealed and sloshing on his back, the muscle striations standing out deeply along the tops of his forearms like metal grooves. He did not look down. He inched his way upward. At times, his cheek lay flat against the stone which warmed his face with its stored heat. Gray tussocks of grass grew from the cracks in the rock; emerald moss with a moldy smell beside his face.

Eight feet from the top of the cliff, he came to a spot whereupon he was unable to move in either direction. The thin slab that he'd hoisted himself by means of had peeled away from the cliff the moment he'd gotten here and nearly sent him plunging to his death. It was only the quickness of his reflexes that had saved him: by digging his fingertips into the hairline crack left behind was he able to hang on. Tiny spalls of rock tumbled through the glassy air beneath him. Nothing he could see above or below afforded him a significant hold. His sneakers clung to the rock wall like suctions, the rubber shoe-tips jammed into a slight indention, but slipping. He was growing tired.

In a kind of fetal position, he clung to the rock facade, afraid to move at all, afraid of death. The sky above him was now a thin green membrane that held the dying light. For a long while, he hung there motionless. He stared forlornly at the draining sky.

He remained in this position for over half an hour, unmoving, hesitating between life and death. His forearms started to cramp. His solar plexus ached. The sun went down. Above his head and slightly behind him, he descried a small, loose-looking projection, about the size of a horse tooth—enough, perhaps, for one finger, two at most. Beyond that, and out of reach to him, grew a tuft of moss, which he didn't think would hold his weight. But he had little choice. His digits, all wedged into the narrow crack at his chest, were weakening by the second. He knew he must act now or fall. With his right hand, he reached up and at the same time partly lunged for the tooth-sized rock; in the same motion, he clamped his first two fingers around that rock. He felt it wiggle beneath the tips of his fingers, but the rock held—for a moment. As he started pulling himself up, clambering simultaneously with his feet, the tooth-sized rock came loose from its socket, and the hand that held it dropped. Pain tore through his torso.

The fingers of his other hand were still wedged into the fissure at his chest, his feet still scaling the stone below, so his balance was all off. When his arm dropped, therefore, his weak grip was demolished.

This took place in an instant. And in that instant, he saw himself sailing down to his death. But the moment before the tooth-sized rock broke, Joel managed to pull himself high enough to clutch at the tuft of moss above, and with his falling hand, he swung for it. And caught hold of it.

The moss held.

Even as the relief poured through him, though, the moss began tearing away from the rock. He could hear it: a slow protracted rip, like splitting cloth. He pressed himself tightly against the rock, as if he would burrow into it, and then, as lightly and as rapidly as he could, he eased himself upward by means of the slow-tearing moss and his scrabbling feet. Piecemeal, that moss shredded away beneath his fingers, but he was high enough now to reach a single solid piece of stone, which he clutched with a metal grip. From here, he hoisted himself fully to a stable rock projection, and then after a full hour, he came to the top of the ledge.

By now, the twilight was accomplished. Joel lay on his back on solid ground. His upper abdomen was in great pain, and each breath came with difficulty. The land below him was sunk in leathery shadows. At the end of five minutes, when his heart rate slowed, he raised himself on his elbows and looked about for his blanket roll. He saw it not far away. It was caught in a woody thicket. The moment he moved to retrieve it, two things happened at once:

A dim silvery shape emerged from the woods above him and then went gliding into the high hills. From the very opposite direction, down below, came the startled cry of a bird. And then something else.

Joel spun over onto his battered stomach and inched his way forward to the cliff ledge. He looked down, his heart hammering against the rock beneath him. He cast his eyes along the base of the cliff and then outward. He scanned every inch of the shadowy land.

Something was coming through the woods, creeping in by stealth. Whatever it was had managed to follow his circuitous path. A chasmed terror gripped his heart. He flattened himself more completely against the ground. He stared through the lattice work of his bangs.

The light was poor, yet he was able to see. And what did he expect? A large lank hellhound snuffing the ground, tracking him by his scent alone, padding on its strong unhurried paws down the labyrinthine way he'd laid? Yes, exactly that. So that when the thing actually came into view, and he saw what it was that had pursued him all this time, all this way, Joel's mind blanked at the monstrousness of it.

"It is you," he whispered.

Indeed it was.

It was his old man.

42

Joel lay on his stomach, on the stony earth, and stared down in wild surmise. He didn't move.

He thought: the old man must have powers beyond belief if he's able to trace me through the caves and over that path I laid.

With his ancient limp, his father came. One hundred feet below, Joel could see the moon-colored hair drifting through the crepuscular light. His father's gaze was fixed steadfastly on the ground, a look of deep concentration pleating his forehead. Joel saw also the thin drooping mustache, pure white now, and his father's face a wan ashen pallor. He heard the soft swish of grass brushing against the old man's knee-high boots, saw the glint of the boot buckles. His father wore a long-sleeved shirt the color of kidneys, and no jacket. He carried a dark shapeless object like a hat in his hand.

When the old man came to the exposed roots beneath the fir tree, he genuflected and began investigating the ground. The roots lay like a cluster of boas in the dirt. As the old man bent down, Joel heard the creak of his boot leather. The old man studied the roots and the ground all around them, the imbricated pinecones, the rusty needles that lay thickly between the roots. He studied everything. Nothing got past his laser-beam eyes. Once, he even leaned over and sniffed at the roots, touching them with his snout, like a dog. His scowl deepened.

Joel held his breath and was motionless.

Slowly, his father rose from his genuflected position. His boots creaked. Joel was even now struck by the awesome stature of the man, who looked well over seven feet tall. The old man tipped his head back incrementally, eyeing every inch of the tree. At last he was staring directly over his head, at the treetop that swayed above, not far from the cliff ledge where Joel was lying concealed.

As Joel looked down, he saw his father's scowl replaced with a grin. The big teeth shone phosphorescent in the half-light. Joel's scalp went numb.

The old man stared for several minutes into the green tree heights, scanning the boughs. A Lethean mist oozed in about him; it hung low above the ground, silken vapors rotating around his boots. Gradually, then, and to Joel's wonder, the scowl crept back over his father's face. His gaze went back to the ground, then back up the tree. The frown deepened. The old man dropped onto the ground the shapeless object he held. He was so tall that when he stood on the tree root, he was nearly able to touch the lowest-hanging limb: the limb that Joel had leapt to. With hunter's eyes, the old man studied that limb, the grooved bark. And still he glowered in concentration. Joel watched him and did not breathe. His mind the whole time was fixated on the black vessel that rested partially concealed three-quarters up the cliff ledge.

After a very long while, his father stepped down off the root and faced forward. He bent down and picked the shapeless object up off the ground, and then he strode away into the trees ahead, pinecones cracking like walnuts beneath his big boots. Joel shut his eyes and released his breath. He did not wait a second longer. He drew back silently from the edge of the cliff and retrieved his blanket roll. Then he removed himself deeper into the mountains.

43

He did not walk but ran. He ran far into the night, tugged along by the tireless moon. The Purple Mountains he moved toward were draped in shawls of mist that glowed in the silver moonlight. He ran over the hills and over the labyrinthine ways. In the dark, he passed through groves of black juniper and pinon trees; their astringent odors watered his eyes. The ground was dark, but the moon drew long shadows from the mountainside and penetrated the eerie caverns beneath the rocks. His course now was clear: put as much distance as possible between him and the old man, who would not be overcome so easily, however.

Joel ran in a cold sweat and did not rest. The pit of his stomach felt pummeled. The image of the X on his mother's map loomed continually before him.

The autumn season was well advanced in these higher elevations. He could see yellow leaves gleaming everywhere in the light of the moon. Faint game trails wound away before him and vanished into the dark timber above. The autumn stars burned overhead with a mineralized gleam. And each time he looked up, Orion was stalking the heavens right above him.

He pushed on. He knew that his father would never rest. For a long time, Joel could hear, off to his right and below him, the anfractuous river yelping away through a sheer-cliffed gorge. The dusty stars cast a bluish glow across the rocks. He ran with the army blanket draped over his shoulders. Finally, toward morning, when a small quadrant of the east was a smear of ashes, he came out onto the lip of a vast volcanic bowl. Here he stopped running. He could see miles in every direction. The minty hills behind him fell away, all hoary and heather. He crouched under an igneous bluff and breathed roughly the morning air. His windpipe felt seared. His entire midsection pulsed with pain. He crouched down and watched the land to the east, out of which he'd just run. Far off, an endless phalanx of evergreens fell over the mountain. Joel surveyed the entire countryside. He saw nothing move, and suddenly, because of this, he felt his fatigue drain out of him, replaced with a sense of euphoria— euphoria over the fact that no one was following behind him.

Perhaps I outran the son-of-a-bitch after all, he thought. Perhaps I ran him into the ground.

He allowed himself a moment of relief and rest. He turned and faced west.

Down below, in the valley of that dead volcano, a string of beaver ponds lay smoking like pools of hot milk; the morning stars were drowning within. A plexus of narrow streams webbed the entire valley. These streams were deep and sinuous. Above, a pair of shark-shaped clouds swam down from the north and then continued on, their midsections tinged with rose. Joel watched them. He had not eaten anything since Lauren had fed him, however long ago that was. The inside of his stomach felt barren and cold. A small wind blew over him. In the southwest, below the setting moon, the purplish stones of Equity Peak fluctuated in the developing light. Joel stood shivering. His breathing slowed and slowed. He glanced once more over his shoulder. At first he saw only the eastern sky, alight now and clear, pale yellow, the fading stars gleaming like snake eyes, a cloud-wrack churning across the horizon; but as he was watching, a black speck emerged on the landscape below, still very far off, and yet coming with what seemed to him abnormal rapidity. This figure was traveling a different path from the one which Joel had followed to get to this point, but that path led to this spot. All at once then, Joel grasped the magnitude of his miscalculation. He saw how much he had underestimated the old man, who indeed would never stop pursuing him—ever—and so it was now that Joel looked on in horror as that gigantic figure articulated from the iron dawn.

That's when Joel knew that straight flight was futile.

44

You must stay calm, he told himself, you must think.

There was still time but not a lot. He picked his way down into the volcanic valley, toward the pearly ponds, where green frogs gibbered on the shores and brook trout were leaving water-scrolls all along the surface. He inadvertently scared up a flock of birds, bottlenecked waterfowl who scared him even more than he scared them. They came splattering out of the water and then ascended low over his head on dripping wings. The valley grass was damp and fiery-green. Diamonds of dew lay nested among the blades. A smell of morning mulch came to him on the air. He hurried through. The sun was not yet up.

Two hundred meters beyond the ponds, around a slight eminence of land, he came before a black wall forged of mud and silt. He stood for a moment facing it. A thread of silver water crackled down the center of the wall, with long cuspidine blades of rock-hard sludge rippled like drapes on either side. Rodents and birds had come to sip at the bottom of this wall. He could see their fresh prints stamped everywhere across the mud. The water emptied into a narrow flume, which branched off into a spring-fed brook, which in turn branched off into another, and then again, and again, until soon a multitude of streams laced the lower valley, each one leading to the distant river he'd heard in the night.

Joel shrugged off his blanket and folded it twice vertically. He placed the flashlight and the sealed bag of matches in the middle of the blanket. Then he rolled it all up and tied it with twine. When he was finished, he flung the blanket as far as he was able into the house-high grass above him, atop the muddy wall. He looked over his shoulder.

He saw nothing upon the ridge.

Still, it was with excessive haste that Joel went loping down the stream banks. He studied, as he loped, the swirling waters, so limpid and so green. The flowing water cut far beneath the mossy banks, the banks overhanging the water like miniature cliff ledges. Exactly how far back into the earth the water went, he was not sure, and yet it was this that he sought to discover.

Peering down into the prasine pools, he caught sight of the blurry wobble of yellow tadpoles swimming deep into the subsurface currents, spatulate feet churning away like tiny paddles. The topwater of the stream skated upon the surface in an oily way, as if all the water beneath were thicker and more gelatinous. After approximately three minutes, Joel felt that his time was up.

He stopped and gazed back one more time at the top of the volcanic ridge.

It was still empty.

The sun was not yet risen.

He turned back to the stream and eased himself into the jade water which robbed him of his breath.

45

The water was like slush; it encased him. It was so cold that it cut through his whole body, like a saw blade. He gasped, and for a very long time he had absolutely no control over his breathing. He was spasmodic. He gibbered loudly despite himself. As soon as he'd entered the water, he tucked his legs up under him to avoid dragging his feet along the bottom and stirring up silt, but it turned out that there was no danger of this: the water was so deep that even fully extended, his legs came nowhere near the bottom, a fact he discovered gradually. His jaw clattered like toy teeth. The flask of water strapped around him floated now upon the surface of the water. He let the stream take him. He thought he might die of cold. Palsied with shivers, he tried once to glance over his shoulder, and did, partially: to his relief, he did not see the old man anywhere. After a while, he began to paddle with his arms and flipper kick, which helped him regain some control of his breath. He was careful not to touch anything around him—not an overhanging bow or even a blade of grass. He knew that nothing would get past his father's all-seeing eyes.

About his entire body there was only the loose silky green water now. Below his feet, along the underwater banks, long beards of algae thrashed in the underwater current. He went on like this for approximately four hundred meters. Then he reached out under the stream bank and grabbed hold of a sisal root, which hung down in the water from the mulchy ceiling of the overhang. By means of this root, he hauled himself out of the stream and back under the ledge and came at last into hidden shadows.

The stream cut much farther back than he'd reckoned. The current here was not nearly so swift. The water felt warmer, though not by much. He made his way farther back into the soft earth, beneath the streambank, switching roots as he went along, swinging beneath the soggy ceiling like an aquatic monkey brachiating on these short gnarled vines. He went back until he could go no farther. He was some ten feet under the banks. His head brushed the muddy ceiling. The water was up to his Adam's apple. The air smelled of mulch and humus; he felt it closing in about him. With frozen hands, he held the root above his head, and then he swiveled around in the water until he faced outward. He stared through a very narrow rectangle at the bright world beyond.

From this vantage, he could see reflected on the surface of the outside stream a partial image of the volcanic lip above and the sky now brimming with light. His body was totally numb. He waited for what seemed hours, his jaw still spastic with shivering. All he heard the entire time was the steady sipe that he was now at one with.

After a while, he began to worry more seriously that he might freeze to death under here. He pumped his legs harder and faster, churning the green water below him. Bubbles rose to the surface. At the same time, he made S's with each arm, one arm at a time, alternating the hand that held the overhanging root that moored him. The green water whispered continuously by. His breath resounded in the enclosed embankment. At length, he started to think that he'd miscalculated again, that he'd misjudged how far off the advancing figure of his father was. After that, he began questioning his sense of time and wondering how he could have gotten so confused. Perhaps it was the cold, he thought, and perhaps he had not waited so long after all. Finally, he began to question the very existence of his father, and whether, in the last analysis, he'd really seen anything coming up the hill after all; whether any of what he was experiencing now could actually be happening, for he felt that his faculties were bleeding out of him and draining away in the current. His eyes closed and opened slower and slower. Also, though he did not know it yet, the ceiling above him was gently collapsing over his head. The water now stood up to his lips.

Looking through the rectangular window at the outside world, he saw in the water's reflection no sign at all from above. Nor did he hear any footsteps. At last, he talked himself into swinging back out, to gain a better perspective, and when he came out from under the bank and into the open water, the first thing he saw was his old man stalking down into the valley.

He yanked himself back under the overhang. Had the old man seen him? He didn't know. He cursed himself for his move.

Now he did not have long to wait. Before he new it, the pound of his father's boots came to him gigantically in the water. Joel pushed himself against the mud wall behind him, and he held tightly to the root above his head. The steps came louder. The water rocked by at his nose, his mouth now submerged. He noticed only then that the water had risen, but at first he didn't grasp the reason for it. He held the root and breathed through his nose, his head tipped back. He saw the mud above moving toward him, and then he understood that it was he who was pulling the soft ceiling down onto himself, by hanging onto the root, inadvertently pushing himself deeper under the water. He cast his eyes about for more space, but he wasn't able to find any, and he didn't have time to look. The sound of the steps grew close.

He tilted his head back as far as his neck would allow. His long hair spilled out like ink around his head, his face a white deathmask on the green current. He stared centimeters at the dank ceiling that would suffocate him. Flecks of mud were beading inside his nostrils, up into his sinuses. He was growing panicked. The footsteps were almost on top of him.With a terrible effort of will, Joel forced himself to breathe slower, quieter, despite the physical awkwardness of his position and the torrent of terror that poured through him. His midsection, at least, no longer hurt: the cold water had anaesthetized his body.

He feared that his father would hear him breathing, and so he made a decision: when the tiny currents sloshed into his nose, he inhaled one final time, as deeply as he was able, and then submerged himself. Underwater, the sound of the footsteps came to him in a more amplified manner. And then the footsteps stopped.

Joel still held to the anchoring root above him, his whole hand underwater now. He did not kick or paddle at all but let himself go slack. He opened his eyes. In the emerald chambers of the stream, he saw a thin blue shadow, a negative of his father, angled steeply into the molecular green water. He pictured his father standing on the bank directly above, looking down. Joel was already running out of breath. The steps did not resume.

Joel waited.

How long? Sixty seconds and then more. Still the steps did not resume. He saw a huge white hand and then an arm come plunging down into the water, groping beneath the bank a few feet away from him. Then the hand withdrew.

Inside his chest, Joel felt his lungs jerk involuntarily, over and over, revolting at his mind's willful deprivation of air. Every part of his body called for him to come exploding out into the oxygenated world, to breathe, and yet the footsteps would not commence. So it was in these cold green keeps that Joel swore he would die of suffocation before he gave the man above him the satisfaction of knowing he had won. Joel therefore willed himself to remain perfectly inert, even to death, even as his windpipe constricted inside his neck, gasping internally, and even as he went partially out of his mind.

He watched what he thought was the long blue shadow that his father cast. The shadow lay motionless in the water.

Joel closed his eyes. Another fifteen seconds passed. All was silent.

Joel was crazed with underwater panic, and he felt on the brink of death. Yet he did not move a muscle.

Abruptly, then, the shadow in the water flickered and the footsteps pounded away.

Joel waited a while longer. He waited until the steps were only a distant thud, and then, before his brain went black, he pushed himself with his remaining strength off the mud wall behind him and out into the open water. He came floating up without a sound, and he sucked in the air as he'd never sucked it in before.

He rolled over onto his back and gasped, floating down with the current. He stared up at the breathing sky above. He turned back over onto his stomach and grabbed hold of the streambank.

He raised himself and looked up over the ledge.

He saw his father's back receding in the distance.

Joel remained here motionless for many minutes. He waited until that mountainous figure was out of sight. Then he climbed up out of the water and staggered back.

46

He slept among the rocks, curled like a fish in the thin solar light. The breeze blew. His clothes dried as he slept. He had the blanket roll beneath his head, and he clutched his knife to his chest in his sleep. When he opened his eyes, he found himself staring up through a spray of pine needles at the pale sky. High above, an eagle wheeled slowly beneath a shrunken sun the color of clay. He closed his eyes again; his retina retained a purple-green image of the light. The nick of autumn was in the air. He opened his eyes and looked around. The autumnal breeze brought to him a feeling he could not name: a feeling of ruin.

He stood up and almost fell back down from dizziness.

He drank from a clear stream in which pins of light bounced off the bluish stones all along the streambed. The water lay silken on his tongue, a taste of dark flora. The cold of it numbed the back of his throat. Mirrored on the surface of the stream was the sky above, marbled with clouds, blue and white, like blue bacon. He knelt there for a long moment and watched the reflected sky tremble and dish.

All that day, he moved westward toward the castle-shaped peak in the distance. Late in the afternoon, he came into a lonely glade that was filled with tall aspen trees and a curious, quaking light. Shadows streamed over the ground. He was dazed with hunger, and he incorrectly believed that the cause of his dizziness was unrelated to anything else but his lack of food. He walked deeper into the glade. Wind blew softly through the treetops. Shabby-looking robins watched him with their golden eyes. He stopped halfway through and stared up at the giant aspen trees. Their beauty reduced him. Light airy bees banged into his body by mistake. The leaves of the trees were changing now, lemon-lime and banana-colored leaves, pumpkin-colored leaves, leaves like ruddy-skinned pears see-sawing down around him as he stared. A ghost of decay entered him through the nose.

The sky was thinly overcast but luminous. A soft tide of light slanted down through a great cleft in the clouds far off and poured out long bars of light. Across the way, at the far end of the meadow, a small pond lay in the mellow sunlight. He walked over to it. The sky was angled across the pond water. Yellow leaves floated upon the surface. A quiet river filled the pond. Trout were coming to the surface, and in the shallows at his feet, blue-black leeches fanned the slate-colored sand.

Joel walked the circumference of the pond. Grasshoppers spurted up with each of his steps, as if he and he alone were ejecting them forward. On the other side, he came to a tiny blue spruce, dead from top to bottom. He yanked it up by the roots. The needles were the color of burnt-sienna. In a shallow cave twenty feet beyond, Joel lit the tree on fire. It seethed and popped. It burned rapidly down to orange embers. He added larger sticks of deadwood. Then he walked back under the towering aspens and found a handful of worms beneath a flat stone. They were long worms, purple and fat, with white saddles on their backs; they lay squirming in the moist earth. He impaled one of them on his fishhook, bunching it up hugely, like shirred fabric, around the curve of the hook. From the hilt of his knife, he unwound the pale-green fishing line. He drew that line through the loop at the end the fishhook. Then he climbed out onto a projecting rock and lay on his stomach above the pond.

The rock was warm. Gray silt covered the bottom of the pool. He lay there for minutes, watching his dark eyes stare back at him in the water. Wild fish burst like shadows beneath the fallen leaves. He swung his short line into the water.

The worm landed five feet from a huge brook trout. The fish lay in profile, and when the worm plucked the water, the fish angled one way and then instantly the other. Joel saw the midsection of the fish clearly. It was stippled with polka dots of pink and blue. The velvet fins swayed like feathers in the clear gray water. Joel waited. He watched the slit cheeks periodically open and close like dampers; he saw the burgundy flare beneath. After a moment, the fish flickered and was gone.

Before Joel had time to care, that same fish smashed into his hook and was thrashing about on the end of the line. Joel lifted it from the water. It came up silvery and dripping. It was twenty inches or more. The big body snapped back and forth, bowing so hugely that the wedged tail slapped at its own torpedo-shaped head. Joel reached down and held the fish by the lower jaw, paralyzing it, extracting the hook, small razorous fish teeth piercing his thumb. The fish quivered and the tail curled. He then yanked the head back until the neck popped mutely and the fish died. Joel came down off the rock and, still holding the fish by the jaw, walked over to the riverbank.

With his knife, he notched out the asshole and then sank the tip of the blade into the white belly. He made a smooth incision from rear to throat. The viscera was hot; much of it plopped out onto his forearm. It was mixed with watery blood. Small orange eggs, basted in blood, came gushing out onto his wrist in a welter of gore. Blood dripped from the fish into the riverine grass. Joel caught sight of his own shadow drifting over the stones beside him. For a moment, the shadow spooked him. He even turned and eyed his shadow warily, and it he: cognate shade, steadfast doppleganger, lean and lilac in the platinum daylight.

Silent grouse sat watching him from the trees.

That was when he understood that his senses were beginning to perplex.

He gripped the entrails of the fish and ripped them out violently, then flung them spinning into the river. Annelidic mass of organs winking in the bright light, and then the flow sucked them away at once. The flesh of the fish was coral. The blue-and-pink polka dots along the skin were so vivid that they looked dabbed there with fresh paint. With his thumbnail, Joel scraped out the wide ream of dark-blue blood encased within a thin membrane along the inner backbone. He rinsed the inside of the fish in the running river. Then he rinsed his knife and finally his hands. By the time he was finished, his hands were pink.

He went back to the cave. The fire had burned down. He laid the fish on its back on the glowing coals. Outside the cave, the clouds had thickened as if whisked. Joel warmed his hands above the embers.

After ten minutes, when the fish had cooked all the way through, he deboned it and stood eating it outside in the open air. He cradled each bite carefully inside his mouth before chewing. The fish flesh was rich and sweet. Two horseflies tangled with each other in a midair ballet, making lemniscates around his wet lips. He waved them away. He assessed five separate gnat-clouds hovering in the distance above the pond. At his feet, a platoon of red ants marched toward him through the sand. Joel ceased chewing and watched the ants. As he stared, one ant stopped and appeared to reach back and give the one behind a helping hand, antennae rotating radially, counterclockwise. Joel scowled at them. Something seemed amiss, but he didn't yet know what it was. By the time he was finished eating, he'd begun to suspect: his old sickness was creeping back, the abnormal acuity of sight and sound and smell, the strange shimmer of reality, had leapt back upon him. As soon as he realized this, the sput of rain sounded on the coals of the fire, just inside the cave. He turned. Small white tracers of smoke were shooting off the embers.

On the other side of the pond, a solitary mountain flower stood as stiff as a cornstalk. It was purple and sun-leached, half-hidden among the reeds. He only noticed it because, from nowhere, a spiky-headed swallowtail alighted upon the stalk, bending it nearly to the ground. Then this bird did something strange: it appeared to impale its own beak repeatedly into its downy breast, stabbing at it rapidly, as if it would pierce its own tiny heart. When the bird lighted off, the flower sprung back to attention. Joel closed his eyes and ground his knuckles into his eye-sockets.

He lashed the coals with lakewater and moved on.

He followed the river up.

The falling rain marked the river rocks with dark hyphens. It dimpled the deep river pools. Shore currents rolled into the sandy banks like little silver breakers. The soft river sounds embalmed his brain. The air smelled dusty and wet at the same time. He followed the river high into the mountains. The rain increased. He soon came to a larger river from which this smaller one branched. He followed the larger river up. He walked under the great riparian cottonwoods and presently entered a wild and isolated landscape, a land of stupefying loveliness, filled with the sad reminder of death and life and the terminal nature of all living things. The rain began to drizzle. The wind blew harder and brought out all the odors of decay. He unrolled the blanket and draped it over his shoulders. He pocketed the matches and the flashlight. In the water beside him, brown rinds of river-lather bobbed against the rocks. The farther up he climbed, the faster the river moved, the colder the wind blew. He wore the wind like a cloak. In no time, the swollen water was thundering away beside him, so white, so black. The blanket across his shoulders became soaked and heavy. He sloughed it off and left it on the riverbank.

An hour later, he came to a game trail that led away from the river toward the crenellated mountains. He followed this path and soon entered a silver bleeding wood. From here, Joel continued forward, pressing toward his mark, the prize of the high calling, although he was purblind now and plagued with chills and alternate flashes of heat.

At twilight, when the sun hung like a salmon lozenge under the dark clouds in the west, the sky above him opened up in earnest. The rain came slanting down; leaves cartwheeling all through the windy air. It was in these conditions that Joel stopped at the base of a grassy hill whose surface was studded with large cubic boulders that stood gleaming like moonrocks in the rain. The grass was long and limey. Creamy fog oozed down from the hilltop. There was no trail anywhere that he could see, so he walked straight up the center of the hill, through the wet grass, his pant legs saturating. At the top of the hill, groin-deep in grass and fog, the sky collapsed around him, and his sense of direction collapsed as well.

He stopped moving. He cast about for the stone crenellations and the thin spire of rock that rose above the rest, but he could not see anything. Clouds were draped over the entire world. After a while, Joel couldn't tell in what direction he looked. Yet he continued moving. What else to do? Just then, the sleek silver shape emerged from the trees above him and went gliding into the hills. The shape flashed once and vanished. Then it reappeared briefly and was gone again. This thing, whatever it was, may have been flying or it may have just been running. In either case, it had a liquidy quality, which for all its ephemerality struck him as indescribably beautiful. He followed after it.

And in so doing, he became irretrievably lost.

Every one of his steps now uncovered slimy patches of tobacco-like leaves. His wet hair hung in ropy ringlets down his back. A flock of ravens pounded lowly by. They called to him hoarsely, wind-muted croaks that struck his heart with a gothic pang. He did not see the quicksilver shape again. He moved on in a lobotomized fashion. The rain did not abate. Night fell suddenly.

Still he pressed on. He felt himself pursued now by the footsteps of the dead, the eschatological terrors of his childhood, something less clear. Beneath him, the ground was soaked and spongy; his sneakers slogged through. In the deep night, he passed through a city of small aspen trees like little ghosts that fell across the slopes. Their leaves reeled down around him in the darkness.

Joel walked that entire night without rest. The mountain storm followed him the whole time. All around him, spasms of lightening flickered on and off. The fog came and went. And came.

Early that morning, in a grainy light twelve thousand feet high, he fell upon the shores of a wide volcanic lake. The lake water was so deep that, even in the early dawn light, the entire lake looked like a pool of turquoise. The shore was ringed about by silver-gray rocks. A cold wind corrugated the surface. Above him, the black sky wept bitterly still. Joel rested on the shore and drank from the lake. The pain in his stomach had subsided to a dull steady ache. As he leaned over his cupped hands, the tips of his hair touched the water. Torn rags of fog blew across the surface of the lake.

He lay back on the rocks, exposed to the rain and the wind. Soon the morning grew as bright as it was going to get, the sun a wan crescent of light. Through the mist, Joel could make out a forest of firs a few hundred feet below. He didn't have any idea where he was.

He looked behind him and scanned the wilds out of which he'd just come. Nothing was there. Nothing moved, no living thing. He felt himself completely alone. He got up and walked around the lake, over a hill of stubble grass.

On the other side, at the bottom of the hill, he came to another lake, identical to the first in every way that he could see.

Again he walked around the lake and then again over a grass hill, and again he came upon a third lake. In disbelief, he gazed out across the water from the silver shores. The glassy wind passed over him. He was very cold and soaking wet. He was near now to despair. Or madness. The wind cut through to his bones. Then he saw something move at his feet. He looked down.

It was a living entity, a tiny salamander crawling off the rocks and arrowing into the water. It was fish-colored and had a tail like a tiny whip, a small snake's head. He watched it paddle away into the blue water. It was very beautiful. When it was gone, he saw a dark face emerge in the water. This face stared straight back at him like a nereid, and it was with shock that he realized this face was his own. He looked skeletal and scarred, yet he was still alive. Seeing himself thus, he suddenly remembered his mother's note, the one she had left inside his book:

You must live. You must always live.

Far below him, and slightly to the left, a parkland, fifty acres in extent, stretched off into the mountain mist.

That open field is where he went. The rain increased.

Coming deeper into the mist, Joel found himself among a forest of moss-draped conifers. Before him on the ground and sprung full-blown from the earth were huge puffball fungi growing out everywhere. They were big bulbous lobes that lay like alien skulls in the grass. All around him blew a boletic stench, and ripe mulchy smells, odors of compost and humus, the autumn earth distilling hot teas and sour brews, velveteen broth. All the evergreens now were sluicing silver water. Joel kicked the heads off inky cap mushrooms, their gills dissolving in dark blood. Horrible beauty. He reached down and plucked up a puffball with both his hands. He held it as if it were a dinosaur egg, membranous and fat, while it discharged a yellow ethos around his body. The grass twitched spasmodically in the rain. He cracked the puffball open. Dry dust exploded into the wet air. Joel stood looking at the torn white muscle in each of his hands. He discarded it. He walked on.

He walked for the rest of that morning and then into the afternoon and then the evening. The fog never lifted. The trees never thinned. It seemed to him that he made no progress. It seemed to him that he was walking in circles. At dusk the wind finally died. Still the rain continued. A weak watery sun bled its last. Joel moved across the twilit plains, over tumulus ground, thirteen thousand feet above sea-level. Fog lay folded over the rocks.

Late that night, in a stupor of sickness and exhaustion, he emerged from mist and stood before a dark cliff at whose base a narrow doorway opened up into the mountain. The top of the cliff was sunk in dove-gray clouds. He stood tottering in the rain. He squinted up toward the summit. He could not see it. He stood for ten minutes and then he entered the rock.

It was an abandoned mineshaft. It smelled of dust and minerals. There was the steady echo-drip of water within, yet the ground beneath him was dry. He saw the dim shapes of two-by-eight planks scattered about; vestiges of old scaffolding and collapsed braces. He checked his sealed bag of matches, whose tips he'd long ago encased in wax. They had remained dry. With his long knife, he split one of the two-by-eights and built a fire. He stoked the fire enormously in the entrance of the mineshaft and warmed himself mindlessly. A continuous breeze poured out of the blackness, coming from somewhere deep inside the earth and traveling back outside, fanning the fire on its way. The flames twisted and sawed. The fire cast an orange glow onto the ground. Joel dried at length. Then he lay down like a dog on the cold earth and fell asleep. The last thing he heard was the sound of underground streams flowing away beneath him like time.

47

He was awakened by the sound of a distant collision. When he opened his eyes, the first thing he saw was a pair of banana slugs copulating beside his face. They were large leopard-spotted slugs, entwined double helix around a mucus cord, like a caduceus. A frothy bubble grew between them. His empty stomach churned; it churned up nothing. The fire was dead. How long had he slept? He was not sure. He was cold and shivering. The cave had the stale odor of a crypt.

The sound of the distant collision came again. He realized only then that this noise is what had brought him out of his long sleep. He picked himself up off the ground and went outside. His whole body felt excessively sore.

The rain had not stopped, and the world was silver-gray. Wild vapors blew across the cliffs. The sun was a thin bloody stain in the east. A mild tinnitus whistled in his ears. The chopping sound came again. What was it? He stood listening. It didn't return. The stain in the east spread gradually. The rain tapped. The air was glassy and thin. The ground about him consisted of sparse gray grass and large patches of bare rock, which lay half-buried in the earth, showing through like the skins of enormous red potatoes. The concussive sound came back: a sharp but distant crack. It wasn't a gun, he knew that for certain, and yet he couldn't figure out what it was. It sounded not quite like anything he'd ever heard. It rebated off the cliff wall behind him. He thought it must be issuing from the woods below, although he wasn't sure of that either; for it also seemed to perhaps emanate from the sky. It came only once every few minutes, but with conspicuous regularity, and still, each time he heard it, it startled him out of all normal proportion.

He turned and looked at the cliff wall behind him. Patches of mauve rock glinted through the shredded rags of fog. Joel could also see stratified water stains, like chalk, high up the narrow walls—vestiges of an antediluvian flood. Tangled gorse grew out of the cliff walls and were clawing now at the low-hanging sky. The collision came again, ricocheting off the rock.

Joel was dangerously lightheaded. He started down into the woods which he believed sourced this strange intermittent sound.

In the woods, the ground was fully saturated. Wet warts of blue lichen gleamed in the rain. The collision came again. It was louder now. He knew he was nearing its source, but he still couldn't tell in exactly which direction it was coming from. The sound filled him with apprehension.

The fog was so thick that he was unable to see more than five feet in front of him. Then for a flash, when the fog blew briefly away, he thought he glimpsed a bearded figure in a stovepipe hat standing off in the rain. But the instant he saw it, the fog swallowed it back up.

Joel flung himself behind a tree and flattened himself against the rough bark. He did not breathe. What the hell was that? Then the concussive crack came again. It echoed all throughout the silent woods. Joel felt something watching him. He lifted his eyes to the tree above. A murder of crows, blue-black and beaded with rainwater, stood staring from among the sluicing evergreen boughs. When his eyes fell upon them, one of the crows resituated its wing, as if that wing had been improperly folded. Then it grokked at him and blinked a golden eye. Joel stared back with dread in his heart.

After many minutes, he peered cautiously around the tree trunk. The fog was still too thick for him to see. He dashed forward silently, his breath pluming. He hid behind another tree twenty feet farther up. The sound came again. He was right on top of it now.

He peered around the tree and at last glimpsed the source of the collision.

It was two bighorn rams knocking heads in a forest clearing.

The ewes stood watching from the mist that partially concealed them. They were wild-looking and eerie. When the sheep sensed him there, they floated soundlessly up the rocks with muscular strides and cornuted heads; then, suddenly, another sound reverberated, a sound that Joel wasn't at all prepared for, and which shook him badly: it was the sound of a great act of violence.

Joel squinted into the shifting fog. He saw nothing for some time. Then the fog whirled away, and he caught sight of his father, fifty meters beyond, kneeling in the wet grass, slaughtering a huge ram, the biggest of the two that had been hammering heads. His father immediately stood when he saw Joel watching. He held his knife at his side. He wore his black cowboy hat now, and he was soaked in blood and water. The knife blade dripped. The two stared at each other for a long moment, and then the old man smiled.

He advanced with his knife.

Joel bolted back up the hill.

48

He was at a dead run when he plunged into the black mineshaft, knowing full well that his father was close behind him. Once again, Joel entered the labyrinthine tunnels, and in so doing he lost his father, but also in so doing, he as well grew hopelessly lost.

He didn't have any good idea how long he was in the caves. He had nothing by which to gauge time, and his own sense of time deserted him early on. For days, he saw nothing but black. Black everywhere. And yet he never stopped looking.

After a certain period of time, his fear left him. He shuffled on blindly through the cryptlike tunnels. He slept among the cold stones, by turns sweating and shivering. He slept in fits and starts. He lay on his stomach over icy pools of water that he could not see, and he drank the black liquid that he half hoped would poison him. It did not. His hunger was absolutely gone. His flashlight no longer cast light. For a while, the wire filaments behind the lens shone with a dull reddish glow, which soon faded away into blackness. After that, the darkness around him was pure. The only thing he saw was the multicolored wands of light generated by his own brain. He still had dry matches, but he'd nothing to light on fire, not even strips of his own clothes, so damp had they grown, so cold in these underground corridors.

Many times Joel was sure he heard voices beside and behind him, voices coming down offshoot passageways. Sometimes he heard other sounds as well, like low growls and grunts, and the inexhaustible footsteps of the dead. He called out. His voice reverberated gigantically around the vacant stone caverns, and that was all. He'd strike matches one after another—only to see his pale fingers shaking from cold, and then the matches winked out and darkness engulfed him total.

At first he moved much through the black caves on all fours, feeling his way by hand, afraid the ground would open up without warning and send him falling into the hot flames of earth's core. Then he stopped caring. He shuffled on.

Near the end, he came to a narrow stone cleft out of which blew an odorless breeze. This cleft he managed to squeeze himself through.

On the other side of it, he found nothing new, at first. Just more blackness piled on more blackness and more, all of it filled with cold empty space. But then, when he moved to the right, he felt the breeze coming stronger from somewhere down below him. He felt around with his feet and then with his hands, until he brushed over something wooden. He investigated it with his fingers.

It was a ladder, an old ladder he didn't trust. Still, he lowered himself cautiously onto the first rung, and immediately that rung split in half and sent him crashing down, rungs snapping beneath his feet even while his hands held each side of the ladder. The drumming sound resounded about him, and then all was silent. He lay on his back on the ground that he'd fallen to. He hadn't fallen very far, yet he hit the ground with an impact that stunned him. He sat up. He felt around among the broken rungs and picked one up. He struck a match and managed to set that wooden rung on fire. Once it was lit, he held the burning rung vertically, pointing it downward, so that the yellow flame licked back at the wood, toward his fingers. The creamy firelight blossomed in the room and hurt his unaccustomed eyes in a good way.

He then lit another rung on fire, and then another. Soon a small strong blaze burned in the room.

In front of him now, he could see a wide passageway that led out of this room. This is where the breeze was coming in from.

He built the fire higher. The blowing breeze fanned the coals. There was plenty of dry wood down here: a pick handle, a shovel, fallen braces, the busted ladder. After five minutes, Joel was even able to discern the black hole above him, through which he'd fallen. He kept adding wood; he warmed himself. After some time, he became aware of a strange object in the corner of that room. The object was black, but there was a small white glow hovering above it, like a halo, or a miniature moon. Joel stared at the object for a long time. He seemed agitated and loathe to approach, as if he'd begun to suspect what it was. But eventually he did approach. And his suspicions were confirmed.

It was a human skeleton, fully clothed but lying intact upon the ground.

The domed skull was faintly phosphorescent, glowing lunar-like above the black jacket.

The skeleton was stretched out nearly supine, the head alone propped up on something behind it, the hollow eye-sockets staring vacantly at the spires of limestone that dripped like teeth from the low ceiling. Beside the spiderlike flanges, there was a metal flashlight on the ground. The skeleton wore a thick leather jacket, which was partially unzipped, the gray sternum shimmering in the ambient light of his fire. The square teeth leered at Joel.

Joel shuddered, and moved closer.

There appeared no external injury, nothing broken that he could see. The skeleton was remarkably well-preserved, pristine even. What had killed this person? Lack of oxygen? A poisonous gas? The bleeding heart within bursting behind the breastbone?

In fact, as he was about to discover, it was this latter thing: the heart breaking inside the body human. When Joel removed the dead man's coat and put it on for warmth, not only did the bones crumble into a heap of rubble, but he also found on the ground, beneath the leg, a slip of coarse paper that said:

Dear William,

I love you and will always love you. You are the one person in my life that could never be duplicated, and from whom I've learned the most. But as you know—as you yourself once said—I could never come back. It's too late for us now. Our time is done. Forgive me this necessary unkindness, even if it kills you, as I fear it will.

Love,
Lauren

Beneath that, in handwriting altogether different, Joel read the following words:

I William Michael Morgan was lost in these caves. I came here looking for a treasure that I did not find. Instead, I found gold, only gold. I got turned around in an endless maze of tunnels and I could not find my way out. My food and water are long gone. I know now, as I write this, that I will die. I was certain I'd find what I was looking for. I was wrong. I write this note in the unlikely event that someone should ever find my remains. I write it so that it can be known that I did this to myself, but I did not do it intentionally. My death is no suicide.
I am no longer afraid of death.

Signed,
William Michael Morgan

Joel, delirious, was not able to grasp the full ramifications of this. He grasped enough, however.
Mon semblable, he whispered.
He tried Bill Morgan's flashlight.
It too was dead.
But he found something else there: behind the piled skeleton, glinting dully in the dark, a huge mound of pure gold.

Joel sat for an hour, throwing more wood into the fire and staring transfixed into the coals, the gooey hearts slowly pulsing. The stalactites above him flickered in the firelight. Now and then, he looked back to the bones of the dead, his half brother reduced to chalky rubble on the floor.
The bones did not frighten him any more.
After a while, Joel slept.

Something cried out. It was a piercing shriek. His eyes flipped open. Joel was stretched out on his side next to the faded fire. He felt a crawling sensation on his face. Although the fire was reduced, he could clearly see what was on him. It was a giant rat perched and squeaking on his shoulder, the pink tail lightly lashing his face.

Joel yelled and with great force backhanded the rat off of him. He sent the rat tumbling across the room. To Joel's horror, a choir of rat screeches followed.

He sat up and looked around him.

The cavern floor was a surging sea of rats. They had come here because of his firelight. They were mean-looking rats. Joel's breath choked; he jumped to his feet, his eyes wild. The rats snuffed him, hissed. He kicked at them. There were hundreds.

Without looking back, Joel ran headlong into the pesthole out of which the black breeze blew.

And Joel was running, running. Entering a deeper darkness, and a thicker stench, he stumbled into a lake of putrescence, a sheet of some foul and foreign ejaculate that sloshed under his shoes like mush. It smelled of hot decay. He could not see anything, but he felt it. He felt it enveloping his ankles. Goddamn, goddamn! He was seized with panic. Then came more squeaking, a different kind of squeaking now that did not sound like the rats, and he felt more things on his body, crawling things, spiders and insects moving over him, leathery wings slapping dryly across his face. *My God, my God,* he thought, *bats.* Bats on their inflight or outflight, he had no way of knowing. He yanked Bill Morgan's jacket like a cowl over his head. There was no way for him to turn back now, even if he wanted to face the roomful of rats: his firelight had been swallowed by darkness, and he no longer knew the direction by which he'd come to this place.

So he waded deeper into the thick viscous pool of sperm. With his free hand, he swatted himself, whacking sightlessly at the things that crawled over him, whacking the furred wings that whooshed past his face. The room now was filled with a rising crescendo of high-pitched shrieks, the sickening reek of rot.

Joel slid forward, one hand holding the jacket over his head. He plunged through the passageway and suddenly smacked face-first into a solid rock wall. The impact almost knocked him down. He staggered in confusion. The squeaking overwhelmed him. He was gasping the mephitic air. He was clawing at himself. *Calm down!* he told himself. *Goddamn it, calm down!* But even as he told himself this, he thought of rabid bats and rats and poisonous spiders all over him in the dark. With gripping terror, Joel plunged farther into the rotted pudding beneath him. He tripped again, fell forward, his fingers sliding through the foul jissom. He stood and continued into the utter blackness, beyond which lay only more blackness and more. He slogged through interminably, fearing and hoping at the same time that the ground beneath him would open and send him plunging into the empty chambers of the earth. Still the creeping things swarmed over him, the high-pitched shrieks like dog whistles in his ears, the pasty sludge sucking at his shoes, the reek assaulting his senses and his brain, stinging his eyes, good Christ, the poisonous air he imagined spreading like a deadly histoplasmosis throughout the bronchial tree inside him, taking root inside his tree of life infecting it with microbes and microparasites and worms. He imagined the rats surging up around his legs, nipping at him, rats the size of swine lashing him with bald pink tails, until at last he pitched forward and fell headlong into a torrent of icy purging water that swallowed him whole.

49

He washed up on an alien shore deeper within the mine. When he opened his eyes, he saw nothing at all; his eyes never acclimated. He felt himself near the earth's actual core, gravity sucking at his bones. He climbed out of the water and stood dripping in the mineral darkness.

He wandered around down here for days. More mazes of stone. He drank from black flowing water. Soon he began to understand that, like Bill Morgan, he would also die here; yet by this time, he was so exhausted from his lack of food that he could not find energy enough to worry. Nor was he able to feel overly surprised by the one image that kept coming back into his mind: the image of Lauren Lake.

He slept and moved on.

He followed this pattern for what seemed weeks.

At the end of it, he came to a large room wherein a block of pure sunlight descended from a hole in the ceiling above him. The opening was too high for him to reach. The climb was not difficult, but he was very tired. So he lay down on the floor inside the light and slept. The light was warm. It was bright. How long he slept, he didn't know. He opened his eyes, and when he did, he found himself looking up through the hole at a sky now absolutely awash in stars.

Joel began scaling the rock.

It was deep night when he finally emerged into the outside world. The air was cool. He breathed it in. Over his head, Orion stood pinned gigantically against the sky, like thumbtacks marking off incomprehensible coordinates. Joel stood in the open air and gazed up. The sky was sagging with celestial light. He'd never seen so many stars. He swayed in exhaustion, but he was also giddy with awe and liberation. There were more stars in the sky than there was blackness of space, and green meteors crisscrossed everywhere in silent arcs. The jellied blackness was alive and burning, long corridors of collapsing matter, stars falling all around him, and more stars, as if the heavens themselves were dismantling. At last, he lowered his gaze and looked around him.

He was astounded to see where he was.

The abandoned monastery, where he'd first emerged from the caves, stood crouched sixty meters away at the feet of the saurian hills.

Joel rotated in a slow circle, gazing around him in wonder. He was free at last in the open air of the world.

All the noctivagant creatures and the wood nymphs with mica eyes winked on in the outlying trees, holding the blackness at bay—or pronouncing it, he could not tell which. The autumnal air smelled intoxicating, a delicate scent of grass and spearmint. The stars fell. He could see his breath expiring faintly into the sky; to him it looked like clouds. Just then, the sleek silvery shape emerged from the farthest building of the monastery and vanished behind the compound. Joel followed after it. He thought the object had gone into the mouth of yet another cave, a mouth partially obscured by trees and lush undergrowth. He went in.

As he entered the stone room, an icy sensation passed over him, a windless chill like the brush of a gleaming blade. This cave was entirely new to him. It was open and spacious. Compared with what he'd just come out of, it was shallow. Ten feet inside the cave, on the dirt floor, there stood a gaping hole that plunged deep down into a dark shaft. This hole was dangerous. For this reason, someone had placed two big sticks across the opening to mark the hole. The sticks were crossed. Joel peered down between them; he peered into the blackness of the shaft. He thought he saw, way down inside, a silvery-blue glow issuing steadily from within, a bluish gleam that was very soft, like a star burning inside the earth.

Joel stood staring at it. He was shivering with cold, but he also felt alive and free. He had survived. And yet he was dizzy and faint. He built a fire near the entrance of the cave and piled on the wood. He stoked a massive bonfire and watched it rage. Tongues of flame rose up and licked at the huge rock ceiling above. He threw more wood onto the fire. He could not get enough of the flames, the heat. His shadow flickered on the stone wall behind him. He added more wood yet. Then he sat upon the ground right in front of the furnace blast and let the warmth blow over him. He grew listless and sleepy. His eyes blinked slower and slower. He realized now that he was beginning to fall asleep, and he stood up and paced in and out of the ring of firelight, seeking to drive the lethargy out of his body. But pacing only made him feel dizzier. At times he thought he might collapse. He even feared that he would fall into the marked-off pit.

Yet it was not exhaustion or dizziness that preoccupied him most now. For some time, he had been looking into the fire, glancing nervously through the leaping tongues of flame. At length, he sat back down and again stared through the fire at something beyond, something sitting on the other side.

In fact, it turned out that someone was indeed sitting across from him, a tall man, no longer young, with long legs crossed Indian style, his enormous hands folded sedately across his chest. Joel could not remember how long this man had been sitting here, and he grew more and more upset with himself because he couldn't figure it out. His anger made him reluctant to speak, and so he sat fuming. He did not, however, remove his eyes from the man opposed to him, the man whose face was twitching with light and shade.

Finally the man spoke:

"It's a fearful thing to fall into the hands of the living God," he said.

"Pardon?" Joel said.

"I said God is a consuming fire, and it's a fearful thing to fall into the hands of the living God."

"I'm sorry," Joel said. "I can't seem to recall exactly when you came here." He looked troubled as he spoke, and almost as if he might for some reason cry. At that moment, a log collapsed in the fire, sending a chain of sparks flying into the ceiling. Joel watched them. He then shook his head, as if to jiggle clarity into his brain. "How *did* you get here?" he said.

"These tunnels all lead to the same spot eventually."

Joel nodded. His seated shadow loomed on the cave wall, and the man nodded to that shadow now. Joel turned to see what he was indicating. "What is it?" Joel said.

"Your shadow on the wall of a cave," the man said.

"What of it?"

"It's a reflection," the man said, "but what's it a reflection of?"

"It's a reflection of what's real," Joel said.

"So the shadow is the negative, and what's casting the shadow is the positive?"

"Yes."

"Reality then reflects itself?" the man said.

"Yes," Joel said. "And everything that exists is reality."

A pocket of pitch thudded deep within the fire. With dilated pupils, Joel stared transfixed into the coals. Silence ensued.

"Did you see the moon tonight, son?" the man said. He gestured vaguely to the mouth of the cave; a slight lift of his index finger.

Joel didn't answer. He did, however, turn his head to gaze outside. There, between the trees, the full moon hung hugely, like a giant egg in sky. It hovered up above the terrestrial curve. For a long moment, Joel couldn't believe his eyes. It was the biggest moon he'd ever seen. Green meteors fell around it. Joel stared in silence; he stared at the fantastically silver shiny moon. The fire raged in the cave.

"The moon is at its perigee," the man said. "That's why it's so big."

Joel turned back to the flames.

"Are you unwell?" the man said.

"Yes," Joel said. "I'm very unwell. To be honest, I've been sick for a long time. I can't seem to shake it, I don't know why. It keeps coming back. And still, after all this time, I don't know for sure what's wrong with me."

"Trouble in the flesh."

"Perhaps," Joel said. He closed his eyes, opened them slowly.

The man lifted his index finger again and gestured back to the ovoid moon. "Do you believe that the earth is an egg that contains all good things in it?"

"Yes," Joel said, "I do believe that."

"Then it is to you," the man said. "For there's nothing either good or bad, but thinking makes it so."

"Is that true?"

"True? No, it's not true. There comes a point—and you reached it long ago—when ignorance can no longer be justified, when ignorance becomes the unwillingness to think, the unwillingness to piece out painstakingly the nature of things, to hammer out your own salvation, and in so doing to become your own master. All of that takes effort and time and work. Most would rather do other things. I don't deny that. But that doesn't alter the facts: Thinking takes effort. It takes the effort of attention, the strain of focus. When ignorance is the result of the opposite sort of act—an act of avoidance—it is bad, objectively, regardless of whether or not anyone thinks it's so. And regardless of whether you're able to convince yourself otherwise. Make no mistake: the human capacity for rationalization is limitless."

Joel nodded again. "I see."

"Thinking is effort," the man said again. "Morality is discipline. Life is work. There's a man whose labor is in wisdom and in knowledge and in equity. Yet not all people are brilliant."

"So what of that?"

"It doesn't matter at all if one is brilliant or not."

Joel didn't say anything.

"If I'd not come and spoken, there would be no sin, because there would be no knowledge of sin. But now that I have spoken, there's no longer a cloak for sin. Ignorance past a certain point can't be justified. Ignorance is a lapse in thought, a refusal to think, a refusal to engage the effort, whether because of busyness, or vice, or impatience, or anything. *That* is no longer so easy to cloak. Or to justify."

"Well, I wonder," Joel said.

"At what do you wonder?" But the man didn't give Joel time to respond. "In a person born healthy, there's always the choice to pay attention or not. Years of protracted avoidance can habituate against it, it can damage the choice, and the chains of thinking can get tangled beyond all untangling so that there's no longer any short way back to sense. But if the person is healthy, the choice to think always exists. If there were not choice, there could not be right or wrong behavior."

"That is true," Joel said. And as he sat there now, clawing back through all the events of his life, he saw indeed that every moment of it could have been different if he would have decided each individual moment differently.

"Yes," the man said, "it is true. But do you know why it's true? It's true because we are each defined by our actions, which are chosen. Actions are shaped by thoughts. Thoughts are processed within a context of knowledge, the body of data we've accumulated, a level of understanding and intelligence, but whether that context is large or small makes no difference. There's nobody who's ever asked for more than he or she is capable of. Do you hear me?"

"Yes," Joel said.

"Actions that can't be chosen are automatic actions. They are neither moral nor immoral but amoral, precisely because they're automatic. That is how the animals live: amoral. But the human brain, which operates by means of thought whose activation is chosen, is not amoral. And the choice to pay attention is the seat of moral agency. Reason, as John Milton said, is also choice. Thinking *is* attention. It must be willed by each—and only each. It's that act, the act of focusing the attention, that no person can perform for another. It's the first and final act of will for humans. It's the locus of human individuation. It's the locus of independence and human freedom—political freedom and psychological freedom. That ultimate choice to pay attention or not is what gives rise to moral agency. That is why humans and humans alone are the ethical primate."

Joel didn't answer.

"If human action were not chosen but automatic," the man said, "there would be no such thing as freedom and no such thing as moral agency, because human action would be unchosen. The grizzly bear who mauls the innocent child isn't evil. The man who mauls the innocent child is. Do you understand the difference between a man who murders and a bear who mauls?"

Joel stared steadfastly into the tongues of fire. "Please," he said, *"please,* no more philosophy."

"What? Now I've become your enemy because I tell you the truth?"

"No," Joel said. "No."

"And who's bewitched you that you shouldn't obey the truth?"

"No one has."

The fire squealed and exploded. A ball of molten scurf went sailing into the ceiling of the cave.

"God *is* a consuming fire," the man said. "And He is not mocked."

"God is spirit," Joel whispered.

"And they that worship Him must worship Him in spirit and in truth," the man said. "Which things are an allegory whose purpose is to make the abstract principles real, to turn ideas into the concrete reality we all live in every day. That is the purpose of myth and art and allegory. But people do error when they take symbology as fact. At some point, we have to get real." The man paused. "So let's get real," he said.

"Yes," Joel said.

"A crime has been committed," the man said. "But a crime against whom?"

The man waited. Joel didn't speak, but he felt himself growing angrier and angrier.

"I don't understand," Joel said at last. "And your question is irrelevant—"

"Is it?" the man said. "Or is it entirely relevant?" He grinned. His large teeth shone phosphorescent in the cave.

Joel closed his eyes and put his face in his hands. He shook his head. They were both silent for several minutes.

"Do you know who I am?" the man said.

Joel opened his eyes and squinted through the fire. "Yes," he said. "I know who you are. How could I not?"

The man nodded.

"You're the person who killed my mother," Joel said. "Of course I know who you are."

The old man reached behind himself and took from his back pocket a small book. He held it up over his head, toward to the firelight. It was *The Secret*

History of the Arche, Joel's copy, the same copy in the hidden vessel, which he'd left on the cliff ledge. The cover glinted, wavier now in the firelight. The man tossed it onto the hot coals. Joel sat there and watched the painted child burn. He watched the delicately rendered face blister and scar. He watched the painted chessboard bubble. Then all the pages and all the knowledge and truth contained therein burst open and collapsed into pure ash. The coals beneath the book looked translucent now, full of hidden caves and grottoes and enigmatic chambers of pulsing light.

"God is a consuming fire," the old man said, "and there can be no light without dark. No up without down. No life without death. No good without bad. Now, Joel, where's the goddamn map?"

Joel didn't say anything. He closed his eyes again.

"I've waited a *very* long time," his father said.

"Is she still alive?" Joel said. "You told me once that you buried her in the mountains that she loved? Do you still have her there, imprisoned in the caves?" Joel opened his eyes.

The old man's pupils widened in incredulity and rage. "Is *that* what you think?"

"Is she?" Joel said. "Is she still alive?"

The old man glared at him ferociously. "You are one simple son-of-a-bitch."

"Please don't say that, father."

"You've disappointed me *so* much, Joel. I can't even tell you how much. You're nothing but a pale criminal. You're a mediocrity who fears blood more and more. Now I'm going to ask you again: where's the goddamn map?"

"I burned it," Joel said. "I burned the map."

"You'd better be lying."

Joel shook his head. "No," he said, "I'm not lying. I promise you I'm not lying." He saw the dangerous-looking underbite suddenly appear on his father's face, and it made his heart race. "What do you care about the map?" Joel said. "It was your mining claim. Your property. Have you forgotten where it is, *your mine?*" Joel spat these last words out with contempt.

"*What?*"

"You heard me," Joel said.

"Are you really so stupid? Do you really not understand anything at all?"

Joel tilted his head: a brand new thought had just entered him. "Tell me," Joel said, "tell me what it is I don't understand. Tell me exactly what's at issue here."

"It's the oldest issue there is: it's an issue of blood," his father said.

At precisely that moment, everything came together for Joel. He understood at last. His eyeballs jerked over to the hole in the ground, the two dark sticks marking the opening, the two sticks crossed like a large X, marking that spot. The hole was only three feet away from him. He could still see inside the silvery gleam throbbing deep down in the earth.

His father did not notice. He continued: "This is about the principal thing. It's about the only thing that matters, in the end: blood, bloodlust."

With that, the old man rose up from his cross-legged position on the ground, something white and glinting in his hand, like the jawbone of an ass. Joel saw then that there were flecks of dry blood on the backs of the old man's wrists and hands.

"Through knowledge shall the just indeed be delivered," his father said. He came at Joel straight through the center of the fire and emerged on the other side.

But this time Joel was ready for him.

He stood up instantly and stepped through the two cruciate sticks and went plunging down into the gaping hole, knowing full well that his father could never survive exposure to that surgical gleam—knowing also that nothing short of death would ever stop the old man's relentless pursuit.

50

Joel fell through.

He came crashing out of the caves, and when he tumbled outside, he landed with a jolt that jarred his entire body. For some time, he lay on his back and stared up into the bewildering light of day. He lifted his head. At the foot of the iron mountains, thermal winds swirled up scarves of dust. In the opposite direction, not ten meters to his left, the melancholy trailer-house stood shimmering under the bright morning sky. Beyond him, the limbs of the ancient apple tree were bent low with their lunar globes of fruit.

Joel jumped to his feet and went running across the yard, up the short porch steps. He burst through the front door and into the house.

"Mother!" he said.

But the rooms were barren and swept clean, and the house was left to him desolate.

"Mother!" he said.

The only answer was the wind.

The windows all stood open. The soft September air poured into the room. The ghostly curtains billowed and popped. Grains of dust blew in from outside. On the kitchen table, the egg stood tilted in its narrow shot glass, the telephone still crouched beside it, waiting to ring, but the big shining orange was gone.

Joel ran to the back of the house, where his father's bedroom was.

The made bed was empty.

A small lump lay under the tight covers, something left there in his father's stead.

Joel went over and stood above the bed, staring down at the lump. Finally he folded back the covers.

On the white sheet was the precious stone Joel had once, many years ago, stolen from his father. Under the stone, as if that stone was weighing it down, anchoring it, lay the delicate watercolor that Joel had found in his own bed the night after his mother's death. The painting was as bright and as beautiful now as on the night when he'd first discovered it. There was a small note in his father's handwriting:

For my son, Joseph Joel Gasteneau.

Joel shut his eyes.

The autumn wind came whistling into the room. It threatened to blow right through him.

And then the telephone rang.

He bolted back to kitchen and picked up the receiver.

"Hello?" he said.

The woman's voice that came through the other end was unmistakable—unmistakable in its happiness, its languorous lilt.

"I've been looking everywhere for you," the voice said.

"How did you find me?"

51

Joel sat alone at a cafe counter and sipped his coffee. A slablike windowpane on his right gave to yellow sandhills. Beyond that, to the north, a bone-white road gleamed in the sharp western light, arterial dirt roads branching off into hidden places.

Joel drank his coffee and stared outside. The sun was sinking. Southward, a large circular cloud stood punctured clean through, like a donut. The sun slanted left and cast shadows which lay perpendicular the highway. A pair of dust devils sprung up among the distant sandhills and then whirled away like twin serpents doing a strange desert dance; they spun themselves out. In the foyer of the cafe, a small fountain splashed and gurgled.

"Hey, buddy," a voice said behind him. "Quit scratching your balls."

Joel turned. He found himself looking into a pair of cobalt eyes. They were the eyes of a young boy, who was smiling. "Hey, buddy," the boy said again. "Quit scratching your balls."

"Quit scratching *your* balls," Joel said.

"Ain't." The boy advanced two giant-steps closer. He had sandy hair and very symmetrical features. His skin was suntanned. "Hey, buddy. What day is it?"

"I don't know," Joel said. "That's a good question."

"Well, I wish it was the damn day after tomorrow."

"Why?"

"Because I get to go horseback riding with my father."

He spoke the last half of that sentence with a rising intonation, so that by the time he'd come to the final three words, he was nigh to screaming.

At which point, a good-looking young lady—his mother—came striding over from the cash register, her slim legs clipping like scissors. "Hey, hey," she said. "Cool your jets, Magellan. There's absolutely no reason to shout. I'm sure the nice man hears you just fine." She winked at Joel. "Isn't that right, monsieur?"

"Oui," Joel said.

"We?" the boy said.

The woman stared at her child, and so did Joel. The woman's eyelashes rose and fell slowly. They were much like her son's: long and black and becoming. She shared his twin pools of cobalt as well. Her brown hair hung in long spirals past the middle of her back. She wore a white tanktop that exposed the lower half of her midsection, which was indrawn and toffee-colored, a tiny gold hoop burning in the delicate skin around the edge of her navel.

"Yes, that's right," Joel said, speaking louder now, more animatedly, and turning from the mother back to the boy. "That is right, sir. What am I, deaf?" Joel then extended his hand to the child. "My name is Joel," he said. "Joel Gasteneau. And your name, sir?"

The boy didn't answer.

"Introduce yourself, Roger," the young woman said. With her hip, she nudged her child forward.

"Roger Brown," he said to Joel. "Ask me again and I'll knock you down." He pumped Joel's hand vigorously.

"One of these days, we'll have to cut that joke open and count the rings on it," his mother said. "I predict it will be a fascinating experiment."

Hearing this, Roger emitted an ear-shattering cackle—or, more precisely, a long series of "han-han-hans" which came, evidently, straight from the back of his throat. So widely did he open his mouth that while he laughed Joel and Roger's mother both saw the little uvula hanging down like a miniature stalactite from the ceiling of that cave, dripping onto the plush carpeting of his protruding tongue.

"Darling, darling" the woman said with a frown, "my God. You're louder than a jackleg. Please give mommy a break before she breaks your face." She then turned back to Joel. "My name is Ashley," she said.

"Actually," Roger said.

She extended her hand, which Joel shook.

"It's nice to meet you, Ashley," Joel said.

"Hey, buddy," Roger said. "Quit scratching your balls."

"Why does he keep saying that?" Joel said.

"Who knows where the wind goes when it's calm?" Ashley said.

"Big news afoot," Roger said. He pointed toward Joel's shoe.

Ashley and Joel glanced down to where Roger was pointing.

An old newspaper was lying on the floor beneath the counter. It was opened to a page that someone had left a dirty footprint upon.

Ashley scrubbed Roger's hair. "Everybody's a comedian," she said. "And Roger dodger the old codger is about as funny as a rubber crutch. Now, then: shall we adjourn?"

Roger nodded: big robotic head jerks. "Oui," he said.

"Your sullen sister's waiting for us in the car," Ashley said.

Roger turned back to Joel.

"We'll see you," Joel said. He lifted his chin. "Don't get bucked off that bronco."

"Not bloody loikly!" Roger said.

Joel turned to Ashley. "Goodbye," he said.

"Goodbye," said Ashley. "Thank you for being so nice."

After they left, Joel swallowed the remains of his coffee and stood up. The newspaper rustled beneath his foot. He glanced down at it. Something there attracted his eye. He picked up the newspaper.

It was an article—or, rather, the continuation of an article—about a child prodigy, of mysterious origins, who had the same last name as Joel. According to the article, this prodigy was believed by some to have possessed the highest raw intelligence ever observed. And yet, said the article, this person went almost nowhere in the end.

The article continued:

No one knew the date of his birth, or even who his family was. He was orphaned as a child, and he'd run away from the orphanage, and from school, when he was still very young. He proceeded to teach himself everything he knew. He never earned diplomas or degrees but went on to pursue his own interests, which, among other things, included astronomy, philosophy, and the study of ancient civilizations. When he was in his thirties, he spent a great deal of time in Africa and the Middle East.

A shudder passed through Joel when he read that last thing. The article continued:

He held blue-collar jobs all his life and was for many years a truckdriver. He eventually turned to mining. He believed that, in his own words, "nothing more than work is fundamentally required for the production of wealth—and I mean real wealth—and productive labor is man's highest purpose. Wealth is production, production is life. Life is work. Money is the symbol of production, and symbols must never replace actuality."

He left almost no belongings behind. Investigators did, however, find a handwritten manuscript that confirms what many readers believed all along: He was the author of an anonymous book called The Secret History, *which was a cult classic, and copies of which are all but impossible to find today.*

The Secret History tells the story of a man named Markeus James Raddick, who is probably the author's alter-ego. Raddick not only traces the origins of the Ark of Jehovah to Ethiopia, but he also brings it back to the United States. It is disputed how much of this story is fact and how much is fiction. A number of archeologists and historians have come to the defense of the book, stating publicly that the book is, in the words of one Princeton scholar, "astonishingly accurate." Others have confirmed facts contained within the book that were once thought pure fancy, but which only recently have come to light: for instance, the identity of the architects who built the monolithic, rock-hewn cave churches in Lalibela (or Roha), Ethiopia, churches carved from living rock....*

Joel tore back to the beginning of this article and found that he was in fact reading a long obituary:

Neil Gasteneau was twice married and a widower two times over. His first wife died of an unknown disease. His second wife was the writer Angela Kristiansen-Gasteneau, who herself, under the pseudonym Jamie Kristiansen, developed a small but devoted following. The two had one child, Joseph Gasteneau, whereabouts unknown.

Joel shut his eyes. When he opened them, he saw this headline:

Local Miner Neil Gasteneau Dies of Old Age

A small picture was posted. This photo was apparently recent, for it depicted an old haggard-looking man with a mass of moon-colored hair and defiant eyes.

Joel searched the top of the newspaper for a date, but he couldn't see one.

He glanced outside through the windowpane. Banked clouds hung low over the western horizon. Beneath the clouds lay a long bar of imprisoned light.

In the parking lot, a blue Mercury cruised slowly by. The car came to a stop at the intersection before the highway. Here, ten meters removed, Joel could clearly make out the driver: it was the young mother Ashley, with her son Roger in the passenger seat beside her. Neither of them, however, were whom Joel focused upon. The person commanding his full attention was the teenage girl in the backseat, a girl he'd never seen before. Her hair was flaxen, and she had braces on her teeth. She stared vacantly out the car window, directly at Joel. Her face was devoid of expression. To him, her face looked like the bottom of a deep dead lake, silent and lifeless. Joel watched her for a long time. She did not once blink. He even raised his hand to her, to show that he was a non-hostile presence, but her expression did not change at all, nor did her eyes move. Her face was filled with an infinite silence which frightened and saddened him. As the car pulled out onto the highway, Joel unconsciously reached out to her, knocking his fingertips against the glass, and then suddenly a disembodied head appeared superimposed over the dead face of the girl in the car. This head was bobbing toward him. Joel's pupils dilated.

It was only a reflection of the waitress coming to refill his coffee.

He turned to her.

She saw his troubled face, and she smiled. He glanced outside once more. The car was disappearing down the lonesome highway, and so was the girl. A horsefly buzzed around the edge of the windowpane.

"Would you like more coffee?" the waitress said.

"Yes," Joel said.

She refilled the cup. The sound of the pouring coffee made a soothing plash. Joel sat back down.

"Thank you," he said.

"You're welcome." The waitress's eyes went down to the newspaper by his hand, and she saw the photo of the dead man. She looked at Joel. "Did you know him?" she said. She was holding the bulbous coffee pot by its brown handle.

"Yes," he said.

"How did you know him?"

"He was my father."

Her eyes dropped to the ground. "I'm very sorry."

"Thank you," he said.

She turned and set the coffee pot on its hotplate. She then sipped from a clear carbonated drink with a barber-pole straw studded with silver beads, like cookie decorations. Above her, on the wall, a two-foot trout hung warped upon a wooden plaque. The fish looked ferocious. Joel stared at the fish and was still staring at it when he spoke to her again:

"Did you know him?" he asked.

"Your father?" she said.

"Yes." His eyes went from the fish back to her.

"No," she said. "I don't think so. Not that I know of, anyway."

"If you knew him, you would know," he said.

"Why do you say? Was he exceptional?"

"Yes," Joel said, "he was. He was very exceptional."

"But?"

"But?" Joel said. "There's no but."

"I'm sorry. I thought I heard some hesitation."

"No, no hesitation. To tell you the truth, my father was so exceptional that I almost can't believe it. He could have been perfect. He came *this* close, but he never made it."

"What do you mean?"

"He was violent," Joel said, "and he couldn't let go of that. But do you know what?"

She shook her head.

"He led me to it after all," Joel said. "The old man came through."

"Led you to what?"

Joel stared at her. Then his eyes went back to the mounted fish, whose mouth was round and gigantic. "The truth," Joel said. "He probably orchestrated the whole thing from the very beginning, probably from the time I was a child."

The waitress didn't say anything. The surface of her soda with its fizzing bubbles looked like a sea spewing out an underground geyser of mist. She glanced down at the newspaper again. She reached over and turned the page. Joel then saw the date: September 28th.

"Is that today's paper?" he said.

"Yes."

"It's my birthday," he said, not as an announcement but as a simple statement of fact, because he had only this moment realized it.

"Happy birthday!" she said. "You're a Libra."

Outside, the peace of shadows lay over everything.

52

He came up out of the thistles and into a clearing beneath the evergreens. He could see the daytime moon hanging translucent in the eastern sky. The graveyard sat upon a high hill, a disorderly necropolis of tilted tombstones most of which were streaked with spinach and sour moss and peeked barely above the tall grass. The ghostly trees croaked above; malformed fungus grew like leather along the tree trunks. There were grasshoppers among the grass blades, green little vaulters of the summer stalks, all sunburned black now—like the season, beautiful and dying.

He wore gray slacks and a new shirt, open at the throat, his chest visible through the thin fabric. He watched from a distance while the process started and finished. It didn't take long. There was no formal service. To the north, just below the cemetery hill, a wrinkled lake lay like a kidney, red with autumn sunlight. The breeze blew. The wind, the water, and the blood.

The gravedigger was a thin man with long hair. He stood smoking a cigarette. He was stripped to the waist, his midsection dark from the sun. He nodded to Joel, and Joel told him to proceed. The earth he shoveled was moist and cakey. A smell of mushrooms hung in the air. Then came the stinging odor of smoke from dry autumn fields burning somewhere unseen.

Joel watched the man shovel dirt into the clean-sliced pit, a pit of raw wet clay. The man had wiry arms and prominent veins. There was an extra spade impaled in the dirt. After a while, Joel went over and got the extra spade and helped the man bury the dead.

He and the gravedigger finished shoveling, and then the gravedigger rounded off a dome of dirt. The rectangular tombstone said simply: *Father*

There were no dates listed.

When the gravedigger was finished, Joel gave him a fifty dollar bill, which the man refused. Joel insisted. The man nodded once and slipped the bill into the back pocket of his Levis. He lit another cigarette and smoked it. His front tooth was chipped. They stood in silence. The sky above was deep blue, a perfect day.

The man took a final drag from his cigarette, then dropped the butt onto the ground and crushed it out with his boot. He shook Joel's hand. All around the cemetery, the tall iron fence stood like spears against the royal sky. Joel watched the gravedigger walk down the dirt road, to a white shed at the very end. The man carried both shovels, one in each hand. There were pigeons strutting along either side of the road. Susurrus of wind passed through the grass like the whisper of souls, and the grasses shone whitely in the breeze—the grass that these human dead had fertilized. Spotted leaves lay here and there among the blades.

Viewing him earlier in his walnut coffin, scrolly with involuted knots and bird-eye dots, his father's moon-colored hair had stood frozen and waved. Two vertical grooves bracketed the parted lips. The marmoreal brow was pleated with a permanent scowl, the drooping mustache tinged yellowish; between the lips, his tongue, just-glimpsed, was the spongy-looking texture of raw lung. To Joel, the old man seemed beyond empty now: he seemed like the case of a huge spirit gone cold.

Deer were in the graveyard. They stood nearby, elbow-deep in the dewy grass; they were browsing from the crabapple trees. The grass beneath the trees was long and wind-bent. Sunlight came through the changing leaves and showed the intricate veins and the fading life flowing chemically within each leaf. To the left of him, behind a black-iron grate, a limestone child stood robed and dainty on a granite plinth. No figure of grief, this smiling child messiah. The stone hair had autumn leaves plastered to it. The hair was weather-pocked and wavy, the lidless eyes staring forever out on this ruined scene, a mouth like a little cupid's bow. The square plinth was mysteriously engraved. Joel squatted down to read it:

In ipso vita erat et vita erat lux hominum

When Joel stood, he felt something stiff in his pocket. He fished it out.

It was a folded piece of paper, covered in cracked white wax. He broke the wax off and shook it out onto the ground. In perfect print were these words:

The path of the just is as the shining light, which shines more and more unto the perfect day.

Presently a green car appeared on the long dusty road which led up the cemetery hill. Quickly the car approached, kicking up a wake of golden dust and a swirl of yellow leaves.

Joel watched it come.

The car slowed as it neared, and then it came to a stop beside him. The bluish exhaust was just visible at the mouth of the tailpipe. The cemetery trees stood reflected upsidedown on the hood of the car. The tree crowns cast cell-like images all across the windows, and the windows were made silver from the mirrored sky. Denuded branches looked like live roots across the glass. In fact, the replicated earth shone so fiercely on the car that the earth almost seemed to penetrate the car, the celestial blue above not diminished at all in reflection.

Mechanically the window dropped, and Lauren's smiling face was there.

She wore mirror sunglasses, a black tanktop, a short brown skirt. Her ash-blond hair was windblown. The skin of her arms and the skin of her chest looked like buttermilk. She shut off the engine. Joel could see himself reflected twice in her sunglasses, like shrunken twins imprisoned in each of those silver lenses, the miniaturized moon hanging behind him. He thought again of her contralto voice coming to him down the mysterious phone lines. He thought of how she had found him there, at his childhood home.

"Hello, Joel," she said.

"Hello, Lauren." He leaned forward, partially into the car, resting his hands on either side of the open window.

"I'm sorry for your loss," she said.

"No life without death," he said.

They were silent.

"No one came," he said.

"To the funeral?"

"Yes."

"Perhaps no one knew," she said.

"That he died?"

"Yes."

A gust of wind passed over him. He nodded. The smell of smoke from the burning autumn fields came to him stronger; it stung his nostrils and lodged itself dryly in the cavities of his head.

"Would you like to drive?" she said.

"Yes, I would."

"I like a man who drives," she said.

"Well, we'll get along just fine, then."

Her lips broke into a smile, and he laughed. It occurred to her then that this was the first time she had ever heard that from him, his laugh. She slid over to the passenger side, and Joel got in behind the steering wheel.

They sat there awhile longer. Neither of them spoke for some time. He stared at the delicate patterns of mirrored light streaming like quicksilver over the roof of her car. She watched him stare. He turned to her at last. Her left hand was outspread on her bare thigh, her spear-shaped fingernails clear-lacquered and glinting. The bluish veins embossed on the back of her hand gave back the pure light, and so did her fingernails. The stretchmarks on her thighs looked like sandbars. Joel leaned over and kissed her on the mouth. Her lips were very warm. He kissed her for a long time. When he drew back, he produced from his pocket the precious stone which looked so unearthly and so beautiful. He gave it to her. Her eyes widened.

"It was my inheritance," he said.

Then he drove out from under the ghostly trees and away from the burning fields. He drove out onto the wide-open highway and accelerated faster and faster into the perfect day.

The End

www.rayharvey.org

ray @ thearmstronghotel.com

LaVergne, TN USA
14 March 2011
219963LV00001B/48/P